# Catherine Dunne

## Something Like Love

PAN BOOKS

First published 2006 by Macmillan
an imprint of Pan Macmillan Ltd
Pan Macmillan, 20 New Wharf Road, London NI 9RR
Basingstoke and Oxford
Associated companies throughout the world
www.panmacmillan.com

ISBN 978-0-330-44250-3

3 5 7 9 8 6 4 2

A CIP catalogue record for this book is available from
the British Library.

Typeset by SetSystems Ltd, Saffron Walden, Essex
Printed and bound in Great Britain by
Mackays of Chatham plc, Chatham, Kent

Visit **www.panmacmillan.com** to read more about all our books
and to buy them. You will also find features, author interviews and
news of any author events, and you can sign up for e-newsletters
so that you're always first to hear about our new releases.

For Shirley Stewart, Literary Agent

*with thanks for a decade of patience, faith*

*— and a lot of fun*

# ACKNOWLEDGEMENTS

My thanks to Audrey McDonald and John Carty for taking time out of a hectic schedule to discuss the finer points of cold rooms, food preparation and snazzy serving ideas. Not to mention the rigours of loading and unloading the van . . .

Thanks, too, to Geraldine Lockhart of Lockhart and Company, Solicitors, for helping me pick my way through the intricacies of Irish family law. Any mistakes in interpretation are my own, and occur despite Ms Lockhart's illuminating insights into difficult, often bewildering, and always sad, territory.

Lia Mills and Mikaela Wiezell read early drafts of this novel and made many welcome suggestions, as did Julia Forster and Shirley Stewart of the Shirley Stewart Literary Agency, and Trisha Jackson of Macmillan. I am grateful to all of them, particularly as they took me at my word and were cheerfully blunt when the occasion demanded.

And, finally, special thanks to my editor, Imogen Taylor at Macmillan, for just about everything. Her interventions have made this a much better book than it could ever have been without her.

# *Prologue*

ROSE PULLS OPEN the heavy outer door that is already slick with rain.

She pushes her foot against the jamb, balances briefcase and handbag, and struggles to fold her umbrella. She almost has it when the wind gusts, slamming down hard against the metal ribs. The fabric suddenly inflates: gaudy pink and yellow roses widen, distort, strain angrily away from her. She tries to get a firmer grip on the wooden handle. At the same time she can feel her bag begin to slip from her shoulder, the briefcase slide from her grasp. It can't be helped: the gaily patterned umbrella wrenches away from her, flails its way across the car park. It bounces occasionally against the puddled tarmac. Rose watches its overblown, full-bellied bid for freedom. She knows that there is no point in chasing it. And so, she lets it go. She is reminded, once again, of this April day, this morning, this time, eight years ago. Her husband stands before her in the kitchen of their home. Eggs boil in a saucepan; she wipes away the splashes. Ben's face is vivid now, his words bubbling just underneath the surface of her memory.

'I don't love you any more,' he is saying. And then he's gone, bag packed with twenty years of marriage. Buggers off, just like that. Rose doesn't think about it much these days. She certainly doesn't try to remember. But once every year she allows herself that one indulgence.

She closes the door behind her now, shrugs out of her damp jacket, hangs it up in the hallway. Sarah appears, keeping the inner door open against her hip.

'Morning, Rose. Foul day. You okay?'

Rose nods and rummages in her handbag. 'Morning, Sarah. Fine, thanks. Just lost my umbrella, though. The wind took it while I wasn't looking.'

Sarah grins. 'Yeah – we saw it leave! Looked impressive in full flight, I have to say. Do you want any of us to chase it for you?'

Rose smiles. She knows how much Sarah hates the rain.

'Nah – I'd say it's blown inside out by now. But thanks.' She looks in the mirror and begins to brush her hair. 'Probably high time I got a new one, anyway.'

Sarah waits while Rose touches up her lipstick. 'Remind me: are you up to full capacity today?'

Rose shakes her head, snaps her bag shut. 'Nope. I'm taking tomorrow and Monday off, remember? I'm mostly fiddling about with paperwork this morning: I've to see Sam later on.'

'Betty or Angela due in?'

'I gave them the day off. Why?'

Sarah looks at her archly. 'Our birthday party for tonight has just increased by yet another twenty. We're already out the door. Can you help? Just for a couple of hours before lunch?' She stops and grins. 'And maybe an hour or so after?'

Rose sighs in mock exasperation. 'You're a slave driver. Did I ever tell you that?' She follows her into the spotless kitchens. 'Bring it on: kill the willing horse.'

Sarah smiles her thanks. 'You're a star. This always happens when you're doing someone a favour, doesn't it? They dump stuff like this on you at the last minute. Let's grab a cup of tea first and then we'll get started.'

Sarah's sisters, Claire and Katie, are already absorbed in their work, standing behind a phalanx of canapé trays. Serried ranks of tartlets, brioches and tiny croquettes line the stainless steel counter to either side. Spice of Life never cuts corners, never compromises. Rose feels that she has learned a lot from Sarah and her sisters over the years: they have done their market research, kept up with food's changing fads and fashions, kept their costs down.

Claire looks up as Rose passes. 'Morning, Rose,' and then her head is bowed again. Katie waves distractedly. She is chopping and grating as though her life depends upon it. The three sisters always work with speed and great economy of movement: perfect teamwork, Rose has often thought, with a twinge of guilty envy.

'My expertise will cost you, of course,' Rose says calmly, pulling the large white teapot towards her. She makes sure to catch Sarah's eye before the younger woman reaches for her mobile. Sarah looks over at her, waits.

'Go on, then,' she says cagily.

Rose pours boiling water, stirs, gives the teabags a final, thoughtful squeeze.

'How about a new umbrella?'

# PART ONE

# Chapter One

Even after five years, Rose still got a small thrill of ownership every time she saw the signs above the door: 'Bonne Bouche Catering' and 'Spice of Life'. She liked it, too, when Sarah and her sisters arrived in the mornings before she, Rose, did. Their presence warmed up the industrial drabness, made her feel almost as though she was coming home.

She sipped at her tea now, flicking through the previous day's invoices. 'How come tonight's birthday party has suddenly got so much bigger – again?' she demanded, as soon as Sarah finished her call.

'Oh, you know how it is,' Sarah was trying not to smile.

'A severe attack of the TFGs?'

'The very one. The "intimate family celebration" has now tripled in size since last week. They've cousins coming out of the woodwork and *everyone* has to be invited or one side won't speak to the other for the next ten years. If it was my family, I'd consider that a bonus.'

'Well, bless 'em all, every one,' said Rose, stuffing papers into her briefcase. 'It's great for business. Don't know where we'd be without Traumatic Family Guilt.' She put on her white jacket, tied back her hair. Quickly, she scanned the list that Sarah had just handed her.

'That's fine,' she said. 'We have most of this in the cold room already. I'll give you a shout if there's anything missing.

Which do you want me to get stuck into first – the salmon roulade or the beef tagine?'

'The roulade,' called Sarah, and lunged across the kitchen as her mobile shrilled again. 'Nobody does it better!'

Rose pulled a fish kettle off the stainless steel hook above her head and caught sight, briefly, of her own distorted reflection, waving and shimmering across the metal's cloudy surface. She hardly recognized herself.

Katie's face suddenly loomed beside hers. Rose jumped.

'I'm nipping out for a smoke. Big Sister Sarah is putting us all under pressure.' Katie grinned, tapping on the slim metal box in her pocket. 'Down to two cheroots a day from ten. Not bad, is it?'

'Not bad at all,' Rose agreed. 'You're becoming a paragon of virtue.'

'Don't worry: I won't get carried away. Claire and Sarah have enough virtue for all of us.' And she was gone, rolling her eyes up to heaven. Rose smiled as the back door slid quietly closed behind her.

Claire looked up from her chopping board across the room and caught Rose's eye. 'I'm doing the first run and the set-up around midday. Will you come with me? That means Sarah can stay and finish the desserts with Katie.'

Rose nodded. 'Of course. I'll be well finished with the roulade by then – and I'll leave the tagine on low. It can look after itself while we're gone. Just give me a shout when you're ready, and we can load the van.'

Claire smiled her thanks.

Three hours later Rose manoeuvred her van as close to the kitchen door as possible. Then Claire began to pass her boxes of plates, bowls, cutlery, ticking each one off her list as she did so. 'I *hate* this bit,' she said, with a vehemence that surprised Rose. Claire was normally the quiet one, the non-complainer.

'Loading and unloading the van's a killer on the back, it really is.'

'I know. I have to confess, I usually get Betty and Angela to do it. There have to be some compensations for being their boss.'

Claire laughed, her good humour restored. 'They're not *that* bad.'

Rose made no comment.

'That's the last of the white wine – that's got to go in the fridges as soon as we get there: remind me in case I forget.' Claire consulted her list once more. 'Just the tablecloths and napkins and all the usual party paraphernalia left. At least they don't weigh much.'

Rose looked at her, alarmed. 'We don't have to decorate the place and blow up a million balloons, do we?'

Claire shook her head. 'No – we're just supplying the bits and pieces. The birthday girl's friends are supposed to be meeting us there in half an hour. The marquee was set up last night, and they've already started on the balloons.'

'Oh, thank God for that,' said Rose. 'Okay, let's go. Let's see if we can beat our record for set-up.'

Claire finished counting. 'That's fine – twelve trestle tables, each seating ten. Let's give the surfaces a rub-down and then we can begin to get them ready. The cleaning stuff is in box number ten, the last one to go in the van.'

'I have it here,' said Rose, 'along with the cloths, napkins and centrepieces.'

Claire grinned at her. 'Now you see why I wanted you with me!'

They worked quickly and with concentration, pausing only to corral the balloon-blowing girls into the furthest corner of the marquee. Quietly but firmly, Claire insisted that they stay where their raucous good humour would not interrupt the work in progress. 'It's that, or come back at seven tonight,' she told them. 'We can't have you under our feet.'

'They can sure shriek, can't they?' remarked Rose, reminded of her own teenage daughter, Lisa, and her high-pitched friends.

They smoothed the white tablecloths, made sure the settings were spaced adequately, even made allowances for awkward table legs. Claire consulted her seating plan, matching place cards to her numbered list. Finally, she nodded, satisfied.

'Okay, let's do a walk-around and make sure there are no hazards for the waitresses.'

'I think this is pretty tight,' said Rose, indicating a group of tables in front of the stage. A young man with very long hair and arms crowded with tattoos was setting up the sort of disco equipment that Rose knew would make her ears bleed.

Claire frowned. 'It's a very difficult angle for turning. We'd better get the most sylph-like girls to serve this end of the marquee.' She made a note on her floorplan. 'Okay, I think that's it for this run.'

'Wine,' said Rose suddenly. 'White wine – in the fridges here. You said to remind you.'

'Done and dusted,' said Claire, putting her pen in her top pocket. 'And,' she paused, looking at her watch theatrically, 'I think we can say our record remains unbroken. Let's head for the hills.' She looked at Rose archly. 'That's only because *you* don't need to slip away for a secret smoke every half-hour.'


Back at the Bonne Bouche, Rose took a chair outside into the early afternoon sunshine. Without a word, Claire brought her a mug of tea. 'That's it, Rose,' she said. 'We've caught up with ourselves. We'll bring your roulade and the tagine when we're on the last run tonight. Thanks a million. You really made a difference.'

'A pleasure,' said Rose, smiling up at her. She sipped at her tea gratefully, and Claire disappeared back inside.

*What I used to do for love I now do for money.*

The sudden thought surprised her. She hadn't felt like that in a long time, not for years, not since the early days after Ben left. Back then, her life had been filled with loaves, bread rolls, pizzas: all that leavened dough rising steadily in the heady, emotional heat of her own kitchen. Her days had become a steamy routine of mixing, kneading, proving. All around her, while everything else rose and grew and doubled in size, she watched herself shrink and shrivel, disappearing onto the sidelines of her own life. After almost two years she'd had enough; she needed to be somewhere else, somewhere she could breathe. She'd grasped at the first straw that floated her way: premises for rent, somewhat run-down and ill-equipped, to be sure, but close to home, cheap and just meant to be hers. She knew it; she could feel it.

'I have to get out, Pauline.' Rose remembered the way she'd paced the floor of her solicitor's office. It had been a long, discouraging meeting. 'I can't stand being cooped up inside my own four walls any longer. I'll go mad. There's no distance – no dividing line between home, work, kids, life. I feel like one of those horrible gerbil things on a treadmill, just manically going round and round and getting nowhere. Besides, the Health Board regulations are getting tougher. I *need* a proper place.'

Pauline had been calm, professional, just like her father. 'I understand that, Rose, but these premises you're considering just aren't suitable. Think about it for a minute: why are they so cheap? Why have they been on the market for such a long time? As your solicitor, it would be remiss of me to let you sign this lease. There are more holes in it than a colander.'

Rose had flung herself into the old-fashioned armchair then, angry, defeated. Pauline was right, of course. And that was just one of the many things that made everything feel so much worse. They'd sat in silence until Rose's impotent fury had crackled and fizzled its way to nothing, like a child's cheap sparkler at Halloween.

Pauline had waited her out, and then remarked mildly: 'If Lisa sat there with a face like that, you'd kill her.'

'How come you're *never* wrong?' Rose had demanded, laughing in spite of herself at the thought of her daughter's bright, open face.

Pauline smiled at her, looking over the tops of her glasses. 'That's what you pay me for. Let this one go, okay? Trust me. There'll be others.'

Rose had given in, not without a show of reluctance. But had she been really honest, she would have had to acknowledge that relief had already begun to take the place of frustration. She couldn't allow herself to be cheated, not then, not ever. She'd already had enough betrayal to last her a lifetime.

Pauline's voice had remained quiet, reassuring. 'Let's draw up a list of what you need, and a budget. Then you can do some systematic searching. Right now you don't know what you want. All you can think about is escape.'

It had taken almost twelve months, but Rose eventually did it: she found what she'd been looking for.

'It's perfect, Pauline. This time I've got it just right, I'm sure of it.'

Then she'd been unable to sleep, lying rigid throughout the anxious nights, waiting for Pauline to close the deal. Attention to detail, she'd kept insisting every time Rose phoned her, tried to hurry her. 'It'll pay off in the end, I promise you; it'll be so watertight you'll hear it squeak. But these things can't be rushed. Now just get back to work and let me do my job.'

Finally, they'd sat together in Pauline's office once again, Rose perched on the edge of the old leather chair. Her arms were folded; she hugged her elbows close to her body, trying to contain her excitement.

'You're right: this one's the business.' Pauline was looking very pleased. 'It's the first let, a great location, plenty of private parking.' She leafed through the pages of the lease, referring to her own pencilled notes in the margins. 'After a bit of horse-trading, we've got nine years nine months with no breaks, and the rent is reasonable. I think it's good you'll be sharing, too. Keeps costs down all over. The only thing we haven't yet considered—'

Rose looked up at her, concerned.

'—is how you'll get on with the other tenants.' Pauline took a sip of her coffee, watching Rose steadily as she did so.

'I think it'll be okay, I've already spoken to them.' Even to her own ears, Rose's voice sounded too eager, almost childlike. She caught Pauline's look. 'I'll be careful, don't worry. I know that sharing could be a minefield. And if I'm not happy about something, I'll get in touch with you straight away – *before* it becomes a problem.'

Pauline raised her cup. 'Well, here's to you, then: new premises, a full order-book and a few quid in the bank for a rainy day. Go get 'em, girl.'

Rose could still recall the first morning she'd arrived at the new premises in Santry, apprehensive, excited, terrified all at once. Sarah and the others had arrived before her on that occasion, too, their van parked right outside. Spice of Life, it proclaimed, the words unfurling across its side like an old-fashioned banner rippling in the breeze. The letters were cinnamon-coloured on a cream background, shaded by paintings of tiny nutmegs, allspice, cardamoms.

Rose had felt instant dismay. Their name was so much more professional, so much catchier than hers. Bonne Bouche Catering had seemed tired, somehow, almost cumbersome, old-fashioned by comparison. Even her van looked discouraged: grimy, rain-streaked, in need of a good wash.

I can't just stand out here all morning looking at vans, she'd thought finally. I'll have to go inside sometime. She took a deep breath, settled her bag more firmly on her shoulder and went for it.

When she opened the door, she'd been met by a blizzard of activity. Tiny white nuggets of styrofoam – thousands of them – had launched themselves onto the stainless steel counters, the floor, even into the sinks. The draught from the open door seemed to give them a life of their own and they took sudden flight, scattering everywhere on Rose's entrance. She looked around her, surprised. Whatever she had expected, it certainly wasn't this.

Three women were unpacking cardboard boxes with a speed that reminded Rose of the rapid, jerky movements of old home movies. They were calling out to one another at the same time, opening and slamming cupboard doors, answering mobiles. There was a cloud of energy in the room so intense that Rose could almost taste it.

One of the women looked up, as though sensing Rose's presence. She wiped her hands quickly on a paper towel and made her way down towards the door, smiling. Rose had felt a sudden wave of relief. The other woman's hand was extended in greeting, her face open and friendly.

It's okay, thought Rose. We're going to get along.

'You must be Rose Kelly. I'm very pleased to meet you. I'm Sarah Greene. We spoke on the phone.'

'Pleased to meet you at last, Sarah. I've just been admiring your van – and your logo: what a great name!'

'Yeah, well, the name's ours all right, but that's about the only thing. All the rest belongs to the bank! Come and meet the other Lifers.'

Rose shook hands with Katie and Claire, momentarily confused at the similarities between them: the same dark hair, fine angular features.

Katie grinned at her. 'It's all right – everybody thinks we're triplets.'

'Here, steady on,' objected Claire. 'I'm the youngest – less of this triplets business.'

'And I'm the eldest,' said Sarah sternly, 'so these two do what I tell them.'

Rose had looked from one lively face to the other. 'In your dreams,' she'd said.

All three laughed.

'I can see we're going to get on just fine,' said Sarah. 'We've the kettle on. Cuppa before we all get stuck in?'

'Yes, please,' said Rose.

'Have you others starting today?' Katie asked, as she rummaged for mugs in the box in front of her.

'Yes, two part-timers – Betty and Angela.'

As though on cue, the door opened and two young women entered. Betty hovered uncertainly by the door. Angela pushed past her and made her way towards Rose. Her small face was bright, confident.

'Morning, Ms Kelly.'

'Morning, Angela,' said Rose. 'Meet Sarah, Katie and Claire. They call the shots around here. This is Angela, everyone.'

Rose looked around. Betty still hadn't moved. The girl looked uncertain, almost frightened. 'Come and introduce yourself, Betty,' Rose called. Awkwardly, the younger girl made her way into the kitchen. She's like an unmade bed, Rose had thought, filled with sudden misgiving. She'd taken a chance on the girl, moved by her air of eager thoroughness, her willingness to please. Now she wasn't so sure.

'Hello,' said Betty, looking down at her scuffed shoes. Her voice was barely audible.

'O-*kay*,' said Katie briskly, after a small silence. 'Let's have this first, then we can all muddle about together.' She handed around the mugs of steaming tea.

Sarah lifted hers in mock salute. 'Right, everyone, here's to the start of a beautiful friendship.'

'Amen,' said her sisters.

I'll drink to that, Rose had thought.

Now she felt that these days, more often than not, she hovered somewhere on the margins of cautious happiness. She'd kept the roof over her children's heads. And she'd plenty of work for the next six months.

Not a bad place to be, eight years later.

She could only hope that Sam had no nasty surprises waiting for her that afternoon.


'Okay, Sarah, I'm off. Katie, Claire, see you all on Tuesday.' Rose called out to the various corners of the kitchen as she hung up her white jacket, searched in her handbag for the keys to the van.

Sarah emerged from the cold room, her arms laden with vegetables. 'Half four already! God. Where does the day go?' She grinned at Rose. 'I know, I know, I sound *just* like my mother. You have a great weekend – and thanks a million for the roulade. It looks wonderful.' She dumped scallions, peppers, tomatoes onto the counter in front of her.

Rose reached out quickly and caught a large red bell pepper just before it fell.

'No problem. Don't forget to check on the tagine. It dries out if you take your eye off it.' She looked at Sarah slyly. 'Enjoy the celebrations this evening, won't you?'

Sarah snorted. 'I'll be out of there just as fast as I can. Friends of the family can be very dangerous animals: they're always the first ones to complain, even if there's nothing wrong.' Grimly, she began tearing the outer leaves off the lollo rosso. She looked up at Rose for a moment. 'It's their way of keeping you in your place, you know? In case you'd get above yourself.'

Rose smiled. 'You have my sympathy. I'll spare you all a thought this evening as I read my book – with my feet up, sipping a glass of good red wine.' She started to make her way towards the door. 'Just the one thought, mind you,' and she waved, theatrically, over her shoulder. 'Bye, now! I'm off to rediscover weekends!'

'Have a good one!' Sarah called after her.

'See ya, Rose!' called Claire and Katie. In unison. As ever.

Rose pulled out into the late-afternoon traffic. A passing motorist flashed his lights and slowed down, allowing her into the long line of cars ahead of him. She waved, surprised at this small courtesy. Such gestures were thin on the ground in Dublin, these days.

She glanced at her watch. Half an hour with Sam, collect Lisa from swimming, pick up a few things in the supermarket and then home. Shoes off, feet up.

No baking. No brewing. No boiling. No cocktail parties to cater. Just peace and quiet.

She could hardly wait.

*

Rose made her way carefully up the steep flight of granite steps. At the top she paused and combed her hair energetically with her fingertips. She pushed open the door. As she did so, watery afternoon sunlight glanced briefly across the glass and she suddenly saw herself again: a little wind-blown, a little startled this time. What is the matter with me? she thought. That's the second time today. As soon as she stepped inside, her reflection disappeared, slipping away into the hush of the closing door. She couldn't help grinning to herself. Now, what sort of an omen was *that*?

A young woman looked up as Rose approached, smiling at her, too brightly, from behind a vast mahogany desk. Must be new, Rose thought. Haven't seen her before. 'Good afternoon,' she said firmly. 'I've an appointment to see Sam McCarthy at half past three. My name is Kelly; Rose Kelly.'

She waited while the receptionist consulted her screen. The young woman's face was a mask, a smooth palette of perfectly applied make-up. Rose wondered where she'd got that shade of lipstick.

'That's fine, Ms Kelly. Please, take a seat. Mr McCarthy will be with you in just a moment.'

'Thank you.' Rose sank into a comfortable armchair, glad of the opportunity, finally, to do nothing. But Sam was there instantly, smiling warmly, his hand already extended in greeting.

'Rose – good to see you!'

She stood up and shook hands, wondering what this sudden display of formality was all about. He seemed a little nervous this afternoon, almost flustered, as though she had just caught him off guard.

'Hi, Sam. Keeping well?' She had to say something, to dispel the sudden awkwardness she could feel hovering like a fine mist somewhere above their heads.

'Fine, fine,' he replied. 'Come this way.'

She followed him across the blue carpet and into his office. Once he'd closed the door, he seemed to regain his composure.

'Would you like a cup of tea, or coffee?'

'No thanks, Sam. I'm okay. A bit pressed for time, to be honest.'

'Have a seat – this won't take long.' He eased his large frame into the swivel chair opposite, and looked at Rose inquiringly. 'So, how have things been at the Bonne Bouche?' He began to rummage on the desk for his reading glasses, still looking over at her.

Rose grinned at him, wrestling a sheaf of papers from her briefcase. 'I thought *you* were going to tell *me*!'

He pulled a thick manila file towards him, opened it and handed her a couple of pages stapled together. 'That's the account summary for the past few months. I think you'll see lots of room for optimism.' He smiled at her as she took the pages and scanned them quickly. 'There's no need to look so terrified – you're making good money again. The bad old days are over.'

Rose ran a finger rapidly up and down the neat rows and columns. She could hardly believe what she was seeing. Almost a year ago she had come to Sam, looking for advice. His prescription had been brisk, blunt, no-nonsense.

'Stop all these dinners for ten and twelve people,' he'd told her. 'Your profit margins are way too small, particularly when you look at all the work involved, *and* the fact that your overheads stay the same no matter what size the party is. Go for the bigger events: weddings, corporate entertaining, trendy food.'

Rose had looked at him in dismay. 'But I've never done that sort of work – I couldn't possibly handle that kind of volume on my own, with just two part-timers.'

'I agree, but hear me out. First of all, let's look at the current situation. The market is changing, Rose: you've told me so yourself. You've already seen that your kind of home entertaining is becoming less fashionable – people are eating out more.' Sam had leaned back in his chair, watched her carefully.

Rose hadn't answered at once, but she couldn't deny the impact of his words. The past five or six years had seen an explosion of restaurants all over Dublin: all fashion and fusion, and all stuffed to the gills with impossibly beautiful people. Rose hardly recognized her native city any more. It had had some sort of a designer makeover while she wasn't looking, become a place for the dotcom *wünderkinder* with brash cash in their pockets and an appetite for some serious spending.

Nobody seemed to want her First Communion lunches any more, her budget birthday parties, anniversary buffets for friends and family.

'You might be right,' she'd admitted, finally. 'I'm not sure what sort of change I can bring about, but I can't just go on as I am, with money leaking away as if there's no tomorrow.'

Sam had raised a cautionary hand. 'Don't get too despondent – you have the basis of a very healthy business here, still. You just need to do some tweaking. Why not see if Sarah and the others would be interested in joining forces, particularly for the bigger events?'

Sam had drafted some rough figures on the page in front of him. 'I think it could be profitable for everyone. If you wanted to, you could still retain a measure of independence by holding onto some of your own, more profitable clients as well.'

Rose had nodded thoughtfully. 'That's a very interesting suggestion. It could well be the best of both worlds.'

As it happened, Sarah had been more than pleased to have Rose join forces with her and the other Spice of Lifers. It was an arrangement that quickly grew to suit everybody. Rose did decide to hold onto some of her loyal, more long-standing clients, but more and more, she and Sarah worked as a team. Now, almost a year later, it seemed that the strategy was finally paying off. She looked over at Sam, who was watching her intently.

'You're sure I'm really out of the woods?'

He nodded. 'Positive. You're back on track – in fact, you're ahead of yourself. Your contracts are solid and your cash flow is very healthy. You've really turned things around. Congratulations.'

Rose sat back in the chair, conscious of a powerful wash of relief. 'You've no idea how glad I am to hear that. I mean, I knew I was getting there, but I wasn't sure I'd done enough. I was afraid I might have run out of time. Of course, I should never have let it happen in the first place.'

She shifted a little, uncomfortably aware once more of the sneaky proximity of financial failure. She should have been able to see it coming: it had stalked her once before, in the wake of her husband's departure. She couldn't afford to hope that it would never do so again.

'Stop beating yourself up,' Sam said gently. 'Business isn't an exact science, you know. Losses happen to the best of us.'

'Maybe.' Rose inclined her head, only in half-agreement. 'But I certainly took my eye off the ball. And with three hungry mouths at home, I was in no position to make mistakes.'

'"A woman of genius makes no mistakes. Her errors are volitional and are the portals of discovery."' Sam was grinning at her widely now.

She looked at him in astonishment. 'What? Who said that?'

Sam tried to look offended. 'I just did.'

Rose laughed at his expression. 'I know, but who said it before you? And I bet they weren't talking about a woman, either!'

Sam sighed. 'It was James Joyce, actually. Someone once

quoted it to me after I'd lost my shirt. I took a small measure of comfort from it. And you're right.' He rubbed both hands through his shock of greying hair. 'He did say "man of genius", meaning himself, I suppose. But what would you expect? It doesn't mean that it can't apply to you.'

'Well, well, what do you know?' Rose teased him. 'A literary and philosophical accountant: whatever next?'

'A self-forgiving mother and businesswoman?' Sam shot back.

They both laughed. Rose put the stapled pages into her brief-case, folding them carefully first. When she looked up, she was aware that the room had grown suddenly still. She spoke quietly, her words carefully measured out and weighed beforehand.

'I haven't ever thanked you properly for all you've done over the last few months, Sam. I couldn't have got through them without your help.'

He spread his hands, palms upward: an expansive, inclusive gesture. 'It's all part of the service. You did the donkey work yourself, you know. Don't ever forget that.' He pointed towards the bundles of pages in Rose's hand. 'Is that more paperwork for the bookkeepers?'

She slid them across the desk to him. 'Yes. I checked everything earlier today and there's nothing missing. Things are looking very solid for the next six months. They're even verging on the hectic. We've no big events on until next week, though, so I'm taking a long weekend off while I still have the chance.'

He nodded in approval. 'Good for you. You deserve it. Any particular plans?'

Just then, the phone rang, startling them both. With an exclamation of irritation, Sam answered it. 'Yes?'

Rose was surprised at his tone. It was brusque, almost curt. She busied herself needlessly with her briefcase, checked her watch, looked out of the window.

'I asked not to be disturbed. Tell him I'll call him back within the hour.' He hung up abruptly. There was something in his expression that Rose had seen once or twice before, had failed to read. Whatever it was eluded her this time, too. She stood up. Time to go. The man was under pressure: so was she.

'Must fly. Thanks again, Sam. See you next month?'

He pushed his chair back. 'Same time, same place. Keep up the good work. You know what to do.'

Rose began to itemize, using her fingers. 'One, write everything down, no matter how small the transaction; two, daily internet bank balance reconciliation; three, keep on top of credit control; four, keep on top of credit control. It's my Wicca-word, my morning mantra.'

Sam looked at her, puzzled. 'Wicca? Isn't that some sort of old crone?'

Rose shook her head in disapproval. 'Modern, Sam, modern. No such thing as an old crone any more. Witches are young and vegetarian these days. "Wicca" is how I remember my homework: Write, Internet, Credit Control, and then Credit Control all over again.'

'What about the final "a"?'

'Can't you guess?'

He shook his head.

She looked at him, trying hard to be serious. 'You're in the wrong profession, then. It's "a" for "Be anal" about it.'

He laughed. 'I can see I've taught you well. I can relax now, my duty is done.' He opened the door for her. 'Drive safely.'

'I will.' Rose made her way back down the steps towards the street, feeling lighter, happier.

No matter what, it was always a relief to have your survival confirmed by somebody else.

*

'Mum? Is it okay if I go over to Carly's?' Lisa was at the kitchen table, texting frantically, her long fingers whizzing around the keypad of her mobile phone.

Rose was trying to fit too many vegetables into the bottom of the fridge. She looked up, surprised. 'I thought you said you had a load of homework to do. You were grumbling about it all the way home from the pool.'

Lisa's phone beeped. She began texting again almost at once.

'Lisa – I'm speaking to you.'

'I know, I know. I was just in a bad mood. None of it is for tomorrow.'

'Lisa . . . ?' Rose's tone had an edge of warning to it.

'I'm serious, Mum. Look, I'll show you my homework journal, if you like.' Lisa leapt up from the table and dived onto the sofa, where she began rummaging at once in her schoolbag. Rose knew the routine. Soon, her daughter would produce incontrovertible evidence of no homework. She'd fill the kitchen with her energy, circle her mother, move in for the kill. Rose sighed. Sometimes she didn't know whether she had the stamina for yet another fourteen-year-old.

She looked at the blank page her daughter now waved in front of her.

'See? I told you. There's nothing due for Friday.'

'So, how long do you need to spend studying over the weekend, then?' Rose demanded. She felt it was time to seize the advantage. 'Let's agree it now, in advance, so that there's no argument. Don't forget, you've three tests next week – you told me so yourself.'

Lisa opened her mouth, took one look at her mother's face and closed it again.

'I mean it, Lisa. It's my first long weekend off in ages and I've no intention of spending any of it fighting with you.'

'Okay, okay – don't go off the deep end,' said Lisa crossly.

She tossed her long hair back from her face, grabbed a pen off the kitchen table and scribbled something in her homework journal. She thrust it at her mother.

Rose looked at it quickly. ' "Saturday morning, eleven to one; afternoon, four to six. Sunday, provisionally, eleven to one." Why provisionally?'

'Cos I might get everything done on Saturday, mightn't I?' Lisa looked at her mother, head cocked to one side, smiling wickedly.

Moods like the weather, Rose thought. As changeable as an Irish summer. 'Here, sign it,' she said, handing her daughter the rather dog-eared journal.

Lisa sighed. A very eloquent sigh, Rose thought, indicative of her daughter's great disappointment at having a mother who neither understood her nor trusted her.

Lisa signed her name with a parliamentary flourish. 'Satisfied?'

'Don't be cheeky. Give it here to me, please. There – I've signed it, too. That means it's a deal, okay? And deals thus agreed cannot be broken. Right?'

Lisa rolled her eyes. 'Yes, mother. You're *always* right.'

Rose grinned at her. 'You'd better believe it. Now give me a kiss. Back home at nine, okay?'

Lisa almost strangled Rose in a bear hug. 'Ten.'

It was a well-worn routine. They both knew the drill.

'It's a school night. Half nine.'

'Okay.' Chirpy again.

'What about dinner?'

'Can I have it later? I'm not hungry.'

'Fine. In that case, definitely home by half nine – not a minute later.'

Lisa blew her a kiss from the doorway. 'Admit it: you're *thrilled* to be rid of me for a few hours. You'll snooze on that sofa there all evening.' Lisa suddenly struck a dramatic pose, threw her head back, placed the back of her hand on her forehead. It was perfect silent-movie-speak for female distress. 'Then you'll tell me: "I never slept a wink."'

Rose threw the tea-towel at her. Lisa ducked, catching it easily, and flung it back at her mother, who missed. Shrieks of laughter as the cloth landed on Rose's head and draped itself over her eyes.

'Nice burka, Mum!' And she was gone.

'Don't you be late!'

The front door slammed.

Rose put Lisa's journal away safely and left her schoolbag in the hall. She picked up the plastic swimming bag, full of damp towels, and thought about loading the washing machine. Then she hesitated, changed her mind. She kicked off her shoes, loosened her skirt and sank gratefully onto the soft cushions of the old, familiar sofa.

She decided to close her eyes and rest, just for a few moments.


The tapping was insistent, coming from somewhere very far away.

Rose jerked awake, her heart pounding for no good reason. She felt dislocated, groggy. She must have slept for far longer than she'd intended. The tapping started again, more insistent this time. Then she realized: there was someone at the front door. Whoever it was had no intention of going away. Rose scrambled off the sofa, her knees obeying her with difficulty. As soon as she put her foot to the floor she could feel the numb, warm tingling of pins and needles.

Crossly, she made her way down the hallway, ready to shout at Lisa for forgetting her key. As she approached the door, something about the silhouette of the figure on the step made her pause, made her heart speed up. Only then did she realize that she was clutching the bag of towels close to her chest, holding onto it as if there was no tomorrow.

It couldn't be.

It was the milkman – someone collecting for charity – a political canvasser. Rose reached out slowly, cautiously, as though something was about to explode in her hands. She saw his face through the glass a split second before he saw hers. From nowhere, the most tremendous feeling of calm descended upon her.

Ben. It was Ben.

In slow motion, she dropped the towels into the corner, until later. Everything around her seemed to have liquefied; it was like running under deep water. All she could think of was putting down the towels. She couldn't handle this and dirty laundry at the same time. Something had to give.

She noticed her hand shook as she reached up to open the door.

She was conscious of nothing else but him and her, standing there, each facing the other in a perfectly ordinary way on a perfectly ordinary evening. Time was full of the present moment; there was no room for anything else. No past, no future, no anger. Not yet.

No recriminations, no distress.

All she knew was, he was back.

Some part of Rose had been waiting for his return, had prepared for it, for eight long years now. Seeing him there on her doorstep was a shock, but she couldn't say it was in any sense a surprise.

'Hello, Rose,' he said.

Was his tone gentler than she remembered? There was a lightness around the corners of his mouth. Not quite a smile, but something that could perhaps become one in time. He looked smoother than he used to: his thinning hair sleeker, darker than she would have expected. Rose thought of the shiny-headed seals she had recently seen on a nature programme. She had a brief, blinding vision of her husband standing on that step, just as he was now, more than eight years ago. Then, his face had been brick-red with astonishment and disbelief that his wife had, finally, locked her door against him.

'Hello, Ben,' she said now, quite coolly.

There didn't seem to be anything else to say. She looked at him with mild detachment. She had been married to this man. She had loved him and minded him and relied on him, once upon a time. She had had her children with him, and now he seemed to her like someone she had once met long ago, briefly, in another, previous life.

She kept probing to see if she felt anything, any emotion at all. Like a tongue worrying a sore tooth, she would have been reassured to feel the pain of its presence. Instead, all feeling seemed to have been extracted, just yanked out of the way, leaving not even the smallest gap as a reminder of its previous troubled existence.

What do I do now?

The question was suddenly clear in Rose's mind, as though some inner voice had just articulated it rather sharply, prodding at her, impatient at her lack of action.

'May I come in?' he said. 'Or perhaps . . . we could . . . go out . . . somewhere for a drink?'

She stood back, opening the door wider, aware of some absurd emotion just beginning to stir deep inside her chest. It was like the hopeful, frantic flapping of a caged bird. 'Please, come in.'

He followed her down the hallway into the kitchen. Rose indicated the sofa, hoping that her voice had acquired confidence, the easy authority of ownership.

'Take a seat.'

She watched him carefully before he sat, as he smoothed out the warm wrinkles on the cotton throw. He kept pulling and straightening until the whole surface was bland and featureless, all traces of warmth and familiarity disappeared. By the time he sat, his face was almost as smooth, but disapproval lingered where the contours of a smile had, almost, recently been.

He can't help himself, she thought abruptly. The shard of realization sliced through her resentment like a scalpel through flesh. He hasn't changed a bit. He still thinks I'm nothing but wife and housekeeper – keeper of his house, wife to some long-ago, ever-present Ben: discarded, unwanted, but still, somehow, irrevocably his.

Stop it, she told herself severely. You don't know what he's thinking.

Nevertheless, the small voice that sometimes refused to be silenced, whose presence had grown more and more insistent over the years, now whispered sadly to the inside of her head: *Oh, but you do, you do.*

Ben handed her a bottle of wine. The movement was an abrupt one, coming out of nowhere, like a conjurer's trick. She almost expected to see a bunch of fake flowers blossom suddenly in his outstretched hand, or a startled, pink-eyed rabbit, suspended by long white ears. Slowly, she took the bottle from him. She hadn't noticed it in his hands while he stood at the doorway.

'I'll get the opener.' Rose walked over towards the cupboards, glad of the opportunity to turn her back on her husband. She felt cold all over. Memories crowded all around her, their clarity splintering like ice. When Ben spoke again, his voice was quiet, almost hesitant.

'How are the kids? How's Damien?'

Rose opened the drawer, rummaged noisily for the bottle opener. 'Damien doesn't live here any more.'

What else could she say?

It was a bottle of good red wine, but the cork was plastic, she noticed. That was more and more common these days. Something to do with contamination, she'd heard . . . Stop it, she told herself. Get a grip.

'He's had a place of his own for the past year or so. He's sharing with a couple of friends.' Let Damien tell his father, if he wanted to. She wasn't going to fill in all the years for him.

'Really?' Ben looked surprised.

Rose began to pour. The glass shuddered for a moment, and she steadied its base with her free hand. The fingers were trembling slightly, she noticed. She considered the information in a detached way, as though the hand belonged to someone else.

'He's twenty-four years of age, Ben.'

'Of course, of course.'

Rose saw his face tighten. Watching the expression she knew so well, it seemed clear to her that she had a choice: she could kill him now, either with the corkscrew, or arsenic in his wine. Or she could instead pretend to be calm, blasé, woman-of-the-world. It wouldn't be too difficult. She already had the impression of watching herself from a frozen distance, waiting while her emotions skulked somewhere in the wings. She took a long sip of her wine, tried harder for chattiness.

'And Brian is quite the academic star. He's just finishing first year at college – computers and languages. He's hoping for a first. He'll be working with IBM in Paris for the summer.'

Ben looked gratified. Rose understood that look. My son, it seemed to say. My favourite child. Of course he'd do well.

Didn't he have me for a father? Rose felt rage flare suddenly, a bright coil of it, spooling upwards from the depths she'd kept so carefully covered for eight long years.

'And Lisa?'

Did he really find it all perfectly normal, to learn like this about his children's lives, strangers' lives, in a polite but cursory telegrammese that acknowledged no absence, no sense of anything at all *missing* on his part?

Rose's smile was bright and brittle. 'Quite the young lady. Fourteen going on forty. Thinks the world was created for her entertainment. She's fine – as self-centred and moody as the next fourteen-year-old.'

'I'm looking forward to seeing them.'

Rose thought there was a question in there somewhere. She decided not to acknowledge it.

'More wine?'

She poured recklessly, wishing he would go, wishing he had never come back, wishing she had never known him, that her children had somehow been transported to her through the medium of the spirit world. She could feel her thoughts becoming wilder. Her fear of what her husband's return must mean grew and grew beyond her control. The frozen air she'd wondered at earlier had now begun to thaw. It felt like a hole in the permafrost, a hole in the ozone layer – an unwelcome, almost toxic return of sensation that brought her dangerously close to tears.

'Why have you come back, Ben?' The directness of her question surprised even her. Something – perhaps the wine – had given her false courage.

He placed his glass carefully on the coffee table, even more carefully not looking at her. 'Things have changed for me, as I'm sure they have for you.' He ran his finger reflectively around the rim of his wine glass, making it sing.

The sound was somehow inappropriate, Rose thought: this was not a night for musical accompaniment. This was all harsh lights, hard words, harder feelings.

'I'd like to move back to Dublin. There are some ... opportunities ... here I'd like to pursue. Celtic Tiger, and all that.'

His smile was ghastly, Rose thought, like a death's head. He had paused slightly before and after the word 'opportunities' too, as though giving the word a capital letter, allowing it to occupy a larger, more significant space than usual.

He needs money, she thought suddenly, shocked by the brutal clarity of her realization. That's why he's back. He wants me to sell the house.

'Opportunities.' She nodded, seeming to consider this. 'I see.' She said nothing more, comfortably allowing the silence to grow between them. It could grow for as long as it wished, now that she knew.

He shifted a little on the sofa. When he spoke again, his voice was softer. He's been practising this, she thought. Someone has schooled him in how to get what he wants. By negotiation, this time.

'I believe ... I feel that it's time we ... regularized our position – financially ... and ... with regard to the children, the house – everything, in fact.'

These were not his words. They did not fit comfortably inside his mouth. They tumbled out as soon as he spoke, recklessly, glad to escape. He must have held them prisoner ever since he first came across them, planning to use them as hostages in getting what he wanted: what he believed to be his, felt was his due. Rose could imagine him leafing through some awful American self-help manual, perhaps with a title like *Divorce: Negotiating So Everyone Wins*. Except that everyone couldn't win. Everyone hadn't won. She'd already lost more, far more, than anyone could ever give her back. Particularly Ben.

'Really? And what "position" might we be in need of regularizing?'

Careful now; careful. Don't blow it. Keep your temper.

The corners of his mouth drooped. His shoulders hunched a little as he leaned forward, literally on the edge of his seat. He examined the dregs of his wine, his eyes fastening the rich, red liquid as it swirled its way around his glass.

'I didn't behave well, Rose. I know that. But I felt backed into a corner. I felt that I had no choice.'

He looked at her directly now, his eyes not flinching from hers.

'And what do you think it was like for me, Ben?' Rose kept her voice even. 'A rather crowded corner with three children in it, don't you think? No support – financial or otherwise – and the need to keep a roof over all of our heads? How do you think *that* felt for the past eight years? And you have the gall to talk to me about choice!'

She couldn't stop herself. She hurled her final words across the table at him, filled suddenly with enraged astonishment at all the assumptions, all the expectations that had had to underpin his return.

He stood up abruptly, his hands raised as if to ward her off, to push back the force of her fury. 'I didn't come here to fight. I know things were tough for you, and I'm sorry the way it all worked out, sorrier than you can imagine, but—'

'You know nothing about my life, nothing at all.'

Rose cut across him, already moving towards the kitchen door. She'd have to negotiate with him sooner or later, she knew that. She'd always been aware that this day would come, that part of this house was his, whether she liked it or not.

She'd often fantasized about leaving it all behind, moving on somewhere else, closing the door on memory, on failure, on the precarious notion of 'family home' – whatever either of those words meant now, or had ever meant.

'Financially, I've survived.' She put her hand firmly on the handle, opening the door into the hallway. 'The children have survived. This *house*, as you like to call it, is our home. Not some property portfolio, some kind of spoils to be divided once the dust has settled. I seem to remember making this point to you before, when you walked out on us, but you chose not to listen.'

Boiling water, sharp scissors, carving knives . . . She had never been angrier in her life.

'Calm down, Rose. This is my house too, you know.'

'It may be your house, but it's my home. Now, get out of it.'

She paused for a moment. The force of sudden memory made her slow down, draw one quiet breath. She was surprised at how calm she became. Her voice, when she heard it again, sounded brisk, almost businesslike.

'And what you call my "position" is quite "regular", thank you. Yours is your own business. Now leave.'

I'm getting good at this, she thought. Throwing people out. It gets easier the more you do it.

He hesitated, as though he was about to try again.

'Don't, Ben,' she said quietly. 'Don't say another word.'

'We have to talk.'

The world collapses, years spiral into turmoil, lives are shattered. Rose knows now that all these disasters were once heralded by that phrase. *We have to talk.*

She opened the front door.

'I seem to remember the last time you said that, too. You've made me wait for eight years. Now you can wait a little longer.' She opened the door wider. 'Go.'

He looked at her helplessly. 'I . . . we . . . can't we just—?'

'We'll do nothing until I'm good and ready.'

In a strange replay of the day her world had changed for ever, Rose ushers her husband out of the house and locks the door firmly behind him. For several moments, she is unable to move. She watches the stiff, angry set of his shoulders as he makes his way down the driveway without once looking back.

Behind her closed door, the house reeks of silence. Bright shards of a shared past cut through the empty stillness. Christmases, birthdays, anniversaries. Twenty years of her life, her children's lives, telescoped into Kodak moments – all mocked by the astonishing return of one man in a suit.

Rose stoops to pick up the bag of damp towels in the hallway and makes her way back into the kitchen. She opens the washing machine, piles in the towels, adds the soap tablets and slams the porthole closed. She pushes the sixty-degrees button, sits down on the rumpled sofa and waits for her heart to stop pounding. She feels it pulsing painfully against her ribs.

It had to come to this; she'd always known that. And now that it was here, she longed suddenly, violently, for closure. Divorce, freedom, drawing a line in the sand. She would do it; she was ready.

But one thing was sure: she would do it on her terms.

Rose sat at the kitchen table, occasionally topping up her wine glass. She was fascinated by the dislocated, alien image of herself that she could see there, all moon-like cheeks and forehead; small, wavering eyes; sharply pointed chin. She remembered how she had caught sight of herself earlier, too: once in the smoky depths of a fish kettle, and again in the watery sunshine of Pembroke Road. Had both of those moments been sly reflections of a rapidly approaching future? Were they sudden premonitions that her life, once more, was about to become unrecognizable?

Every time a car passed, or voices were suddenly raised in laughter in the dusky neighbourhood gardens, Rose stiffened, all senses on the alert. She was waiting, again, for Ben's insistent knocking at her door.

Lisa found her, surrounded by dim, grainy light, at almost ten o'clock that evening.

'Mum! You gave me a fright! I thought you'd gone out! Why didn't you ring me back?'

Rose looked up at her daughter blankly. 'What?'

'I sent you a text, ages ago, but you didn't ring me back. I . . . Mum – are you all right?' Lisa snapped on the kitchen light and Rose winced, covering her eyes from the sudden, merciless glare.

Should I just tell her now? Should I just say, 'Your father is back,' and wait to see what happens?

Lisa put her arm around Rose's shoulders. 'Mum, you look exhausted. Would you like me to make you a cup of tea?'

Rose immediately sat up straighter. 'Yes, please, love – that would be great.'

She watched as her daughter filled the kettle, trying to imagine her as she once was. A shaky, tearful six-year-old, her only certainties the pink, plastic world of her Barbie dolls. Her childish universe had been rocked by the blinding flash, the grey mushroom cloud of marital fallout. What would Ben see, looking at her now? A tall, slender fourteen-year-old, all long legs and blonde hair. Would he recognise her if he met her in the street? Would she recognize him?

'And you're right, I am tired – very tired. Think you could bring me that cuppa up to bed?'

'Yeah, of course. You're not working in the morning – sure you're not?'

Rose shook her head. She stood up very carefully, making sure her heels were planted solidly on the floor, able to take her weight. She had the feeling that with Ben's return, the ground might suddenly begin to shift beneath her feet again. She needed to test it, to make sure that nothing was giving way without her knowledge. 'No, not tomorrow, or the next day, nor even the day after that. In fact, I might never go back to work again.'

Lisa looked at her strangely. 'Are you sure you're okay?'

Rose smiled. 'I'm fine – just feeling a bit ... defeated tonight. Thanks for looking after me, pet.' And she kissed her daughter's cheek lightly. 'By the way, aren't you late?' She glanced at the clock on the kitchen wall. Had the hands moved at all? Or had they completed one whole revolution without her noticing?

'That's why I was texting you earlier.' Lisa concentrated on filling the teapot with boiling water. 'Carly invited me to stay for dinner. I just wanted to make sure that that was okay with you.'

Rose nodded. 'Oh. Right. Fine.'

'Her mum and dad are giving us a lift to school in the morning – they're going into town early. Will I hang out those towels for you before I go?' Lisa pointed to the washing machine, which Rose had no memory of filling.

Towels. Dirty laundry. All those years of hanging out the washing.

She tried to clear her head. It was getting cluttered again

CATHERINE DUNNE

with the smoke of tiredness, the present, the future, and all the lowering clouds of Ben's return. 'Yes, please, do that. I'll see you straight after school tomorrow, then, okay?'

Lisa pointed to the teapot. 'Do you still want that cup of tea?'

'Absolutely – see you upstairs.'

But she couldn't keep her eyes open. She tried to wait for Lisa's light step on the landing, but her eyelids wouldn't let her.

She slept, dreaming of bread baking, wine spilling, crystal smashing. She dreamed of standing by her open bedroom window, watching sheets hanging on the line.

They were being blown back and forth, back and forth, by the gusty summer winds off the bay.

# Chapter Two

Rose slept deeply, dreamlessly, until eight o'clock the following morning. She woke only when she heard Lisa close the front door carefully behind her. Her first thought was: Today is Friday; yesterday was Thursday. She needed to locate herself, to make sure her life was rooted firmly in the present. She needed a universe of logic, order, ordinariness, where the unexpected didn't take her by surprise.

In the dim, curtained light of her bedroom, Rose allowed herself to wonder whether she had imagined the events of the previous night. Had Ben really come back? Or was his return instead one of those waking dreams – the ones that crawl just underneath the surface of sleep, insinuating themselves into the mind's eye, inducing paralysis, voicelessness, the jerky fear of falling from a great height.

Rose pulled herself up to sitting. Her shoulders ached, her head throbbed. Part of her was glad: at least that was real. Even though she knew that her husband's return belonged entirely to the waking world, Rose felt that there was still something unreal, something strangely insubstantial, about his startling presence in her home the evening before.

She showered, dressed, put on her make-up. She needed to do all of these things very slowly, deliberately. Once downstairs, she opened the kitchen door, waited for the evidence. Two wine glasses stood on the draining board; there was a careless plastic cork in the sink. She opened the window and saw towels hanging heavily on the line. Then, she knew for sure. The flesh and blood man who had once been her husband had indeed returned and had stood inside this house again. And now, this morning, no matter where she looked, she couldn't stop seeing him, seeing herself, seeing their children as they used to be. Every corner of her suddenly unfamiliar kitchen seemed to be populated with edgy, restless ghosts. This was not where she needed to be, not now. This warm and comfortable space had, overnight, become fractured, fragile, poised on the edge of uncertainty. She needed to get out.

Rose made a physical effort to shrug off the lethargy, picked her keys up off the hall table, and pulled the front door closed behind her. She had to come back to check it twice, forgetting each time that it had been secured already, made safe and solid: her fortress. Halfway down the street, she noticed that it was starting to rain again. She'd left the house without her coat. And she had no umbrella.

Jane answered the door almost at once. She smiled broadly when she saw Rose on her doorstep. 'Rose! Great to see you. Come on in. Goodness, you're wet!'

Rose followed her into the kitchen.

'Take a seat. I was just about to fill the kettle. Your timing is impeccable.'

Rose looked around her, as though seeing this kitchen for the first time. She'd stumbled in here a lifetime ago, a briefcase stuffed full of credit card statements, receipts, Post-its, all the forgotten detritus of her husband's pockets. She'd sat for hours at this table, over endless cups of tea. In the evenings, she'd sipped wine while she pieced together the garish jigsaw of her husband's betrayal. How many times since then had she come here looking for solace?

Rose sat, feeling all at once that there was no substance to her below the knees. Jane handed her a towel and she patted her face, hiding, just for a moment. Then she blotted dry the ends of her hair.

'You great ninny – out on a day like that without an umbrella! Fancy a cup of coffee?' Jane turned to look at her as she flipped the switch on the kettle. All at once, she seemed to notice something in Rose's expression. 'Hey – are you okay?'

Rose hung the towel on the back of the chair and tried to smile at her. 'You asked me exactly the same thing – and I mean those *exact* words – eight years ago. "Fancy a cup of coffee?" you said.'

Jane sat down beside her. 'Rose, what is it? You're like a ghost. Tell me – what's wrong. You're scaring me.'

'It's Ben. I'm sorry. How can I say this? It's . . . Ben's back.'

Jane looked at her strangely. 'What about his back?'

'No, no, no, not *his* back – *he's* back: Ben's here, in Dublin, right now. Landed on my doorstep yesterday evening.'

Jane leaned forward in her chair. She looked at Rose, her face suddenly paler. 'You are joking.'

Rose shook her head slowly. 'I wish I was. But he's back, large as life.'

Jane's tone was guarded, deliberate. 'And do you know why? I mean, why has he turned up now, rather than any other time?'

Rose smiled at her sadly. 'My thoughts exactly. He's back to "regularize our position", according to him.'

The kitchen went silent, just for a moment.

'What does he think you are? After all this time?' Jane's words were heated, indignant. 'A set of accounts!'

Rose looked at her in surprise. 'Why, yes, yes I believe that that's exactly what he thinks I am.'

Jane stood up suddenly and busied herself with the coffee-pot. 'Sorry, Rose. I shouldn't have said that. It kind of . . . slipped out.'

'Jane, look at me.'

Jane turned around, leaning against the sink, her arms folded. She had never been very good at hiding her feelings. Right now, her face was flushed; her expression hovered somewhere between disbelief and outrage.

'I want you to listen to me, now,' Rose said quietly. 'You do not have to be careful of what you say, you do not have to censor your thoughts. Ben and I will not be getting back together – not in this lifetime, not ever. I wouldn't have survived these past years without you. If we can't be honest, and angry, and say what we think to each other after all this time, then what's the point?'

Jane moved over to the table, started to stir the coffee carefully. 'It's just – it's always such a minefield. Particularly when couples separate. I don't want anything I say to drive a wedge between us.' She pulled cups and saucers out of the cupboard, set them carefully on the table, fished the milk jug from the back of the fridge.

Rose smiled as her friend sat down again beside her. Jane must have forgotten how, together, they'd once developed a sliding scale of domestic disasters and their signifiers. They'd joked that mugs were for the banal, the friendly, intimate everyday: rows with children, temporary shortages of cash, the minor, recurring frustrations of family life.

Cups and saucers, on the other hand, were for times of crisis; for mothers-in-law, for children's poor exam results, for all the unwelcome distresses of formality. Painted china became something to focus on, a welcome, delicate distraction. Jane had also insisted that that the scale of the crisis could be further judged by the presence of milk jugs: once they took the place of cartons, or plastic containers hefted onto the table, then the world was declared officially to have shifted, unsteadily, on its axis.

Rose looked directly at her friend. 'You did everything absolutely right when Ben walked out. Now he's back: that doesn't mean he's in my life for any longer than it takes me to get rid of him for good. Okay? Nice cups, by the way.'

Jane grinned at her, suddenly remembering. She shook her head, started to pour the coffee. 'Jesus, I still can't believe it. I just can't believe it. You must have been gobsmacked.'

'I was. I'd fallen asleep on the sofa after work, and I woke to find him pounding on my front door. Just like that.'

'What do you think he wants then, really? I mean, what does "regularize a position" actually mean?'

'Well, he didn't say so in so many words, but then he wouldn't, being Ben – but I know he wants money. Oh yes, the Celtic Tiger has brought him home, according to him. My guess is he wants to sell the house.'

Jane frowned. 'But he's been gone for ages.'

'I know. I'd imagine he knows I could have gone ahead and sold up without his consent last year, but I didn't, did I? I was too busy trying to make a living and keep the roof over my kids' heads.'

'What are you going to do? I mean, is he even entitled to anything at this stage?'

Rose shrugged. 'I don't know. But one thing's for sure: he's going to keep pushing for whatever he believes is his. And that's fine by me. I want to put this behind me, once and for all. I want a divorce. I'm prepared to pay to make it all ... just ... go away.' She paused for a moment. 'I'm not going to tell *him* that – not yet, at least. But I am going to handle this. I'm going to manage it.' Shakily, she raised her cup to her lips. 'I know I don't look as though I can manage much right now. But by the time this weekend's over, I'm going to have a plan.'

Jane grinned at her. 'Good woman. Are you going to contact your solicitor today?'

Rose shook her head. 'I could, but I'm not going to. I need the rest of this weekend just to let the dust settle. Pauline will always fit me in, even if it's after hours. I need the time to work things out before I get in touch with her. I need to think about what I want. This is not the time to be a headless chicken.'

'Do the kids know?'

Rose drained her coffee cup, and shook her head. 'Absolutely not. Lisa didn't come home from Carly's until after Ben had gone, and Brian'll be away until Sunday night. According to Ben, he does want to see them; I just don't know whether they'll want to see him. I mean, two of them are adults, but Jesus, that doesn't mean that they won't be affected. I dread to think what all of this might do to Damien.'

Rose pressed the heels of her hands into her eyes. She could feel another, awful headache just starting. 'In fact, I'm terrified of what this will do to all of them. I am *not* going to have them thrown into turmoil all over again on what might be just a whim.'

'Anything I can do?'

'Just keep on doing what you've always done,' Rose stood up and hugged her. 'You might get in some good red wine, though.'

'No problem.'

'It's ironic, isn't it?' Rose paused on her way out of the kitchen. 'Me sitting here all those years ago, wondering how on earth I was going to tell my kids their father had left. Now, here I am again, wondering how in God's name I'm going to tell them that he's back.'

'I'm so sorry you've got to go through this all over again. And I feel so helpless. If there's anything I can do, just shout. You need anything for this afternoon, for tonight?'

Rose shook her head. 'No, thanks. I'm going home to try

44

and get my head straight. Then I think I'll lie down for an hour or so before Lisa gets home. I'm barely up out of bed and I'm exhausted already. I have to get a handle on this. I'll talk to you over the next couple of days, okay?'

'Any time. You know that.'

Rose opened the door of the kitchen.

'Rose?'

She turned around. 'Yes?'

'You do know that any time means any time?'

'I do. I do indeed. See you tomorrow.'


Once Rose came home from Jane's, she crawled up the stairs to bed and pulled the duvet around her, pausing only to kick off her shoes. But she couldn't stop shivering, couldn't get warm. Finally, she lay there, pinned under the armour of a heavy, restless half-sleep.

She dreamed, watching herself as she waded through some swampy place, surrounded by the chill fogs of memory. There were lights everywhere, but they were pallid ones, their beams shifting and multidirectional. Untrustworthy light, all of it. Elusive, evasive light. There was no way out that she could see, apart from the path she hacked at for herself.

She struggled into wakefulness in time for Lisa's return from school.

'Hi, Mum!'

Good. She was home, and by the sounds of it, in high good humour.

'How was today, love?' Rose called down to her, scrambling out of bed.

Lisa dropped her bag in the hallway. She looked up as Rose began to make her way downstairs. 'You okay? You look very pale.'

'I'm fine, thanks, love. Just still very tired. How was school?' She followed her daughter into the kitchen.

'Fine. Same old same old, as you'd say yourself.'

'I was wondering . . .'

'Yeah?' Lisa was rummaging in the fridge, not looking at her.

'Are you doing anything tonight?'

Lisa shrugged, made her way over to the table with a tub of yogurt. Rose followed. 'I was supposed to go babysitting with Carly, but her brother's little fella is sick, so I don't think we'll be going anywhere.'

Rose decided to seize her opportunity. 'How about dinner out, then? Just you and me?'

'Tonight?' Lisa looked surprised.

'Yeah – why not? Whole weekend off, ain't nobody here but us chickens . . . I haven't treated you in ages.'

'Can Carly come, and maybe Alison?'

'No, not tonight. Next time, and that's a promise. I want to talk to you about a couple of things.'

'What sort of things?' The spoon stopped halfway to Lisa's mouth. Her expression was immediately suspicious.

'Family things, Lisa – what your plans are for the summer, what money you'll need, clothes . . . that sort of thing. We haven't really had a chance to chat in a good while.'

It wasn't a lie, Rose thought, but it wasn't really the truth, either. The whole truth could wait a little longer. It wouldn't spoil.

'Oh, okay. Yeah – that would be good. What time?'

'Let's say we leave here about half six? That'll give me time for a bath – and you, too, if you want one. I've the water on.'

'I'll wear my new black trousers with the pink top – what do you think?'

'I think you'll look just gorgeous.' Rose planted a kiss on top of her daughter's fair head, hugged the slim shoulders from behind. 'I'm going up now for a good soak. See you in about an hour.'

'Mum?'

'Yes?'

'Don't use up all the towels.' Nonchalantly, Lisa licked strawberry yogurt off the back of her spoon, then scraped the inside of the carton, not looking up.

Rose grinned. 'That's my line.'

'I know. Just wanted to get it in before you did.'


Rose drove into the Temple Bar car park at exactly seven o'clock. There were plenty of spaces still: the surrounding bars and restaurants didn't really begin to fill up until about eight. She turned to face Lisa, hoping that her anxiety about the evening ahead wasn't already obvious.

'Well? Have you decided?'

Lisa made a face. 'I still dunno whether it's Thunder Road or the Elephant and Castle.'

Rose stayed silent. Please, she thought, please not Thunder Road. It was all too aptly named: within half an hour the loud, relentless music would give her a thumping headache. She'd never liked loud music, not even as a teenager. She liked it even less now. She pulled a coin from her jacket pocket.

'Toss?'

'Okay.'

'Heads for Thunder Road, tails for Elephant and Castle – all right?'

Lisa nodded. Rose flipped the coin in the air, smacking it onto the back of her left hand, covering it with her right.

'Ready?' She took her hand away, revealing the map of Europe on the face of the one euro coin. She sighed inwardly. 'Thunder Road it is.'

'Nah – let's go to the Elephant. We haven't been in ages!'

'You sure?'

'Yeah.'

Rose led the way quickly from the car park and crossed the cobbled street to the restaurant, praying that Lisa wouldn't change her mind again. She wondered whether this ritualization of bad news was such a good idea after all; perhaps she should have told the child at once, at home, that her father had suddenly reappeared. Perhaps there would be tears, tantrums: and how would either of them cope with such obvious distress in a very public place?

It was more and more difficult to tell how Lisa would react to anything these days. Rose hoped that she hadn't chosen the wrong option. Well, we're here now, she told herself, and at least we're away from phones and friends. Just make the most of it. And it was always possible, of course, that in Lisa's teenage eyes, Ben's sudden return might not be such a bad thing after all.

'Two, please.'

The waiter darted away to clear a table and Rose turned to smile at her daughter. 'Good choice, Lisa. There's plenty of room and it's not too hot.'

'The music isn't too loud either, is it?' There was an arch innocence to her daughter's tone that took Rose by surprise.

'No – it's not; it's just the way I like it.'

Lisa grinned. 'I know you hate Thunder Road – I was just winding you up.'

'You monkey!'

Rose suddenly relaxed. This was going to be fine between them; she could feel it. There was such an extraordinary change in Lisa when she wasn't fretting over things. Freed from the anxieties that frequently bedevilled her during the school day, her young face was now smooth, glowing, her eyes bright with anticipation and mischief. She looks wonderful, Rose thought, even allowing for the fact that a mother was allowed to be prejudiced. When Lisa smiled, as she had just now, her expression was impish, irresistible. Silently, Rose thanked the god of mothers that her youngest child was continuing in one of her sunny moods; she didn't think she could have coped with a hormonal moment just now.

She watched, amused, as Lisa regarded herself in the restaurant mirror while they waited for their table. She tugged at her fair hair, tucking strands behind her ear, pulling her fringe down over her eyes. Her vanity was a completely unselfconscious one: absorbed by her own reflection, she was unaware of the scrutiny of the four young men sitting directly behind her.

But Rose wasn't. She suddenly saw her daughter through their eyes, rather than her own. With a shock of recognition that almost took her breath away, Rose realized that her daughter looked older than her years, almost grown up and profoundly, innocently . . . *sexy*. How had that happened? How had Rose taken her eye off her youngest child long enough for such a transformation to have taken place?

I can't think about that right now, she thought. Not with everything else that's going on. But I'd better file it away for later, crisis or no crisis.

The waiter showed them to their table and Rose waited patiently, sipping at her glass of water, until Lisa had ordered their food. Then she began, obliquely, leading up to the issue that had already set her heart thumping.

'So,' she asked casually, 'how do you feel now about your summer exams?'

Lisa shrugged. 'Okay, I think. They're still a month away.

And they're not all that important, so I'm not doing too much study.'

Rose checked the automatic response that came to her lips, ignoring the imaginary filial red rag that had just been waved at her maternal bull. All your exams are important, young lady, and need to be taken seriously. Instead, she said lightly: 'Well, you've worked hard all year, so I'm sure you'll do fine. And it's good that you're not too stressed about them.'

There's no easy way to say this, Rose thought. Just go for it.

'I had some surprising news . . . during the week,' she said. 'Last night' or 'Yesterday' sounded too dramatic, she thought, too sudden. Lisa looked at her mother, mild curiosity puckering across her forehead.

'Yeah?'

'I had some news of your dad.' That was enough. Rose didn't need or want to share any of the emotion that had accompanied the personal delivery of such unwelcome news.

Mercury winged with malice.

'*Dad?*' said Lisa, in a tone of such incredulity that Rose's heart was gladdened. No upset, no distress. Keep on going.

'Yes. It seems he's considering coming back to Dublin. Some sort of business opportunity has come up, so he got in touch.'

'What does he want?' Lisa's tone was guarded now, almost suspicious.

A girl after my own heart, thought Rose, feeling relief like sunlight. A perfectly appropriate response. 'Well, I don't know yet that he *wants* anything in particular – except, of course, to see all of you guys.'

'Why? He's been gone since I was in first class in *primary*.' Now her tone was edging towards indignation, her blue eyes suddenly huge, luminous.

The waiter arrived with their food and provided a welcome interruption. Rose waited until he'd gone before answering.

'I know, it's been a long time. Lots of water under the bridge, as we say.' She smiled at her daughter. 'I don't know all the details yet – we haven't really spoken at length, but I do know that he is particularly anxious to see you and Brian and Damien.'

'Do I have to?'

Lisa was pushing the food around her plate, her expression suddenly troubled, older, somehow.

'No,' said Rose carefully. 'You don't have to do anything. But I wouldn't dismiss something so important without having a good think about it first.'

'Are you going to see him?'

I can't tell her that I already have, thought Rose. Too much for her to take in, all at once. Too much. 'Yes,' she said firmly. 'There are still some things we need to talk about, to sort out between us.' She paused, waiting for Lisa to break the silence.

'Are you two going to be getting back together again?'

For the instant it took to half-form a thought, Rose intended to say something soothing, childproof. Then she changed her mind.

'Absolutely not,' she said firmly. 'There's no chance of that; neither of us wants it. But he is still your dad, and I think you should give some serious thought to seeing him.'

'He hasn't given much serious thought to seeing me, though, has he? He's been gone since I was *six*.'

'I know. But things change, people change, circumstances … move on. I'm certainly not going to force you to do anything you don't want to do, Lisa, and you can take your time thinking about it. But please don't shut me out – we need to talk about this so that whatever decision you make, you're happy that it's the right one.'

Lisa stared at her plate. Rose's heart ached for her young, suddenly pale face. 'Are you all right?'

'Do you think I should?'

'I'll tell you that after we've talked some more about it. But, right now, if I'm honest, I think you should at least keep a very open mind about it. He's never stopped being your dad, you know, never stopped loving you. Parents generally don't.' Rose smiled across the table, stroking her daughter's hand.

'He'd a funny way of showing it.'

Yes, thought Rose. Yes, he had.

'Well, let's just see what happens. Just don't close off anything, okay, love?'

Lisa nodded, her blue eyes grave. Too much, thought Rose suddenly, too much adult stuff at such a young age. I could wring your bloody neck, Ben Holden, I really could – hard and tight and without female mercy.

'Now, that's all we need to say for tonight. Let's park it until you've had time to think about it. We'll talk again tomorrow, and you don't need to make any decision until you're ready. Deal?'

'Deal.'

'Except, of course, the decision about dessert. What's it to be, mademoiselle? The health-giving benefits of fruit salad, or, just this once, a chocolate frenzy?' Rose kept her tone light, teasing.

Lisa brightened immediately. 'Yeah – Heart of Darkness!' She grinned. 'A zillion calories – and who cares?'

'Who indeed?' Rose was giddy with love, relief and optimism.

One daughter down, two sons to go.

*

Rose pulled a notebook out from under the microwave, rummaged in the drawer for a pen that still worked. She found one, finally. A pink Barbie pen, chewed and disfigured, a brave feathery boa still clinging grimily to its top. It was almost two o'clock in the morning and she had, for now, given up on sleep. Lisa had finally gone to bed, the kitchen was quiet, the house long settled into its night-time repose. Even the normal creaks and groans were suddenly, strangely silent.

I need to make a list, she thought. Of what I need for the kids, for myself, for everyone's future. After Ben left her, Rose's whole life had seemed reduced to an exercise in list-making: shopping lists, catering lists, childcare rotas, moneys owed and owing lists. Back then, such a careful, deliberate process had made her feel that she could put some sort of shape to her life; that, able to wield pen and paper, she wasn't completely at the mercy of forces beyond her control.

But it wasn't working tonight. She couldn't concentrate. A list was too much of a paltry thing: a paper shield in the face of the unknown. She threw the pen onto the kitchen table, refilled her cup with lukewarm, tannin-tasting tea. No matter what she did, what she thought, in these quiet hours of the early morning, nothing could comfort her. Nothing could make her feel secure.

She stood up from the table, restless. For something to do, she filled the kettle again, noticing as she did so that the blind on the kitchen window was grubby, its ends sad and fraying. She could feel herself shrug. Years ago – even just one year ago – she would have regarded that as something important, something she would waste no time in fixing. Now it was just another sign, along with shabby furniture and fading paintwork, that the past belonged to another planet, one that simply orbited hers every few years, reminding her of how things used to be.

Right now, glimpses of that past kept merging with the new

future of Ben's return, and all Rose could see before her was Damien.

How was she going to tell him? Was there any point even in hoping to guide his response? Rose rubbed her hands across her forehead and closed her eyes for a moment. It was no use. Eyes closed or open, her eldest child was everywhere.

The eldest, the firstborn, the repository of all parental hopes . . .

Poor kid, she thought. No wonder he went off the rails.

She could still see him, as a two-year-old, walking along the sea wall in Clontarf. He used to love dipping the toes of his red wellies into the little pools where seaweed and greenish salty water gathered. She remembered how he'd pull hard against her, straining to run on ahead, his bright yellow oilskin creaking against her hand. His strength and determination had always surprised her.

Then, years later, the great toothless grin of triumph as he'd mastered his first bicycle. Later still, his young face filled with shy pride on his first day at secondary school. Rose tried to shake away the image. She had a sudden, violent longing for all the busy, uncomplicated years of her children's childhoods. They had been hard work but no trouble: all the difficulties of mothering amply rewarded by just one sunlit smile.

How quickly things can change, she thought. What had once been the certainty of love and connection had somehow been transformed overnight into anguish, alienation, and just about every kind of trouble. Rose began to recall now that seismic evening when she'd discovered with brutal, bitter clarity that her carefully tended, lovingly nurtured family had finally begun to implode.

She'd been late back from the Bonne Bouche, laden with supermarket shopping, struggling to get her key into the lock.

She remembered pushing open the front door with her foot. And the feeling of relief: home. At last.

She elbowed her way into the hall, struggling to manage the four plastic bags full of groceries. She could feel the handle on one of the bags begin to elongate, as it stretched itself to its limit, digging its way painfully into the soft flesh at the root of her fingers. She was hot and cross.

She hurtled down the hallway towards the kitchen, arriving just before the seam on the heaviest bag gave way and dozens of potatoes bounced gleefully out of their sweaty captivity, tumbling across the kitchen table and onto the tiled floor. Thus released, they then made it their business to seek out the most awkward, least accessible hiding places where, eventually, they came sullenly to rest. Small nodes of grit and clay launched themselves into orbit everywhere like tiny satellites. Rose swore loudly, and only then noticed the state of the kitchen. Every surface was crammed with plates and glasses, bowls, mugs – all the detritus of breakfasts and snacks and lunches strewn carelessly everywhere. How many young men had there been *this* time, eating her out of house and home?

She pulled open the door into the sitting room. The curtains had not been drawn back, the lights were still on. More glasses and plates had been catapulted everywhere and the room was stifling. There was no sign of Damien. Rose rushed upstairs. She found him lying on his bed, eyes closed, completely oblivious to all around him. She watched, paralysed for a moment, as music from his headphones poured itself into his body, filling the whole length of him, it seemed, as first his arms, then his hips, then his feet gyrated in time to its rhythm. The volume was so high that Rose could feel the drumbeat and hear the tinny, scratchy sounds of distant vocals. She'd *told* him not to have the setting so loud, that he'd damage his eardrums.

'Damien!' She'd stood in front of him, calling his name. She was reluctant to touch him, to startle him – it was obvious that he was in another world. There was no answer. Eventually she had to shake his shoulder before she got any response. He sat up immediately, pulling the headphones down so that they encircled his neck like some strange tribal necklace. Relief vied with anger, anger with impotent frustration.

'*What* is going on?' she asked him sharply.

He looked at her blankly. 'Nothin'.'

'It's seven o'clock, Damien – where are Brian and Lisa?'

'What do you call her – Margaret, Carly's mother, called for Lisa. They've got some drop-dead gorgeous new DVD, or somethin'. She invited Lisa over to her house, said she'd feed her. Brian's around in John's. Said he'd be back around nine.'

'And what about downstairs?'

Rose wanted not to feel the rage that was building up inside her. She'd had a long, loud, angry day and all she'd wanted was to come home, put her feet up for half an hour and have a cup of tea. Instead, a mess not of her making awaited her, colonizing her kitchen, cluttering up her living space. Damien was twenty-two, for Christ's sake, well old enough to clean up after himself.

That had been only the tip of the iceberg, though – the hard, cold, dishonest point of her anger, the bit that gave her the excuse to get mad. The real reason was well below the surface, had been floating along for the best part of two years now, frozen, impenetrable, slow-moving – and always, simply, there.

That evening was just another incident in a long line of conflicts. Rose stood in her son's bedroom, rigid with anger, determined, this time, not to yield.

'Relax, relax, will you? I'll clean up and fill the dishwasher in a minute.'

'Do it now, Damien, please. I'm worn out working and I'd like a breather before I start the dinner. I presume *you* haven't made anything?'

Stop it, stop it, before this all becomes too much.

Even as she spoke, she had seen the situation spiralling out of her control: a red dust seemed to be gathering in the room between them, shaping itself into some sort of deadly vortex into which they'd both be sucked, each made blind and deaf to the other until spat out again spent, useless, impotent.

He'd looked at her coldly, fury gathering across his eyes. She noticed more and more as he grew older how much he physically resembled his father.

'No,' he said belligerently, 'I haven't. Why should I?'

That did it.

'Because last time I looked, you were still living here, eating, drinking and generally enjoying all the comforts of home.'

They were out on the landing now, facing each other. His head was thrust forward, Rose's fists were clenched.

'What comforts?' he shouted. 'There's nothing here but rules and petty restrictions and I'm sick of it. Don't worry – you won't have to provide for me much longer. I'll be gone just as soon as I can!'

He pushed past her, taking the stairs two at a time.

Rose called angrily after him: 'You'll have to practise getting up off your arse before six o'clock in the evening, in that case!'

The front door slammed, making the bits and pieces of pottery on the hall table tremble a little. Motes of dust danced crazily around each other in the shafts of light that came through the window.

Perhaps he'd heard, perhaps he hadn't. It hardly mattered. More and more during those days, there had seemed to be no way of reaching him.

And things had got steadily worse.

There was that awful night when she had woken suddenly, hair prickling, the back of her neck tingling. It had taken a moment or so to adjust her focus, to understand where she was, what she was hearing. She'd looked around her, grappling with the unexpected sensation of fear. Her bedside light was on, her book open on the pillow beside her. There was a distant pull of pain across her shoulder from resting too long against the headboard, the angle an awkward one. She'd had no idea what time it was, what day it was, or why she had awoken so abruptly. Then she heard it again: a strange, dragging, muffled sound, coming from the hallway below.

Fully alert then, Rose had thrown the duvet back and shoved her arms into the sleeves of her dressing gown. She'd walked quietly, quickly, out onto the landing. Her bedroom door was always open, a deliberate statement to her family that she was there, watching over them, protecting them. It might have fooled her children, but Rose knew that she could never fool herself: she was still nervous whenever she woke during the night. Darkness brought with it those nameless, primitive fears that had never dared claw at her insides as long as Ben was in her bed. Now her heart began to hammer against her ribs and from some distant viewing point, she saw herself leaning over the banisters, terrified that the magnified drumbeat was echoing throughout the whole house.

There it was again.

Her hand shaking slightly, Rose reached out for the light switch. At precisely the same moment, someone below her coughed, and the spell was broken.

'Damien!' she cried, unsure whether relief or anger was the stronger emotion. Light flooded the stairway and the hall below. Damien stood halfway between the front door and the kitchen, his rucksack dragging against the wooden floor. That's the sound, she'd thought, her heart beginning to return to normal.

Nothing sinister; nothing supernatural; just a rucksack. It took a moment before her gaze reached Damien's face. She was unhappily conscious of what stood in front of her, even before her son spoke. His face seemed peculiarly out of proportion, dirty, formless somehow. The features were no longer his: they belonged to some alter ego, some fairy child that had magicked its way into his place. He had deserted his own body, filtered himself away somewhere into the darkness, leaving her with the changeling child. He began to sway then, very gently, back and forwards, back and forwards.

'Hi, Mum,' he said thickly.

Then she knew for sure, of course she did.

'You're drunk,' she said bluntly. 'Again.'

He said nothing, just continued to make his unsteady way towards the kitchen. Rose followed, almost tripping on the belt of her dressing gown in her haste to reach her son.

'This has to stop, Damien.'

'What has, Ma?' He was standing in front of the open fridge, just bending slightly as he reached for the orange juice. His stance filled her with sadness, an intense rush of emotion composed partly of memory, partly of regret and partly of a searing, blinding vision of what the future was becoming, unfolding right there in front of her eyes. He tried to keep the teasing, affectionate tone he always used when he called her 'Ma', but she could hear the strain in his voice. And he kept his back to her, his unsteady gaze still directed towards the contents of the fridge, the carton of juice apparently forgotten.

'Look at me, Damien. I mean it.'

He turned, his gaze glassy, hostile. 'I've just had a few pints with the lads. First time we've met up in a while, for God's sake. I'd no dinner, so . . .' he shrugged, allowing her to reach her own conclusion. *It was the empty stomach, your honour. I'm not to blame. No responsibility here, your honour, not on my part.*

'It's not just tonight, and not just the start of the new term, or the end of the old one. This is happening far too often. It's dangerous – can't you see it's affecting your whole life?'

Even as she spoke, Rose realized how useless her words were. Who thinks of their whole life when they've only recently celebrated their twenty-second birthday? Their whole life is the here and now, living for the moment. Years unfurl in front of them, rushing full-bellied before the wind, heading towards an unconsidered future. All of life is now: growing older happens to other people. As though he'd just read her mind, which her elder son had always had the uncanny ability to do, Damien looked at her mockingly.

'Forgotten what it's like to be young, Ma, eh?' And he tipped the carton of juice to his lips, throwing his head back, almost keeling over in the process. Rose turned away without a word. She should have left him until morning, shouldn't have bothered trying to reason with him. But he had frightened her with his sneaky, shuffling entrance, had reminded her of some furtive animal, intent on evading capture. He had been slipping away from her for over two years now – not with the independence of a grown-up, but rather, elusively, resentfully, shielded by a hard carapace of anger.

She left the kitchen, closing the door quietly behind her.

And it wasn't as if she could have kept this from her other two children, either. On another, later occasion, Brian had looked on shocked, white-faced as his elder brother lurched sickeningly down the hallway, his face twisted into an ugly parody of a smile.

'All righ' there, bro'?' Damien had tried to high-five his younger brother, but Brian had simply stepped out of the way. The sudden lack of connection with the hand he'd been expecting, the emptiness of the air as he swung downwards, had disturbed whatever was left of Damien's fragile sense of equilibrium. He'd stumbled forwards and come crashing down onto his knees. He'd looked up at both of them, stunned, puzzled to find himself on the floor. There seemed to be a moment when he'd realized what had happened before his eyes closed and he slumped into a heap outside the kitchen door. Brian had looked at his mother, his eyes wide and horrified.

'Is he drunk?' he asked in a whisper.

'He certainly is. Again.' Rose had been filled with impotent fury. There was no point in pretending. She couldn't shield Brian from this, and she couldn't shield Damien from himself, either. She had the familiar, ashen taste of failure in her mouth. 'Not a pretty picture, is it?'

Brian had shaken his head, slowly.

'Come on,' she'd said briskly. 'Leave him.'

'What – here? Like this?' Brian's expression was appalled.

'Yes, just like this. This can't go on. I'm at my wits' end. Let him sleep there and sober up. Maybe he'll learn a lesson.'

'We can't just leave him here!'

'Yes,' she'd said firmly. 'We can, and we will. I believe it's called "tough love". Come on – step over him.'

Reluctantly, Brian had stepped over his brother's prone form. Rose had thanked God that Lisa was already asleep. This was something a twelve-year-old girl should not have to see.

Later on, she crept downstairs in the darkness. Damien was lying on his back, snoring. Gently, but firmly, Rose turned him over onto one side, making sure his airways were free. He'd been sick on one previous occasion: her terror was that he might choke in his sleep. She stroked an escaped lock of hair back across his pale forehead. Something in the ghostly vulnerability of his face as he slept stirred a deep well of sadness within her.

She saw him in front of her with a bucket and spade, saw

him smile up at her from his buggy, from his first tricycle. The face before her was still that child's and, despite herself, she felt filled with the all the aching tenderness of grief.

'Damien, Damien,' she whispered, tears welling and falling uncontrollably. 'What on earth am I going to do with you?'

She realized that she was crying again, quietly now. The tears surprised her as she sat at her kitchen table, a cup of cold tea in front of her. She'd never before allowed herself to dwell on those times in all their excruciating detail. She knew that she already carried them inside her, their insistence dulled a little by the act of not remembering. Rose had always felt that if she journeyed there, she might not be able to find her way back. Instead, she had been intent on survival: something that belonged to the present, that focused the future.

If you kept on looking over your shoulder, she'd told herself, the danger was that something, somewhere, would eventually trip you up.

But now Ben's return had stirred more than just the memories of his leaving. Everywhere she looked, there was something prodding at her, reminding her of loss, of missed opportunity, of all the failures and fractures of maternal love. I'm not at my wits' end, she used to think, during those long nights when she'd sat up, waiting, hoping, for her elder son's safe return. I left Wits' End a long time ago: it was a chilly, deserted place, a mere stopping-off point along the road. I'm much further on than that.

'That's enough,' she said now, out loud. 'Stop it.' She stood up, literally dusting herself off. She opened the dishwasher and put her mug inside. Firmly, she emptied the teapot, threw the teabags in the bin. She tore a piece of kitchen towel off the roll, wiped her face briskly. 'That's quite enough for one night.'

Wallowing was not part of the plan.

Go to bed. Pandora's box would wait until tomorrow.

She turned off the lights, checked the alarm, climbed the stairs slowly to her bedroom. Exhaustion claimed her even before she took off her dressing gown. She half-pulled the duvet over her, and sank gratefully into the merciful oblivion of sleep.

# Chapter Three

ROSE PULLED UP outside the local supermarket at ten o'clock, just as it opened. She'd slept little the previous night. Too many cups of tea, she'd scolded herself, trying to be matter-of-fact, no-nonsense. But she knew, of course she did, that tea had had nothing to do with it. She'd dreamt of Damien whenever she did sleep, and then lurched awake, head pounding, palms sweating. Once awake, she could think of little else. Her son's face ambushed her at every turn: that pale forehead, the defiant lock of hair.

But despite two restless nights, Rose could now feel a welcome return of energy. She relished the feeling, getting stronger and more insistent with every hour, that now was not the time to be tired: now was the time to be smart, alert. Saturday had been spent, *wasted*, in a fog of inertia, of listless worrying. But some time around three o'clock on Sunday morning she had been jolted awake by a shock of realization. It was nothing new: nothing she hadn't felt a hundred times already, since Ben's return. But in the darkness of her silent bedroom, the thought had acquired a new clarity.

These were not the days to fill with *waiting*. She was a woman on a mission: she had things to do, days to organize, people to handle. She needed to act, to make things happen. The old Rose, the one who'd spent so much of her early adult life in a state of passive animation, had no place here. She'd had a sudden surge of will, one that had kept her awake until dawn. And now, all the remaining lethargy of the past two days disappeared somewhere between the tinned tomatoes and the cheese counter.

She made her way quickly up and down the broad aisles, mindlessly calculating what household supplies were critical, what was running low, what could wait for another day. This was the one thing she no longer needed a list for: it was as familiar to her as breathing.

Briskly, she emptied the contents of her basket onto the sluggishly moving belt at the checkout.

'Are you collectin' the stamps?'

Rose looked blankly at the checkout girl. Her young face was a white wall of boredom, its sullenness strange against the glint of a nose stud, the defiant gleam of an eyebrow ring.

'Pardon?'

The girl sighed. 'The stamps, for the fryin' pan and saucepan set?'

Rose almost laughed out loud. 'No – no thank you. I think I'll pass.'

The girl suddenly grinned at her: a bright, broad ray of feminine complicity. For some reason, the exchange cheered Rose enormously.

Frying pan? Saucepan set?

Rose had no clear idea of where she wanted her life to go next. As yet, she didn't know in what directions Ben's unwelcome return might point her. But wherever it was, she was damned sure that she, and the checkout girl, would both bring with them something a lot more interesting than a frying pan and saucepan set.

*

Later that evening, Rose pulled up outside Heuston Station. She parked behind the long line of taxis queuing for passengers off the evening trains. Just at that moment, her mobile rang.

'I'm outside, Brian – just down from the taxi rank. Yes, I'll wait for you here.'

She didn't want to meet him inside the station, knew that his sharp eye would see that all was not well. She'd a fighting chance of fooling him in the fading light, but fluorescent lamps would only highlight the dark circles under her eyes, the normally pale complexion now red and blotchy from lack of sleep.

Dad's favourite son: how would *he* take the news of the prodigal father's return? She remembered how, in the early days after Ben left, her middle child had had difficulty even looking her in the eye. She had played a deliberate waiting game with him, knowing him well enough to hope that he would, eventually, emerge from his chrysalis of hostility. And he had – at about fourteen years of age, in a cloud of deodorant and hair gel, demanding to be seen, insisting that she notice him, his clothes, his hair, his brand-new personality.

He'd seemed willing, finally, to shed his coat of sullen silence, his air of lofty grievance. Almost overnight he'd turned into a noisy, in-your-face, up-front adolescent. Rose had grown used to the sound of his large feet taking the stairs three at a time, landing with a thump on the wooden floor of the hallway. She'd greeted every loud outfit, every new haircut and colour, no matter how outrageous, with the same mild mantra.

'Well, well,' she'd remark. 'What can I say? You take my breath away.'

Choose your battles, she'd learned. Fight only the ones worth winning: passing fads and fashions were not one of them.

He'd display each of his new outfits in the hallway, twirling dizzily, the soles of his trainers squealing against the floorboards. He'd always finish his dance with a flourish, his hands extended in a music-hall 'ta-da' for her entertainment.

'Give me a hug,' she'd demand, every time.

And he would. On cue, he'd lope towards her, much taller even then than she was, and lift her up in a bear-like embrace. When she insisted he put her down, he'd be delighted to oblige: suddenly, and with some force.

Damien had never cared for that sort of experimentation, and Lisa had only ever wanted to be the same as everyone else. But Brian, it seemed, had been driven to express enough individuality for all three of them. His became a sartorial rebellion which Rose hadn't minded in the least: she had welcomed its brash, colourful ordinariness with a huge sigh of relief. Often it had brought with it a measure of fun and frivolity to a household sometimes sadly lacking in both.

She smiled to herself, now. She used to ruffle his hair back then, too, before the days when gel and wax and *product* had taken over. Now his locks were permanently constructed into complicated peaks and valleys, the texture unwelcoming – spiky on the hills and gooey in the lowlands. She had learned not to travel there.

She waved now as her tall, gangly son approached her, hunched over from the weight of his rucksack. Where did I get such tall children? Rose wondered idly. It's a complete mystery to me.

Brian grinned at her, his face unshaven, shadowed by three days' dark growth. He pulled open the door, dumped his rucksack into the back of the van.

'Hi, Mum! Thanks for collectin' me. You on your own?' He struggled into the passenger seat, folding his long body to fit into it.

'Hello, love. Yes, Lisa's watching something on television.' She leaned towards him, met his kiss halfway. 'Did you have a good time?'

'Wicked.' He nodded. 'Absolutely brilliant. Great party.'

'Good,' said Rose, pulling away carefully from the kerb. 'So John's no longer a teenager. He's a mature old man now, don't you think?'

Brian grinned. 'Well, I don't think I'd ever accuse John of being mature. But at least he's older: and boy, has he turned twenty in style.'

'Were there many there?'

'Yeah, about eighty, I think. We didn't get to bed until six on Saturday morning. And when we got up, we just started the party all over again.' He looked at her quickly. 'Don't worry, I didn't overdo it. Believe it or not, I was sensible.'

She glanced over at him and smiled. 'I do believe it. I'm glad you had fun.'

'Are you okay?'

'Yes,' said Rose. 'Why?'

'You look as though you're the one who's been up for two nights in a row.'

'I haven't been sleeping.'

She didn't want to tell him: not here, not in the car. She wanted to take him home, to the comfort of her own kitchen, somewhere he could be angry, or silent, or indifferent. He deserved at least that. She had a bright, brittle vision of sitting in the little wicker chair by the window in Brian's bedroom. Her eleven-year-old son had sat before her in complete silence. She'd tried to explain to the white, pinched face, all the usual stuff about Mum and Dad still loving the children, while her tongue felt like a dried fish in her mouth. When she'd faltered her way to a finish, Brian spoke. His words had been stony.

'Can I watch television now?'

His grief had sliced at her heart. On that day, her son, her baby, had become a human scalpel with spiky hair and grubby trainers. It had taken until the following morning for him to cave in, to weep into his porridge like there was no tomorrow.

'Mum – you're very quiet. Are you sure there's nothin' wrong? Mum?' His tone was suddenly anxious, urgent. 'Tell me.'

Rose hesitated, just for a second, but it was a second too long.

'There *is* somethin' wrong, isn't there?' He leaned forward in the passenger seat, straining against the seatbelt. At that moment, in that position, he looked unnervingly like his father. 'It's Damien, isn't it? He's at it *again*!'

Rose shook her head, tried to keep the tears at bay. 'No, no,' she protested, 'Damien's fine. It's nothing like that.'

'Then what is it? Pull over!'

'I can't, Brian, that's a bus lane.'

'I don't care! Look – there's a space there, over on the right. Drive in there.'

Rose parked, the lights of the Liffey shimmering just below them. She turned off the ignition.

'Now, tell me. If it's not Damien, then what is it? Has somethin' happened to you, or to Lisa?' He clutched at her sleeve, his eyes alarmed.

God, thought Rose, I'm making a right mess of this. 'No, Brian, it's okay, truly – there's nothing wrong with anybody, I promise.' She fished in the sleeve of her sweater for a handkerchief.

'Then for Christ's sake, what is it? Tell me!'

She turned to face him. 'It's your dad. He's here, in Dublin. He came to see me on Thursday evening.'

Brian sat back suddenly. He looked as though someone had just punched him. His five o'clock shadow was starker than ever against his pale skin. 'Dad?' he said.

Rose nodded. 'Yes. I wanted to get you home before I told you. I'm sorry to do it like this.'

'What does it matter where you tell me? Why didn't you *ring* me? Why didn't you let me know?' His tone was more incredulous than angry. He struggled to change his position in the passenger seat, but the seatbelt locked, preventing him. He released it abruptly and turned to glare at his mother.

'And you'd have done what, exactly?' Rose kept her voice very quiet. 'Left your party, come home to find your dad already gone? What would have been the point of that?'

'I don't know – but I could've *been* here, done *something*! What . . . why didn't he . . . When . . . How long is it since I've seen him, anyway?' Now his tone began to grow angry. 'I stopped countin' long ago.' He patted his top pockets furiously, searching for something. 'Why's he come back? I mean, he's not lookin' to *live* with us again, is he?'

Rose shook her head. '*I'm* not lookin' for him to live with us! No, of course he's not. He's talking Celtic Tiger opportunities and tying up all the loose ends between the two of us. And he wants to see the three of you.'

'What sort of loose ends?'

'Well, we're only separated, not divorced. It's probably time to do that now, and settle things properly, legally. But he does want to see the three of you. He's made that very clear.'

'Has he now?' said Brian grimly.

'Yes, he has. And he was very glad to hear how well you're doing.'

Brian snorted. 'He coulda heard that any time he wanted. From eleven to nineteen is a bit of a gap, isn't it?'

Rose felt weary all over again, her palms clammy, eyes gritty.

'I know, I know, but he's here, and he's still your dad. You need to see him.'

'Oh, I'll see him all right. Out of curiosity, if nothin' else. There's a couple of things I'd like to ask him.' Brian rummaged angrily in his jeans pockets now, pulled out cigarettes and a lighter. He raised one hand in his mother's direction, as though to push away the words she hadn't spoken. 'I know you don't like me smokin', but I don't care just now, right?' He lit a cigarette, inhaled deeply.

Rose saw that his hand was shaking. She tried to smile at him. 'Smoke away. I think you can have a special dispensation for tonight.'

'Have you told Lisa?' He opened the window, blew a long thread of bluish, ghostly smoke out into the night air.

'Yes.'

'How did she take it?'

'She was puzzled, a little bit upset – but she was only six when he left, so I don't think her memories are anything like yours. It's very different for each of you.'

'Does Damien know?'

'Not yet. And don't tell him, please. I'll call him later tonight, invite him over for dinner as soon as he's free. I want him where I can keep an eye on him, hold onto him for a few hours.'

Rose pulled her hair back from her forehead again. It felt as though it grew too tightly there, too close to the skin: its very presence made her head begin to ache.

Brian nodded in agreement. 'Yeah. Sounds like a plan. Don't want him goin' off at half-cock. Jesus, I can't believe it.' He turned away from her, flicked ash out of the window.

Rose reached out her hand and rubbed her son's stubbled cheek gently. 'I haven't done that to you in a long time.'

'I'll let you away with it, just this once.'

They sat in silence for a few moments.

'It's kinda hard to take in, isn't it? I mean, it's the last thing I'd have expected.' He crushed the end of his cigarette into the ashtray, turned to look at Rose.

'You and me, both.'

'Are you sure you're all right? You look like the Bride of Dracula.'

'Thanks a lot. I've been better. I feel a bit shocked, a bit unsteady. And I can't seem to switch my brain off.'

'Does this mean that he'll be livin' in Dublin for good?'

'I honestly don't know, Brian. I have so many questions, I don't know where to begin. As soon as I have any answers, I'll tell you. I said I'd let him know when I was ready to talk.'

Brian grinned faintly. 'That could be pretty open-ended.'

Rose smiled back at him. 'No, I want to do it sooner rather than later . . . I think. Maybe towards the middle of next week. I want it to suit me: I don't want to be taken by surprise again. And by the way, I've disconnected the house phone. Right or wrong, I'm going to leave it like that until I've got in touch with Damien. So, if you need me at any time tomorrow, just call my mobile.'

Brian nodded, looking down at the lights of the river. 'When do I see him? Dad, I mean?'

'Whenever you want. I'll get his mobile number, the number of wherever he's staying, his address, whatever you want. And then you can take it from there.'

'I *am* entitled to some answers, amn't I?' he asked, suddenly.

'Of course you are.' But you may not like what you hear, she thought.

'His timin' could have been better. Exams are only a month away.'

'This is your decision, Brian – *you* arrange something that makes *you* feel comfortable.'

'A ratio of one to ninety-six.'

Rose glanced over at him. 'Sorry? I'm lost.'

'I've had to wait for him for ninety-six months. I can make him wait for one, can't I?'

'Well, yes, I suppose so – if that's what you want. Can we talk on the move? I don't want to leave Lisa on her own for too long.'

He nodded. 'Yeah, sure.'

'Okay – put on your seatbelt.' Rose pulled out into the sparse moving traffic. They drove the rest of the way home in silence. I should have waited, she thought anxiously, given him more time to talk. I should have sat there for longer. But what can you do, pulled from one child to the other?

Your best, said her mother's voice inside her head. Only your best.

At the very least, it was now two children down, one to go. Rose knew that she now needed time and solitude to marshal all her forces for Damien.


'Lisa?'

She came out of the living room at once, looking quickly from her mother's face to her brother's.

'Did you tell him?'

Rose looked at her daughter in disbelief. 'Lisa – try the indirect method from time to time. A little tact goes a long way, you know,' she said, dryly.

Brian grinned at his sister. 'Yeah, Mum told me. No big deal.' He shambled his way towards the television, dropping his rucksack on the floor. Rose bit back the urge to tell him to bring it upstairs, to put his dirty clothes in the laundry basket. It could wait; it could all wait.

'Tell me about the birthday.' Lisa threw herself onto the

sofa beside her brother. 'How many were there? Was John's sister at it? What did she wear?'

Party animal, thought Rose in amusement. I've given birth to the ultimate party animal. God help me when she's old enough actually to *be* there.

Brian held up both hands in mock surrender. 'Whoa – steady on! I've no idea what she wore—'

'Liar!' shrieked Lisa in delight. 'You fancy her, I know you do!'

Okay, thought Rose. This is as good a time as any. I'm not needed here. 'Right, you two. I'm going for a bath, and bed. Did you leave on the hot water, Lisa?'

Lisa nodded. 'Yeah. There should be a full tank.'

'Good girl. Brian, there's some cold meat and potato salad in the fridge. Help yourself. If you decide to have one of your troughs of cereal, make sure there's enough milk left for the morning. That's all, folks. I'm gone.'

Lisa reached up and kissed her. Brian grabbed her hand. 'You okay, Mum?'

She bent down and kissed the top of his head. 'I'm fine. Oh, my God – your *hair* is revolting! What on *earth* are you using?'

He shrugged, looking embarrassed. 'I forgot my gel. Ciara said that a mixture of sugar and beer would make a good substitute . . .'

'See?' Lisa shrieked in delight. 'I *told* you you fancied her!'

Rose didn't wait for his denials. 'Right, I'm off. Lisa, bed by ten. Brian – you know the drill.'

She left before either had the chance to argue.

Once upstairs, she switched on the light in her bedroom and closed the door quietly behind her. She searched in her handbag for her mobile, becoming convinced that she must have lost it: one after the other, the different compartments of her bag yielded nothing other than notes to herself, change, purses, keys, glasses, at least half a dozen pens. Finally, exasperated, she upended the bag, spilling all its contents onto her bed. The first thing she saw was her mobile phone lying there, all silver and innocent. She grinned to herself. It was the same every time.

She'd joked lately with the Spice of Lifers about hanging her belongings around her neck so that her things could no longer manage to mislay themselves while she wasn't looking.

'Think about it,' she'd said to Sarah. 'A new line in jewellery – all very tasteful, of course, but chunky and practical. Look at all the time women would save: no more rummaging for reading glasses or seeing glasses; no more swearing at the missing car keys. And no more reaching the top of the stairs wondering what the *hell* you'd come up for in the first place. It'd be a winner.'

Sarah had laughed at her, but Rose wagged an admonitory finger and growled: 'Give it twenty years and you'll thank me, my girl, mark my words. I'll call my new range "*Fun*-ctionals" – what do you think?'

I'd be my own best customer, Rose thought now, bringing Damien's number up on the screen.

'Hiya, Ma.' He answered at once.

Rose closed her eyes for a moment, feeling the familiar tentacles of anxiety loosen suddenly, allowing a watery sense of relief to take their place. It was the same every time she called: she never knew what would greet her. For now, he sounded normal. And that was all she wanted. No great gifts, no great achievements, just the everyday blessings of the safe, the healthy, the ordinary.

'Hello, love. All okay with you?'

'Yeah, great. Just watching a DVD with Kev an' Andy. You okay?'

'Yes. I've just collected Brian from the station. I'm off to bed early, so I wanted to catch you now. Would you be able to join us for dinner tomorrow night? I know it's short notice, but I'd love to see you. You haven't been in a while.' Rose winced. That sounded very much like a guilt trip. What the hell, she didn't care. Whatever worked, whatever got him here, under her roof, safe – all was fair in love.

He hesitated. 'I've . . . somethin' on tomorrow. How about Tuesday?'

Rose swallowed her disappointment. He spoke again quickly, before she had time to reply.

'It's all good stuff, Ma – nothin' to worry about. I'll tell you when I see you. I'll be there at exactly six o'clock on Tuesday, okay?'

Nothing to worry about? Rose smiled to herself. If only he knew.

'Tuesday's fine, love, just fine. I'll look forward to seeing you then. Go back to your DVD – tell Kev and Andy I was asking for them.'

'Night, Ma. Take care of yourself.'

'You too. Love you lots.'

'Yeah – me too.'

Rose hung up. Right. So she'd have to wait until Tuesday.

She went out onto the landing and listened for sounds from downstairs. She could hear the banter between Brian and Lisa, could hear Ciara's name being mentioned, and the bass rumblings of Brian's denials. She stepped into the bathroom and closed the door quietly behind her.

They're fine, she thought, as she emptied a full bottle of bubble bath under the running water. Both of them.

They're really fine.

*

Sometime later, Lisa tapped on the bathroom door. 'Night, Mum.'

'Night, love. Sleep tight: don't let the bugs bite.' Rose sang out the refrain of her daughter's childhood.

Lisa giggled. 'You're sad, Mum, d'you know that?'

'Absolutely,' Rose said. 'May I always be. See you in the morning.'

She could almost hear Lisa grin.

Rose lay back, allowing the warm bath water to soothe her. She smiled as she remembered how the bathroom had once been her refuge, in the early days after Ben left. She remembered hiding behind the sound of water, the comforting blanket of steam. Back then, it was the only place her children hadn't come looking for their mother. Some things never change, she thought.

She closed her eyes, sliding further under the hot water. There would be more emotion to come for Brian and Lisa in the coming days, no doubt about it, but for now they were better than she could have hoped.

What was it Damien had just said? *Nothing to worry about.* What a malignant little word, worry. Persistent, paralysing, pernicious. It was the one constant of parenthood, she thought. Membership of the Worry Club was handed out to all parents, particularly mothers, along with the cutting of their children's umbilical cords. It must be the largest organization in the world. Lifetime benefits accrued: grey hair, shortages of cash, the multifaceted terrors of the night.

And Damien had brought with him more than his fair share of those. Even now, Rose could vividly recall his face on the morning, well over a year ago, when she'd finally managed to corner him in the kitchen. She'd been determined to confront him, to block yet another one of his sneaky, shuffling exits. She had finally had to admit to herself that she could no longer handle her own son, no longer shield her younger children from the ugliness he brought home with him almost every night.

'I want you to leave, Damien.' She had said this very quietly.

He'd just looked at her without speaking.

She had continued to unload the dishwasher, standing by the sink, looking out over the winter garden. She very deliberately wiped the pools of water off the bases of the mugs, concentrating on the tea-towel in her hands.

'You can stay until after Christmas, but I want you gone by the New Year. There's plenty of casual work around, if you don't want a proper job, and if you can afford to drink yourself into a stupor on a nightly basis, you can afford to live somewhere else.'

She waited, begging the silent air for some reply.

'Fine.' He scraped the chair loudly away from the table, his face set in an expression she knew so well from another, past life.

'Do you want to know why?'

He was standing, not flinching, staring her down.

'You're not only damaging yourself, you're hurting your brother and sister and you've broken my heart. You have a drinking problem, Damien. Get help for it and we'll talk again. Until then, I don't want you upsetting the whole household.'

'Are you finished?'

'Oh, yes,' she said quietly then, her voice close to breaking. 'I am most certainly finished, more than finished.'

'I don't have a problem. *You're* the one with the problem. I'm twenty-three years of age, for fuck's sake, I'm entitled to go out with the lads at Christmas and have a good time. Just because *you* don't have a life.'

Rose closed the door of the dishwasher very carefully. 'It's not just Christmas, Damien. It's Fridays, or Wednesdays, or then again, maybe Monday afternoons – it's been any time and every time, just getting worse and worse over the past couple of years. You scraped through college by the skin of your teeth, you've never been able to hold down a job, you can't even get up before midday. You have a problem. Deal with it and I'll help you. Otherwise, you'll have to find somewhere else to live in January.' She faced him then, leaning against the counter top, glad that there was something solid at her back.

'I don't want your fuckin' charity,' he hissed. 'If you want me to go, I go now.'

Rose drew a long, slow breath. She moved away from the window, hung the tea-towel over the back of one of the kitchen chairs and rested her hands on the table.

'Then go.'

He left the kitchen at once, not even bothering to slam the door behind him.

There were scuffling noises from upstairs, cupboard doors banged. She could hear him speaking loudly on his mobile. And then he was gone, front door swinging wide open behind him, wind and rain lashing into the hallway in the wake of his departure.

'Happy fuckin' Christmas!'

She heard the shout as he walked angrily, stiffly, down the driveway.

Slowly she made her way to the front door and closed it quietly behind him. She caught a glimpse of him as he crossed the road to the bus stop, hair wild, rucksack like a monkey clinging to his back.

He's no coat on, she thought. He'll catch his death.

Then she returned to the kitchen table, put her head down, and wept.

*

It hadn't ended there, of course.

There was the morning the police had come. Rose had become suddenly aware that someone was shaking her by the shoulder roughly, almost painfully. Lisa's small, pinched face was all she could see as she'd struggled into consciousness. Her instincts were already firing, ready for trouble. Lisa's blue eyes were staring directly into hers and Rose could see a tiny version of herself reflected in the dark, frightened pools.

'Mum, Mum, wake up! There's a policeman and a lady downstairs. They want to see you now, Mum!'

Rose had thrown back the duvet, grabbed her dressing gown from the end of the bed, shoved her feet into rather raggedy-looking pink slippers.

Jesus, she thought. What now? Turning to Lisa, she said: 'What time is it, Lisa?'

'Eight o'clock.'

Eight o'clock on a Saturday morning: and already the police were at her door? Damien, Damien, the voice inside her head had kept repeating. Dear God, just don't let him be dead. That's all I ask. Please don't let him be dead.

She made her way downstairs, conscious of the effort it took to put one shaky, reluctant foot in front of the other.

'Mrs Holden?'

Rose hadn't bothered to correct the young, blue woman standing in her hallway.

'Yes.'

'I'm Sergeant Finlay, this is Sergeant O'Connor. May we have a word?'

Her eyes had glanced over Rose's shoulder. Lisa was still hovering at the bottom of the stairs.

'Of course.' Her voice was close to breaking; the catch at the base of her throat suffocated all the other words that lay there needing to be spoken. Not in front of Lisa, she thought. Not like this.

She led the way to the kitchen, kissing Lisa on the forehead as she passed. The child's face was grey with fear. 'It's okay,' Rose told her. 'I'll be out to you in a few minutes. Go into the living room and wait for me there.'

Lisa obeyed instantly.

Once inside the kitchen, Rose turned to face the two Guards. My God, she thought, they look about twelve years old. Wasn't this yet another one of the irrevocable signs of ageing? When doctors, policemen, firemen all looked like children in their dressing-up clothes?

'Is he dead?' Rose's hand made its way to her mouth, covering the trembling it had discovered there.

'Damien Holden is your son?'

'Yes,' said Rose.

She'd said 'is' – not 'was'. Damien Holden *is* your son. Could it be possible that the worst had not happened, not yet, after all?

'Please, Mrs Holden, sit down.'

The woman has a kind voice, thought Rose, kind but firm.

Rose held her ground. It was her son, her kitchen, her home. She was damned if she was sitting down until they'd said what they came for. 'Not until you tell me.'

'Damien has had an accident.'

Rose thought her words were deliberately slow, careful, and still she felt that some other event, something worse, was looming in the background, waiting its turn.

'It's nothing too serious – it just looks worse than it is. He's in Beaumont Hospital for observation. He's going to be fine, Mrs Holden. Now, will you sit down?'

Rose hesitated. If she stayed standing, was that the worst of the news that these two uniformed people would deliver? If she sat, would they then reveal what no mother should hear while on her feet? Was that how they did these things, waiting until they caught you unawares? Her knees made the decision for her, giving way just at the crucial moment. She sat heavily onto one of the kitchen chairs, burying her face in her hands, not capable of stopping the sobs that escaped hoarsely, wetly, between her fingers.

'It's not a serious accident, Mrs Holden. Your son will recover completely.' That measured voice again, slow, compassionate words.

'Would you like a cup of tea?' Sergeant O'Connor's voice was brisk, gruff almost. Rose took a surprising strength from it – its blunt, no-nonsense ordinariness in the midst of chaos. It was a pull yourself together kind of voice. But young. Far too young to be so full of no-nonsense.

'Tea. Yes, why not? Let's have tea.'

The sense of absurdity that Rose was already feeling began to grow as she watched the young man's large frame lumber its way to the sink, grasp the kettle in its left hand, turn on the tap with its right. There was a rush of water; the figure stepped back abruptly. Rose almost laughed out loud: she'd forgotten to tell him that that was a particularly splashy tap.

'Mrs Holden?'

Somehow, Sergeant Finlay had sat herself down on the chair beside Rose's. Rose hadn't seen her do that; she was surprised to find her at her side. Somehow, too, her hand was on Rose's forearm. A pale hand, Rose noticed, freckled; the sort of skin that went with red hair.

She seemed to be speaking again. 'Damien is all right, Mrs Holden. His injuries are superficial. He is not in any danger. Do you understand?' Gentle tones, soothing ones. The sort parents used to calm their children's night-time terrors.

The woman's face swam suddenly into focus in front of Rose's eyes. She did have red hair, and pale green eyes. And she was telling her that Damien was alive, not dead after all. Rose felt a great wave of love for this young woman sitting beside her, an urge to kiss the pale freckled hand, to show gratitude for the gift she had brought.

'Thank you, thank you,' she whispered.

And then there was a cup of curly-steaming tea in front of her. A cup with a saucer. Rose tried hard not to smile at that. She must tell Jane. But the twisting sensation around her mouth as she thought this did not feel like a smile, not like a smile at all. She felt something mould itself around her features like warm plastic. A murmured conversation between the two Guards resulted in milk from the fridge, spoons rattling from the drawer, sugar from the bowl at the end of the kitchen table.

Rose looked at the teapot, now hugely unfamiliar in its familiarity. Everything else around her felt dislocated somehow, curtained in spots of black light. Even the table was different, shifting away from her as she tried to reach for her cup of tea.

'I think she's going to faint,' were the words she heard from a very great distance before everything around her slipped from her grasp.

Rose's last thought was that this kind young woman would look after her.

There was something cold pressing down on her forehead. Rose tried to fight it off – she felt cold enough already: why was her forehead insisting?

'Take it away, Lisa,' she heard herself saying. 'It's too cold.'

'Mrs Holden?'

Something snapped in Rose's mind. Suddenly, her memory was perfectly clear: the police at her door, Damien's accident, the untasted cup of tea. She tried to sit up. Strong hands kept her down.

'Mrs Holden – can you hear me?'

Rose opened her eyes. 'Yes . . . what happened? Did I pass out?'

The pale face with the green eyes nodded. 'You did indeed. Now, if you want to sit up, I'll help you do so – but slowly, very slowly.' The woman – Finlay, wasn't it, Sergeant Finlay? – took the cold cloth away from her forehead and hooked her arms underneath Rose's.

'Is that better? Feeling any steadier?'

Rose nodded. 'Yes, I think so. I'm sorry. I'm not usually given to fainting. Where's my daughter?'

'We sent her upstairs to get a blanket. You were only out for a minute. Ah, here she is now. Good girl.'

Lisa brought the blanket over to the sofa and tucked it around her mother's knees. Rose smiled at her. 'I'm fine, love – just got a bit weak, that's all.'

Lisa nodded, biting down hard on her lower lip. Rose could feel herself fill with love, guilt, the dull ache of tenderness. This child is only twelve. She's had far too much grief in her young life. I'd do anything to make that go away. She pulled Lisa down onto the sofa beside her, put one arm around the slender frame. Lisa rested her head on her mother's right shoulder. Rose took a peculiar comfort from that childlike, trusting gesture.

She turned to Sergeant Finlay. 'Thank you for looking after me. Now, can you tell both of us how Damien is?'

'He's fine. He had a fall outside a club last night, or rather, at two o'clock this morning, to be exact. He's got a lot of cuts and bruises to his face and arms, but otherwise he seems to be absolutely fine.'

'Then why's he in hospital?' asked Lisa, sharply.

Sergeant Finlay turned to her. 'Some people there thought

that he might have hit his head when he fell. They called for an ambulance because they were afraid he might have concussion. It's something that can happen after a blow to the head, and it can make people feel very sick.'

'I know what concussion is,' said Lisa. 'Does he have it?'

'In a minor way, yes. They want to keep him in hospital for observation, just in case. The doctors want to make sure that no damage was done.'

'Was he drunk?' Lisa was meeting Sergeant Finlay's gaze, eye for eye.

There was barely perceptible pause. 'I can't say. The hospital contacted us because all he had with him was his passport, no address. We had to track down his home.'

At that moment, the phone rang.

'Lisa, will you get that upstairs in my bedroom? Take a message and say I'll call back later.'

Lisa ran from the kitchen.

'Well,' said Rose. 'Was he? Was he drunk? You might as well know that I threw my son out six weeks ago. I felt he had a drinking problem that he wasn't addressing.'

How cold that sounds. Hard and cold. Mothers shouldn't behave like that. I'm supposed to be the responsible one, the eternally loving one. I should have kept him here, close to me, kept an eye on him. This might never have happened.

'There was alcohol involved, certainly. But you'd need to talk to the doctors about the amount. Can we give you a lift to the hospital?'

'Was he fighting?'

'No – as far as we can tell, it was just a fall. The bouncer saw him sort of lurch forward and then fall down the steps. It's conceivable that he was pushed, of course, but not certain. We've no evidence of that, no evidence at all.'

'We can bring you to see him straight away,' said Sergeant

O'Connor. His deep voice startled Rose: she had almost forgotten he was there. 'You shouldn't drive for a while, not until you've recovered from the shock.'

Rose stood up. 'I'm fine,' she said, with a firmness she didn't yet feel. 'I'll have some breakfast and a bath and I'll make my own way up later. I won't go just yet, thank you. I need to spend some time with my daughter. She's very upset.'

She met the Guard's level gaze and he nodded, a little abruptly. 'If we can do anything else to help, just call the local station. Here's the number.'

Rose accepted the card from his outstretched hand and put it in her dressing gown pocket without looking at it. 'Thank you.'

'Sure you'll be all right? Is there anybody here with you?'

Rose thought that Sergeant Finlay had put the question very delicately. No, indeed, Sergeants Finlay and O'Connor, there is no Mr Holden here.

'My daughter, Lisa. And my son Brian will be home very soon. He's almost eighteen – a sensible adult. I'll be fine, thanks.'

Both Guards shook hands with her and moved towards the front door.

'Thanks again,' said Rose.

'You're welcome, Mrs Holden.'

And then they were gone. Rose felt surprisingly calm. So, Damien, she thought, this is what we've been leading up to, is it? And you've got away with it. You're alive, a few cuts and bruises, nothing serious. If you don't get your act together after this, I'll do more than throw you out of the house.

I'll throw you out of my life.

\*

Later that morning, Rose and Lisa had pushed their way past the groups of people in the hospital garden, all dragging deeply on cigarettes. Rose wondered what calamities lay behind the faces there, some haunted, some resigned, some convulsed into spasms of grief.

I've been lucky this time, she thought gratefully. Either way, it's such a very fine line.

The corridor was long and sterile, a faint but identifiable smell of illness lingered everywhere. Lisa had been grimly determined: she didn't care what Damien looked like, she wanted to see her brother. Rose checked her mobile one last time before she switched it off. She hadn't been able to contact Brian, so she'd left a non-committal voicemail about contacting her as soon as he picked up his messages.

She still wasn't sure what she was going to say to him. Sometimes she felt that Brian actively relished his elder brother's fall from grace. Oh, what a good boy am I.

At least with Lisa, things were still comfortingly straightforward: the child was angry with her big brother, but more than that, she wanted to see him safe.

I can cope with that, Rose thought, that's all reassuring, free from ambiguity. I can help her with that.


In the large hospital lift, there was no chance of conversation: packed uncomfortably close together, the vertical travellers looked up, or down at their hands, or stared straight ahead. Once the lift doors opened, they spilled out onto the second floor as though escaping from some nameless pursuer.

'Okay, Lisa – your call. Do we go in together, or one at a time?'

'Together.'

At the nurses' station, they were directed to Damien's ward. Rose could feel her knees, and her courage, begin to weaken.

Bed seven.

The ward was full, hot and heady with central heating. Lisa tugged at her mother's sleeve.

'Over here, Mum.'

Rose looked down at the boy in the bed. She was about to say – no, no, no – that's not Damien, that's not *my* boy, when something about the forehead gave it away. There it was, that unruly lock of hair that would never lie flat, no matter how much it was persuaded into submission.

'Jesus, God,' she said aloud, her eyes drawn to the pulpy flesh that had once been her son's face. Superficial? she raged. They call this superficial? One eye was badly swollen, crushed to a dark slit by the pressure of the black flesh all around it. The chin was criss-crossed with raw, angry grazes.

Lisa pulled a chair up to the side of the bed. 'Sit down, Mum.'

Rose obeyed, unable to draw her eyes away from the sleeping form in front of her. Her eyes filled. She needed to cry, but not here.

'Will he be okay?' Lisa's voice was suddenly very small, all the determined courage of earlier evaporated.

'I'm going to find a doctor, love. Will you sit here and keep him company? I'll be back in a few minutes.'

Lisa nodded.

Walking towards the nurses' station, Rose wiped away angry, impotent tears. What a waste. What a dreadful, awful, savage waste. She would not allow him to throw his life away like this. She would fight like a lioness to save him. Gloves off. She'd hound him and challenge him and fight him until she was no longer able to draw breath.

Twenty-three years of her life – and his – would not end

like this, with a slide into drunken wastefulness. She'd pull him back from that brink with every ounce of what was left of her strength.

Dr Keane was, to Rose's relief, somewhere in her mid-fifties. Surrounded by all the cheery youthfulness of nurses, Rose felt that she had strayed onto another planet, one where the signs were different, confused, alienating. How could any of these people help her handle her son? They were barely older than he was. At least Dr Keane looked as though she might have picked up some of life's experiences along the way.

'I know the injuries look bad,' she was saying, 'but actually your son has been very lucky. All the damage will heal, in time. I don't believe that there will even be any permanent scarring.'

'How drunk was he, Doctor?'

Dr Keane looked at her notes. 'Not drunk at all – he'd had maybe the equivalent of three pints of beer over the entire night: quite a modest amount, in fact. You should see what comes in here most weekends: seventeen, eighteen pints, shots of tequila, you name it.' She looked at Rose quizzically. 'Why, has alcohol been a problem?'

Rose nodded, barely trusting herself to speak. She could feel her lower lip begin to betray her again. 'Yes, for almost three years now. Not enormous at first, but kind of . . . incremental, if you know what I mean.'

The doctor nodded. 'The curse of sudden affluence, I'm afraid. He's not alone in that.'

Rose looked at her in surprise. 'I thought I was the only one to feel that. He used to get so mad at me – called me old-fashioned, Victorian, whatever. He said I should "get a life" – he was only having a "good time".'

'Yes, well, a good time with all the brakes off. There's a lot more pressure around these days – none of the certainties of other generations.' She leafed through her notes. 'Young people have trouble coping. I have twin boys myself; well, they're not boys any longer.' She smiled. 'They're almost thirty, so they've settled, in all senses. But I do understand your concern. The wild phase is particularly difficult to deal with.'

A wild phase? Was that all it had been?

Rose felt that she'd be profoundly relieved if she could believe that: that her son was not following some imprinted behaviour that would lead him towards inevitable desolation, loneliness, all the isolation of the drunkard. She'd never done this before: been mother to a twenty-three-year-old. How did parents know whether their child's trajectory was a normal response to twenty-first century adolescence, or whether it was an intimation of self-destruction?

'I threw him out of home before Christmas. I feel desperately guilty about that, now.' Rose could feel the tears gather. She gulped, her nose ran and she searched uselessly for a handkerchief. 'I'm sorry. The past year or so has just been so awful.'

Dr Keane handed her tissues. 'You probably did him a favour – gave him a wake-up call.'

'But how is he so cut and bruised if all he did was fall? I mean, you can't really fall flat on your face if you're sober, can you? You'll put your hands out instinctively to break the fall, surely?'

'His injuries are only partly consistent with a fall, Mrs Holden. My guess is that his eye, as they say, came in contact with someone else's fist in the nightclub. There was probably some girl involved – there usually is. You may want to follow that up with the Guards yourself. The notes here indicate that he lurched forward and then down the steps. I suspect that he was pushed. But you'll never get any proof. See no evil, hear no evil.'

'How long will you keep him here?'

'Probably just for tonight. He's stable. We gave him pain-killers earlier this morning, and he'll need to keep taking those. You can take him home tomorrow, if you like. Would you like me to have a word with him?'

Rose felt a small tug of hope. 'About his drinking?'

'Yes. There are some signs of damage to his liver – very minor signs as yet, but nonetheless, a cause for concern.'

'Can you frighten the living daylights out of him?'

Doctor Keane smiled. 'I suspect he's already done that to himself. By all accounts, he was a very quiet and contrite young man in the early hours of this morning. My guess is that he's already started to process the slippery slope he's found himself on, and has discovered that it's not to his liking. I'll encourage him to keep thinking that way.'

'When do young people finally grow up?' Rose asked suddenly. 'I was married, working and keeping house at his age. Not that I want him doing all of *that*,' she added hurriedly. 'I was far too young: I know that now. But these kids are so different from my generation, my experience, that I feel like a stranger, someone from another country trying to learn a new language.'

'You're not alone. You'll be glad to know that the American Psychiatric Association has recently decided that the official end of adolescence – in young Western men, in particular – is now thirty-four.' Dr Keane stood up, smiled briskly and closed Damien's file. 'You've a good way to go yet.'

Rose shook hands with her. 'That's if I last that long. God Almighty, I've got two others at home. I won't be out of this mire until I'm seventy, at this rate. What a prospect – I'll be able to retire, my kids will be off my hands and I get to relax at seventy? Life's a bitch.'

Dr Keane laughed. 'Don't worry, it gets easier. Is Damien the eldest?'

'Yes.'

'The oldest one tends to blaze a trail. May I ask if there's a Mr Holden?'

'Mr Holden deserted us. He walked out on all of us six – almost seven – years ago now. He and Damien never got on. I've often wondered if that's what part of this rebellion is all about. Mind you, I'm the one who stayed and I get to deal with all the fallout.'

'It was ever thus. That may be part of the explanation. But make him work that one out for himself. Don't give him any answers; make him find his own. Anyway, it helps me to know that bit of the jigsaw before I talk to him.'

'Thanks, Dr Keane. It's been good talking to you.'

'Look after yourself, Mrs Holden. Don't forget – you have a life, too. Get yourself some space, and above all, don't blame yourself. And don't allow your son to blame you, either. Guilt is a wasted emotion.'

Rose walked back down the corridor, the doctor's words having stirred a nugget of something significant inside her mind, something that would become a thought to give her comfort, later, whenever she managed to form it.

She'd figure out whatever it was, whenever she found the time, away from all these smells of sterility and mortality.


Rose sat down again by Damien's bedside and sent Lisa off in search of tea.

Moments later, he started to stir, opened one bloodied eye

and looked up at the ceiling, groaning. Rose waited. She knew that he would sense her presence eventually. She wanted him to be the one to make the first move. Her whole being strained towards him. She longed to cradle his head in her hands, to kiss his pale forehead, to whisper, 'My lovely boy, I'm here, I'm here.'

She resisted, some older, wiser, grimmer part of her making her sit still and silent. Perhaps it's tribal memory, she thought. All those mothers before her clamouring to make themselves heard: Be strong! Be silent! Have the courage to wait!

Slowly, he turned his head towards her. Her hands had already begun to tremble; a light film of sweat developed above her upper lip. God, kids were hard work.

'Ma?'

The voice was his own again, the tenderness tentative, but unmistakable. He reached out one searching, bandaged hand towards her. She took it, unable to speak, filled with sorrow, hope, all the impotence of furious love.

'I'm sorry, Ma. For everything. I'm going to make it right, I promise.' And he wound his arm around her neck, pulling her gently towards him.

Then she sobbed. She didn't know if she could believe those words, if this was the start of yet another nightmare journey, if she would be locking her door against him in another month's time – but for now, none of that mattered. She buried her face in her son's warmth, the soft, baby-smelling space between neck and shoulder, filled with a desperate longing to make things different.

'It's all right, Ma – I love you. I'm so sorry for everything.'

She pulled back from him, unwilling to be the easy target, ready to blaze out again in anger, in grief, in all the frustration of thwarted love.

But, even as she searched for clues, her son inhabited his own eyes again. He was, despite his grazed and swollen face, more recognizable than at any other time in the past three years.

'Can I come home, just for a while?' he asked, eyes filling.

'Are you going to behave yourself?' she said, trying to be fierce, eyes overflowing despite herself.

He nodded and she hugged him close, knowing exactly what she might be letting herself in for. But he was young. He deserved just one more chance.

And she was his mother, after all . . .

Someone tapped on the bathroom door, sharply.

'Mum, are you okay?'

Rose started. The bath water had cooled and the skin on her fingers had wrinkled. How long had she been lying there?

'I'm fine, Brian.'

'You've been in there ages. Can I use the bathroom before I go to bed?'

'Of course. I'll be out in a minute.'

Hurriedly, Rose pulled the bath sheet off the radiator and wrapped herself in its warmth. She was shocked to find that it was after midnight. She met Brian on the landing.

'At least you've got a bit of pink in your cheeks,' he grinned at her. 'I was afraid you'd fallen asleep.'

She kissed him. 'Thanks for looking out for me. Sleep tight.'

'Yeah. You too.'

She slid between cool sheets. Sleep, she thought. Let me check out, just for a while.

# Chapter Four

IMMEDIATELY AFTER an early breakfast the following morning, Rose made her way to Ben's old desk in what had once been his office. She ran her hands over the scratched wooden surface, remembered how many times she had polished it in a previous existence. She pulled her address book out from under a pile of cookery books, and leafed through the well-thumbed pages until she found the number she wanted.

'Pauline? It's Rose Kelly. Sorry about the unearthly hour, but I know you're an early bird. Have you a minute?'

'Of course, Rose. How are you? Everything all right?'

Rose smiled at the question. How could she even begin to reply?

'Oh, I've been better. Ben is back.'

There was a moment's silence.

'I see . . . Okay . . . I have a free slot tomorrow afternoon – someone's just cancelled. Three o'clock suit you?'

'Three's perfect. Thanks, Pauline. See you then.'

She walked out into the hallway.

'Lisa? I can give you a lift to school if you're ready now!'

'Coming!' Lisa jumped down the last three steps and grabbed her schoolbag off the floor in the hallway.

'Let's go. It's not too early for you to go in, is it?'

'No – I was just about to ask you for a lift. I forgot that I'd told Alison and Carly I'd meet them there. We're working on our book project.'

'Did you make your lunch last night?' Rose searched in her handbag for the keys to the van, at the same time crumpling up old supermarket receipts, notes to herself, sweet wrappers – why did she keep on stuffing the same old rubbish back in again? She had learned a long time ago that cleaning out a handbag was a ritual, one which had to take place in tranquillity, at regular intervals. Spontaneous or disorderly throwing out meant that the one necessary receipt, the one essential phone number would go missing, necessitating hours of fruitless rummaging.

'Yeah, I've a sandwich and a banana in my schoolbag. Here, Mum – catch.' Lisa found the keys on the hall table and tossed them over to her mother.

'Good girl. Thanks.' Rose followed Lisa out of the front door and into the van.

'I thought you said you weren't working today?' Lisa pulled down the visor above her seat and scrutinized her face inch by inch in the small mirror.

'I'm not working. I've just got a lot to do, so I decided to get going early. Put on your seatbelt, sweetheart.'

'Did you ring Damien last night?' Lisa clicked her belt into place. She readjusted the mirror and immediately started to apply lip gloss. The whole car filled with the smell of sweet, synthetic fruit.

'Are you sure it's okay to wear that into school?'

Lisa nodded. 'Yes, Mother.' Her tone was weary. 'Lip gloss is allowed.' She put the cover back on the pink tube and turned to Rose. 'Well, did you? Did you ring him?'

'I did. He's something on this evening, so he'll be eating with us tomorrow night instead.'

'Cool. So I guess it'll be homemade lasagne for dinner, then?'

Rose smiled at her daughter. 'Got it in one. Any objections?'

She shook her head. 'Nope. Can we have fajitas tonight?'

'Sure. How can you think about food so soon after breakfast?' Rose teased her.

'Look who's talkin' – you do it all the time.'

'Only because I have to make it!'

'I'm a growing girl; you said so yourself. Are you telling Damien tomorrow night? About Dad?'

'Yes,' said Rose. She glanced over at her daughter. But she seemed to be fine. More than fine for a Monday morning. Maybe this was all going to be a lot less difficult than Rose had feared. Perhaps she'd underestimated her children's resilience, their ability to handle an uncertain future. So far, both Lisa and Brian had been surprisingly adult. 'Keep that news under your hat, just for today. All right?'

Lisa looked guilty. 'I've already told Carly . . .' She looked at her mother, her expression tentative: half abashed, half questioning. 'And Alison.'

Rose sighed. 'Well, just leave it at that, okay? I don't want Damien hearing about this from anyone but me – all right?'

Lisa nodded. 'Yeah, but I don't think he'll be talking to either of them, do you?'

Rose laughed. 'I think they might be just a little bit on the young side for your big brother! But you know what I mean.' She pulled up outside the school gate. 'Off you go, now. Have a good day.'

'Thanks, Mum. See ya later – bye!'

Brian was walking down the driveway just as Rose arrived home. She rolled down her window and waited for him to reach her.

'Want a lift to college?'

He looked at her in amazement. 'Have you totally lost it? It'd take you *hours* at this time of the morning!'

She shrugged. 'We could talk along the way.'

'Mum – I'm fine, really.' He settled his rucksack more firmly on his shoulders. 'It all came a bit out of left field last night, but I've had time to get used to the idea. Don't be worryin'. I'll see Dad when I'm ready.'

*Don't be worryin'.* That word again. 'Okay. I'm glad you're fine.'

'Is Damien comin' tonight or tomorrow?'

'Tomorrow, about six.'

'Do you want me to be here when he comes?'

'Do you want to be?' She smiled at him.

'I don't really care, one way or the other. There's a gang goin' to the cinema straight after lectures, so I'd prefer to do that, if it's okay with you.'

'That's perfectly okay with me. Will you be home for dinner this evening?'

'Depends on what it is,' he grinned at her.

'Your sister has just requested Mexican.'

'Yep, I'll be home. See ya later, Mum. Mind yourself.'

'You too. 'Bye now.' She watched his tall, confident progress down the driveway, and smiled into the rearview mirror.

She locked the van and made her way towards the front door. As an afterthought, she opened up the garage door, moved Brian's bike out of the way and folded the clothes horse against the wall. She caught sight of Lisa's tattered old runners, nestling in a pink bucket in the corner, a fluorescent yellow spade standing guard nearby. All the charms of childhood. It made her smile.

She drove the van in, parking carefully in the tight space, then eased herself out the door, trying not to get her jeans dirty. Then she closed the garage door and locked it.

No harm, she thought. Just in case.

*

Rose made her way into the kitchen, making a mental note to pick up the dry-cleaning, take the clothes off the line, make time to go to the bank. She was just beginning to scribble her tasks for the day into one of the many notebooks she carried with her, when her mobile rang. It began to vibrate, the sound shuddering along the surface of the wooden table, and turned itself gently in her direction, a technological genie sensing the presence of its owner. She pulled it towards her and glanced at the screen.

Sarah's name popped up. Relieved, Rose answered. 'Hi, Sarah. Thanks for getting back to me.'

'No problem. Is everything all right, Rose? Your message sounded worried.'

'Well, I am worried, and upset and angry. My missing husband landed back on my doorstep last Thursday night.'

'What!'

'Yep. How about that for a good start to my weekend off?'

'After all these years? Jesus, Rose.'

'Eight, to be precise.'

'What does he want?'

Rose grinned, despite herself. 'Aren't we a suspicious bunch – that's what everyone asks. In a nutshell, to draw a legal line under our separation, and to see his kids.'

'I see.' Sarah's tone was wary.

'Anyway, I'll talk to you when I see you, but I need a favour.'

'Shoot. Anything we can do, anything at all.'

'I've a meeting with my solicitor tomorrow afternoon at three. I know we're going to be under pressure with Friday's party, but—'

Sarah cut across her. 'Consider it done. Take all the time you need. We'll manage.'

'Thanks, Sarah. I really appreciate it. Don't forget, Betty

and Angela should be back this morning at about ten: keep them as busy as you like. I'll come in tomorrow, as usual – I can't even remember if I've anything on before Friday; my brain's addled. Either way, I'll have to go about two.'

'It's not a problem, Rose. Take the whole day if you want. It'll give me an excuse to light a fire under everyone. No harm, every so often.'

'Well, work could be a good distraction, to be honest. Anyway, the next couple of days are pretty full, but I'll play it by ear.'

'Good luck, then. Shout if there's anything you want. And don't worry – we'll tick over without you. Just do what you have to do.'

'Thanks again, Sarah. See you in the morning.'

Rose hung up thoughtfully.

Just do what you have to do.

And what is that? she wondered. What is it I have to do? I wish I knew.

She finished writing in her notebook and stood up briskly. No matter what else, housework had to get done. Then dinner must be made and money must be lodged to the bank. That was this morning looked after.

The twin pillars of being a domestic goddess: make the bread, manage the dough.

On an afterthought, Rose added a further item to her list: Ring Sam. Start looking for advice.

That was enough for now.


Rose folded the dry clothes carefully and left them on the bed in the spare bedroom. Thus folded, they needed less ironing. It had been one way of coaxing Damien, in the early days, then Brian, and now Lisa to do that chore for themselves: that, and the permission to play music as loud as anyone wanted, as long as nobody disturbed the neighbours.

'How the mighty have fallen,' she'd once observed to Jane, some years back. They'd been sitting in Rose's kitchen over their customary glass of wine on a Friday night. 'To think that I used to iron knickers and socks. Now the stuff is pulled out of the tumble dryer, or off the line, a quick smooth, a quick fold and, as often as not, that's it. Nobody bothers any more with the finer details.'

Jane had laughed at her. 'Your secret is safe with me. I promise never to tell anyone that you used to iron socks!'

Still, Rose reflected now, even though the domestic routine had been reduced to a mere holding mechanism, it was still extraordinary how long it all took. Shopping, cooking, cleaning: even the barest essentials demanded extra, energetic hours from an already crammed week. There were many times when she missed that leisurely aspect of her old life; times when she longed to do all of the old necessities at a slower, more thorough, more measured pace. She missed the homemaking; now everything she did seemed, at best, like caretaking. At worst, it had all the hallmarks of staying ahead of the posse, keeping your head above water.

Well, she thought now, at least I still have a home. Better make sure I take care of *that*. She scooped the dirty laundry out of the basket on the landing and made her way downstairs. She filled the washing machine, keeping a weather eye on the darkening sky outside her kitchen window. Should she risk the clothes line this afternoon, or just go with the tumble dryer?

She dialled Sam's number and measured detergent into the soap drawer while she waited for him to answer.

'Rose?' His voice sounded alarmed. 'Is everything all right?'

She laughed. 'You wouldn't believe the number of times I've been asked that question in the past few days!'

Suddenly, Jane's face appeared at the back door. Rose waved her in, pointed to the kettle. Obediently, Jane filled it and pulled the teapot off the shelf.

'Anything wrong at the Bonne Bouche?' Sam's voice was curious now.

'No, no, nothing's up at the Bonne Bouche. I need your help with something rather different.'

'I'm listening.'

'My husband-that-was came to see me last Thursday night, after a rather long and silent absence of eight years.'

'I see. Thursday? Wasn't that when you were in to see me?'

'Yes indeed,' said Rose, grimly. 'He appeared on my doorstep just when I thought I was starting a long, lazy weekend.'

'And how can I help?' Sam's voice was more neutral now, Rose thought, as though he had just applied a quick-drying veneer of professional concern.

'Well, I'm not sure yet. I've to see my solicitor tomorrow afternoon. But from where I stand, there are some pretty complicated financial details to be worked out in advance of my divorce. I was wondering if you could help me come to grips with all of those.'

'Certainly. I'd be happy to. Why don't you come and see me after you've discussed things with your solicitor – Pauline O'Brien, isn't it?'

'Yes,' said Rose, surprised that he remembered.

'She's great,' he said warmly. 'I've worked with her before on cases like this, so we both know the territory.'

Despite her best efforts to keep upbeat, Rose felt a sudden, treacherous stab of depression. No matter how human and friendly their faces, she, Rose, was nothing but a 'case' to all these professional bodies, her life no more than disputed 'territory'. The United Territories of Marital Disharmony. She shook the thought away impatiently.

'Okay, Sam, that sounds good. I'll call you in the next day or so, and we can take it from there.'

'I'm sorry, Rose. I don't quite know what to say. Anything I can do to make this easier, I will. I know what an upheaval it can be.'

'Thanks. I appreciate that. Talk to you soon.'

'Bye, Rose.'

She hung up, watching as Jane warmed the teapot, watching as she swirled around the hot water before throwing it down the sink. It was a peculiarly calming ritual, the sacredness of tea-making.

'Hi. Sorry about that. That was Sam, my accountant. Something tells me I'm going to need him.'

'No problem. I didn't mean to barge in like that, but I hadn't heard from you, and I was worried.' Jane stirred the tea and took their usual two mugs from beside the microwave.

'I should have called. I'm still not sure whether I'm coming or going, to be honest.' Rose rubbed her hands across her forehead, trying to dispel the fuzzy tentacles of headache that seemed to lodge there permanently now.

'Hey, you weren't supposed to do anything,' said Jane, firmly. 'We're not talking about good manners here, you know. I just wanted to make sure you were all right.'

Rose grinned at her. 'Isn't it funny how "all right" shifts from one extreme to the other, depending on the context? Given the last ninety hours or so – and who's counting? – yes, I am all right. Confused, maybe, exhausted, definitely, but still all right.'

'So, what's on the agenda for today?' Jane filled their mugs and took the carton of milk out of the fridge. 'Anything I can do to help?'

Rose looked at her curiously. 'How come you're not at work?'

Jane shrugged. 'I took the day off. Lots of leave due. I didn't feel like going in.'

'Jane,' said Rose gently.

The other woman looked up, suddenly busy pouring milk into her mug. 'What?'

'You're the best friend, ever.'

Jane smiled. 'Cuts both ways, you know. I thought we could . . . you know, get some of the housey stuff out of the way, give you a bit of breathing space. I'm going to the supermarket anyway, why don't you give me a list?'

'Like the lists we used to make?'

Jane laughed. 'We did, didn't we? Jesus, we'd lists for everything; collecting kids, delivering kids, days for football, days for basketball, days for ballet, days for swimming: all those kits to have ready the night before!' She shuddered. 'There are some benefits to them growing older, after all.'

'Speaking of growing older – I spoke to Damien last night. He'll be here tomorrow evening.'

Jane nodded. 'Did you give him any hint of what was up?'

Rose shook her head. 'No. I need him to be here before I tell him anything, I have to feel that he's safe. I don't care if he lets off steam; in fact, I expect him to. I'd be terrified of the silent treatment.'

'How did the other two take it?'

Rose pulled a packet of chocolate biscuits out of the cupboard. She tore open the cellophane and pushed the packet towards Jane. 'Here, special occasion; to hell with calories.'

Jane grinned. 'I was never any good at resisting temptation.' She looked apologetically at Rose, and dipped the biscuit into her tea. 'I know, it's a revolting habit. I only do it when I'm among friends. So, any major fallout with Lisa and Brian?'

'No, they both took it pretty well, considering. Brian was furious at first, but he calmed down almost at once. I'd say he has mixed feelings, and happiness is definitely one of them. There was a very strong bond between himself and Ben, always.'

'What about Lisa? Did she remember Ben?'

'Oh, yes, she remembered him all right. Wasn't too eager to give him any quarter, though. I think she was astonished, more than anything else: eight years is more than half of her life, don't forget. She was puzzled as to why he's come back after all this time but there was no anger there, not on her part. I'm trying to keep it that way.'

Jane reached for another biscuit. 'I knew you shouldn't have opened these. Will you send Lisa down to me for dinner tomorrow night, if you need space with Damien here? I know it's not going to be easy. Send Brian, too, if he'll come.'

Rose leaned over and squeezed her hand. 'Thanks. This shouldn't be allowed, you know, my husband leading us all this sort of merry dance. Not twice in the one lifetime.'

Jane put down her mug, grinned. 'Yeah, well maybe this time you're the piper: you get to call the tune.'

'Maybe. Remember *Groundhog Day* – the film that all the kids used to watch time after time?'

Jane threw her eyes up to heaven. 'How could I forget? Being doomed to repeat the same day over and over again, until maybe somewhere, somebody finally got it right?'

Rose nodded emphatically. 'Well, this is *my* last chance, my groundhog day. I have to get it right.'

Jane looked at her directly. 'You already have. For one, you did a great job of bringing up those kids on your own. I don't know how you did it – do it. It's a very lonely station. I've always felt that you were very brave.'

Rose smiled at her. 'Bravery is when you have a choice; I don't remember anyone giving me one. And the jury's still out on the "great job", don't forget.'

'Brian and Lisa are solid as a rock; Damien's had his

troubles, but fundamentally he's a great kid. I've a lot of time for him. He really did the business when Ben left: I guess a bit of rebellion was inevitable. Anyway, you can't have all your kids being good at the same time. It's against the laws of nature.'

'And speaking of being good, how's James?' asked Rose, quietly.

Jane smiled. 'Not bad, not bad at all. Made it to school three days last week. I'll take any improvement I can get.' She stood up, took the mugs off the table and put them into the dishwasher. 'Anyway, that's a problem for another day. You're looking as white as a ghost again. You should go back to bed for a while.'

'I've only been up five hours!'

'So? Wasn't this always supposed to be your day off?'

'Well, yes, but I guess Thursday night changed all of that. Look, don't worry about going shopping: I got most of the essentials in the supermarket yesterday morning and the rest can wait, honestly.'

Jane shrugged. 'I'm going anyway. I can pick up some easy-to-prepare stuff for you to stick in the freezer. It's not a big deal. Why don't you turn off your mobile, unplug the phone and take a book back to bed?'

Rose waved as Jane reversed out of the driveway, and closed the door behind her. As she climbed the stairs to her bedroom, she felt overwhelmed by a sense of the familiar, the déjà vu that had been thickening all around her over the past few days, like daylight before thunder.

*

It was almost three o'clock that afternoon when she woke. She could hear someone downstairs, smell food cooking. Puzzled, she got up, pulled on her jeans and sweater.

'Lisa?' she called, just as she reached the kitchen door. She didn't want to startle the girl by appearing suddenly out of nowhere. But what was she doing home from school so early, anyway?

Rose pulled open the kitchen door. The dishwasher was humming, the floor had just been mopped, and there was a large, rectangular dish of lasagne on the kitchen table.

'Jane!'

The other woman jumped, busy arranging things on the glass shelves of the fridge. She turned around and her hand flew to her throat. 'Jesus, Rose. Don't creep up on me like that.'

'What are you doing?' Rose looked around her in astonishment.

'What does it look like?' Jane grinned at her. 'Don't worry – I made double the quantity at home, and brought one dish for you. It was no trouble. I'm just heating up soup for lunch.'

But Rose wasn't listening any more. She was staring out of the window, not wanting to believe what her eyes were telling her. Over Jane's shoulder, she could see a solid, familiar figure pause at the end of the driveway.

'Rose? What is it?' Jane turned to follow her friend's gaze.

'Quick,' said Rose, urgently. 'Come with me. It's Ben. I don't want him to know I'm home.'

Jane nodded. 'Okay.' She turned off the hob. 'Let's go.'

Rose moved swiftly out into the hallway, pulling the kitchen door closed behind them. 'Come on, quickly, up to Lisa's room. We'll be able to watch from there.'

Jane followed her up the stairs. They both crouched at the window, barely lifting their heads above the sill.

'What's going on, Rose?'

'I don't know,' she said grimly. 'I made it very clear that I would contact him when I was ready. At the very least, I think I'm entitled to that. I don't know *what* he's doing here. As far as he's concerned, I'm at work.'

'Where's the van?'

'I put it in the garage after I left Lisa at school. Don't ask me why; I just did. I had a gut feeling he wouldn't be able to keep away.' Rose could feel herself beginning to grow angry again. 'Who on earth is that with him?' She craned her neck, trying to make out the figure standing beside her husband. Ben was oblivious to her presence, she was sure of it. He was looking up at the house, gesticulating, turning back from time to time to talk to his companion.

'*I* know who that is,' Jane whispered.

'Who?' asked Rose, turning to look at her.

'It's Richard Murphy, the estate agent. I know his wife.'

Rose felt a buzzing in her ears, a great white heat building up behind her eyes. 'He's *what?*'

'Yeah,' said Jane, nodding slowly. 'He has his office near the shopping centre. Look – it's definitely him. He's measuring something.'

Rose watched as Ben held one end of the tape, the younger man the other. She watched as they measured the length of her garden, the width of her driveway. The agent made occasional notes on the clipboard he held in his hands. Rose turned to Jane, keeping her voice quite calm. 'What is it you said I was, the other day? A set of accounts? How right you were.' She struggled to stand up, not knowing what she wanted to do, but feeling that she couldn't just crouch there, doing nothing.

Jane put a restraining hand on her arm. 'Don't, Rose: don't engage with him now, no matter how mad you're feeling. Let it go. He's no idea you've seen him. Doesn't that give you the upper hand?'

Reluctantly, Rose bent down again. Perhaps Jane was right. She needed to stay cool, keep her wits about her. She watched as the two men made their way back down the driveway to their cars. They stopped, shook hands, took a last look at the house, and then they were gone.

She turned again to Jane. 'Can you believe that? God, Jane, I want this over; you have no idea how much I want this over. What if Lisa had been here? What if she'd had a half-day from school, or something?' Rose's hands began to shake, her mouth had gone suddenly dry.

Jane stood up. 'Come on. Let's have a cup of tea.' She held out one hand to Rose, pulled her to her feet. 'It's only twenty past three. You've time to gather your senses before Lisa gets in. Let's go downstairs.'

Rose allowed herself to be led. She was aware that some colder, more calculating part of her brain had just been kicked into action.

Jane's words lingered, resonating with her anger.

'You sit down,' Jane said, as she pulled open the kitchen door. 'I'll make the tea.'

Mechanically, Rose watched as Jane filled the kettle, took mugs out of the dishwasher, engaged in the ritual that was as familiar as family. Her friend's quiet movements around the kitchen made Rose suddenly feel that she was watching *herself*: a different self, a very young self rooted firmly in the past. Her life had seemed fixed back then, its contours already shaped and mapped and plotted by the innocence of all her expectations: a husband, a home, the deep thrill of children to come. She remembered feeling grateful that the flux and uncertainty of young adulthood was finally over. All grown up, proudly married, she was now where she belonged, for ever and ever.

She recalled vividly the first day she and Ben had made this house their home, sitting crosslegged on the kitchen floor, opening their wedding gifts. She saw a young bride, in love with love and all it had promised.

'Happy?' Rose had asked her brand-new husband, leaning forward for a kiss.

Ben had smiled at her then, taken her hand, squeezed it. 'Of course. We were so lucky to get this house at the price we did.'

She could still remember the sting of disappointment, that childlike falling-down-inside feeling, as her moment of perfect happiness slowly deflated. She'd chided herself then, for being selfish and shallow. After all, Ben had worked so hard to get them this house, in this neighbourhood. Instead of wounded pride, she should be feeling admiration for his skills of nego-tiation, his persistence, his vision.

And so she'd brushed off her disappointment, smiled brightly and said: 'Will I put on the kettle?'

She'd never thought about that day again until now. It burned behind her eyes, crowding together with the sight of her husband and his estate agent in her garden, measuring up her home.

'You okay?' Jane asked. She poured tea into their mugs.

Rose nodded. 'Fine, thanks. Still sitting here, nearly thirty years later.' She waved a hand, taking in all the air of the kitchen. 'Sometimes, I wonder who those people were who married each other all those years ago – me, as well as Ben. They're complete strangers to me now.' She felt her eyes begin to fill, looked away from her friend's gaze. They sat in silence until they'd finished their tea.

Jane glanced out of the window. 'Here's Lisa now. I'd best be off.' She pushed back her chair and rested a hand on Rose's shoulder. 'You know where I am.'

Rose nodded, arranging her face to greet her daughter's noisy entrance as she burst through the kitchen door.

'Hi, Mum – oh, hi, Jane.' Lisa raised an eyebrow in mock disapproval. She dumped her schoolbag on the floor, made her way to the fridge, throwing her words over her shoulder. 'You two being the ladies who lunch again? Thought you never got a *minute* to yourselves.'

'You go right ahead and torment your mother,' said Jane, grinning at her. '*I* have my own hooligans. I don't need you as well.' She blew Lisa a kiss. 'You look stunning, kiddo. What's your secret?'

Lisa looked at her archly. 'Youth, perhaps?'

Rose and Jane smiled at each other, and at Lisa.

'That's me told,' said Jane. 'See you both tomorrow.' She sashayed towards the back door, making Lisa giggle.

'Thanks,' Rose called after her.

Jane gave her the thumbs up, and closed the door behind her.

'You have a good day?' asked Rose.

She shrugged. 'Not bad. I'm going to watch telly for a bit before I start my homework.' She bent down and hugged her mother. 'Okay?'

'Okay,' Rose agreed, touched at her sudden rush of affection. 'Just for an hour or so.' She watched her youngest child bound out of the kitchen, and smiled after her. She should have had her father, Rose thought, for all these years. All my children should have had their father. He could have left me, if he'd wanted, but he shouldn't have run out on them.

She stood up, gathering the mugs off the table.

And now he's back, the man with the measuring tape. The man who calculates the price of everything, knows the value of nothing. And he thinks he has the upper hand?

He hasn't seen anything yet.

# Chapter Five

SARAH WAS WAITING for Rose the following morning as she drove into the Bonne Bouche parking space. It was just before eight o'clock. It looked as though Sarah and her sisters had just arrived. Damn, thought Rose. I'd really hoped to get here before her. She waved, making her smile brighter than she felt.

'Hi, Sarah! Thought I'd beat you to it, just for one morning!'

Sarah looked at her keenly. 'You've to be up very early to catch me.'

Rose locked her van and walked straight over to her. She gave her a quick hug and said: 'I'm okay, really. There's no need to worry.'

Sarah looked at her. 'You look well, but that doesn't fool me for a moment. You've been hit by a truck.'

Rose smiled. 'Good description. I was thinking of a runaway train myself – the pummelling lasts longer. Must be something to do with all those wheels.'

They walked together towards the door. Sarah put her hand on Rose's arm. 'You know, you don't have to be here this morning. We *can* manage.'

'Thank you, Sarah. But I do need to be here, and I can get six good hours' work done before my appointment this afternoon. I need to keep the routine going, the normality. If I don't, I'm finished. I may need to take time out later on, but for now, it's business as usual.'

Sarah smiled. 'Weekends off like that one, we can all do without. How are the kids?'

'They're fine, actually. I deliberately left them to their own devices this morning. I don't want to start hovering over them. I'll only make them nervous – especially Lisa. Brian'll just get mad at me. And I do want to be here. I actually feel quite rested. A very kind friend shopped for me yesterday, made lasagne and even left me with a spotless kitchen, all while I slept. There's nothing for me to do at home, except wallow.' Or think about murder, she thought, seeing Ben's face again as he dismissed her home with a wave of his hand, reduced it to something that could be measured, calculated in square metres, defined by narrow columns on a balance sheet.

'Oh, well, a little wallowing never hurt anyone. I'm all for it, myself. Along with industrial amounts of chocolate and an old movie on the telly . . . sure I can't tempt you?'

Rose laughed. 'Not today. I'll see Pauline this afternoon, and then I've Damien later on. I've no time to be tempted, just yet. And it really is a case of one day at a time.'

'Okay, if you say so. But just shout if you come unstuck.' Sarah pulled open the outer door. 'And when you're ready, you can tell me all about it. I can only imagine what you must be feeling.'

Rose stopped her. 'Sarah – did you tell the others?'

'I told Katie and Claire only that Ben had come back, out of the blue. I told them to take their cue from you, that you might not want to talk about it. They were great. Their only response was to ask how they could help out. I hope that's okay.'

Rose smiled. 'That's more than okay. And of course they'll need to know if I suddenly disappear for a day. I'll talk to them later, but not while Betty and Angela are around. I don't feel like sharing this news with either of them.'

Rose hung up her coat and brushed her hair. Just as she'd finished touching up her lipstick, Sarah turned to her and said quietly: 'Betty was great yesterday, by the way. Did everything she was asked to do, and more. Angela was a different story. She spent a lot of time on her mobile, once she came back from shopping. I pretended not to notice, but Claire overheard bits and pieces of conversation and she's convinced that Angela's chasing another job.'

'Jesus,' said Rose, groaning. 'More great timing. I need to start looking for staff like I need a hole in the head.'

'Don't worry about it for now. There's always the three of us and I've a couple of nieces up my sleeve, if things get tight. Ellie and Julia are always open to earning a few quid.'

Rose grinned. 'Must get a bit crowded, that sleeve of yours, with all the other things you've stashed up there.'

Sarah winked. 'Nothing like having a Plan B. Now, let's show them what we're made of.'


Betty had already arrived and was tying back her hair when Rose greeted her.

'Morning, Betty, you're in early.'

The girl looked at her shyly. 'You told me on Thursday to come in early this morning. I've to start the stock for your lunch party tomorrow. I'm in charge of the soups and the desserts, remember?'

Rose looked at her. Lunch party? Told her on Thursday? Didn't the girl realize that some things had changed since last Thursday, even since yesterday? And then she remembered. The tennis club ladies who lunch – well, twice a year, anyway. Faithful clients of seven years' standing. How could she have forgotten? The date had slipped well below her radar. Not surprising really, given the amount of enemy activity over the past few days.

'So I did. I'm very glad you remembered, very glad you're here. Did Angela do the shopping for it yesterday?'

Betty nodded. 'All the stuff is in the cold room. I think she said she'd to collect the ducks and the tuna from the suppliers this morning, so she won't be here until about ten.'

That's interesting, Rose thought. Collecting ducks and tuna? Particularly as I have the van. She said nothing to Betty. Let Angela explain herself.

'Okay, let's you and I get stuck in. You go ahead with the stock, and I'll make the breads.' She pulled a ledger from the drawer under the counter. 'Before I check, can you remember the menu?'

Betty nodded, eagerly. 'Yeah – I went over everything again yesterday. I'd to work out all the quantities for Angela.'

'Okay; let's hear it.'

'Almond and courgette soup, chilled gazpacho. Brown rolls, fennel loaf. Main course of glazed spicy duck, or marinated tuna, usual selection of vegetables. Dessert is orange and chocolate mousse or hazelnut meringue. You said to assume mousse *and* meringue: that these ladies have a sweet tooth. There'll be approximately thirty guests, numbers to be confirmed this afternoon. Coffee and petits fours, red and white wine same as last time.'

Rose smiled at her earnestness. 'Well done, Betty. Right, off we go. If you're in any doubt, let me know as soon as possible. I won't be here after lunchtime today.'

'I'll be fine; I've the notes I made from before. Don't worry.'

Rose watched her begin to work, glad that her instincts all those years ago had been proved right. She was solid, reliable. Angela, it seemed, was another matter. With a pang, Rose remembered that young Betty had a four-year-old daughter to support: something that tends to concentrate the mind. It seemed that they had more in common than either would have thought.

An hour later, Rose was up to her elbows in dough. The more she mixed and kneaded, the more she relaxed into her task, forgot about what was waiting for her in her real life, that other life waiting in the wings. She remembered all those breads she used to make in her own kitchen: all those thousands of loaves over the years. She remembered the first batch of samples she'd put together, trying to bring in money just after Ben left. Trays of brown rolls, soda bread, almond buns, Russian Easter bread. Dozens of quiches, pizzas, apple pies. They'd all been a success, but she smiled now at how dull they seemed in comparison to the fashions of today. Now it was all tomato bread, olive bread, tortes and truffles. No matter what, though, there were still few culinary activities to beat the kneading of bread: all that punching and rolling and knocking back had a soothing effect on the nerves, she was convinced of it.

It was almost eleven when Angela arrived. Rose decided that a cool reception would be appropriate. She looked pointedly at her watch.

'Bit late this morning, Angela. Anything wrong?'

Angela looked at her in surprise. 'No, there's nothing wrong. I told Betty to tell you I'd be late.'

Rose wiped the flour off her hands. She signalled to Angela to follow her, took her to one side. This was no time to take prisoners, she thought. These days, everything counted, at work, at home: nothing could be taken for granted any more.

'First of all, you do not communicate with me through

anybody else. Secondly, you cannot have been collecting anything from the suppliers, because I have the van. Thirdly, if you have anything to tell me about your future plans, you tell me now, right now, so that I know what I'm dealing with. After five years, we owe each other that much courtesy.'

Angela looked at her, her face colouring – whether with embarrassment or anger, Rose couldn't yet tell. Right now, she didn't care.

'I'm sorry. I had some personal stuff to deal with this morning.'

'And you couldn't call?'

'It wasn't . . . appropriate. I'm sorry. It won't happen again.'

Rose watched her closely. I'm a mother of three, she thought: I've had lots of practice reading faces. This one shows defiance, discomfort at having been caught, and not one trace of remorse.

'Okay,' said Rose, slowly, deliberately, still looking at Angela. The girl flinched, looked away. 'We're all under a bit of pressure here, this week: lunch for thirty tomorrow, and the party for a hundred and fifty on Friday night. Don't let anybody down, Angela. If there's something that needs your attention, tell me now. We can work something out. Otherwise, I'll expect a hundred per cent from you over the next few days. You're due a bonus: earn it.'

Angela said nothing. Her stance reminded Rose of Lisa on one of her bad days.

'Take the van now and collect the ducks and the tuna from Maguire's, please. Our preparation schedule is already tight.' Rose walked away from her and pulled the keys of the van out of her handbag. 'I'll see you back here in an hour.'

Angela took the keys and turned on her heel without a word. Rose watched her go. When she turned back to the counter where she'd been working, there was more than the trace of a smile on Betty's face. Rose groaned inwardly. Not only do I have it in spades at home, she thought, now even my employees are in conflict.

It looked like things were shaping up for an interesting few weeks.

'Come in, Rose. Good to see you.' Pauline's handshake was firm, friendly. 'Sit down. Can I get you a cup of tea or coffee?'

'Coffee would be great, thanks.'

Pauline lifted the phone and said: 'Two coffees, please, Joan.'

Rose settled herself into the large leather armchair, remembering its creaks and blemishes from before. She stroked the fine old mahogany armrest.

'Couldn't throw it out.' Pauline grinned at her, replacing the receiver. 'It would have felt too much like throwing out the old man. That's where he sits whenever he condescends to come and dispense his much-needed advice. Much-needed in his estimation only, I hasten to say.'

Rose smiled. 'I've a lot to be grateful to your father for – and to you. Is he keeping well these days?'

'Almost too well. He rings me up on a regular basis telling me to get out of the rat-race, that the only worthwhile living is country living. He still likes to wind me up. Ah, here's the coffee.'

Rose smiled at the motherly woman who entered. At nearly seventy, her face was still smooth, almost unlined. She balanced the tray in one hand and opened the door with the other, having already managed to knock. She brought an air of calm competence with her.

'How are you, Joan? Keeping well?' Rose smiled at the older woman.

'You don't know what I have to put up with,' Joan murmured, casting her eyes in Pauline's direction. 'Even worse than the old lad, this one.'

Rose laughed. 'And he was a hard act to follow!'

'Indeed he was. But we don't get too much of a chance to miss him, do we, Pauline?' And Joan left, grinning, her ample frame adding a comforting, solid dignity to her surroundings. She'd always had the ability to make Rose feel completely at ease; more than that, she made her feel as though things could never really be as bad as they seemed.

Pauline smiled after her.

'She still loves the last word. I know, I know,' she groaned in mock-anguish, her hands waving away what she could read in Rose's expression. 'Don't tell me how lucky I am to have her – not you as well.'

Rose smiled and looked innocent. 'Okay. If you say so.'

Pauline poised the milk jug above Rose's cup, her arched eyebrow questioning.

'No, thanks, Pauline, I'll take it black. I'm in need of a caffeine hit right now.'

Pauline sat easily on the edge of her solid, old-fashioned desk. Rose was glad she hadn't thrown that out, either, in favour of the light, minimalist furniture, all tubular stainless steel and clear, clean lines, that seemed to be furnishing offices everywhere else in Dublin. Northern European décor certainly had its place, but something more grounded, more substantial, more *experienced* seemed to be required for those quiet, grave rooms where the fates of men and women were decided on a daily basis.

'So,' said Pauline, her tone telling Rose that she had absorbed all the implications of their phone conversation of the day before. 'Mr Holden has returned, has he?'

Rose smiled. On paper, Pauline's words would have been perfectly proper, supremely innocent, devoid of rancour. Spoken now, as they were, with a wicked expression on her face, the words contained a just discernible edge of contempt for Ben and support for her. Rose found it all immensely comforting. There was something very reassuring about feeling the warm, verbal embrace of the supposedly impartial interpreter of the law.

'He has indeed. I believe from out of the "wide blue yonder" is the suitable expression.'

'Well, his timing is certainly interesting. Has he given you any reason why he's here now, rather than at any other time?'

'Well, no, not directly, but I think it's fairly clear, particularly after yesterday afternoon's performance.'

Pauline didn't speak; she simply gestured to Rose to go on.

'He told me last Thursday that he was back to chase up some business opportunities in Dublin. He wants to see the kids, and "regularize" our position, as he puts it – financial, family, everything. That's what he says.'

'And do you believe him?'

'Well, I did believe him that he was back in Dublin for business – in fact, I hadn't even questioned it. I took that bit at face value. But of course, it might not be the truth. I can't explain it properly, but I feel that someone has been teaching him what to say, how to get what he wants without a major row.'

'And what is it he wants, do you think?'

'Money,' Rose said with certainty. 'Maybe it's not for business here, maybe he intends to disappear all over again, maybe it's for another woman – even another family – what do I know? Most of me doesn't care.' She paused. 'He brought around an estate agent yesterday, when he thought I wasn't there. They couldn't get in, of course, but they did a lot of measuring outside. So,' she said briskly, 'he wants to sell the house, take his share of the cash and . . .' Rose shrugged. 'After that, who knows?' she paused again. 'He says he wants to see the kids, too, and I have to believe him, for their sakes.'

'How do you feel about all of that?'

Rose hesitated. 'Furious. On the one hand, I resent him for coming back, pretending to be all reasonable. Then, behind my back, he goes and does what he did yesterday, full of the sort of assumptions that make my blood boil. On the other hand, I always knew that some day I'd have to negotiate with him. I always felt that he'd come looking for his share of the spoils at some stage.'

'And how would you feel about selling the house? Just another gut reaction here – I'm not expecting you to have any worked-out position.'

Rose paused for a moment, trying to gather together all the impressions of past and future that had bombarded her ever since Ben's return. 'The house isn't really the issue: I don't care about it in any loving way any more, not like I used to when the kids were younger. It just always seemed too complicated legally to try and leave. I know I could have sold up and moved on, once Ben had been gone for seven years, but the last twelve months have been so hectic that selling my home was the last thing on my mind. And anyway, where would I have gone? Lisa is still at school, all her friends are around her – why would I have wanted to disrupt that? Particularly when it took *so* much hard work for me to keep it all together in the first place, after he walked out on us.'

Rose stopped. How *dare* he come back with such expectations, such demands? That small, spiteful voice inside her head had begun to rage again, stirring up all the old, tired angers.

'The real issue for me – for all of us – is the emotional upheaval. I'm really worried about the kids. God knows, Damien is a grown man, but I've had so much trouble with him over the past few years that I'm terrified of anything knocking him off balance again.'

She took a sip of coffee, steadying herself. Pauline stayed silent. Rose breathed deeply and continued.

'Brian has taken the news of Ben's return pretty well so far, considering. And by the way, he's very attached to where we live. He's become a real old home bird. I just don't know how he'd react if we had to move.'

'Well, you don't *have* to – not in any legally compelled sense. We'll talk about that in a minute. What are your particular concerns about Lisa?'

Rose looked up at the ceiling, and back again at Pauline. She sighed. 'What can I say? Lisa is your average, hormonal teenager: some days she's great, and other days she's impossible to deal with. I just dread anything else rocking the boat.'

Rose felt like putting her head in her hands. She didn't want to cry, but she could feel the tears precariously close to the surface. Speaking all of her fears aloud had suddenly given them an added dimension, another layer of complexity that she wasn't sure she could deal with. Ever since yesterday, potential treachery now seemed to hover around every word Ben had spoken, every intention he might have towards his children, towards her, towards what remained of their home.

'And me? I'm just worn out. My home, such as it is, is now in jeopardy; my business is finally getting there but it still needs an awful lot of minding, and now it feels as though everything is up for grabs all over again. I just feel – overwhelmed.'

'Okay,' Pauline's tone was brisk, kindly. She walked back to her chair behind the desk and put on a pair of glasses. It gave Rose the time to gather herself, to pull back a little. She was grateful to the other woman for her sensitivity in re-establishing, literally, her professional distance.

'Stop me if I'm wrong,' Pauline began, looking at Rose over the tops of her glasses.

The image of her father, Rose thought. Somehow, the thought made her feel better.

'Your home was originally bought in both your names in 1975. In 1988, you remortgaged, taking out a significant amount of money, based on the equity in the house. Correct?'

'Yes,' said Rose. 'There was some business deal Ben was really excited about, and he needed working capital. To be honest, it was one of those pieces of paper I used to sign without paying very much attention. I trusted him – trusted his business judgement. We'd done very nicely up to then.'

'Forgive me – this is purely for background – did you question his judgement on that occasion, or disagree about the amount of money to be borrowed for whatever project he might have had in mind?'

'No. I'd given up on that, probably for the last ten years we were together – if not more. If ever I questioned him, which I did on a couple of occasions in the early days, he'd become angry very quickly.' Rose shrugged her shoulders. 'We had a dreadful row about it one time, and I ended up feeling guilty. I suppose I didn't feel I had the right to challenge him: I wasn't earning any money of my own, after all. I was between a rock and a hard place, although to be fair, I didn't see it like that then. I just deferred to him, to his business experience, his . . . acumen, I suppose. My province was our home and the children. That's what both of us wanted. Until he came unstuck, of course.'

'The mortgage continued to be paid until 1995, isn't that right?'

'Yes, and I didn't know how much financial trouble he was in back then. He'd stopped paying it without saying anything; that was around the time of his affair with Caroline.

When all that ended, I kept chasing him for money, to keep the roof over our heads. Once he disappeared, that was it. I had to restructure the mortgage, start my own business and learn to survive.'

'Have you ever defaulted on the mortgage repayments?'

Rose shook her head. 'No, never. I've basically kept my head above water for the past eight years. I've always kept up the monthly repayments. In a funny way, it became a matter of pride. And having three hungry young people at your table tends to focus the attention. It was a struggle but I did it; I'm still doing it, for God's sake.'

Pauline made some notes on the pad in front of her. 'Let's deal with one issue at a time. If I am correct, your husband has paid no mortgage, no family expenses, no child support in eight years.'

Rose nodded. 'Yes, that's right. Well, seven and a half years, maybe. I did manage to get him to pay up for a few months after he left us, before he disappeared for good to England.'

'If he's looking for his portion of the home, there are a few things you must remember. The first and the most important one is that Ben can't force you to sell. This is the family home and Lisa is not yet eighteen. You are entitled to stay for another four years – that's the law. Longer, if she decides to go to college. If you decide to accede to his demands – assuming he makes demands – you are entitled to fight for a much larger portion of the estate than he is. You're going to start divorce proceedings, I presume?'

Rose nodded. 'Yes, please,' she said grimly. 'Today. Now. This very afternoon. Should have done it years ago.'

'Okay. Let's leave future maintenance aside for the moment and deal with the past. Should you decide to go ahead and sell the house, we would make a case for eight years of child support at a minimum, plus eight years' mortgage repayments. The division of the spoils, as you so succinctly put it, would probably end up as a seventy–thirty split in your favour, or maybe sixty-five–thirty-five. We wouldn't tell *him* that, of course. We'd start off by offering him, maybe, fifteen to twenty per cent. But the real question is, do you want to sell?'

'I have to put it another way, Pauline, to be honest.' Rose spoke quickly, breathlessly, feeling the clash of emotions with which she'd become all too familiar, all over again, during recent days. 'More than anything else, I want to be rid of him. I want rid of Ben out of my life. That's my only certainty, and I've become more and more convinced over the past few days that that's what I want, that's what I need.

'If getting rid of the house means that I cut all connection with Ben, then that's what I'm prepared to do.' Rose paused for a moment. 'Maybe I'm selfish. Maybe I shouldn't even consider disrupting my family all over again.' She looked Pauline right in the eye. 'But I know this man. I know that he won't leave me alone until this issue with the house, with money, is sorted out. I can't explain to you how . . . significant that house always was to Ben. It was like a symbol of his success, a sign that he'd made it, become someone important. It was like taking out a full-page advertisement in the newspaper: "Look at me! I've arrived! I'm somebody!" Sometimes I wonder if he stayed with me for far longer than he wanted, because leaving me would have also meant losing the house.'

Pauline opened her mouth to speak, but Rose silenced her with a wave. 'I'm not feeling sorry for myself, and I'm not proud of how Ben's return is making me think. I feel mean-spirited and small. I hate the way he's made me angry again, and spiteful. I can't go on like this, not knowing what's going to happen next to me and my family. I need to survive – and my best chance of survival is to cut the cord and move on. If that means moving house, so be it. It's only bricks and mortar to me. Home is a completely different thing: I'll make another one.'

Pauline spoke quietly. 'I admire your honesty. And I know what you're saying. But surely the children mean that you can't completely cut the cord: assuming that Ben does want a relationship with them?'

Rose looked at her steadily. 'I'm more than happy for the kids to have contact. It would be good for them to reestablish their relationship, to have a dad again; that's fine by me, more than fine. Maybe they can all salvage something: I never wanted them to be without their father in the first place. But all that's apart from what I want for *myself*. You have no idea the grief Ben's coming back has caused me. It's made me doubt myself, my right to be angry, my own ability to survive. Don't ask me how, but just the very fact of his presence has already started to undermine any bit of self-confidence and self-belief I've managed to build up in the last few years. I want to draw a line in the sand, move on, get my divorce. And I don't want him turning everybody's life upside down again. I want to be in control of this, to manage it. I don't want any more surprises.'

Pauline let the silence settle around them for a few moments. Rose used the time to breathe deeply, to stem imminent tears.

'Does Ben have a solicitor?'

'He hasn't said.' Rose rummaged in her handbag for a tissue. 'All of this just blindsided me last Thursday. I never even asked. Talk about a week being a long time in politics: the past few days have been interminable. I can't believe it's only Tuesday. I was so shocked to see him standing on my doorstep last week that I just went numb, and kind of fumbled along. Then he made me so mad I threw him out of the house and said I'd talk to him when I was ready. I haven't spoken to him since.'

Pauline grinned. 'Good for you, for throwing him out, I mean. I hope you . . . enjoyed it?'

'Yeah, well, maybe the words were braver then than I feel now. I was so furious – his arrogance really got under my skin. And then yesterday: standing in my garden with a tape measure. Only for a sensible friend, I'd have rushed downstairs and hurled abuse at him. Would it sound daft if I said that this was the first time I've ever felt truly middle-aged? I mean, I know I am: but I've never felt it until now. It's made me feel stale and tired and I think I'd do anything for a quiet life.'

'Over my dead body,' said Pauline sharply. 'The one thing I want you to do is to stay keen and sharp and angry. They say, "Don't get mad, get even," but in my experience getting even means getting mad, at least at first. You've got a good accountant, haven't you, someone you trust to look after you?'

'Yes,' said Rose, feeling a shock of recognition at Pauline's words. 'Yes, I do indeed. I've already contacted him. It's Sam McCarthy; I think you know him?'

Pauline smiled at her. 'I do. You couldn't be in better hands. I want you to talk to him as soon as you can. Put figures on what things have cost you over the past eight years, mortgage, kids, the works. Let him do his magic with inflation and bank charges and interest rates, all the stuff accountants are good at. I want you to get started on that right away. I also want you to promise me that you'll talk to me before you talk to Ben – and I don't just mean the first time – every time. You need to manage each and every conversation, to take hold of the reins. I'm sorry, Rose, but this is not the time to give in. You know what his real intentions are, particularly after yesterday. You must be ready for one more fight, or everything you've worked so hard to hold onto will be taken away from you. Your worst enemy, your most dangerous adversary in all this is inside this office, right now.'

Rose looked at her, puzzled.

'Yourself.' Pauline's voice was firm. 'You cannot allow yourself to be taken advantage of. As your solicitor, I won't let you. Simple as that. Besides, Dad would kill me.'

She reached over to the mountain of manila folders on the side of her desk, pulled the top one towards her and rolled off its elastic band.

'Now, let's start drawing up a wish list. Your must haves, your negotiables and your nice to haves. Once you know what each of them is, you'll know when to push, when to concede, when to chance your arm. Your husband – soon to be ex-husband – is not the only one who can be tutored in the royal and ancient Irish art of negotiation. You can, too. So. Are you ready?'

Rose emerged from Pauline's office feeling exhilarated. The woman was right: this was not the time to whinge, to plead tiredness, to give in because giving in was easier than winning. How she behaved over the next few weeks and months would shape the rest of her life. She would go back to the régime of the early days following Ben's departure. She had thought nothing then of getting up at five in the morning, cooking up a storm, fitting her own life in and around the gaps that might or might not emerge during any given day. Damien had once told her she was like Boxer in *Animal Farm*: to every difficulty, every challenge, every potential disaster, her response had always been the same – *I will work harder*.

She had learned subsequently, but forgotten again in the tornado of events that followed, that working harder was often not the point. Working smarter was. If Ben Holden could learn the art of negotiation, of getting what he wanted at any price, then so could she.

Now she was ready: now she knew who she was again, what she wanted, what she needed.

Now she could go home and deal with her eldest child.


'Mum, Damien's here.'

'Hiya, Ma. Hiya, little sister.'

Rose could feel the material of her blouse already sticking to her back. Strands of hair began to cling to the base of her neck; her palms were clammy. She opened the kitchen window. But she knew that what she felt now had nothing to do with the heat of the kitchen.

Damien walked in, looking immensely self-conscious in dark chinos, dark jacket, white open-necked shirt. There was a tie peeping from his top pocket, but Rose pretended not to see it.

'Well,' she remarked, observing the transformation. She didn't quite know what else to say. Where had the raggy jeans gone, the T-shirts crowded with logos, double-entendres, skulls and crossbones? 'Such formality. To what do we owe the honour?'

She could see him struggling to be calm and understated, but he couldn't wait. 'I've got a new job,' he blurted, 'a proper job. I start on Monday. I've just come from meeting my supervisor.'

'Damien! Congratulations – that's wonderful!'

Rose felt a rush of delight at his news. A new job, a proper job: did that mean that the bleak hand-to-mouth days of counting spare parts in a storeroom were finally over?

In the year or so since he'd been discharged from hospital, Damien had insisted on finding his own way in everything. He'd stayed at home for a few restless months only, determined to begin again: new flat, new friends, new job. Rose had learned to say nothing about what she saw as his unwise decisions, his apparent lack of ambition. Standing on the sidelines of your child's life, she'd decided, was one of the coldest and most inhospitable places she'd ever been.

'Where? Who's it with? Will you be earning loads of money?' Lisa was dancing, circling her brother, eyeing his new clothes, his shiny shoes.

'Lisa! Give him a bit of breathing space.'

'It's with Freeman's, the advertising agency. It's not much to start with, but they give training and there's loads of opportunities. I didn't want to tell you until I was sure I had it.'

Rose looked at him, seeing his shining eyes, the faint beads of perspiration along his upper lip, his pride bursting at the seams. She knew by him that he had rushed here tonight with his news, could see by the pinkness of his cheeks.

How am I going to tell him? she wondered. How in God's name am I ever going to tell him that his father's back? His first, real, grown-up balloon: and I have to be the one to burst it.

She tried to play for time. She hugged him hard, pulled his head towards her, kissed him soundly on the cheek. 'That's the best news I've had in a long time. Come on, tell us all about it! What will you be doing? When was the interview?'

He shrugged. 'I've had two – one was three weeks ago. I didn't know if I'd made it through to the next stage: to be honest, I didn't think I'd done all that well. But they called me for the second round; that was yesterday evening at five. That's why I couldn't come for dinner. I'd to bring them a portfolio – and,' here he grinned, 'I'd pretended at the first interview that I'd more prepared than I actually had. I've been burning the midnight oil all week.'

Rose smiled at him. She was remembering his college days, when he was always the last to submit everything, sometimes with only minutes to go to the close of stern, unforgiving deadlines. She was going to remark lightly, 'Some things never change,' but stopped herself just in time. It seemed, right now, to be a wholly inappropriate thing to say. Things had changed; *he* had changed. And the best and most compelling evidence was standing right here before her in her own kitchen: dressed to the nines, reeking of pride and aftershave.

Damien fumbled now in his inside jacket pocket and took out two envelopes. He handed the first one, awkwardly, to Rose.

'What's this?' she asked him.

'Open it and see.'

She opened the flap carefully. 'Damien! What on—'

He raised his hand to his lips: a pleading gesture to silence her. 'It's to say thanks. For everything. You can relax. I'm on my way now. Got my shit together.'

She could swear she heard a catch in his voice. 'But five hundred euro – for Brown Thomas?'

'You deserve it.' He kissed her quickly, turned away.

'Here you go, little sister. This one's for you.'

Lisa ripped the envelope open. 'A hundred euro!' She jumped up and down in delight. 'Thanks! What's it for? Can I spend it now?'

He grinned at her. 'Aren't you going to the Gaeltacht in August?'

'Yeah.'

'Well, put that towards your spending money. Give your old ma a break.'

He looked at Rose's face, misinterpreting what he saw there. 'It's all right, Ma, honestly. I took out a Credit Union loan to get clothes and a yearly bus ticket and some bits and pieces that I needed. I can afford it. Stop worryin'.'

Rose was about to answer, to begin obliquely, to let him down gently, when Lisa broke in: 'Have you heard about Dad?'

It felt as though the entire room had just been punctured, emptied of air.

'What?'

'Lisa!' said Rose angrily. 'I thought I'd told you to leave that to me?'

'Leave what to you?' asked Damien, slowly looking from one to the other.

'Sit down, Damien,' said Rose, quietly.

'I'll stand, thanks. What's goin' on?'

Rose sat down. She had a blinding, nuclear flash of memory as she did so. Blue uniforms, bad news, words that could not be spoken as long as a mother remained on her feet.

'That's the main reason why I asked you here this evening. Your dad came back . . . just appeared on the doorstep, out of the blue, last Thursday. He's anxious to . . . sort out everything between the two of us, and he wants to see each of you.' She waited, folding her hands on the table to contain the slight trembling that had already started.

When it came, her son's outburst was more or less as she had expected.

'What does the old *bastard* want with us after what – eight years?' Damien's voice was instantly, completely angry. He was shrugging out of his jacket, the old, impatient gesture she remembered so well from his schooldays. It was as though the extra layer of clothing could not contain his rage. He needed to let it loose.

'Just what I've already told you,' said Rose quietly. 'I know no more than what I've already said.'

Damien sat down abruptly at the table, facing Rose. Lisa had gone very quiet.

She's going to take her cue from her big brother, Rose thought now, and there's not a damn thing I can do about it.

'He's lookin' for money. He has to be lookin' for money.'

All traces of pink had disappeared from Damien's cheeks. His face looked suddenly darker, almost middle-aged.

'As I said, he wants to finalize things. So, yes, money would be part of it.'

'But he left you – left us – with *nothing*!' Damien slammed his hand down hard on the table. The cutlery trembled a little. Rose wondered at how explosive the sound was in the still kitchen. So much anger, she thought sadly. Still so much anger. Would it ever go away? Lisa sidled over towards her mother.

Rose nodded. 'I know. But we have to move on from that. I started divorce proceedings this afternoon, because we need to sort all of this out legally, once and for all. Everything is up for negotiation.' She looked at Damien warningly, her eyes darting in Lisa's direction.

He understood, took the cue, nodded imperceptibly. She smiled at him gratefully. Instantly, his voice became quieter.

'Well, he can wait until hell freezes over before I see him.'

'That's up to you. You don't have to make any decision now – Lisa and I have already discussed the same thing. You wait, you take your time, you think about it. Any contact will be initiated by you: you're an adult. For what it's worth, I think he does want to see all of you.'

And that's as much leeway as I'm giving you, Ben Holden, you miserable shit, Rose thought, angry at having to be the one doing all of this.

Feeding, cleaning, minding, soothing: and still handling Ben Holden's dirty washing, in all the ways that counted.

'Well, tough on him. Sorry Ma – I've no interest. He was never here when I needed him.'

Fair enough, that's fair enough. At least you now know that you needed him.

She smiled at him. 'Don't apologize to me. I'll support you no matter what you decide.' She turned to Lisa. 'Now, madam, that was not the way to break difficult news to anyone. Don't do that again.'

'Sorry.' Lisa looked down at her shoes. 'I forgot.'

'Hey – at least it's over. What's for dinner, Ma? I'm starvin'.' And Damien ruffled Lisa's carefully brushed hair until she squealed and tried to push him away. Naturally, he was easily able to keep her at a distance, so that both her arms windmilled uselessly in the air around her.

'Okay, that's enough. Sit down, both of you. Lasagne's ready.'

That wasn't too bad, she thought. Considering it's Chapter One. She took plates out of the oven, served food, tossed the salad. He was angry, yes, but that was to be expected. But he was also in control.

She felt grateful, relieved. That was what was unexpected.


Four hours later, she and Damien were still sitting at the dinner table, yet another pot of tea between them. Lisa had earlier made her escape to Carly's, despite her mother's protests. Rose's instinct had been to keep both son and daughter close to her just now. But eventually her son's white, drawn face had been the deciding factor.

One at a time, she'd thought, one at a time. She filled Damien's cup again. 'Are you okay?'

'Have you told him about me?'

'No,' said Rose firmly. 'I simply said you didn't live here any more, which is the truth. The rest of it is up to you.'

Damien pulled a packet of cigarettes out of his jacket pocket. 'Sorry, Ma, I just can't . . .'

'Go on,' she said. 'It's all right. Special dispensation for you, as well, just for tonight.' Rose couldn't help remembering her sons' indignation when they were younger, their absolute abhorrence of smokers, cigarettes, pipes, cheroots: it was a high moral ground that had grown increasingly boggy and treacherous once they'd begun to teeter on the brink of adolescence.

'Does Brian know?'

'Yes, I told him on Sunday night, after I picked him up from the station. He was at John's party in Mayo over the weekend.'

'How was he?'

'A bit like yourself: astonished, angry, confused. I think he'll see Ben, though. He said something about being entitled to some answers.'

'So am I,' said Damien grimly. 'Maybe even more than he is.'

'Well, all you can do is ask.'

The friction between her two sons had always saddened Rose. It had become more and more apparent over the years. The two boys had developed some sort of strange, symbiotic, inverse relationship with each other. It was as though Damien's disturbing antics had lifted a burden, an imperative of bad behaviour, from the willing shoulders of his younger brother. It also seemed that she couldn't have both boys on an even keel at the same time: when one stepped out, the other stepped in again.

'I haven't said I'd see him, yet,' said Damien quietly.

Rose forced herself to stem an exclamation of irritation. 'I'm not forcing you either way, Damien. You're twenty-four years of age – you can make up your own mind about things like this.'

Things like this? What other things could there possibly be, *like this*? She stood up abruptly and went in search of an ashtray.

'I'm sorry, Ma, I know this is tough on you.'

'Yes, it is.' She pushed the ashtray towards him, sat down

again. 'All I want to do is the right thing, and then somehow find the way to live a quiet life. That's all I want. A quiet life.'

He leaned across the table and squeezed her hand. 'I gave you a really hard time over the past few years, and you know how sorry I am about all that. I'm not going to make this one any tougher than it has to be.'

Rose felt her eyes fill. 'Thank you. That's a huge comfort.'

'Remember when you came to see me in the hospital?' His voice was suddenly quieter, the tone softer. He concentrated on tapping his cigarette on the ashtray in front of him.

Rose nodded. How could she ever forget?

'You gave me the chance to get back on my feet. It made me realize, more than ever, all you had to do on your own. I'm not going to let you down. And I will see the old git, of course I will.' He grinned at her, and his face was suddenly a five-year-old's again: cheeky, challenging. 'Doesn't mean I won't make him wait, though.'

Rose smiled at his expression. 'Well, I think we're all entitled to play the waiting game. After all, we've been taught by the master.'


It was three o'clock in the morning before Rose finally crept, shivering, into bed. She wrapped the duvet tightly around her, making sure there were no gaps anywhere, no opportunities for the still chilly night air to catch her unawares.

And so morning came, the sixth day: the thought surprised her, caught up with her out of nowhere. She felt wide awake still, not in the least drowsy. It was as though one full phase of this other new life had just been completed: as though the chapter entitled 'The Children' had finally been written.

Now, she thought, let battle commence.

# PART TWO

# Chapter Six

ROSE COULD HEAR the phone ringing as soon as she turned off her hairdryer. She took her time, allowing the answering machine to pick up. Some sixth sense told her that it was Ben. Earlier still that morning, there had been two calls: one she'd missed while in the shower, the other Lisa hadn't bothered to answer, or simply hadn't heard over the blare of the television. She checked the messages now, fairly sure of what she was about to hear.

Nevertheless, despite her preparedness, despite her sense of calm certainty, Ben's voice on the answering machine still took her by surprise. It was a few seconds before his tone registered with her as one that she knew, one that was already all too familiar to her.

'Rose, it's Ben calling. I just wanted to make some arrangement to meet up with Brian and Lisa and Damien, and I think we should talk before I do. Maybe you could give me a call at—' And the line went dead. Rose erased the message, overwhelmed by the pedestrian normality of his words.

The second call was Ben successfully leaving his mobile number, the third again urging Rose to contact him at his hotel as soon as possible. Rose wrote his numbers rapidly into her notebook and erased both messages just as Lisa came into the living room.

'Was that a message? Was it for me?'

'Yes, it was a message, and no, it wasn't for you. Are you ready to go?'

'I can't find my book of maths questions.'

'Do you need it for this morning?'

'Mum! That's the whole *point* of this morning! We've a double revision class before our test tomorrow! I *have* to have it!'

Rose refused to rise to the bait. Moments like this one made her believe that she had another shape-shifter under her roof, another changeling child. Lisa seemed to be possessed by at least two conflicting personalities, each cohabiting uneasily with the other. Sweet, helpful Lisa of the past week was now anxious, truculent Lisa of early Wednesday morning. A school morning. But at least Rose was beginning to get used to it. First Brian, then Damien, now her. There was a certain comfortable, predictable symmetry to it all.

She reached into her handbag and pulled out her lipstick. Very deliberately looking in the mirror, and away from her daughter, she said, her voice quite calm: 'Where do you think you had it last?'

Her affected nonchalance only seemed to send Lisa's anxiety register soaring even higher.

'*I* don't know! Doing my homework—' she trailed off abruptly.

Rose zipped up her handbag briskly. 'Exactly – homework ou insisted on finishing at Carly's yesterday evening, even though I specifically said I wanted you to stay at home.'

'But she was *helping* me with stuff I didn't under*stand*.'

'Damien offered – and you turned him down.' Rose began to walk towards the front door. 'Ring her on her mobile,' she said sharply. 'Tell her to bring your maths questions with her to school.'

'But she'll have left by now!' Lisa's voice ascended to a wail.

Jesus, thought Rose. How many variations of this must I endure on a daily basis? 'Ring her anyway. If she's only just left, she can go back for it and you can meet her at school, no harm done. If she's too far away, I'll pick her up, we can go back to her house together and I'll leave you both to school.' She raised her hand to stem Lisa's protest. 'We're not going to argue, Lisa – that's how we're going to handle it. If we're late, I'll tell your tutor what happened: that you were too disorganized to have discovered this earlier. Now let's go.'

And she walked out the front door, leaving her daughter for once with nothing to say. Get used to it, kiddo, she thought grimly; this mother's not for turning. These days have far too much depending on them.

The journey to school was a silent and indignant one, as soon as the call to Carly had been made. Rose pulled up at the school gates and turned to her sulky daughter. She spoke gently to her, but firmly, not wanting to leave with this spiky silence prickling the air between them.

'Let's not be like this, Lisa. We're both dealing with some difficult stuff at the moment.' She leaned over, tucked strands of Lisa's hair behind her ear, lifted up her chin with one finger. The girl had no choice but to look her mother in the eye. 'Let's try and help each other,' said Rose, smiling at her. You can do your bit by looking after your things, and I'll do my bit by looking after you. Deal?'

Lisa looked down, away from her and examined her finger-nails. 'Are you seeing Dad today?'

Rose sighed inwardly. 'No, not today. But I will be speaking to him later on. Would you like me to give him a message?'

Lisa shrugged. 'No – I mean, not yet.'

'That's fine. Whenever you're ready. Now, do we have a deal?'

She nodded. Then the words came out in a rush. 'I'm sorry,

Mum. I just feel ... nervous and cranky.' She turned away from Rose and stared out of the window. 'I'm feeling really rotten this morning, and it doesn't have anything at all to do with Dad being back.' She looked down miserably, picking at her fingers. 'I feel like this too much of the time.'

Rose squeezed her hand. 'There's lots of things going on in your life right now. And you're due a period soon, aren't you?'

Lisa looked at her, her eyes a surprised blue. Two large tears trembled on the lower lashes. 'Yeah, but how did you know?' She wiped her eyes hastily, using the back of her hand.

Rose grinned. 'You'd be surprised at the things I know. But keep that in mind when you feel bad and just keep on talking to me, won't you? We'll make those nerves go away together.'

Lisa looked thoughtful.

God bless your innocence, child, thought Rose, amused. 'Now, come on, give your old mother a kiss and have a good day. You always do, once you get inside, don't you?'

'Spose.'

'And you're really lucky with your friends, aren't you?'

Lisa's face brightened at that. 'Yeah.'

Rose leaned towards her. 'Hang onto them, girl. Nothing like your friends. They're God's apology for your family: did you know that? Now go.'

Lisa giggled, despite herself. 'Thanks Mum. See ya later.'

'Bye.'

Rose watched her go. She bit her lip, remembering all too clearly her daughter's experiences of the adult world: how familiar certainties had shifted, without warning, and hurtled her towards calamity. No wonder she felt on edge, poised for the next wave to strike. Rose tried not to think about it.

And anyway, there was a lot to be grateful for: Damien was holding, still steady. His reactions last night to his father's return had been enough to give her great hope. The heat of his initial anger had given way to sadness, sadness to the cooler waters of reflection.

By the time he'd climbed the stairs to his old bedroom, at three o'clock in the morning, Rose had had the feeling that her eldest child finally understood the poison of unfinished business.

'Ben? It's Rose.'

How strange her own voice sounded, Rose thought. For so long now, she had only ever uttered Ben's name to other people. He had become somebody who existed only at second-remove, somebody to be referred *to*, spoken *about*. Saying his name now, over the phone, it acquired a directness, a peculiar intimacy that unnerved her, made her feel somehow off-guard.

'Hello, Rose. Thanks for getting back to me.'

She was intrigued by his tone. He was subdued, less combative than she had expected. Rose was immediately suspicious; she couldn't help it. She decided to kick to touch.

'You're welcome. Can I ask you a favour, Ben?'

There was a brief, surprised silence.

'Of course.'

Rose smiled to herself. Pauline had been right, after all. Conciliation was the way to go, she'd insisted. Avoid conflict at all costs in the early stages: there'll probably be more than enough of it later on.

'Can you leave it up to me over the next while to get in touch with you? I think it would be better if you didn't ring or call to the house just now.'

Rose allowed an uncomfortable silence to gather. She sensed surprise, perhaps even shock, at the other end of the line. Good, she thought. Let him wonder. She wasn't going to show her hand just yet. When she continued, she was careful to keep her voice neutral. 'Lisa is at a tricky stage, particularly with school exams looming. To be honest, she can be a handful. I need the time to talk to her before she meets up with you. I don't want anything sprung on her suddenly.'

Still Ben said nothing. He cleared his throat, as though about to speak, and Rose waited. If he wouldn't keep away for her sake, then perhaps he'd do it for his daughter's. Time; they all needed time. Rose tried to remember where she'd heard, or read, or absorbed recently, that the average teenager spent an hour and a half alone with a parent in any given week. What influence could a father or mother possibly have, what positive difference to a young person's life could you even begin to make in less than fifteen minutes a day? And right now, Lisa's life was far from average.

'Okay,' he said finally. 'That sounds all right. How long do you think you'll need?'

Definitely suspicious: mildness, reasonableness – these were not the traits Rose remembered of her husband. She stopped herself, mid-accusation. You're dealing with a *father*, now, only a father. Maybe this was just the simple parental imperative: a clear, flowing instinct unmuddied by the white-water rapids of separation. She had to believe that Ben meant well towards his children. This was pure fatherly concern, chiselled away from all the bonds of marriage, the ties of failure. Rose decided to give him the benefit of the doubt.

'Give me another few days. I need to be sure that she feels ready to meet and talk. But I don't want to make a big deal about it, either – I don't want to fuss her.' Rose paused, but again, there was no response. Despite her best intentions, her husband's silence made her begin to feel exasperated, on the defensive. 'I'm really trying to find the right balance here, Ben, and it's going to take me a bit of time.'

'Okay,' he agreed. 'I know it's tough on you, Rose, and I appreciate you taking all this trouble. I'd love to see Lisa as soon as possible, of course, but I'll wait to hear from you. You let me know when you think the time is right.'

Ben? Trusting her judgement? Rose missed a beat.

'Yes, well, I'll keep in touch. Today's Wednesday – I'll definitely get back to you before the weekend. And just in case you need to speak to me beforehand, I'll text you my mobile number. You can always get me on that.'

'Okay, fine. What about Brian? Have you told him?'

'Yes, I have, immediately he got back on Sunday night. He's nineteen, Ben, an adult. I'm leaving him to do the running for himself. Now that I have your numbers, I'll pass them onto him. He'll get in touch in his own time.'

'Right. I did try the house over the weekend, but I couldn't get through.'

And the day before yesterday, she thought. What about the day before yesterday? She couldn't let it go. She struggled with the instinct to blurt it all out: how she'd seen his calculated arrival, how angry his man with the measuring tape had made her. She stopped herself just in time, imagining Pauline's advice. *Under no circumstances*, she'd have said. *Keep your counsel.*

All Rose knew right now was that she was in the grip of some ferocious, perhaps unreliable instinct: the overwhelming need to protect her children from all threats, real and imaginary. It was as though she had reverted to living in the shadow of the cave, alert for the stranger's footstep crackling on branches, the dim, steady thrum of danger in the distance.

With a start, she realized that Ben was still talking, his tone a little more hesitant now.

'I don't want to put you in the middle, Rose, but how did Brian take the news?'

Didn't want to put her in the middle? Where else had he put her? Where else could she have possibly been for all these years?

But she didn't say that. She knew she'd have to try and avoid all those old, intimate angers: angers that were hers and Ben's alone, which did not belong in any of the forgiving spaces between parents and their children. 'That's for you and him, Ben. All I will say is that he was very taken aback. Your return has been somewhat . . . sudden.'

There was a small silence. When Ben spoke again, his voice was distant, almost brittle, as though it had retreated behind a suddenly treacherous emotion. 'Ah. Yes, of course. There is that. They don't know that I've never . . . that I've always . . . thought about them, all the time.'

Despite herself, Rose could feel her own eyes begin to fill. She swallowed, stood up from the table, walked around the kitchen. She felt suddenly trapped in a tangle of emotions, all clamouring like loud music inside her head. It was as though she'd been sitting for hours beside a loudspeaker, the orchestra's notes jangling and discordant now that the concert was finally over. She was angry that she had to do this all over again. But even more than that, she felt cheated, filled with an enormous grief that this man was suddenly, once more, warm and fatherly. Why couldn't he have stayed like that? Why couldn't he quite simply have *stayed*?

'I presume Damien doesn't need warning, does he?'

The steadiness of Ben's voice made her calmer. This wasn't about her, about him, about the two of them, any longer. This was only about the three young people who had once made them a family. Rose didn't know what to say. She felt suddenly at a disadvantage. If this were a game of Ben's, then she couldn't read the rules. He gave no hint of remembering all the difficulties between himself and his elder son all those years ago. Had he forgotten all the shadows of conflict, the differences that had spontaneously ignited every time each found himself in the company of the other?

Rose bit down hard on her lower lip, remembering the earlier times, too: Damien on his father's shoulders, holding on for dear life, shrieking with laughter as Ben careened around the back garden, making loud, stuttering motorbike noises.

'I've already told him. I met up with him yesterday evening.'

'And?' His tone was anxious.

'He'll be twenty-five on his next birthday – a grown man. I'm certainly not going to answer for him. I'll call him tonight and give him your numbers.'

'That's fine – thank you for that. Please let him know how keen I am to see him.'

'I will.' Rose felt suddenly exhausted. And she used to think that catering was hard work. 'And, by the way . . .' It wasn't by the way at all, of course. It was right to the heart of the matter, but she couldn't think of any other way to say it. 'I haven't forgotten that you and I need to meet, but you're going to have to trust me on that one, too. Give me a little time with Lisa, let the dust settle, and then we'll talk again.' She made sure that her voice was firm, her final words calm and deliberate. 'I'm every bit as anxious as you are to have all the practical, financial things sorted out between us, once and for all. But please don't rush me, Ben: I'll get back to you as soon as I'm ready.'

There, that felt better.

'I'll leave it up to you, then. There's just one more thing.'

'Yes?' She felt suddenly wary again.

'I know that this is really difficult for all of us. My hope would be that . . . you and I . . . that we . . . might be able to sort things out without being at each other's throats. I know I have a lot of explaining to do . . .'

'Don't, Ben. Please don't – not yet.' Rose couldn't bear the sudden break in her own voice. 'Not today. I'm not ready. Remember that you knew you were coming back, you had all the time in the world to prepare yourself for it. I didn't. I've had time to process nothing, nothing at all. It hasn't even been a week yet.'

'I know.' His words were suddenly quieter. 'I am aware of that. Take whatever time you need.'

'Thanks. I will. Bye, Ben.'

'Bye. Take care of yourself.'

Take care of yourself? Rose switched off her phone, filled the kettle. When had Ben ever cared, during her last lifetime, whether she, or anybody else, took care of herself?

She stood at the window now, her heart beginning to pound again. What was happening here? Was her husband's return going to be even more traumatic, more tangled, than his leaving?

Rose dragged her hands through her hair, smoothing out the dull ache in her forehead. Here I am, dressed up in my suit of armour – all dressed up and nowhere to go.

She waited for the kettle to boil and stared, unseeing, out of the kitchen window. She needed to get going: she had a lunch party for thirty-three women at two o'clock, less than five hours away. But she stayed standing by the window, couldn't tear herself away. Her eyes gradually began to focus on the world outside. The tide was in full, the water a rolling mass of gull-wing grey. Could she and Ben possibly have got it all wrong? Could they have worked things out back then, becoming sadder and wiser people in the process, but at least managing to stay together, to keep their now fractured family somehow intact? Rose pressed the heels of her hands into her eyes, trying to relieve the pressure that was beginning to build there, throbbing relentlessly across the top of her head.

Surely the time for re-evaluation was long past? She been over it all too many times before, and the answer had never been any different. Ben was gone, long gone, and their marriage had been over and done with even before he left. So what was all this emotional turmoil about? How could she reconcile the calculating man who had stood in her garden two days ago, with this quiet voice on the phone: a voice full of kindness, of fatherly concern? She couldn't. She felt unsteady again, filled with confusion, ambushed over and over by all the remembered tendernesses of the past.

Then it hit her. What if this was all part of the game?

*Negotiating So Everyone Wins.* The week before, when Ben had spoken about 'regularizing' their position, Rose had been struck by the strangeness of her husband's vocabulary. The words he had spoken were not words she had been accustomed to hearing him utter; they had sounded strange as they tumbled from his mouth, released in a rush as though he'd been afraid of forgetting them. She remembered, too, that once confronted by her anger, Ben's reasonable exterior had begun to crumble very rapidly: he'd behaved as though the intervening years had never happened, as though he was still at the centre of his own discarded domestic universe. Leaving aside their three children, what if this unexpected *niceness* towards her was all part of the plan? Perhaps there really was someone standing in the wings, prompting, whispering, schooling Ben in the art of getting what he wanted. Had he managed just now – almost – to fool her again, to put her once more firmly on the back foot?

'Eight years,' she said now, out loud, to the seething sea in the distance. 'Eight long years of silence, of worry, of sheer, lonely drudgery. That's a long time, Ben Holden. It's long enough for me to be entitled to be furious, and not to believe a single word out of your mouth.'

May God forgive me if I'm wrong, she thought, but I don't believe I am. You will not do this to me again, Ben Holden – never unsettle me again once all of this is over. I was even beginning to lose trust in my own anger.

Quickly Rose gathered up her bag, her coat, and made her way out to the van. She felt energized again, as though the sudden whiff of potential treachery had become some sort of fuel to keep her fired up, keep her moving. She indicated left, pulled out into the thinning morning traffic. At this rate, she should be at the Bonne Bouche in under twenty minutes. Load the van, head off to the tennis club, feed the hungry. Some time later this afternoon, she'd make sure to find the time to call Sam.

There was a living to be looked after here, and a home, and children. She'd felt all of this before, and she felt it even more strongly now: all that she had worked for would not be taken away from her without a fight.

'Rose? Is that you?'

'It is indeed, Sam. How are you?'

'Good, thanks – and yourself?'

Rose was standing outside the back entrance to the tennis club, making sure that she was hidden from sight. She didn't want the ladies in the dining room to think that she was slacking. Just around the corner from her, three women were dragging deeply on their cigarettes, all unwilling outcasts from the smoke-free zone inside. One of them grinned and waved at her, and Rose waved back: one outlaw to the other.

'I'm okay, thanks, Sam. I had a meeting with Pauline O'Brien yesterday, and I just wanted to touch base with you.'

'How did it go?'

Rose paused for a moment, searching for the right words. 'Well, I suppose these things are never pleasant – but the upshot is that I'm now fairly clear about what I want, and what I need to do to make that happen.' She paused, kicking at the pebbles with the toe of her shoe. 'I had another telephone conversation with my ex-husband this morning, and it's helped to make things even clearer.'

'Good – then let's meet up soon and have a preliminary chat, at least.'

'Some time this week?'

There was a brief pause. 'How about this evening? I'm free from five o'clock on. My last appointment has just been cancelled.'

Rose did a quick calculation. It was almost four o'clock now: a few minutes to check on Betty and Angela's clean-up, a quick call to Lisa to say she'd be late. Yes, she could do it, why not? Why wait any longer than she had to?

'Actually, Sam, that sounds great. I'll take a taxi and I should be with you in, say, an hour or so?'

'Good. I'll meet you in the Espresso Bar around the corner from the office. That way we won't be disturbed.'

'See you there, then – and thanks.'

'No problem.'

Rose put her mobile into her jacket pocket and hurried back inside. Most of the lunch guests were still lingering over their coffee, but the tables were almost clear.

'That was wonderful, Rose! You spoil us!'

Rose stopped and greeted some of the women, waved over at others, noticed how the usual suspects were settling into their corner of the bar, wine glasses still full. She felt a sudden ooze of envy: wouldn't she love to be the one waited on, rather than doing the waiting – in all senses. A leisurely afternoon, no timetable squeezing her between the incessant demands of work and family, family and work. A quiet life. That's all she wanted. Just a quiet life.

She pushed open the door into the kitchen, already hearing the raised voices.

'I *saw* you!' Betty was standing at the sink, her plump arms glistening with soapy bubbles. 'Don't try to let on you didn't!'

Angela was standing just behind her, forcing Betty to address her over one shoulder. Rose thought that both girls looked most uncomfortable.

'Why don't you shout louder, Betty?' Angela folded her arms and glared over towards the sink. 'They can't hear you in Australia!'

'I'm warnin' you, Angela, and it's not the first—'

'*You* are warning *me*? Who do you think you are? You're nothing but a . . .'

'Stop it!' said Rose sharply, moving towards them. 'Both of you. What on earth do you think you're doing!'

Both young women stopped instantly. The silence between them was shocked, sudden. Angela's face was flushed, two spots of colour sat high on her normally pale cheeks. Betty was looking almost bewildered, as though this was happening somewhere else, to someone else. She looked down into the sink, pushed the plates further under the frothy surface.

Oh, get a hold of yourself, girl, for God's sake, Rose thought crossly, feeling a familiar surge of impatience. 'I don't know what you're fighting about, and right now I don't want to know. Finish the clean-up, both of you. Get everything into the van – now. I said now, Angela. I don't want any arguments. I have a meeting across town in an hour. You two finish up here and bring the van back to the Bonne Bouche. Empty it completely: put any leftovers into the cold room. Now, get moving.'

Rose watched as Angela threw a contemptuous glance in Betty's direction. The other girl flinched. Rose was taken aback at the venom in the air. It was a dark, almost palpable presence, hovering in the hostile space between them. She'd have to find out tomorrow what was going on, but for now she had just about more than she could handle.

'You can leave the van in the car park overnight. I'll pick it up tomorrow. I'll need you both in for eight in the morning. Are there any questions?'

Betty shook her head, subdued. 'No, Miss Kelly.'

Angela didn't reply. She continued to stand her ground, arms folded tightly across her chest, eyes too bright in her small face.

Rose looked from one to the other, careful to make an equal amount of eye contact with each. 'Jenny's outside: she's the club secretary. Report to her before you leave, both of you, please, and make sure she's happy with everything. And whatever it is you're fighting about, can you keep it out of the workplace? Thank you.'

Rose pulled her jacket off the hanger and left the kitchen immediately. She was unwilling to be drawn. Let them sort it out between them.

After all, she wasn't *everybody's* bloody mother.

Sam was already there when Rose arrived, sitting with his back to the wall, facing the large plate glass window. She pushed open the door of the café, smiling in response to his raised hand. He stood up as she approached and she had the fleeting impression of something old-fashioned, almost courtly, in the way he took her jacket, pulled out a chair for her.

'Good to see you, Rose. What can I get you?'

'Whatever you're having looks good.'

'It's an excellent espresso – and a piece of strawberry shortcake with cream, which I neither need nor deserve. There, I've expunged my guilt, like a good Catholic.'

Rose sat opposite him and laughed at his expression. 'Well,' she said, 'I'm fresh out of guilt – I've been told that it's a wasted emotion. Besides, that cake looks too good to miss.'

'Sorry for starting without you, but I missed lunch and my stomach was getting restless.' Sam caught the waitress's eye. 'So. How was your day? You sounded under pressure when you called.'

Rose shook her head, a gesture of disbelief. 'Oh, when I called, things were fine – just the usual flat-out activity that goes with being a caterer. It was only *after* that that I realized all the gods must be against me, these days. Not only am I fighting with my ex-husband, I'm also fighting with my staff. I don't know what it's about, but Betty and Angela were close to armed combat when I left them an hour ago.'

Sam turned to the waitress. 'Same again, please, Beatriz. We've agreed that your shortcake is far more appealing than our guilt.'

The young woman smiled. 'With cream, too, Mr McCarthy?'

Rose was charmed by her voice. All those elongated vowels seemed so redolent of innocence, somehow. Spanish waitresses in Dublin: why? Rose wondered now. What could possibly bring them here: the high cost of living, the miserable summers? It must be yet another one of those signs that her native city had secretly changed its clothes while she'd had her back turned, slaving away in the suburbs. The baggy, unfashionable cut of its old suit had been transformed overnight into smart Armani, all razor-sharp creases and matching metallic ties. Dublin, it appeared, was now as exotic to the ambitious youth of Madrid, Paris, Rome, as all of those cities had once seemed to her. Except that I was never ambitious, thought Rose abruptly. She felt a sudden, sharp sense of loss. There were so many things she had never been.

She smiled at the young girl. 'Yes, please,' and she sighed theatrically. 'Lots of cream. The whole hog.'

Sam chuckled as Beatriz retreated, puzzled. 'Don't think that her English is quite up to that.'

Rose grinned. 'What the hell – stretch her a little. I have to say, she's a lot more pleasant than my two.'

Sam finished his cake. 'That was truly excellent. Tell me, would Betty and Angela normally get on well?'

Rose shrugged. 'I suppose they don't really get on at all. I mean that in the sense that they have very little to do with each other. They work independently, kind of side by side, rather than as a team, if you know what I mean.'

Sam nodded vigorously. 'I'm afraid I do know what you mean – all too well, as it happens. Are they likely to become a liability, do you think?'

Rose looked at him in dismay. 'God, I never even thought about it like that. I think that Betty's solid enough, but Angela's been a bit flighty lately. I'm keeping a very close eye on both of them.'

Sam nodded his approval. 'Good. The last thing you want right now is either of them taking advantage of your distraction.'

Sam's words stirred something at the back of Rose's memory, that primitive, reptilian part of her brain that was always alert to trouble, poised to recognize betrayal of any kind. She didn't know what it was that was trying to swim to the surface, struggling its way up from the depths. But it was something that she *knew*, without knowing: something that she recognized instinctively, but couldn't put a name to. She shook her head, hoping to dislodge the clutter that seemed to jam up her circuits more and more these days. Sometimes she felt as though her brain was made of porridge: thoughts got formed only sluggishly on many occasions, then failed to make connections, or else simply gave up the fight before they reached any kind of coherent consciousness. She felt that some vital firing of her neurons was missing, that rather than fizz and crackle as they did in a normal person, with her, they simply flared briefly and went out.

'Distraction. That's a good word. Sums up just what I feel.'

Beatriz returned and put Rose's coffee and cake on the table. Rose looked at the large plate with something akin to delight. The lush red of the strawberries formed a perfect contrast with the white porcelain. The ornamental swirl of blue and black berries, the delicate dusting of icing sugar, the soft white comma of the cream – she stopped herself, mid-rhapsody, aware of Sam's puzzled gaze.

'Is there something wrong?' he asked.

She grinned, feeling herself come back to reality again. 'No, not at all, quite the opposite. My mind has just become a speaking menu, that's all.' She shrugged apologetically. 'I can't see any sort of food with an uncritical eye, and I'm always looking for simple serving ideas. This one is stunning, and it's the large, white plate that pulls it off.'

Sam wasn't getting it; she could see by his face that he wasn't getting it at all. She tried again.

'Look – put these same ingredients onto something smaller, and you have – well, the difference, let's say, between singing scales and singing an aria. It's the same voice, but the effect is quite something – a lot more high voltage, if you know what I mean.' She stopped.

Shut up, Rose. Just shut up.

'I see.' Sam appeared completely at a loss. He hesitated for a moment, seeming to consider her words. Then he scratched his head, a comical expression of bafflement spreading across his features. 'It's bloody good cake, you know.'

And they both laughed.

'I won't complicate it any more than I already have, I promise.' Rose paused and took a deep breath. 'Thanks for seeing me so quickly, Sam. I really appreciate it. The Bonne Bouche aside for the moment, I really need to start working out some domestic financial details very soon, and Pauline tells me you're the man to do it.'

He inclined his head, a silent acknowledgement of Pauline's compliment. Rose thought that he looked very pleased. For some reason, his evident pride touched her.

'Well, we'll certainly do whatever it takes to make this as easy as possible on you and your family.' He reached into his shirt pocket and took out his reading glasses. 'Now, tell me whatever you think will help. Once I have the broad outline, I can go away and work on the figures. But it's very important that we overlook nothing. You get one shot at this, and we have to get it right.' He waited, seated patiently across the table from her, pen poised. At that moment, he bore an unexpected resemblance to David O'Brien, Pauline's father. Rose remembered how much he had helped her all those years ago: he'd brought her by the hand through the treacherous financial quicksand that had filled all the spaces left behind by her husband's abrupt departure.

Déjà vu, she thought, and not for the first time. I suppose I'd better get used to it. Telling my life all over again, as though it belonged to someone else; as though it was composed of nothing other than random acts of arrival and departure.

Rose took a deep breath. It felt strange, imposing a reasoned, chronological narrative on her previous life, particularly the events of the past eight years. Reason, order, storytelling: these all seemed completely out of synch with those events which, as she had lived them, were composed only of chaos, anger, shock – all the fractured component parts of emotional freefall.

'Well, Ben and I married back in 1975. I was twenty-two, he was twenty-five.' She caught Sam's sidelong glance and smiled at him. 'I know – mere children.' She looked down at her hands, caught in a sudden grip of emotion. Its blunt force took her unawares: she had thought that Ben had long ago lost the power to surprise her. 'It's hard to explain, but it was as if . . . as if it was *expected* of us; do you know what I mean? Or, at least, expected of me.'

Sam nodded, but said nothing. Rose felt grateful for his silence, encouraged to continue. His matter-of-fact expression seemed somehow to reduce the treacherous well of emotion inside her to a mere muddy trickle, an insignificant puddle after rain. 'And the truth is, I *wanted* to be married. I wanted a home and children of my own: I was never bright enough, or brave enough to follow a career.' She could see Sam about to interrupt, had watched the quizzical lift of his eyebrow. She shook her head at him. 'No – let me continue, please: I've only recently come to understand all these things. Last year was the seventh anniversary of Ben's rather sudden departure from my life, and seven seems to be some sort of magic number. I've been able to tease things out since then that I wasn't able to do earlier.

'I did love Ben – at least, in the way I understood love thirty years ago – but there was also a measure of escape in my marrying him.' She looked at Sam steadily. 'My mother had died when I was quite young. I was the Miss Responsibility of the family. Somehow, I knew that if I didn't make my own life when I was offered the opportunity, I'd end up being my father's housekeeper until he died.' Rose swallowed. She'd begun by needing to tell Sam the facts: *just the facts, ma'am, nothing but the facts*. And now, here she was, unburdening herself to a man who wanted only the figures, nothing but the figures.

'I'm sorry, Sam – I'm blathering on here with stuff that's of no possible interest to you. I apologize.'

Sam waved one hand in the air, a gesture that could have meant anything from forgiveness to mild interest to crucifying embarrassment. Rose decided not to let him speak: she could already feel the warm prickles of mortification caused by such an inappropriate exposure of her private self in such a public place. To a man, moreover, accustomed only to dealing with clients' profit and loss statements, balance sheets and revenue demands, not the subtler profits and losses of their emotional lives. She sat up straighter.

'Anyway, the facts are that we had three children – Damien, Brian and Lisa – and we kept things together for the best part of twenty years, in the way that married couples do. But about ten years ago, I sensed that something was wrong: I mean, really wrong, apart from all the daily "wrong" stuff we'd both just learned to live with. Things had gone stale, I suppose, and disappointing. Ben had become more and more obsessed by his business deals – he was really into property back then, and I just retreated into the family. Then, out of the blue, eight years ago, I discovered he was having an affair.'

'Oh,' said Sam. 'That must have been tough.'

Rose nodded. 'It certainly was. Even though things hadn't been good for a long time – I'd learned very early on that I was way down Ben's priority list – being dumped for someone else is quite another story. Suddenly, you miss all that you never truly had, and a real emotional roller-coaster begins. I'll cut to the chase: one April morning eight years ago, he comes into the kitchen and tells me he's leaving, that he doesn't love me any more. His bag was already packed and that was it. Off he went.'

'And you never saw him again?' Sam's tone was incredulous.

'Oh, I did – he was off on a Spanish holiday with the other woman: that's why the bag was packed. Pathetic, isn't it? Wife of his business partner: the glamorous Caroline. Actually, she's a very nice woman. We mended fences later on; she even sent me clients when I started catering on my own. I think falling for Ben was her one serious lapse in a lifetime of otherwise impeccable taste.'

Sam grinned at her. 'So she dumped him, then?'

Rose laughed. 'She did indeed – in fact, she lost no time in putting him in his place. He was a passing fancy for her. She was horrified when he told her that he'd left me and the kids: she'd no intention of anything permanent with Ben. She got rid of him pretty damn quick and went back to her husband. So much for their romantic holiday. And the rest, as they say, is history. I came to my senses with astonishing speed and decided I didn't want Ben back, even if he asked. It was like a wake-up call, like something I'd been unconsciously waiting for for years. I wanted to finish things between us, make sure the kids were looked after and get on with my life.'

'So what happened?'

Rose had the strange sensation that the events of the previous years were growing less, rather than more, familiar every time she related them. 'He was in financial difficulties back then, his property deals all collapsed more or less at once, and he left the country, just like that: without a word. Disappeared to England. "Divorce Irish Style" it used to be called then, before we got our own.'

'I remember,' said Sam grimly. 'I knew quite a few victims of that particular brand of marriage breakdown myself.'

'Since then – apart from him turning up on my doorstep the other night, of course – I heard nothing from Ben. Not a word. Ever. Not even a card at Christmas for the children, or a birthday present. Nothing.'

'Did you chase him for maintenance?'

Rose shrugged. 'No. Too busy getting on with things. And for what? Spending money I didn't have to secure money I'd probably never get? Seemed like a mug's game to me at the time. Still does. No, my best chance of closure is this present negotiation. Time to draw a line in the sand.'

Sam was looking at her thoughtfully. 'Right,' he said, after a moment. He became suddenly brisk again. 'I have more than enough here to be going on with. Think you could go ahead and get valuations on the house for the next time we meet?'

Rose nodded. 'Of course. Any particular firm you'd recommend?'

'Use a few of the big names, for a start. Then get at least one local agent. They're all pretty well linked these days, but the local guys usually have a private list of people looking for property specifically in their area. You might just get lucky, and have a buyer-in-waiting.'

Rose drained her coffee cup and pushed the empty plate away from her. She remembered the man with the measuring tape: couldn't bear the thought of having to consult him. Don't be silly, she told herself. It's nothing personal. He was just doing his job.

Sam looked at her closely. 'You don't have to do this: you don't *have* to move, you know. I'm sure Pauline's told you that.'

Rose nodded. 'She has, and I know all that. But I think it's best that I do. I've come to the conclusion that selling up is what's right for *me*.' She paused for a moment. 'Mind you, I can't help feeling that the logistics will be a bit of a nightmare. Can you imagine – almost thirty years' worth of hoarded junk, and all the goods and chattels of three children who threw out even less than I did?' She shuddered. 'What a prospect.'

Sam smiled at her, his brown eyes full of sympathy. 'Good chance for life laundry, though. I did a lot of that when I left Australia.'

Rose looked at him with interest. 'I *thought* there was something in your accent – particularly the first time we met. How long did you live there?' She felt ridiculously pleased with herself; after that first meeting, she'd wondered idly whether

Sam had spent time in Australia, New Zealand, or, at a push, South Africa. There was an absurd sense of satisfaction in having got it right.

'Fourteen years, in Melbourne.'

He stopped. Rose felt at something of a loss. There it was again, just a fleeting presence across his eyes: that ghost of some half-familiar expression, something she couldn't pin down, couldn't seem to grasp. It stopped her from asking him the obvious, the conversational questions. So why did you leave sunny Australia? Why did you come back to Dublin? What significant arrivals and departures are there in *your* life that I know nothing about?

'I came back to Dublin two years ago. Dónal and I were at college together, oh – a lifetime ago, and he was expanding the business. We'd always kept in touch, mostly by email, and he let me know that he was on the lookout for a new partner for the firm.'

*Paahtnah.* Rose tried not to smile at the broad, open vowels that slipped into Sam's speech from time to time. It was an intonation that made her think of barbecues, bright beaches, kind blue weather.

'As it happens, that particular piece of information came to me just around the time I needed to leave Melbourne.' Sam put his pen and notebook away and smiled ruefully at her. 'My previous business partner, who also happened to be my life partner, ripped me off after almost ten years of harmonious co-habitation. She took our business, our bank accounts, our clients – even our dog. Left me high and dry. Took me four years to recover.'

Rose didn't know what to say. Before she had time to cobble together some sort of a reply, anything at all, he interrupted her. Grinning broadly, he leaned across the table and said: 'It was a real shame – I was awfully fond of that dog.'

Rose couldn't help laughing at his conspiratorial air. 'Is that what you meant when you told me you'd once "lost your shirt"?'

He nodded and looked surprised. 'I didn't think you'd remember that. But, yeah, that's what I meant. I never even saw it coming – think I was in shock for about a year.'

Rose smiled at him. 'I know what you mean. I felt for so long that being *left* was like a bereavement, except worse. There was no body to bury, no sense that something was *finished*, so that you could move on.'

Sam looked at her and nodded his head slowly. 'Yeah, that's for sure. It took months before I stopped leaping up every time the phone rang, or the doorbell went, or a dog barked. But mind you,' he said quickly, 'I had no children depending on me. My survival – my economic survival – was not all that difficult to organize.' He shrugged. 'And here I am.'

'And are you happy to be back?'

'Yeah.' He seemed to consider her question for a moment. 'I am. "Home" suddenly started to mean something completely different, once I'd been on my own for a few years. The ties I'd felt were to Susanna, not to Australia. It took a while for me to make the decision, I didn't want to rush into anything. But yeah, it's good to be back.'

Rose felt her mobile begin to vibrate. She sighed. Sometimes the technological leash was just that bit too tight for comfort. She glanced apologetically at Sam as she fished it out of her skirt pocket.

'Hi, Lisa, what's up?' She listened for a moment. 'When?'

Rose became aware of Sam watching her keenly, knew that her face had already begun to betray her.

'Don't do anything until I get home. Lisa – listen to me. I'll be there in half an hour. I'm leaving right now to get a taxi.' She snapped her mobile shut and met Sam's troubled gaze.

'Are you okay, Rose?'

'I'm sorry, Sam, I've got to go. Ben has just called to the house. He was around on Monday, too, when he thought I didn't see him. I *asked* him not to do this.' She struggled into her jacket. 'And he agreed, he actually agreed. Lisa was in the shower when the doorbell rang. She hasn't let him in, but she's upset because she doesn't know what to do.' Rose grabbed her handbag, checked that she'd left nothing on the table. 'He *promised* he wouldn't do this; he *promised* he'd give me the time to make sure she was ready. And now, just when my back is turned . . .'

Sam was already on his feet. 'Let me give you a lift, Rose – my car is parked just around the corner.'

She shook her head. 'No, thank you – please don't think me rude, but a taxi will be faster – there's a bus lane all the way to Fairview.'

He nodded. 'Okay. Let me help you hail one, at least.' He threw a note and some coins onto the table and signalled to Beatriz, who waved and hurried towards them. 'Come on.' Sam put one hand under Rose's elbow. 'With any luck we'll pick one up straight away.'

They almost ran out of the café and made their way back towards Pembroke Road. Rose couldn't speak. She hardly acknowledged Sam as he opened the taxi door for her, barely heard what he said.

All she was conscious of was Lisa's high-pitched voice, the memory of Ben on her doorstep and the feeling, once again, of her heart leaping into her mouth.


Lisa was watching TV when Rose got home.

'Hi, hon. You okay?'

She shrugged. 'Yeah, I'm okay,' she said, and continued to gaze at the screen. Rose said nothing more. She sat beside her daughter on the sofa and allowed her heart to slow down, her eyes to drift, unseeing, towards the television.

It was a technique she had refined over many years. Teenagers – at least, the teenagers in her family – seemed to communicate their difficulties more freely if no eye contact with the parent was required. Rose remembered how she used to address the top of Brian's head while he concentrated on hand-held computer games. She had, also, in the past, become all too familiar with the sharp contours of Damien's shoulder blades as she'd follow him around the kitchen. She used to keep several careful steps behind him, coming as close as she dared, waiting patiently as he'd rummage for food in the fridge, or open and close the kitchen cupboards. In such circumstances had the most profound, the most difficult, the most revealing of all conversations with her children taken place.

I can wait, she thought now. I can wait another five minutes. Rose knew that with Lisa, the trick revolved around the TV. The girl would talk while keeping her eyes locked on the manic, noisy antics of MTV.

'I didn't answer the door,' she said eventually.

'That's okay,' said Rose.

Pause. 'He put something through the letterbox for you. It's in the hall, on the table.'

'Okay.' Rose didn't move.

'I just didn't know what to do. He kept ringing and ringing at the doorbell. I didn't know who it was until he started to walk away. I'd got out of the shower and watched from my bedroom window, and it was like, you know, I was six again, watching him go off to work, or something.'

Now Rose turned and looked at her. 'How did it feel?'

Lisa shrugged. 'It was weird – that . . . feeling like a little girl again. Just totally weird.'

'What would have happened if you'd opened the door, do you think?'

Lisa met her gaze. 'I dunno – I s'pose we'd have talked.'

'And?'

'I wouldn't have known what to say. I mean, what do you *say* to a dad you haven't seen in eight years?'

'How about "Where the hell have *you* been?"' suggested Rose, smiling at her.

Lisa giggled. 'Yeah – or, like, you *owe* me, big time: eight birthday presents and eight Christmas presents and I want them all *now*!'

Rose laughed. 'Cut to the chase, why don't you!' She paused. 'On the other hand, you could say something like "I've missed you."'

Lisa frowned. 'You can't say something like that – not right away, anyway. And I don't know if I *have* missed him. I mean, you only usually miss someone who was always there and then goes away for a little while. If they go away and never come back, it's like they were never there in the first place. Isn't it?'

Out of the mouths of babes, Rose thought.

'Perhaps. But he was here for all the years when you were a little girl. I think you'll find things to talk about. And I think you need to decide sooner, rather than later, when to meet up. You don't need to hide from this, Lisa; you've done nothing wrong. And there really is nothing to be afraid of. He's your dad and he loves you.'

'Will you be there, too?'

'If that's what you want, yes. For the first time, anyway. After that, you can always change your mind.'

'Do we have photographs of when I was little?' asked Lisa suddenly.

Rose felt something fall down inside her. It made her feel anxious, cautious, in need of a long, careful breath. Pandora's box again, she thought. What am I letting myself in for? Or rather, what am I letting *out* to wreak havoc on an unsuspecting fourteen-year-old?

'Sure,' she said easily, nodding. 'I put a great big pile of them into the attic only last year – we didn't have room on the shelves with all your books. Do you want to get them?'

Lisa nodded. 'Yeah. I'll root them out on Saturday. Are they all in albums?'

Rose laughed. 'You must be joking! What do you think I have, an *organized* life, or something?'

'Can I do that, then? Can I put them into albums?'

'You certainly can. Go into town tomorrow afternoon after school and buy a truckload of the nicest albums you can find.'

'Okay.' Lisa nodded, happy. Her mobile bleeped beside her on the sofa, and she dived on it, hooting with laughter as she saw the new text.

Rose kissed her daughter on the cheek and went out into the hallway, wondering what message Ben had chosen to leave her *this* time.

There was a large, brown envelope on the hall table. She slid her finger under the gummed flap and looked inside. Puzzled, she went to slide the contents into her hands, but they slithered out much too quickly, falling onto the floor before she could catch them. They lay there, all primary colours, like the large pieces of a child's first jigsaw. Curiously, she bent down to look.

Brochures. Estate agents' brochures. Dozens of them, with bright happy houses for sale. Houses for auction, houses for sale by private treaty, unbeatable investment opportunities: invitations to 'Buy Now! There's never been a better time! Interest rates at an all-time low!'

And there, adhered to the top left-hand corner of the most expensively produced glossy photograph, was a square yellow Post-it. 'Just thought this would give you an idea of what we could be looking at, value-wise. Ben.'

For an instant, Rose felt stunned. We? Value-wise? What 'we' was he talking about? There was no 'we', no 'us' – he had seen to that. And to what 'value' was he referring? The value of commitment, of love, of the security and stability of children? The value of home?

Then it came again. That spool of anger, winding its way through her, filling her chest, her head, the space behind her eyes. She felt caught in a tornado of fury, a tidal wave of rage that saw her gather the leaflets off the floor and fling them into the bin in the kitchen, slamming its swing top down hard so that it flew back and forth, back and forth, finally settling into a white lopsided torpor.

She rummaged furiously in her handbag, looking for the notebook with Ben's number. This time she'd had enough. First Monday, now this. Her mobile rang, just as she was about to call him. She answered at once. It had to be him. 'What the *fuck* do you think you're doing?'

'Rose?' The voice on the line was familiar, startled.

'Yes, Ben.' She kept her tone curt. She had no time for social niceties, not now, not ever again. He had really blown it this time.

'Ah . . . it's Sam, actually. I said I'd give you a call in an hour or so, just to make sure things were okay. Are you all right? Am I interrupting anything?'

Rose felt the balloon of anger deflate suddenly, its heat begin to leak away. 'I'm sorry, Sam. I thought you were Ben.'

'I think I'm . . . rather glad that I'm not, right now – if it's all the same to you.'

Rose could almost hear him grin. His tone made her smile, just a little. 'Well, on balance, it's much safer that way, believe me.'

She sat at the kitchen table, feeling suddenly weary, suddenly very troubled by the strength of her anger, the intensity of its grip. Something was squeezing her, making her breath short, her head light. This had to stop: she had to calm down, think sensible thoughts.

'Things are okay – I think I might just have overreacted.' She paused for a moment, feeling the rest of her anger seep away, leaving ragged, hollow spaces behind it. 'Ben left in some brochures from – oh, I think just about every estate agent in the city. I saw red. And I mean that, literally – lost all sense of proportion. I think it's all the *assumptions* that just get me going. I mean, we haven't even *discussed* the future yet. He agrees not to push me and then he goes and does something like this? It makes me so mad.'

'In the circumstances, that's not too hard to understand. Is your daughter all right?' Sam's voice was light, easy. Its very ordinariness reassured her.

'She's fine. I think I just picked up on her panic. I guess I should know better, but these days I can't distinguish between what's important and what's not. I'll have to try and . . . be more measured.' There was a brief pause. 'Sam?'

'Yeah, I'm still here.'

'Sorry, I thought I'd lost you.'

'No, I'm here. Why don't you pour yourself a glass of wine and watch a mindless midweek movie? I think there's a great selection of nonsense on this evening.'

Rose smiled. 'Sounds like just what the doctor ordered.'

'Let's meet up again towards the end of next week. I think our conversation today was somewhat interrupted. Would that suit, do you think?'

'Yes, I'm sure it will. I won't have time to breathe until after the weekend: we've a big party on Friday night. But I should be able to give you a call early next week.'

'May I make a suggestion?'

'Sure,' said Rose, surprised at the sudden, serious change in tone.

'Have you thrown out all the estate agents' stuff that Ben left in for you?'

Rose looked over at the kitchen bin, feeling its plastic malice, feeling the urge to kick it all the way up and down the back garden. 'Yes. Well, no – it's all here, in the kitchen bin.'

'Excellent. Then how about a three hundred and sixty degree revolution in your thought processes? Come around full circle.' He paused.

'You've lost me,' said Rose. 'Please, go on.'

'Well, think of it as Ben having done you a favour. He's obviously done a lot of legwork around the agency offices: use it for yourself. Bring all the brochures with you when we next meet, and we'll have good, general information to go on before we get down to specifics.'

'That's a rather charitable interpretation of this particular brown envelope,' said Rose dryly.

'Maybe so,' said Sam firmly. 'But it costs you a lot less emotional energy if you think like that. Save your anger. In my experience, you'll probably need it later on.'

Rose couldn't help smiling. 'You're a wise man. Pauline said something very similar to me a couple of days ago.'

'There you go, then; we told you you were in good hands.' There was a small silence. 'How are you feeling. Any less mad?'

Warm, thought Rose. I'm feeling very warm indeed towards this man. And that is not something I need right now.

'I'm fine. About to follow your prescription, in fact, and become a couch potato.'

'Good. There's just one more thing.'

'Yes?'

'I'd switch off your mobile, if I were you. Your greeting might be a bit off-putting to friends, not to mention your family.'

Rose had to laugh. 'Not my normal style, I assure you. But these are not normal times. I can't believe it's not even a week since all this started up again.'

'You'll be fine, I promise you. Now go open that wine.'

Rose hung up thoughtfully. She went over to the bin, tipped it on its side and retrieved all the shiny brochures from among the teabags. She toyed with the idea of ringing Ben anyway and tearing a strip off him. But she dismissed it.

Why bother? It really wasn't worth the effort.


Lisa bounced into the kitchen. 'Mum, I forgot to tell you. Jane called. It's little Katie's birthday and she wants me to go down for cake and lemonade. I said I'd go, but I'll be back well before half nine.'

'Little Katie – do you still think of her as that?' Rose teased her.

Lisa shrugged. 'She's only ten: that's still little to me.'

'That's fine, love. Enjoy yourself. Tell Jane I'll probably call her later.'

'Don't you want to come with me?'

'Not tonight. I'm going to have a shower and then veg out with a glass of wine. Tell Jane she's welcome to join me later on, when the party's over.'

Lisa bent down and kissed her. 'Okay. See you later, then. I'll go down and watch Katie blow out her candles. You have a nice time.'

Rose hugged her. 'You're the best, do you know that?'

Lisa grinned at her. 'Rumour has it.'


Rose stood under the hot water, feeling a curious, unaccustomed sense of anticipation. It was as though she had something to look forward to at last, something waiting for her once all this mess was over. She hadn't felt anything like this in a long time, and the feeling reminded her of Mike. Rose was surprised at that: she hadn't thought about him in ages. How many years had it been since they were together – four, five?

When they'd first met, she and Mike had felt like kindred spirits. It was as if each had been lying in wait for the other to emerge slowly, safely, from the wreckage of their previous lives. Ben's treachery, they had quickly agreed, was equalled – perhaps even surpassed – only by Mike's wife, the lovely Sally, who had locked him out of his own home; who'd tried to deny him access to his two daughters; who'd shacked up with someone to whom Mike would only ever refer as the Golfer.

For almost two years, Rose and Mike had tried to negotiate the wide open spaces between their fractured families: five children, three parents, one absent father and one Golfer. As lovers, they'd each been pulled and pushed by the needs of the family calamities around them. Finally, it all became too much. Mike missed his girls, grieved for them with an intensity that had made Rose feel ever more tenderly towards him. In the end, he had succumbed, wearily, inevitably, to Sally's tearful entreaties to come back to her, once the Golfer had finally gone back to wherever it was he had come from.

And the rupture had hurt, there was no point in denying it.

Rose shampooed her hair vigorously now, surprised at the clarity of the memories that were emerging from the steam. Bathrooms again, she smiled to herself. Somewhere to think, somewhere to pick through private memories, discarding the ones that hurt too much, cherishing the ones that didn't.

She remembered now the last time she had run into Mike, remembered clearly the sense of loss that had accompanied that painful, final meeting.

It was Christmas Eve. Rose had gathered up the presents for Alison, James, Derek and little Katie and made her way down the road to Jane's. The December night was foul: that stinging mix of icy wind and driving rain. She had had to concentrate hard on keeping her umbrella intact. When Jane answered the door, Rose was taken aback at the look of alarm on her face. The normally hospitable, warm and giving hostess was now visibly panicked, white-faced.

'What's up?' Rose had asked lightly, standing her dripping umbrella in the corner of the porch. 'You look like you've just seen the ghost of Christmas past.'

'Mike's here,' Jane whispered. She'd glanced over her shoulder nervously. There was an audible murmur of conversation from the living room.

Rose froze. 'Shit.' She had been about to turn, to run blindly from the house and escape whatever humiliation lurked in wait for her. Was Sally there, too? What could she possibly say to her – to either of them? How would she, Rose, look? Fraught? Lamped, like a rabbit in headlights?

Jane had pulled her by the elbow. 'Come on – wait in the kitchen. He's just going. I presume you don't want to meet him?'

Rose shook her head. 'Absolutely not. Is Sally here?'

Jane had given her a look. 'Over my dead body,' she hissed. Well, at least that was one small mercy. Sally's presence in this house, even if an uninvited and unwelcome one, would have felt somehow akin to the most enormous betrayal. Rose wasn't quite sure how she would have coped with that. She allowed Jane to hurry her towards the kitchen.

'Make yourself a cup of tea, or there's wine in the fridge if you need to steady your nerves. I'll see you in a few minutes, after he leaves – okay?'

Rose nodded. Her heart was racing, and she could feel perspiration creeping down her back, making her blouse cling. With some warning, some sort of preparation, she could have done it, she thought, but not here, not now, not with other people looking on. It would be awkward for everyone. One of those occasions for strained smiles, false politeness: all the sharp, hot restlessness of acute discomfort.

She took a glass from the draining board and poured herself some white wine, noticing as she did so that her hands were trembling, the palms clammy. *Steady on*, she told herself. You're a sober, sensible, middle-aged woman, not a hormone-driven teenager. She slipped off her coat and sat at the table sipping her wine, waiting for her body to stop speeding.

Suddenly she heard his voice, and footsteps approaching, walking rapidly down the hallway. She sat absolutely still: it couldn't be Mike. Jane wouldn't do that to her.

Then she saw it. Folded innocently across a kitchen chair was Mike's raincoat. She had seen it before, so many times. Hanging in the hallway of his apartment, thrown on the back seat of the car, folded carelessly across the chair of one of their favourite coffee haunts. It lay there, all beige and innocent, a waterproof ghost conjuring up images of unbearable intensity, a whole cloud of stunned, lost intimacy.

The door opened and Rose stood up. Over Mike's shoulder she caught a glimpse of Jane's horrified face before she fled back down the hallway again.

There was nothing else for it. Rose put her hands into her jeans pockets, hiding their trembling even from herself. Abrupt though it was, she at least had had a little more preparation than Mike. His face had drained of all colour, his eyes widened into a sudden, startled navy.

'Rose!'

'Hello, Mike,' she said quietly. 'I didn't feel able to meet you, so I'm . . . hiding.' She stopped, nodding to herself, as though at the wisdom of her decision. 'I thought it would be easier for both of us.'

His face softened at once.

'I'm so sorry – I never would have burst in like that had I known.' There was a brief, not uncomfortable pause. 'How are you?'

'Yeah, good,' she lied. She attempted a smile and could feel it instantly go all wrong. Her mouth felt suddenly unfamiliar, as though it didn't belong on her face any more. 'And you?'

He shrugged. 'Okay. You know.'

She paused, seeming to consider this. Her heart was thumping painfully against her ribcage. 'And the girls?'

'Bit of a nightmare, to be frank, but we're getting there.' He nodded now, too, as if mirroring her response. 'Yeah, we're getting there. And your crew?'

'Good. They're all well.'

'Rose—' he took a step forward.

At exactly the same moment, she took a step back. It was a tiny step, a barely perceptible movement. Afterwards, she wasn't sure whether she had actually *taken* the step, or had simply initiated a process that would, eventually, have led to one. Whatever it was, it was enough. Mike had stopped in his tracks.

'I hope it works out for you, Mike, I really do. Have a good Christmas.'

She watched him struggle, could almost see the words

forming behind his lips. If he spoke, what would he say? The next couple of moments could propel both of them into a new chaos. She willed him to speak, willed him even more strongly to be silent.

'Yeah. You too.' He shoved his hands into his trousers pockets.

Somehow, Rose knew they were shaking every bit as much as hers. God, let this be over, please. I can't bear it. 'It's been good seeing you again,' she said finally, quietly, telling him to go now, quickly. 'Take care of yourself.'

His half-raised hand had hovered somewhere between a handshake and a hesitant, truncated wave, trapped in mid-air. Rose was struck by how eloquent his body language was. There was a fog of incomprehension in the air between them. He didn't know how to be with her any more – they didn't know how to be with each other. There was nothing even of the familiarity of betrayal here, for either of them. There was no awkwardness either: more a sadness, tinged with a little desperation. There was nothing that could be said to make anything any better. He turned away, reluctance spelt by every measured step. He paused for a moment and gathered his raincoat up off the back of the kitchen chair. And then he was gone.

Jane reappeared in an instant. 'Rose, what can I say? I'm so sorry – I'd no idea he'd left his coat in here. Are you okay?'

She nodded. 'Fine. You've done me a favour, actually. Now I've met him, so I don't have to go through all that again. How is he, do you know?'

Jane shrugged, her face still pale with distress. 'Okay, I think. He never mentions Sally, and I don't ask. I mean, the Golfer is definitely gone, but I don't know how he's coping with the fallout. He drops in to see Jim from time to time, all I ever hear him talk about are Aoife and Ciara. So I really don't know.'

'Right – well, there's nothing more to be said, really.'

'You miss him, don't you?'

Rose nodded, not trusting herself to speak. She cursed the bad timing that had usurped such a promising chance of a real, loving relationship. She was tired of pain and grief and loss, tired of all of it. All she wanted was a quiet life. Work, home, children. That was it. No more entanglements. Loneliness had to be easier to bear than this.

'Will you stay and have a drink with us?' Jane's hand rested tentatively on her friend's arm.

Rose shook her head. 'No, thanks. I'd better be going. Brian and Lisa are on their own. I just wanted to drop in these few bits for the kids. I'll see you tomorrow.'

She hadn't waited for a reply, knew anyway that Jane wouldn't press her. She'd pulled her coat around her tightly, a gesture that felt curiously protective of herself, and walked down the hallway.

'Night, Rose – take care.'

'Yeah. Say goodnight to Jim for me.'

She'd stepped out into the wet December night, feeling peculiarly in sympathy with the weather. And that was the last time she'd seen him.

Now, as she applied lots of body lotion, Rose kept reminding herself: a quiet life. That's what I said then, that's all I want now. A quiet life. Maybe when all of this with Ben is finally over, that's what I'll have: ease, contentment, serenity. With a bit of financial security thrown in for good measure. No more entanglements, she told herself sternly. Remember that: no more entanglements.

In the meantime, before the days of gracious living began, a glass of good red wine and an indifferent Wednesday night movie would have to do.

# Chapter Seven

ROSE ARRIVED AT the Bonne Bouche by taxi at seven thirty the following morning. She felt more rested than she had in some time. When she'd awoken at six, it was as though something had shifted in her consciousness overnight.

Week Two, she'd thought, as soon as she opened her eyes. I've done it. I've got through it.

She felt energized, washed clean, as though the tidal wave of anger the previous evening had signalled the end of something, the beginning of something else. What that might be she still didn't know, but a new optimism had sprung from somewhere, making her look forward to whatever challenges lay ahead. She was surprised at the feeling: its presence was as welcome as it was unexpected, as delightful as it was unheralded.

She had, of course, fallen asleep on the sofa the previous evening while George Clooney and Jennifer Lopez chased each other across the screen in her living room.

Lisa had come home from Jane's just after half past nine and turned off the television. Rose had immediately woken up. 'Hey,' she'd protested, 'I was watching that.'

Brian and Lisa just grinned at each other.

'You've been asleep since half past eight, Mum,' said Brian, taking her wine glass from her. 'Why don't you go to bed?'

She'd grumbled at each of them in turn – who did they think was the mother around here, anyway? – kissed them briefly, and made her way upstairs.

Just for a moment, she'd observed the jars and bottles on her bedside locker: night cream, eye cream, moisturizer. All those new year's resolutions, standing there like soldiers at attention, but seldom summoned into battle. She hesitated, but only briefly. Tomorrow, she thought. I'll definitely start a night-time routine tomorrow.

Almost at once, she'd fallen into a deep and untroubled sleep.

Angela and Betty arrived at work promptly at eight o'clock, each keeping a careful distance from the other. Rose said nothing about the previous day to either of them. She simply pulled out the ledger from the drawer and sat down with both of them at the counter.

'Right, Angela, you're in charge of the first lot of canapés for tomorrow night: the mascarpone tartlets, the risotto balls, the crispy crabcakes with aioli. Check the final quantities with Sarah and then you can start. Everything you need should be in the coldroom – Claire and Katie did the shopping yesterday while we were at the tennis club.'

She flicked over onto the next page, ignoring the sullen, frosty silence in the air.

'Betty, I want you to make a start on the chocolate truffle cakes, the lemon crème brulée, the apricot tarte tatin.' She snapped the book closed. 'You check with Claire for numbers, and I'll get started on the beef satay. That's it. Off you go.'

Rose watched their subdued progress across the kitchens to the small office she and Sarah shared. She realized, as she watched their departing backs, that she didn't care about any of their simmering hostilities this morning. She was not going to deal with anything else right now: they would wait until she was ready. It seemed that nothing could unravel the cocoon of bright, surprised optimism that had spun itself around her during the night.

The two young women returned almost immediately, faces closed and unreadable. Betty spoke quietly.

'Sarah wants to know can you come over to the office in about fifteen minutes' time.'

Rose nodded curtly. 'Thank you.'

The two girls occupied different counters and began working at once. It's an ill wind, thought Rose. Maybe being pissed off with one another will increase their productivity: they're certainly not going to waste time sharing jokes.


Sarah, Claire and Katie were waiting for Rose in the office, the three of them crowding against Sarah's desk, arms folded.

'What's this?' asked Rose, looking from one to the other. There was a curious air of expectation around the three women. 'What have I done now? Am I on trial?'

Sarah shook her head. 'Nope. We feel you've had your trial – all last week, in fact. Every day was a trial.'

Rose smiled. 'That's for sure. So, what's going on?'

They all stood back from the desk at the same time. It appeared to Rose to be one fluid, practised movement. Her eyes were immediately drawn to where the computer keyboard should have been. There, in its place, was a cake: iced, decorated with dozens of tiny, tumbling yellow roses, candles clustered into one corner.

'Oh!' she said, surprised. She hadn't known that they were to produce cakes for Friday night: had she forgotten that, as well? 'What a beautiful cake! When is it for?'

Katie took her by the elbow. 'Have a look.'

Rose bent down, trying to make out the elegant script.

'Do you need your reading glasses?' demanded Claire. 'Why aren't they hanging around your neck, like you promised?'

The others laughed.

'No,' said Rose slowly, feeling something begin to gather at the base of her throat. 'No, I don't need my glasses. I can read it okay.'

Her eyes began to fill, and the words wavered a little. Nevertheless, she was able to make out, in pale blue script on a white background: *The Survivor's Prayer: for Rose. 'The worst is done: may the best be yet to come.'*

All she could do was stand there; she concentrated on the smooth icing, the intricate sugar roses, the slender white candles. She was suddenly very afraid to speak.

Sarah lit the candles one by one, their pale yellow flames leaping suddenly, then settling into a brave, steady glow. 'There are seven, in case you're wondering,' she said, smiling. 'One for every day of last week. If you got through that, you'll get through anything.'

She blew out the match and Rose suddenly burst into tears: she couldn't help herself. 'Oh, what am I like?' she said, half-laughing, half-crying, feeling her nose begin to run, imagining the dark smudges of mascara on her cheek.

Claire handed her a box of tissues. 'Ready for all emergencies,' she said, grinning.

Rose wiped her eyes, blew her nose. 'It's just lovely – thank you, all of you, so much.' She felt choked, in the heady embrace of real emotion: one that wasn't anger, this time. She felt grateful for that. Lately, she'd begun to be afraid that the heat of anger was the only true thing she would ever be able to feel.

'You're the best, you really are. It's the nicest thing that's happened to me in a long time.' She blew her nose again and took another handful of tissues from the box beside her.

Sarah handed her a cup of coffee. 'Unfortunately it's too early for champagne. But' – she pointed to a bottle beside the computer, festooned with gold roses and ribbons – 'that's for when you have the moment, and the occasion. A very happy occasion, once all of this is over.'

The three women raised their cups to Rose. 'To better times,' said Sarah.

'To friends and better times,' said Rose, raising hers.

Katie cut small slices of the cake and handed it around on paper plates.

'I knew this was going to be a good day, just as soon as I woke up,' said Rose. 'You have a great knack of reading my mind. I really do feel that the worst is over. I mean, all those years it was always at the back of my mind: "What if Ben comes back?" "How will my kids cope if he does?" And "How will we survive if he doesn't?" And now, suddenly, there's no more waiting. He's here, and the kids are fine, and we're all . . . still managing, just like we did before.'

'You're doing a lot more than managing,' said Sarah firmly. 'Give yourself a bit of credit.' She refilled Rose's coffee cup.

'By the way, the champagne stays,' said Rose. 'It belongs here. We'll open it together. Let it stay in this office as my lucky charm.'

'With pleasure,' said Katie. 'We'll even have real champagne flutes – no nasty plastic cups for us.'

'We thought it better to leave Angela and Betty to their own devices for the moment,' said Sarah, with a sidelong glance at Rose. 'The temperature felt a bit on the chilly side this morning.'

'Damn right,' said Rose grimly. 'I haven't either the time or the headspace to find out what's going on, so they'll just have to keep on keeping on until I'm ready to deal with them.'

'Have you sorted them out for today?' asked Katie casually. 'I mean, have they got enough work to keep them occupied?'

Rose nodded, finishing her cake. 'Yes – and probably for tomorrow, too. If they get through that lot, I'll be happy. And I really don't want to have to talk to them right now. I'm going to engage as little as possible.'

'Okay,' said Sarah, 'here's the deal.' She turned away and took Rose's jacket from Claire, who'd been hiding it. 'We're all agreed: you got no proper time off last weekend, and the last seven days have been the week from hell. Go home. We've parcelled the work out among the three of us, and it'll give us great pleasure to kick your two in the arse whenever they need it over the next two days.'

Rose looked from Sarah to Claire to Katie. Each of them looked uncannily alike in their common mission: determined, ready to take no nonsense.

'No . . . absolutely not! I can't do that and leave everybody in the lurch,' she protested. Katie began to ease one of Rose's arms into the sleeve of her jacket, Claire the other.

'Yes, you can,' said Sarah, 'and you will. And by the way, there's no lurch to be left in. We're all on top of things; we don't even have an excuse to panic.'

'No, no – that's not fair.' Rose tried to struggle against her captors. 'Tomorrow night's party is huge, and I've the beef satay and the lamb . . .'

'Go,' said Sarah, again. 'Remember those nieces I once told you I had up my sleeve? Ellie and Julia? Well, they're arriving in half an hour, delighted at the prospect of earning a few quid coming up to the summer holidays. It'll be good for them,' she said, nodding at Rose as she buttoned up her jacket, reassuring her as she would a child. 'They both want a career in the catering industry, may God help them. We figure that the next two days of pulling and hauling, loading and unloading the van, will put them off for good.' She shrugged and grinned mischievously at Rose. 'Their parents are delighted: we're all just doing our duty as aunties.'

'But . . .'

'No more "buts" – time to go. Remember – you pulled us out of a hole for last week's birthday buffet. We owe you: think of it like that.'

'Go on,' said Katie gently. 'Live a little.'

'Yeah,' said Claire. 'Go and visit those bookshops you're always complaining you never get to. Go to the National Gallery, or an afternoon movie.'

'Go and drink champagne, even, if that's what you feel like,' said Sarah, handing Rose her bag, waving her out of the office. 'Do something daft for once, for God's sake, why don't you?'

'Yeah,' agreed her sisters. 'Something daft.'

Rose looked from one to the other. She tried to stop her eyes from filling again. 'I can see you're not going to take "no" for an answer.'

Sarah shook her head. 'You've got that right. See you Monday. Don't even bother with those two witches out there – we'll tell them we've sent you off on urgent client business. Now just go, will you, before one of us changes our mind?'

Rose hugged each of the sisters, briefly. She couldn't trust herself to say anything more. She turned on her heel, never even glancing over at her corner of the kitchens.

Now she just had to go and figure out something daft to carry her through the weekend.

*

Rose hadn't walked up Grafton Street on a weekday in years. Where are all these people coming from? she wondered. How come they're not at work? I know why *I'm* not – what's their excuse?

She wandered in and out of Brown Thomas, the Dublin Bookshop, drank cappuccino on the mezzanine in Bewley's, and watched the crowded street below her. The constant parade of people fascinated her. Ethnic diversity, she thought suddenly, the phrase coming at her out of nowhere. So *this* is what it means. The street below her was a wash of colour: white, middle-aged faces, youthful brown faces, tiny black faces. It was a mix as vibrant and potent as any she had experienced in London on her one visit there, ten years before. It had struck her forcibly then, and it struck her again now: how relentlessly dull and colourless the Dublin of her youth and early adulthood had been. The city had always felt like the poor relation of everywhere else: standing on sullen street corners, always with its hand out. It had been a place of grey skies, grey prospects, grey faces. Now, the midday shoppers below her all milled together, crowding their way up and down the street, in and out of shop doorways: a shifting, multi-hued palette of change.

Rose brought her gaze back to the interior of the café. She looked around at the polished wood, the bright open space that was Bewley's. She felt glad that it had been rescued from the threat of closure. An arrogant new city like Dublin needed an old institution like this: something to remind itself of what it had once been, something to stop it getting above itself. She smiled at the echo of her mother's words. When Rose was growing up, one of her mother's stricter injunctions to her daughter was *never to get above herself.* In those days, 'know yourself' meant 'know your place'.

Back in the poorer, grimmer eighties, Bewley's had always

been *the* place – in fact, almost the only place in Dublin – for coffee, or a cooked breakfast on a leisurely Saturday morning. Mind you, Rose remembered, it had been plain old tea and coffee back then: none of your lattes, or mochas or fruit infusions. There had been nothing remotely fashionable about it. Instead, it was somewhere warm and solid where you met boyfriends, girlfriends, or other young mothers pausing in between bouts of shopping. Rose was glad that Bewley's was there to stay.

She became suddenly aware of a young waiter hovering by her table. Over by the cash desk, a dense queue had already gathered: the lunchtime rush had started. Rose glanced at her watch and realized with a start that she had been sipping coffee and people-watching for over an hour and a half. She smiled apologetically at the young man, stood up and collected her things. She'd enjoyed that.

The Lifers were right, she thought. It *was* fun, doing nothing.

Rose came back down into the street, a dozen of Bewley's almond buns in a bag, two packs of ground Java. There was a sudden sense of spring everywhere. The smell of roasting coffee, the sight of the street sellers and their vast bunches of tulips and daffodils, the young women pushing babies in buggies. On impulse, Rose bought four bunches of flowers, enjoying the heady blue and yellow scent of freesia.

Something daft.

She could still see Claire's and Katie's faces before her, urging her on.

Before she'd time to think, to talk herself out of it, Rose slipped her hand into her jacket pocket and pulled out her mobile. Balancing her handbag and a large, wilting paper cone of damp flowers, she keyed in Sam's number.

'Rose?' He sounded surprised. 'Good to hear from you. Did Doctor Sam's prescription work last night?'

She laughed. 'Only too well. Except that I fell asleep in the chair after one glass of wine. Now I'll never know whether J-Lo and George got it together: there's a huge, gaping hole in my life.'

He sighed. 'Some you win, some you lose. You'll just have to learn to live with the loss. What can I do for you?'

'Well, I have an unexpected afternoon off – Sarah and the others insisted. I was just wondering if, maybe, you'd be free for coffee later on?'

No . . . that wasn't how she'd meant it to sound, not at all. The tone was wrong. It wasn't at all clear whether this call was business or social. She shouldn't have done it.

'Sorry, Rose, I should have told you. I meant to yesterday, but we got . . . interrupted. I'm off to London this evening for a conference. I won't be back until the middle of next week. Can it keep until then, or can Dónal do anything to help?'

No, she thought, it'll keep. It'll definitely keep.

'No, no, there's nothing urgent, Sam, thanks. It's just that as I was in town, I thought I'd call you on the off-chance.'

'I'm glad you did. Let's arrange a time for next week, now that we have a minute.' She could hear the rustle of pages in the background. 'Let me see – I'm back Thursday afternoon. How about Thursday evening, say six o'clock: would that suit you?'

'Yes,' she said. 'Yes, that's fine. I'll see you as soon as I can make it in from Santry.' She wanted to get off the phone now, quickly.

'Why don't we have a drink then?' His voice was as usual, light, casual. She couldn't read him.

'Okay,' she said.

He was speaking again. 'Do you know Neary's in Chatham Street?'

She smiled. 'I do, indeed. I'm standing very near it at the moment – just beside the flower sellers, in fact.'

'Excellent. Then I'll see you there next week, as close to six as you can manage. Upstairs, if it's open. That sound okay?'

'That sounds fine, Sam. Thanks.'

'See you then. Have a good weekend.'

'You too. 'Bye.'

She hung up. What was she doing? She was having trouble enough getting rid of one man out of her life: she certainly didn't need another.

A quiet life, remember? Just a quiet life.

Quickly, she selected Pauline's number. Joan answered at once.

'Hi, Joan. It's Rose Kelly here.'

''Afternoon, Rose. What can I do for you?'

'I just wanted to leave a message for Pauline.'

'Certainly. She's in court all day, but I'll make sure she gets back to you tomorrow.'

Rose hesitated. 'I'm not really sure why I'm telling her this, but she asked me to keep a note of everything, no matter how trivial.'

'Go ahead, Rose.'

'Just let her know that Ben arrived at the house last night, even though he promised he wouldn't, not until he'd met with Lisa. I wasn't there, but my daughter got very upset.'

'Did she let him in?'

'No. She had the sense not to. So, in a way, there's nothing to tell – other than the fact that he's broken our agreement already. Oh, and he left some estate agents' brochures as a guide to the value of *our* house. Pauline'll know how I reacted to *that*.'

'What time was this, Rose?'

'Oh, about six, I suppose.'

'So, there was no conversation, no meeting as such?'

'No,' said Rose, beginning to feel a little foolish. 'As I said, I'm sorry if it's trivial, but it's not the first time.'

'I'll certainly pass it on. As far as Pauline's concerned, nothing is ever too trivial.'

'Thanks, Joan. See you soon.'

'All the best, now.'

Rose hung up, wondering what her husband's next move would be.

When she arrived home, Brian was already in the kitchen, pulling clothes out of the tumble dryer. She was surprised to see him. 'Hi, love. You're home early.'

'So are you.' He glanced briefly over one shoulder, kept his back to her.

'Yes. Sarah insisted I take some time off. Last weekend didn't exactly work out as planned.'

He concentrated on smoothing his new black jeans, folded them carefully over one arm. He seemed busy, preoccupied. He wouldn't catch her eye. 'I won't be here for dinner tonight.'

'Okay. That's fine.' Rose put her handbag on the table. She filled a large vase with water and started to trim the stems of her flowers.

'I spoke to Dad.'

She stopped, a bunch of daffodils in one hand, kitchen scissors in the other. 'When?' She couldn't think of anything else to say.

'This morning. I'm meeting him for dinner at seven.'

'Good; I'm glad.' She began arranging the flowers, hoping he'd say something else. He didn't. 'You okay?' she asked, finally.

He slammed the tumble dryer shut. 'Oh, leave it, will you? Just leave it! Stop fussing!'

He walked quickly out of the kitchen. Rose looked after him, taken aback. He hadn't spoken to her like that in a very long time. His expression was a sudden, unwelcome reminder of the old days.

She heard him shuffle about upstairs in his bedroom, open and close his wardrobe doors, talk repeatedly on his mobile. She wondered what he could possibly be hoping for. Well, whatever it was, it was out of her hands. She was going to keep her distance. He was nineteen, almost a grown man. She trimmed the remainder of the flowers, placed them carefully among the others and topped up the water in the vase.

This was one he'd have to sort out for himself.


'Mum? I'm off, now.' Brian poked his head around the living room door.

Rose looked up from her book. Her son's expression was neutral now, his face paler than usual.

'Okay. You look great, by the way.'

'Thanks.' He hesitated in the doorway, his hands and feet restless. The clothes he wore were neat, pressed, unfamiliar: not Brian at all. He owned one tie and one jacket – part of his Interview Outfit – and he was wearing them both now. 'I'm really sorry about earlier. I suppose I'm just a bit nervous about tonight.'

Rose smiled at him. She put her book down. 'Don't worry about it. We're all a bit on edge. Where are you meeting your dad?'

'The Westbury.'

'I'm sure it'll be fine. I'll be thinking of you.'

She stood up now and walked towards the door, keeping her hands by her sides. This handsome young man had once been her troubled eleven-year-old, all spiky hair and sagging socks. Right now, he seemed to be waiting for her to do something, say something more. Awkwardness was all over him, like fine rain.

'Good luck. You'll be grand.' She made to smooth the shoulders of his jacket. Just as she reached out her hands, he pulled her towards him into a clumsy embrace.

'See ya later, Mum,' and he was gone.

Rose didn't want to watch him walk down the driveway, didn't want all the unwelcome associations that went with it. Damien, striding away from her in the lashing rain, rucksack like a monkey clinging to his back.

She heard Brian's key in the front door just before midnight. He opened the door into the living room, then into the kitchen. Minutes later, his heavy footsteps were on the stairs. There was a gentle knock on her bedroom door.

'Come on in,' she said. 'It's open.'

He looks better, she thought. The pallor had gone, his eyes were brighter.

He came in and sat on the side of her bed. 'I was afraid you might be asleep.'

She shook her head. 'I'm still trying to finish this book – I've been reading it ever since Christmas.'

He peered at the cover. 'Is that the one I gave you?'

She nodded. 'Yes.'

He grinned at her. 'You don't have to finish it if it's crap, you know – life's too short.'

Rose pointed to the unsteady pile of books on the floor by her bedside locker. 'It sure is – as this leaning tower of Pisa keeps on reminding me. I don't know when I'll ever be able to get through them all. No, this one's very good; I just haven't had too much time lately.' Nothing like understatement, she thought.

Then, not able to put it off any longer, she asked quietly: 'Well, do you want to tell me how it went?'

Brian put one hand in the air, rocked it back and forth a few times. 'What is it you say – like the curate's egg?'

She smiled at him. 'That's the one. So, it was good in parts?'

He nodded. 'I think so. I mean, we were a bit stiff and awkward at first, but things loosened up after a couple of glasses of wine. Once I got there, I forgot all the things that I thought I wanted to ask him. And then, on the way home on the bus, I remembered them all again.' He shrugged. 'It was almost like meeting somebody I didn't know. We were very polite, I suppose. Anyway, we're going to meet again some time next week, for coffee or something. I told him I'd a lot of studying to do for the exams. He understood.'

She waited, in case there was more.

'We talked mostly about my college course, my Leaving Cert, all that sort of stuff. He said he knew that there must be things I wanted to ask him, but that for now we could take things slowly. I just said okay.'

'And how do you feel, now that it's over?'

'Yeah, okay. It wasn't so bad. I didn't feel any . . . closeness, or anything. I was really nervous on the way in, but when I saw him standing there I kind of felt . . . detached, or something. I dunno, I suppose it'll take time. We'll see. Anyway, I'm knackered. I'm going to bed.' He bent down to kiss her.

'Oh, and he gave me this, for Paris.' Brian reached into his jeans pocket. 'It's a cheque for a thousand euro.'

Rose felt a dark flash of fear. She saw Brian looking at her face, at the expression she hadn't been quick enough to control.

'It's just money, Mum. That's all. I took it because I don't want you to have to give me any more than you already have. I know exactly what this could be, but it's only money.'

She held onto him tightly. He returned the pressure of her hug, kissed her soundly on the cheek.

'Now, I'm going to bed. I've a shedload of programming to work on for tomorrow.'

She smiled at him. 'Rather you than me.'

He paused at the doorway. 'Oh, and by the way, he said that he's beginning to make progress on his business deals, and that he's on the lookout for a good solicitor. I told him that you found O'Brien's good – Paula, isn't that her name?'

'Pauline,' said Rose, quietly.

'Right. I thought it was Paula. See you for breakfast?'

'Absolutely. 'Night, Brian, sleep well.'

'Night, Mum.'

Now she understood. Now she knew what Ben's next move was. It had only been a matter of time.

Early the following morning, Rose made her way up to the attic. She looked around her at the dozens of boxes everywhere, black plastic sacks, paper carrier bags. Those she could see were all crammed to overflowing with books, baby clothes, Christmas decorations.

No time like the present, she thought.

She pulled the boxes towards her first, opened the flaps and looked quickly at their contents. Old ornaments, crockery: surviving remnants of an earlier, slower life. They could all go. She piled the boxes at the top of the attic stairs, ready to be brought to the van.

Over the next few hours, she divided the remaining sacks

and bags into separate piles: some for the bin, some to keep, some for someone else to use. It felt like giving away the last part of her life, making room for something new.

The charity shops were going to have a bonanza.

At six o'clock Rose heard the front door open, and there were high, girlish voices in the hallway.

'Mum?' Lisa called.

Rose went down onto the landing. She looked over the banisters into the hallway below. 'I'm up here, love,' she said. 'In the attic. Have a good day?'

'Yeah, great! I got all the photograph albums in town this afternoon. Alison came with me.'

'Good – I've put three boxes of photos into your bedroom, so you're all set. We can bring them downstairs later on, if you like. You've taken on some job, do you know that?'

Lisa smiled up at her. 'It'll be fun. Me an' Alison are coming up to my room, now, okay?'

'Hi, Alison!' Rose called.

There was some shuffling in the hallway while Alison and Lisa struggled against each other, giggling loudly.

'Hello, Rose – get out of my way, you!' Alison elbowed her way in front of Lisa.

Rose smiled down at the two fair heads below her. 'Stay for dinner, Alison?'

'Depends on what we're having,' interrupted Lisa, cheekily.

'Oh, the usual – spinach, Brussels sprouts, liver – all your favourites.'

'Nah, I've to go home. I've just remembered I'm needed,' said Alison, grinning.

Rose laughed. 'Relax – I've got quiche, a couple of pizzas and some salads. There's some spicy potato wedges, too, if you want. Oh, and there's some wicked chocolate cheesecake for dessert.'

Lisa turned to her friend. 'I guess you're not needed at home, after all.'

'Thanks – I'd love to stay.'

The two girls raced up the stairs, each trying to push past the other, hurrying to get there first.

'See you later, Mum!'

'I'll call you when dinner's ready. Don't forget to ring Jane, Alison! Your mother needs to know where you are!' Rose called after them.

And they were gone.

Two days ahead, thought Rose. Two days, finally, of doing nothing. A proper weekend, at long last. Once Lisa was ready, they'd ring Ben and make an appointment for the three of them to meet.

Right now, no matter what else might be happening to the rest of her life, it was time to make the dinner.

# Chapter Eight

SARAH WAS TAKING some boxes of vegetables out of her van when Rose arrived on Monday morning.

'Hi, Sarah, need a hand?' she asked.

'Hi, Rose. Thanks. They're not heavy, just a bit awkward.'

Rose went to lift one. 'You're right,' she complained. 'Why don't they make them with handles?'

'Hang on a minute, before you do that.' Sarah rested one of the boxes on the bonnet of the van. She leaned her arms on it and looked closely at Rose. 'Did you manage to have a good weekend?'

Rose smiled, putting the box on the ground beside her. 'Couldn't have been better. Brian met Ben and it went well: very low key, no confrontation. I'm bringing Lisa to see him on Wednesday afternoon, and she's fine about it. And I actually made a start at clearing out the attic. It felt very good for the soul, throwing my old life away. I'd a very productive time, thanks to all of you.'

Sarah inclined her head, a gesture of approval. 'Good, I'm glad you enjoyed it.'

'What about you? Were things all right on Friday? Did my two behave?'

Sarah hesitated. Rose could see reluctance shadowing every line of her expression. It looked as though she was about to say something else, but she stopped herself. Rose could feel her own good humour begin to leak away, draining from somewhere in the pit of her stomach. Sarah was looking down: she seemed to find something very interesting in the top layer of vegetables.

Rose couldn't bear the suspense any longer. 'Sarah? What's up? Spit it out.'

The van's indicator lights flashed twice, the locks sprang up obediently.

'Sit in with me for a moment.'

Rose eased herself into the passenger seat and pulled the door closed behind her. She turned to face Sarah. 'What is it? What's wrong?'

'I'm really sorry to do this, Rose, I know you have more than enough on your mind.'

'Tell me, please.'

'We had some bad news after you left. I had a call from Joe Maguire on Friday morning.'

Rose had to think for a minute. 'Joe Maguire? Our supplier?'

'Yes. He asked me to meet him. He said there was something he needed to discuss with me.'

'And?'

'I couldn't meet him on Friday, obviously, so we had coffee together on Saturday morning. He told me that they've just found out that one of their most trusted employees has been ripping them off for almost two years now. They're in the middle of finding out the extent of the damage.'

'I'm very sorry to hear that,' said Rose, puzzled. 'But what has it got to do with us? I mean, they're not going out of business or anything, are they?'

Sarah shook her head. 'No, nothing like that. The whole thing came to light a few months ago, completely by chance. All Joe would say was that someone made a mistake, and he started to get very suspicious. He had a hidden camera installed above the till, and another one outside in the car park. And they now have some very interesting CCTV footage. Our Angela has a starring role.'

'What do you mean?' asked Rose. But she'd already begun to feel that cold, familiar creeping sense of dread.

Sarah shook her head in disbelief. 'Apparently, the young man at the centre of this has been in cahoots with at least three of their customers, and Angela is one of them. There are six occasions, on video, where she, literally, has her hand in the till.'

'What! But how?'

'It's a very clever scam, very simple. This guy – David's his name, I think – charges Angela, for example, a hundred euro, and gives her a handwritten receipt. But he only registers eighty on the till. She pays the hundred – with our money, naturally – and Dave keeps back twenty euro. He gives her ten, puts ten in his pocket, and does that, maybe, three or four times a day. It all depends on how many customers are in on his little deal.'

Rose looked at her, trying to take in all the implications.

'It gets better.' Sarah gripped the steering wheel, and Rose watched her knuckles turn white.

She groaned. 'Jesus, I don't believe this. Go on.'

'On two very recent occasions – that is, two that were caught on camera – Angela and Dave, as brazen as you like, took a pile of stuff from the stores very early in the morning, loaded up a van and just drove off. Obviously, there's no payment recorded through the till on either occasion. This Dave person is in charge of both the ordering from *their* suppliers and the main client accounts. Joe Maguire reckons that his business has lost a fortune.'

Rose's mind was racing. 'Was it my van on either of the mornings?' She could see Angela's face before her, remembered her late arrival, her air of having been caught in the act. Personal stuff, my foot.

Sarah shook her head. 'No. It wasn't your van, nor ours – not on those occasions, anyway. They were able to read the registration off the tape, and the Guards are dealing with it.'

'I trusted her,' said Rose, her mind racing. She still wasn't able to absorb everything that she was hearing.

Sarah nodded, tight-lipped. 'We all did. Joe had taken his young fellow on so that *he* could start to slow down a bit; he's almost sixty. Now he says he must have had the most expensive golf lessons in history. I felt very sorry for him.' Sarah paused.

'You and I are going to have to do some serious digging,' said Rose slowly, her mind unable to keep up with what she was thinking.

Sarah nodded. 'I know. I came in here afterwards, on Saturday afternoon. I just had to go over the Spice of Life records, to see if I could find anything. I did the best I could, but it's almost impossible to pin down – you'd need to be the Fraud Squad, or something. The beauty of their plan was, it didn't matter whether we paid cash, or by cheque, or even credit card. Because they were both in on it, and both trusted by their employers, nobody was likely to query anything. And they knew it.'

'That's what they were fighting about,' said Rose, suddenly.

'Who?'

'Betty and Angela – last week, at the tennis club. They were like two cats. Betty said she'd seen Angela do something, said she was warning her. I didn't pursue it at the time, but that must have been what it was. Stealing. Jesus, I just don't want to *believe* it!'

'I know. I was nearly sick when Joe told me. I didn't sleep a wink on Saturday, or last night.'

'Why didn't you call me?'

Sarah shook her head. 'For what? What could you do over the weekend anyway, except worry? I was doing enough of that for both of us, and I figured you'd had your fill already. Today was time enough.'

'Well, thank you for that; but we are in this together, don't forget. And I'm the one who hired her.'

Sarah turned to look at her. 'And you were supposed to know all this – what, five years ago?'

Rose shrugged. She didn't know what to say.

'Rose, we none of us have a crystal ball, you know. It's done. We just have to try and do some damage limitation. But the whole thing set me wondering. Remember last year, when we joined forces?'

Rose nodded. 'Of course.'

'Weren't you losing a pile of money at that stage, stuff you couldn't account for?'

'Yes,' said Rose, staring at Sarah, seeing her own disbelief reflected in the other woman's face.

'Well,' said Sarah grimly, 'no wonder your profit margins were way down, if all of that was going on. If she's been steal-ing from Maguire's, and from us, I've no doubt she was stealing from you. Joe reckons that at a minimum, they've lost ten thousand euro – and that's the internal auditor's most conservative estimate. At that rate, you wouldn't be long wiping out your entire profit margin, would you? Even *five* per cent of your income going astray would have made an impact on a business the size of yours.'

'The difference between boom or bust,' said Rose, remem-bering Sam.

'And the problem was, it was all invisible. How can you keep track? Do we have to count every prawn, every onion, every chicken wing? We're sitting ducks.'

Rose looked at her. It took a moment for Sarah to realize what she'd said. Both women laughed.

'Sorry,' Sarah said. 'Bad pun.'

Rose shook her head. 'I could kick myself. I remember thinking on a couple of occasions that Maguire's had got quite expensive: I seemed to be paying more and getting less. But I never did anything about it. I just accepted it. Everything else in this bloody city costs a fortune, why not wholesale food?'

'None of us checked, not in that sort of forensic detail, anyway. It's called being busy,' said Sarah. 'Don't blame yourself. We were all duped.'

'There's wine missing,' said Rose, suddenly.

'What?'

Rose nodded. 'Yes. There are bottles of wine missing. I was two bottles of red and two bottles of white short after the tennis club last week. I thought nothing of it, assumed I had miscalculated because I was in such a hurry on the Wednesday afternoon. *That's* what Betty saw – she must have seen Angela steal the wine.'

'Well, if that's the case, then you can be sure it wasn't the first time. She's probably getting careless now, thinks she has it all sewn up. I bet the last thing she thinks about is getting caught. Joe reckons that she and David probably started very slowly, with the occasional fiver, small change, that kind of thing. When nobody copped, they just got bolder.'

'She's a little cow,' said Rose, beginning to get angry all over again. Was nothing safe, nothing what it seemed? 'What on earth are we going to do?'

'Nothing,' said Sarah firmly, 'for now. The Guards want to let it ride for another week or so, to gather as much evidence as they can. It's us and two other catering companies so far – they want to wait and see if there are any others involved.'

'So we can't even fire her?'

Sarah sighed. 'I'm afraid not. We'll have to put up with her for another while.'

'God almighty. How are we even going to look at her? They're going to prosecute, I presume?'

'Damn sure,' said Sarah. 'And so are we. Don't worry: I'll deal with that – it will be a pleasure.'

'How do we know the pair of them won't do a runner in the meantime?' asked Rose suddenly.

Sarah shrugged. 'We don't. But all the signs are that they don't know anybody is onto them. Joe said to keep everything normal, to keep exactly the same routine going. They'll get the pair of them, don't you worry.'

Rose shook her head. 'I hope so. When I think of how much she might have stolen from me over the years . . .'

'Don't go there,' said Sarah. 'We don't know when all of this started. There's nothing to be gained from hindsight.'

'They say things happen in threes. Christ, is there anything else lurking in the bushes?'

'Come on,' said Sarah. 'We'd better go in: don't want to arouse any suspicions. This is sure going to be a fun week.'

They closed the van doors behind them. Rose watched as the lights flashed again and locks snapped smartly into place. She felt strangely calm, shock hovering somewhere in the distance, somewhere on the innocent outer reaches of the car park. It hadn't absorbed her yet.

'Claire and Katie know?'

Sarah nodded, handing her a box full of courgettes and black, shiny aubergines. Rose thought how beautiful they looked; out of place, somehow, amid all the dust and ashes of betrayal.

'Yes. I nearly had to tie Katie down. She's positively murderous.'

'I know the feeling,' said Rose. 'I have the guts of a hit list right now. It's growing longer by the day.'

Sarah grinned. 'Could be worse. We could have gone under. Look on the bright side.'

Rose held open the door for her. 'Right. Let's go. Oscar-winning performances all round. I don't know how I'm going to keep my hands off her.'

Katie handed Rose and Sarah a cup of tea, and left the office without a word. The two women sipped in silence. They had retreated to the office for the early part of the morning, going through the arrangements for the following week. It was a mechanical task, a routine one: something they felt demanded nothing from them, other than their presence. They went through their checklist together, subdued, assigning the various tasks as they went.

Just as they reached the end of the list, Rose's mobile rang. She didn't recognize the number.

'Hello?' she said, cautiously.

'Rose? Pauline here.'

'Good morning, Pauline.' That was fast, she thought. Ben must have been straining at the leash.

'I promised I'd call you just as soon as I had any news. Ben's solicitor contacted me first thing this morning. He's faxed some stuff over to me. We need to go through it together. You told him to contact me, then?' Her tone was crisp, businesslike. As yet, it invited no discussion.

'No, no I didn't. Brian met him the other night. He gave Ben your name, without realizing.'

'Ah. How are you fixed over the next couple of days?'

How, indeed. 'You name the time.'

'Well, this evening around five is free, or we could meet at eight in the morning? Whichever suits best.'

'This evening,' said Rose quickly. Let's get it all over with at once, she thought. I don't like Mondays.

'Okay, that's fine. See you then.'

'Thanks, Pauline. 'Bye.'

Sarah looked over at her and raised one inquiring eyebrow. 'Something else to brighten up your day?'

'Yep. More good news. I told you things happened in threes.'

Joan ushered her into Pauline's office. 'Tea or coffee, Rose?' she asked.

'Coffee, please, Joan. I've a feeling I'm going to need it. That, or something a lot stronger.'

The older woman patted her on the arm. 'You're in good hands here,' she said, smiling.

'Good to see you, Rose.' Pauline stood up and put out her hands for Rose's jacket. Take a seat.'

'Thanks.' She sat, feeling that, for nearly a decade now, the most significant reflections on her life had all taken place in this armchair. 'So,' she said. 'Hit me.'

Pauline pulled a folder towards her.

'Well, it looks as though your ex-husband has decided to up the ante.'

'What do you mean?'

'Have you spoken to Ben recently?'

'Yes – just like you and I discussed. And it's been conciliation all the way. I haven't rowed with him, not even once. Mind you, I had to sit on my hands when he appeared in my front garden last Monday – remember? The afternoon he brought the estate agent with him? He didn't realize I was home, and I certainly didn't let him know that I'd seen him, either then or later. And I sat on my hands *again* last Wednesday, when he called to the house and Lisa was on her own. I didn't mention that either. In fact, I've been remarkably restrained, now that I think about it.'

Pauline nodded, making a note. 'Interesting. So, you've had no conversation about house sales as such, or splitting the proceeds or anything else.'

Rose shook her head vehemently. 'Absolutely not. All we've spoken about is the kids. He agreed to give me time to make sure Lisa was okay with everything, and *then* we'd sit down and talk finances.' Rose accepted the cup of coffee Joan offered her, smiled her thanks.

'He's already seen Brian; he knows I broke the news to Damien – to all of them: he even thanked me for doing it. We spoke briefly this morning and we've agreed that I bring Lisa to meet him on Wednesday afternoon. It was all as clear as day. So what "ante" is he upping, and why does he feel the need to do that? I understood we had an agreement.'

'Well, that might have been before he sought legal advice.' Pauline pulled several faxed pages out of the folder on her desk. 'We'll get the originals of these in a day or so, but I was anxious to know what Ben was looking for, once I got his solicitor's letter this morning.'

'Who is it? Who's his solicitor?'

'A guy called Paul McGowan.'

'What's he like?'

Pauline looked straight at her. 'A ball-breaker. Ben'll be paying through the nose – which is interesting in itself for a man who's claiming to be broke. But McGowan is no fool either – he'll want to hammer out a deal.'

'So, what *is* Ben looking for?'

'Well, for one, he's claiming that you've already agreed to sell the family home and split the proceeds fifty–fifty.'

Rose stared at her. 'You can't be serious.'

'I'm afraid I am.'

'On what grounds?'

Pauline took a deep breath. 'He's saying that he made regular maintenance payments to you over the years.'

'What!'

Pauline raised a cautionary hand. 'That he sent money to you for the children as often as he could, whenever he could afford it – cash sometimes, cheques, postal orders on other occasions.' She paused.

'He's lying. You know that.'

Pauline continued. 'He claims that he was unemployed for long stretches of the time he spent in England, that he was subsequently ill with depression and unable to work. He has come back to Dublin to try and pull his life together – this is his last chance to do so. He is very remorseful about having walked out, but claims he was under intolerable pressure at the time: business pressures, personal pressures, illness. The whole gamut.'

Rose shook her head, numbness crawling into the spaces that disbelief had just left vacant. 'I can't believe this. You should have seen the suit he was wearing when he turned up ten days ago – *and* the shoes.'

Pauline kept on reading, referring to the pages in front of her. 'He also says that he is willing to develop a full relationship with his children. He says that he has initiated discussions with you to make sure he causes minimum disruption to their lives, but that he is very anxious to make amends to them. He looks forward to regular meetings with each of them.'

'Okay – that bit is fine. I've no problem with any of that.'

'Wait,' said Pauline. 'There's more.' She turned over the final page and Rose saw that she had highlighted something in red. 'He repeats himself. Given his difficult personal circumstances in the past, and the fact that he nevertheless made best efforts to maintain his children, he feels it only just that the proceeds of the sale of property are divided equally between both parties.' Pauline looked over at Rose. 'Got that?'

'I'm listening,' said Rose, knowing that there was worse to come.

'Mr Holden intends to make his permanent home in Dublin, and he is very willing to enter into an agreement regarding *future* maintenance of his family. However, his position at the moment is that of starting in business all over again: he has no resources. Conversations with his former wife have indicated that, and I quote: 'Mrs Holden is the proprietor of a thriving business, one whose original development would not have been possible without the use of the equity in the family home as collateral.'

'You're joking. Tell me you're joking.'

Pauline shook her head. 'I'm afraid not, Rose. Basically he's saying that it's his turn now. You didn't need his money because you had plenty of your own, and *he* contributed in the past whenever he could, despite being down on his luck. This is his last chance, and he's entitled to half the proceeds if he's to survive and maintain his children into the future. That's it, in a nutshell. I have to say, even I didn't expect such a blatant tissue of lies. I've seen some in my time, but this one takes the biscuit.'

Rose gripped the arms of her chair. She had the extraordinary sensation that she might somehow take flight if she didn't anchor herself to the old, solid armchair. Her body felt wispy and insubstantial, as though she was no longer subject to the laws of gravity. She tried to focus on what Pauline was saying, tried to make sense through the fog of disbelief.

'Don't worry, Rose – this is just the opening salvo. Don't take it personally. He's going to fight for the best possible deal for himself, so he's going for broke. I asked you to come here as soon as possible so that you'd know what sort of a fight we have on our hands. We're only getting started.'

'Is it actually possible that my "thriving business" is now a liability?'

Pauline looked at her keenly. 'I presume you never told him that you had any sort of business?'

'Absolutely not! I told him that financially, I'd survived, that the kids had survived, and that the house was our *home* – that's all I said before I threw him out that night, the night he came back. Other than that, all I've said is that I'd be prepared to sit down and talk about finances, once the kids were sorted. I'd even have been prepared to go for mediation, but after a communication like that,' Rose gestured angrily towards the pages in Pauline's hands, 'I don't think there's even any point in suggesting it. He has no idea I want to sell the house. This is all just one huge, arrogant demand – assumption – *lie* – whatever, on his part. This is his children's *home* we're talking about! What do I do now, Pauline, for God's sake?'

'I want us to keep this out of court,' said Pauline, firmly. 'I want us to negotiate. And that means you have to keep your nerve. If he's prepared to lie like this now, then he's prepared to lie before a judge, too. Don't forget, our system is an adversarial one: and far too many people in these circumstances are prepared to fight dirty.'

'Court gets you the law, but not justice,' said Rose, remembering something Mike had once said.

'Something like that, yes. That's why I want to get agreement outside of the system, to tie everything down securely without going before a judge. Our best chance is to agree a deal with him now and not to enter the court process at all.'

'But what guarantee is there that he'd keep to an agreement

– to any agreement? He did a runner in the past; what's to stop him doing another one?'

Pauline nodded. 'That's why we've got to negotiate hard around the issue of the house. You want your portion of the sale to cover all the past arrears in maintenance, *and* to look after the kids' future needs. You need to have a full and final financial settlement, over and done with. Because you're right.' Pauline looked at her over the tops of her glasses. 'He could disobey a court order regarding maintenance: for example, if he left the country. Then we'd have to get him back into court, and start all over again.'

'If we could find him,' said Rose indignantly.

'Indeed. Would you believe it if I told you that less than twenty-five per cent of all lone parents – fathers and mothers – are in receipt of maintenance from their former spouses? There's a good chance that a fair proportion of *them* have done a disappearing act: divorce, Irish style – remember Dad used to say that? But don't worry. We have a few aces up our sleeves, too.'

'We do?' said Rose, feeling a small nudge of hope.

Pauline nodded. 'But you have to work hard on this with me: you've to be very guarded, give nothing away. All nego-tiations go through me. When you meet Ben with Lisa on Wednesday, for example, you smile sweetly and talk about the weather. Have you got that?'

Rose nodded, slowly. 'Yes. Yes I do. I really thought he meant well, towards the kids, at least. He even gave Brian a thousand euro towards his Paris trip the other night.'

Pauline looked up sharply. 'Did he, now?'

'Yes. I thought he might be trying to buy Brian's affection, and I was terrified. Then I felt ashamed of myself for being cynical, over-protective. Now, it seems I've got to see it in a far more sinister light. Is there a chance he could get away with this?'

'Not if you do as I tell you. I've said to you before that you were your own most dangerous enemy. McGowan knows Ben's not going to get fifty per cent: but we've a fight on our hands, because he'll also know I'm wary in these cases of rushing into court.'

*These cases.* There it was again: her life reduced to a manila folder full of faxes, valuations, lies, damned lies and statistics.

'Okay,' said Rose. She tried to keep the weariness out of her voice. 'What do you want me to do?'

'Keep your temper. Keep your distance. Keep your business to yourself – even in front of your three children. Well, they're hardly children any more, but you know what I mean. They could easily let something slip without realizing it.'

Rose looked at her in dismay. 'I can't *tutor* them every time they meet him. That sort of pressure would be intolerable – I just won't have it.'

'Then you'll just have to be very careful of what you say. Be aware of yourself and what's at stake. That's all I can say to you. I have to tell you, as well, that Ben might make the divorce awkward if he thinks it's a bargaining tool.'

Rose snorted. 'Well, it's not. I've no intention of ever marrying again. In fact, let me rephrase that: I've *every intention* of *never* marrying again. I don't care about the bit of paper. I just want to know that all the ties are broken, that he can never do anything like this to me again.'

Pauline nodded. 'Okay. I'm now going to fire a shot across his bows. I'm going to ask McGowan for medical evidence of depression, unemployment records, bank statements. They'll be expecting that, of course, but it should keep them busy for a while. Gives you time to get all your ducks in a row. Have you met with Sam?'

'Yes. And I'll be meeting him again on Thursday. He'll have all the figures drawn up – ball park ones – and we're going to look at house valuations, see what sort of a deal is good for me.'

Pauline closed the folder and rested her arms on top of it. 'Now that is one bit of news you keep absolutely to yourself. We don't want Ben to know that you're even *thinking* of selling the house. You say nothing to Lisa, to Brian, to Damien, even to your friends. Talk to Sam, by all means, but no one else. You need someone you can trust.'

Rose stood up and placed her coffee cup carefully on Pauline's desk. 'I trust both of you,' she said quietly. 'And I'll do as you advise. It's just that it's going to be even more difficult than I thought.' She bit her lip. 'I really didn't think it was going to be such a filthy fight. He was the one who asked could we do this without being at each other's throats; do you know that?'

Pauline looked at her sympathetically. 'Keep your nerve, girl. It'll soon be over. I get the feeling that Mr Holden is a man in a hurry. That strengthens our hand.' She stood up and reached for Rose's jacket. 'May I ask how business is, these days?'

Rose pulled on her jacket and looked at Pauline ruefully. 'You don't want to know, right now. At least, I don't want to tell you. One thing at a time.'

'Okay – but don't let anything slide. There's nothing irrelevant at the moment, Rose, nothing that's "by the way".'

Rose sighed. 'One of our employees is stealing from us.'

'Ah. Any idea who?'

'Yes. The lovely Angela. She gives a Hollywood performance on CCTV. The Guards are investigating. Sarah is looking after it.'

'Has Sarah contacted her solicitor?'

'I don't think so, not yet. I mean, I don't know. Will I get her to give you a call?'

'Do, please. Even if I don't handle it myself, I want to know what's going on. It could well have an impact on your "thriving business".'

Rose started. 'I never thought of that.'

Pauline grinned. 'That's why you pay me. Now, go home and put your feet up. You look worn out.'

'I am,' Rose admitted. 'Recently I felt full of beans, really optimistic. Now it's like somebody just let the air out of my tyres.'

'That's how it's going to be,' said Pauline, gently. 'Up and down, one extreme to the other, one day to the next. First the relief that closure was on its way, now the awful prospect of fighting again. Go with the flow. It'll get better, I promise you. This will all be over sooner than you think.'

Rose smiled. 'Thanks, Pauline. I'll keep that in mind.'

'Particularly on Wednesday: talk to Ben only when Lisa is there, keep it neutral. If he arrives at the house, you are not to let him in. If he phones, tell him to talk to his solicitor. That's it, Rose. That's how it has to be. I'll call you as soon as I have any more news.'

Rose left the office, feeling the familiar sensation of the ground unsteady beneath her feet. She wished this was over, wished Wednesday was over, wished Sam was back.

She couldn't bear the thought of a dirty fight on her hands.

# Chapter Nine

'DO I LOOK OKAY?'

Lisa came into the living room, dressed in new pink jeans and a top that stopped just short of her navel. Rose watched as the ends of her daughter's trousers swept the carpet as she walked. The fabric would be frayed, tattered, dirty by morning. She smiled at Lisa now as she stood in front of her: young, shiny, innocent.

'You look absolutely wonderful,' she said.

Lisa's face relaxed. She slumped onto the sofa beside her mother. 'Are you ready? What time are we going at? Where did you say we were meeting Dad?'

Rose took her hand. 'Hey! One thing at a time. We've half an hour yet. We're meeting in Bewley's in Grafton Street, because I thought the Westbury would be too quiet. You're not to be worrying: you spoke to your dad on the phone last night, so the ice is broken. And, by the way, you did a great job of arranging all those old photographs.'

Lisa pulled at the elasticated bracelet on her slim wrist. She looked down at it and spoke quietly. 'I know I told you I was going to bring them with me – the albums, I mean – but I think I've changed my mind.'

Rose felt relief at her daughter's words. Too much too soon, she'd thought, when Lisa showed her the photographs she'd chosen: their intimacy had been stark, unnerving. Now, she just smiled and said lightly: 'Okay – do whatever you feel is right. You'll be seeing your dad again, anyway, you'll have lots of other opportunities.'

Lisa nodded. 'I suppose so. Anyway, I don't want to do it today. It wouldn't be . . . wouldn't *feel* right.'

'If it doesn't feel right, then you've made the right decision. Now, I'm going upstairs for a few minutes, to drag a brush through my hair and repair my slap. I won't be long.' Rose stood up and smoothed the creases out of her navy skirt.

Lisa grinned. 'You look fine, Mum . . . that's a nice skirt. But . . . er . . . aren't you going to change?'

Rose looked at her in surprise. 'Why? I thought you just said I looked fine. Do I need to change?'

Lisa shrugged. 'You look kinda formal. Why not wear your new black jeans with one of your silk blouses? The outfit you bought for your birthday. You look *really* great in that.'

Rose nodded slowly. She began to see her daughter in a new light – watched in amazement as ancient feminine wiles swam cunningly to her youthful surface. 'Lisa Holden, are you saying that your mother should look sexy?' she teased.

'Yeah, why not?' Lisa's smile was conspiratorial. 'Show him what he's missed.'

*Fourteen*, Rose thought, as she climbed the stairs. She's only fourteen: how did she get to know all this stuff?

As she changed her clothes, Rose remembered how flicking through Lisa's albums had made her feel as though she'd suddenly stumbled and lost her balance. It was as if all the images she had chosen to forget had been hiding somewhere, lying in wait for the moment to catch her unawares. Happy family photos, full of toddlers and tenderness: sandcastles, ice creams, swimming pools, all the faded, blurred clichés that should have helped to harden the heart. But they hadn't. In a way, *they* had been the worst, the ones that could have belonged to any family, any father. Their bright promise had made Rose flinch and turn away, suddenly discovering an urgent need to put on the kettle, answer the phone, visit the bathroom. She was glad that such charged memories would be no part of the afternoon ahead.

Armed with Pauline's advice, she was ready to talk only about the weather. No more confrontation, no guilt, no lingering sense of failure. And no photographs.

Rose touched up her lipstick, regarding her face critically in the mirror. Still only a few lines, she thought, despite everything. A forgiving hairstyle, subtle make-up, brown eyes still her best feature. Not bad, she thought, for fifty. You'll do.

Right, Mr Holden. Let's do as your wise young daughter says. Let's show you everything you've missed.


He was waiting for them on the mezzanine. Rose saw at once that Ben was sitting at the same table by the window that she had occupied less than a week earlier. He stood up as they approached. She watched his eyes widen in surprise as Lisa walked up to him.

'Hello, Dad,' she said, her voice strong, confident.

Rose looked over at her, startled.

Lisa looked at her father. 'Where the hell have *you* been?' she said.

A gust of sudden, hysterical laughter threatened, somewhere at the base of Rose's throat. She felt it struggle with the shock of disbelief. Shock, finally, got the upper hand. She sat at the table, almost knocking over the chair beside her.

'Hello, Lisa.' Ben smiled at her. His face was tight, his smile nervous. Rose felt almost sorry for him. She had never seen Lisa like this.

'I'm very happy to see you.' Ben reached out to her, but

Lisa moved away, just a fraction. He succeeded only in patting his daughter awkwardly on both of her elbows.

Lisa tossed her hair back from her face and sat down beside him, opposite her mother.

Ben sat carefully onto his chair. He had almost recovered his composure. 'I must say, you look beautiful. Amazing. A real young woman.'

She nodded, her gaze unflinching. 'Thank you. It must be a bit of a change, all right, from the last time you saw me.'

Jesus, thought Rose, astonishment growing with every syllable her daughter uttered. I never would have expected it. From Damien, certainly; from Brian, possibly; but Lisa?

A waitress approached, breaking the sudden, appalled silence. Rose could see relief flood her husband's features; his shoulders began to relax.

'Yes – Rose, what would you like?'

'Cappuccino, please, Ben,' she said, the words solid, normal, as though nothing much had happened.

'I'll have a Coke, please.'

Rose tried to catch her daughter's eye, to look at her warningly, but the girl deliberately avoided looking at her.

'Tea for me, please,' said Ben.

The waitress disappeared, leaving the air to fizz and crackle behind her. Rose wished she'd come back. She'd keep her there as long as she could, deliberate over every type of tea and coffee; she'd order everything on the menu, do anything she could to put a stop to the teenage thunderbolt across the table.

'I've wanted to ask you that for a long time,' Lisa continued, evenly. 'Cos I'd absolutely no idea where you'd gone to. Do you know that I had to search for photos to find out what you looked like when I was a little girl?'

Don't, Lisa, thought Rose. Please don't do this. She leaned across the table, drew closer to her daughter. 'Lisa—'

But Ben raised his hand in the air. 'It's all right, Rose. She's entitled. Let her have her say.' His face was pale, the five o'clock shadow reminding Rose suddenly, painfully, of her sons.

Lisa continued. 'I was only six when you went away, and now you're back. Why did you go? Did you not want us any more, me and Brian and Damien?' There was only the faintest quiver in her voice at Damien's name.

Ben shook his head. 'It was nothing to do with you, with any of you, why I went away. It was much more . . . complicated than that.' He looked straight at her. 'I missed you, all of you. And I never stopped loving you.'

She leaned towards him, her voice very quiet. 'You'd a funny way of showing it.'

Rose felt her hands begin to tremble. Her voice had deserted her completely. All she could hear was her heartbeat pounding in her ears, racing back and forth across the top of her head. She tried to reach out a hand towards her daughter, but Lisa glared across the table and stopped her.

'Well,' he said, 'I'm back now, and I know I've a lot to make up for. I'd be very glad if you'd let me try.'

'Why should I?'

Ben shifted on his chair. The abrupt movement seemed to release something in Rose's throat: words began to come to the surface at last.

'Lisa, I don't think that this is—'

Lisa turned to face her. 'Mum, I'm fourteen, almost fifteen. Do you think I haven't *noticed* anything since I was six? Did you think I was too young to understand? I know what our family was like without a dad. And now he wants us all back as though nothing ever happened?'

Ben folded his hands on the table in front of him. Rose was reminded suddenly, of the way Sarah had gripped the steering wheel, knuckles showing moon-white underneath the pale skin.

The waitress returned. Her cheerful voice was monstrous, Rose thought, her words fell like stones around the table. 'That's one Coke, one cappuccino, and a pot of tea for one. Is there anything else?'

Rose shook her head. 'No, thank you. That's everything.' We've more than enough to be going on with.

Ben sat very still, looking at his hands. 'I know I have a lot to make up for,' he said again, quietly. 'All I'm asking is to be given a chance to show you that I care.'

Lisa leaned back in her chair. Her voice rose, ever so slightly. 'Did you care when I made my First Communion that I was the only one in the class to have no dad beside me? Or when I won the swimming championship? Did you even care on eight birthdays and eight Christmases?'

Their corner of the café had gone very quiet. Ben's face looked creased, somehow, elderly. With a jolt, Rose realized that she was now seeing how her husband would look as an old man, how her daughter would look as a grown woman. This was too much. It was time to put a stop to it.

Ben spoke then. 'I don't know what your mother has said to turn you against me, but—'

Rose's gasp was audible. She couldn't help it.

Lisa pushed her chair back noisily. 'Mum said nothing. She *never* said anything because there was no need to. I'm not a child; I can make up my own mind, all by myself. And I'm not thirsty. Come on, Mum. I want to go home now.'

She made her way past her father and began walking rapidly towards the stairs.

Ben turned to Rose, eyes blazing. 'Thanks,' he said.

Rose felt fury gather, raise its head, poise to strike. She thought of all the things she wanted to say, all the things she had sat on for years, all the empty calories of half-truths she'd fed her children. Then she thought of Pauline. With a physical effort, she swallowed the words that were fighting their way to the surface of her consciousness, clamouring loudly to escape.

'You can thank yourself,' she said, and followed her daughter down the stairs.

Lisa was several yards ahead of her, striding down Grafton Street towards the car park. Rose followed. She felt as though someone had painted garish, abstract brushstrokes over a delicate but familiar image. The steel in Lisa's demeanour had taken her completely by surprise. Had she planned this, or had it been on the spur of the moment? Rose tried to think, quickly. What had she missed? What was she to say to her daughter now?

I have absolutely no idea, she thought, as she reached the car park. I have no idea at all.

Lisa was standing by the van, waiting. Her face was closed, her eyes looking at nothing in particular. Rose disabled the alarm and Lisa opened the passenger door at once and sat in.

'Put on your seat belt,' Rose said automatically, putting the key in the ignition. Lisa obeyed. Rose didn't look at her.

She pulled out into the afternoon traffic. This was one silence she wasn't going to break. It might take a whole night of television viewing, of averted eyes, of truncated conversation. So be it. This was much too important to hurry.

Lisa went up to her bedroom immediately they arrived home. Rose hung up her jacket, feeling as though every moving part of her had suddenly become numb, jerky, as if some essential part of her machinery had rusted, ceased to function. In the kitchen, she fumbled at the lid of the kettle, dropped it. She left it where it fell and sat down at the table, resting her forehead in her hands.

Why hadn't Lisa told her? Why hadn't she refused to meet her father, or fought about him, or at least given some clue as to how she was feeling? Rose felt suddenly terrified: was this yet another child who was going to blaze a dark and dangerous trajectory, leading to some place where her mother couldn't follow?

I'm giving her another hour, she thought. No longer. Then I'm going upstairs to make sure she's all right.

The kitchen door opened with five minutes to go.

Rose was drinking tea, glad to be able to do something banal, something that occupied one hand, at least. It was reassuring to discover that the parts of the body still worked, after all.

Lisa walked over towards the sink, leaned back against the counter and folded her arms. 'You mad at me?'

Rose shook her head. She put her cup aside, carefully. 'No. I'm not mad at you at all. But I am very concerned.'

Lisa looked down and examined her nail polish. 'Why?'

'I wasn't expecting you to act like that. It was pretty ... dramatic.'

'I hadn't planned it, you know.' She stopped. Rose watched her face as she fought for control.

'I'd been looking at the photographs ever since I got in from school. There were lots of ones from when I was little, and I'd kind of focused on those up until today. Then, while I was waiting for you, I started to look at all the other ones, the ones I haven't put into albums yet.'

'And what did you see?' asked Rose, quietly.

'All the important times – primary school graduation, first day at secondary school, my swimming medals: all that sort of stuff.' She looked up, her eyes beginning to fill. 'And all the times that *you* couldn't be there, either, because you were working.' She swallowed. 'I never told you. On the last day at primary, I was the only one in my class to have my photo taken with no mum and no dad. I tore it up.'

Rose bent her head. She felt the hot, molten lava of guilt begin to swell inside her.

'And then, when we got to the café today, just out of the blue I thought about something you'd said. Remember the day I wouldn't open the door to Dad, cos I didn't know what to say to him?'

*Where the hell have you been?*

Rose groaned. 'I was joking, Lisa. That was only a joke.'

She nodded. 'I know. But remember the comedian we saw interviewed a few weeks back?'

Rose tried to recall his name: blond, outrageous, wearing stunning make-up and precarious high heels. 'Eddie Izzard,' she said, suddenly.

'Yeah. ''Member he said something about how telling jokes meant telling the truth, but in a way that people would listen to, because it made them laugh?'

Rose was speechless.

'Well, that's what I thought of today, just when I reached the top of the stairs. It just felt like the *right* thing to say. So I went for it.'

Rose looked at her, feeling something like admiration. You'll be all right, she thought, suddenly. I don't need to worry about you.

'So, am I in trouble or what?'

Rose felt herself begin to smile. 'No, indeed. You're in no sort of trouble at all. In fact, I caught a glimpse of a very interesting young woman this afternoon. Feisty, no bullshit, able to stand up for herself. I don't call that trouble, do you?'

Lisa grinned. 'Well, not the usual sort, anyway.'

Rose stood up from the table. 'Give me a hug.'

Lisa walked over, wound her arms around her mother.

'I also suggested you say "I've missed you": do you remember that? That's the one that wasn't a joke.' She stroked her daughter's hair.

Lisa nodded into her shoulder. 'Yeah,' she said, her voice muffled. 'And I didn't know I had, until I saw all the empty photographs.'

Rose pulled her closer. It was a few moments before she was able to speak. When she did, she pulled back, looked Lisa in the eye. 'So. Are you going to give him another chance? You've had your say today, in spades, or at least the start of it. What are you going to do next?'

Lisa looked at her thoughtfully. 'Are you saying it's really my decision this time? Or are you telling me I have to?'

'Your decision,' Rose said at once.

'I'll think about it,' said Lisa firmly. Her tone said that the subject was closed, for now. She rested her head on her mother's shoulder again, saying nothing more.

'Right,' said Rose, a few moments later, breaking the silence. 'I'll wait for your decision then.'

Lisa nodded, satisfied.

Rose looked around her. 'I don't know about you, but the last thing I want to do right now is start cooking. I'm not sure I'm up to it after all that. How about we share a take-away, and rent out a video?'

Lisa shook her head. 'I've no homework for tomorrow. I'll make dinner, instead of a take-away. I'd like to. I'll do my special pasta salad.'

Rose smiled at her. It seemed the day's surprises weren't over yet. 'Not too heavy on the chillies, then, okay?'

'Okay.'

'I'm going upstairs to change my clothes. I'll be down in a while.'

'Cool.' Lisa switched on the television in the kitchen and turned the volume up high.

Cool, indeed. Sufficient unto the day.


Rose stretched out on the bed and pulled the phone towards her. She dialled her son's mobile.

'Hi, Damien.'

'Hiya, Ma. Can you hang on a minute?'

Rose waited, heard the sound of a door closing, the blare of music receding.

'Okay. I'm back. You all right?'

'Fine. You?'

'Yeah, great.'

'How's the new job going?'

'It's really good. I love it. Great gang to work with, as well. I think I've fallen on my feet.'

'That's wonderful. I look forward to hearing all about it.'

'Yeah, I'll probably drop in to the house some time over the weekend. There are still a few bits and pieces in my old room that I need to collect. That okay with you?'

'Of course. Just let me know when, so that I can be here. Can I ask you something?'

She thought she heard him sigh.

'Yeah, go ahead and ask, and no, I haven't contacted Dad. To be honest, he's been the last thing on my mind. I've been too busy. We're training all week and I'm knackered at the end of the day. Last thing I want is to have to gear myself up to talking to him. I need the time to sort things out in my own head, first.'

'Okay. Just thought I'd ask.'

'Has Brian met him yet?'

'Yes. It went well. They're meeting up again next week.'

'Good. That'll mean a lot to Brian.'

'Yes,' said Rose, surprised. She wouldn't have expected that flash of generosity towards his younger brother. 'It will.'

'How about Lisa?'

Rose smiled. 'You wouldn't believe me if I told you.'

'Ah, go on, Ma, try me.'

Suddenly, something that hadn't been funny at all as it was happening, became transformed in the retelling. Rose started to laugh: she couldn't help herself. 'It was the most astonishing performance I've ever seen. I nearly fell off my chair.' She paused for a moment, trying to get her breath. 'Without saying a word, Lisa walks straight up to Ben, in the middle of Bewley's, and looks him right in the eye. "Where the hell have *you* been?" she says, without even blinking.' Rose had to wipe the tears from her eyes.

Damien roared with delight. 'Way to go, little sister!'

'Well, I'm not sure about that,' said Rose, laughter finally subsiding, 'but at least she got something off her chest. I couldn't believe my eyes. It was like watching somebody change from the inside out. I've never seen anything quite like it.'

'How did he take it?'

Rose's answer was a considered one. 'Well, that's another story. Lisa marched away once she'd said her piece and I didn't hang around to find out. All I can say is that it wasn't pleasant, for any of us. But she needed to do it. I'm hoping she'll see him again, and maybe mend a few fences. So, please, don't be too enthusiastic when she tells you what she got up to this afternoon.'

'Why, Ma?' Damien's voice was filled with sudden incredulity. 'Please tell me why. What can you possibly owe him? He left you in the shit, you hear nothing for years, and now he's back two weeks and you're suddenly on his *side*?'

'You're missing the point, Damien,' said Rose quietly.

'Tell me, then. What *is* the point? What am I missing?'

'This is not about your dad at all. This is about each of you – what *you* need.'

There was a silence.

'I'm thinking ahead, Damien, for all of you. That's what parents do – it's our job.'

'Well, I don't need him now – and he wasn't around when I did. And I don't think I'll need him in the future, either. But I'll call him at the weekend, if it makes you happy.'

'I don't know that "happy" is the word, but yes, call him.'

'I might do a Lisa on him,' warned Damien. Rose could hear him grin.

'That's up to you. I just want to make sure that you're not closing off any options.'

'Ma, I'm nearly twenty-five. When will you stop being a mother?'

'Never!' laughed Rose. 'We just keep on going forever, hoping that one day we might get something right!'

'You got lots of things right, Ma. More than you know.'

Rose didn't answer.

'You still there?'

'I'm still here.' She made herself breathe quietly.

'Gotta go now, Ma – I think I smell something burning.'

She heard a door open. 'Ah, shit!' and then the line went dead.


'How many have confirmed for tomorrow night, Sarah?'

It was almost midday on Thursday. Rose stood at the

counter, Betty and Angela on either side of her. Rose felt Angela's presence beside her as an outrage: she had hardly been able to contain the wave of revulsion she'd felt when the young woman had arrived earlier that morning. She didn't want to have to see her, speak to her, share space with her. It was an antagonism that was growing stronger by the hour.

Rose waited while Sarah consulted her diary. Trays of beef bones crowded the surfaces around them, ready for the oven.

'Eighty-four, but we're catering for a hundred. They know that some people who haven't bothered to reply to the invitations will definitely be there.'

'Okay, I'm starting the stock now. Once these are in the oven, I can get going on the filo pastry.'

'Great,' said Sarah. 'I've stuff here for prep – can you send Betty and Angela over, when you're ready?'

'We're ready now.' Rose motioned to the two young women. 'Go over to Sarah, please – she'll tell you what we need you to do.' She watched them go, marvelling at her restraint. Ever since Sarah's revelation on Monday, she'd wanted to shake Angela, or shout at her; she had visions of making her suffer, seeing her blush with shame. *We're onto you: you don't fool us for a moment.* Unshared knowledge hung in the air between them, an oppressive presence. Its weight made everybody quieter. Rose hoped that it wouldn't drive Angela away before they were finished with her.

Betty had come to her first thing that morning, her hands uneasy, her face flushed. Angela had just been sent shopping. 'Can I talk to you?'

'Sure,' said Rose, clapping the flour off her hands. 'Do you want to come into the office?'

'Yeah,' she said, glancing nervously towards the kitchen door. Rose thought she knew what was coming. Don't worry, she'd told the girl, silently. Angela won't be back for some time.

She motioned to Betty to go before her. Sarah and her sisters stayed at their counters, looked studiously in the opposite direction.

'Take a seat,' said Rose.

Betty sat, her large frame awkward on the swivel chair. 'I need to tell you somethin' privately, like.'

'Okay,' said Rose. 'Fire ahead.'

'You know that Angela and I are fightin'.'

'Yes. There has been a bit of tension in the air for some time.' Rose waited, careful not to draw conclusions. She hoped that Betty wasn't going to lie.

'Well, I've thought about this a lot, an' I talked to my da the other night.'

Rose nodded encouragingly.

'Angela has been takin' things.'

'What do you mean?' Rose looked at her intently.

'Stealin' things,' said Betty, with a surge of confidence. 'I saw her. Food sometimes, then bottles of wine. And money.'

Rose leaned towards her. 'Betty, you need to be really sure of what you're saying, that there's no mistake. That's a very serious accusation.'

The girl nodded. 'I know. That's why I've said nothin' before now. But I'm sure, I've seen it happen loads of times—'specially since last year. My da said I was to tell you. He said it was wrong, just plain wrong.' She stopped for a moment, adjusted her hands in her lap. 'Angela keeps sayin' you'll never miss it, that you've got plenty anyway. But he says it's still wrong, no matter how much you have, and I'm to tell you just as soon as I can.'

It was the longest speech the girl had ever made. Rose looked at her earnest face, trying not to smile at all the unconscious ironies buried deep among her words. She was glad she'd been right about her, all those years ago.

'We're going to have to take this very seriously, Betty. I want you to think very carefully about what you've just said. If you can remember any particular times when you saw this happen, then all the better. Before we say anything else, I need you to know that I'm going to have to tell Sarah. We'll need to decide together what to do.'

Betty nodded. 'I'll tell you everything I can remember.'

'You've done the right thing, Betty, and I'm very grateful, to both you and your dad.' She smiled at her. 'You make sure to thank him from me – tell him he's got a daughter he can be proud of.'

Betty smiled back, her face transformed. 'I wanted to tell you ages ago, but she warned me I had to keep quiet, or else she'd say it was me.'

Rose felt a rush of sympathy for the plain, solid figure before her. 'I know it's not you, Betty. I've always been very sure you'd never do anything like that. Now, I want you to behave as usual; don't let onto Angela that you've told me anything. Will you be able to do that, do you think?'

She nodded, eagerly. 'Oh, yeah. We're not talkin', anyway, not since the tennis club.'

Rose's curiosity got the better of her. 'What happened that day, precisely, Betty, can you remember?'

'She put four bottles of wine into her bag, and some of the duck breasts that were left over.' She stopped.

'And?' Rose prompted.

Betty began to look guilty. 'That lady, Judy . . .'

'Jenny?'

'Yeah, Jenny. She gave Angela fifty euro, twenty-five for each of us. I know we're not supposed to take it, but . . .'

'It's all right. You won't get into trouble for that.'

Betty's face darkened. 'After we had the row, she wouldn't

give me my twenty-five. Said I was thick and didn't deserve it anyway.'

Rose smiled at her. 'You are anything but thick, Betty. You are thorough, reliable and trustworthy – all the things that count. And I'm very happy to have you working for me.'

Betty's face glowed. 'Thanks,' she said shyly. 'I love my job.'

Rose stood up. 'I may have to ask you to repeat to someone else what you've just told me, but I'll give you plenty of warning if I do, okay? In the meantime, don't discuss this with anyone – except your dad, of course,' she added hurriedly, seeing the girl's worried expression.

They left the office together.

'Now, you start the prep for the soup and just carry on as normal.'

Betty fled.

Sarah turned, raised one inquiring eyebrow. Rose gave her the thumbs up.

Later that afternoon, Sarah called to her across the kitchen.

'Rose? We need to go over the details for tomorrow night. Can you spare ten minutes now?'

'With you in a sec.' She turned to Angela. 'That's fine. Can you put all that stuff away? And then maybe you could make a start on the dips.'

Angela nodded. 'Is the blender fixed?'

'Yes – it's under the counter there. If you need me, I'll be in the office for the next while. Betty – have you enough to keep you going?'

She nodded. 'I've just added the herbs to the stock and now I'm goin' to get stuck into doin' the vegetables.'

'Right. I won't be long.'

Rose walked over to the office and closed the door carefully behind her.

'Well? What happened this morning?' Sarah looked anxious.

'Same as usual. I gave her cash this time, and I have the receipt. It'll be interesting to see the tape of this one – it was a fairly big order, just as Joe requested. But nothing unusual, nothing to make her suspicious.'

'He's just been on. They're winding it up at the end of this week. Guards say they have more than enough for a prosecution.'

Rose sat down. 'Thank God for that. I don't think I can bear the suspense for much longer. I'll give something away, I know I will. I can't even bear to have her standing beside me.' Rose shuddered involuntarily. 'I keep edging away from her, and it feels like she keeps *following*. The whole situation makes my skin crawl. And she's completely blasé.'

'She's a cool customer, I'll give her that. What did Betty have to say to you earlier on?'

Rose smiled at her. 'Strange how these things happen, isn't it? The tennis club was the last straw, as far as poor Betty was concerned. Angela kept the half of the tip that was meant for her, and Betty was furious. I think a little bit of self-interest prompted the confession. I didn't have to ask anything – she volunteered the information that Angela has been taking stuff for well over a year now. She'll make a good witness, if it comes to that.'

'Good. I spoke to Pauline, like you asked, so she's up to speed. She'd no problem with my solicitor handling it.'

'Okay. That's another job off the list. It's just one damn thing after another, these days, isn't it?'

Sarah grinned. 'Keeps us out of mischief. And speaking of mischief, any fallout from your husband after Lisa's stellar performance yesterday?'

Rose glanced at her mobile. 'No, nothing yet. I've been

expecting a call all day. I haven't decided whether to answer when he rings.'

'Are you managing to move ahead at all, towards some sort of a settlement?'

'Well, Sam's been working on figures, so we should be able to put a shape on things pretty soon. I'm meeting him tonight for a drink to discuss it.'

Sarah raised her eyebrows. 'Are you, now? You're getting quite cosy, the two of you. Since when did accountants take their clients out on dates?'

Rose blenched. 'Oh – it's not like that; it's not a date, not at all . . . I'm just . . .'

'Rose Kelly: I do believe you're embarrassed. Have I hit a nerve, here?'

Rose groaned and waved her away. 'Please, Sarah, don't. I'm in enough of a mess as it is. I can't afford any more entanglements. I promised myself I'd have a quiet life once this is over.'

'Two can have a quiet life together, you know? Pete and I do.' Her tone was mock-serious and she was smiling broadly.

Rose shook her head. 'I can't even think like that. He's a lovely man . . . but I have to keep my distance. I don't think I can handle any more complications.'

'Why? You know as well as I do that to be *alive* is to handle complications and – what's your word? – entanglements. Stop kidding yourself.'

'I'm not listening to you. I'm not having this conversation.' Rose stood up, pretending to put her fingers in her ears. 'I'll start singing now, like kids do when they don't want to hear.'

Sarah switched on her computer monitor and swivelled her chair around to face it. 'Okay. I'll be quiet. But remember, you heard it here first.'

\*

233

At exactly three o'clock Rose's mobile rang. She looked quickly at the screen. Relieved, she answered. Sam, not Ben.

'Hi, Sam.'

'Rose, how are you? Have you a minute?'

'Sure.'

'I'm stuck at Heathrow. The bloody plane is delayed by at least two hours. We were due to take off at four, but now it's going to be six, at the very earliest. Some mechanical problem.' He sounded tired, exasperated. 'I'm not going to make it for this evening, Rose. God knows what time I'll get home.'

Rose was glad that Sarah couldn't see her. She was even happier that Sam couldn't see her. The delightful anticipation of seeing his name on the screen had just evaporated: she could feel her shoulders, and her face, slump into disappointment. She glanced around her, quickly. No one was watching.

'That's a pity. Never mind. There's nothing you can do about it. We'll catch up soon.' She tried to stay casual, neutral.

'Rose?' All the background noise had disappeared, as though Sam had just stepped into somewhere quieter. The connection between them was suddenly clearer, sharper. He might have been standing beside her. 'I'm sorry about this. I was really looking forward to this evening.'

His tone was unmistakable. Who was she kidding, indeed.

'Yes. So was I.' She winced. Shouldn't have said that.

'Were you?' His voice was very quiet.

'It can't be helped,' she said quickly. 'I have to go, Sam. I'll talk to you tomorrow.'

But he wouldn't let her go. 'Are you free tomorrow night?'

'No. We've an event at seven o'clock, for a hundred people.'

'Right.' That was all he said. But Rose could hear all the significance underneath it. The unspoken hovered in the air between them. She decided to stop, before she made things any worse.

''Bye, Sam.'
''Bye, Rose.'
She hung up. Sarah was right.
She was going to have to get off the fence, sooner or later.

# Chapter Ten

'WHAT A SIGHT for sore eyes,' said Damien, grinning at Rose as she came into the kitchen on Saturday morning.

She jumped. 'Damien! You startled me. I didn't hear you come in. What are you doing here?'

'And I'm very glad to see you, too, Mother.'

'Sorry – I didn't mean it like that.' Rose pulled out a chair and sat down beside him. She fixed her dressing gown, ran her fingers through her hair. She didn't need her son to tell her she looked a mess. 'To what do I owe the pleasure?'

'Didn't Lisa tell you?'

Rose shook her head. 'No, I haven't seen her yet. I was working until two o'clock this morning. She and Brian were both in bed when I got home. So, what's up?'

'I called last night to say I was coming over to collect that stuff from my room. I've to work late all next week, so I decided to drop over this morning.'

'Right. Well, then; you can put on the kettle and make your mother a cup of tea. Make yourself useful.'

He pointed to the teapot on the table. 'I already have – freshly brewed, just for you. I heard you getting up. The middle floorboard in your bedroom still creaks, just like it always did.'

Rose yawned. 'Sorry – I'm getting too old for these late nights. What time is it anyway?'

'Half ten.'

Rose looked at him in surprise. 'Is it really? I slept longer than I thought.'

Damien filled her cup. 'You're working too hard,' he said quietly.

She reached for the milk. 'That's for another day. Don't fight with me this early in the morning, Damien. I'm not awake yet.'

He smiled at her. 'I've no intention of fighting with you at all. I still have the scars from the last time.'

She looked at him now. He made her remember that other life, the one that was receding more and more rapidly every day. Sometimes, in moments such as this, she caught a glimpse of it as it slipped from underneath her fingers, sped past her mind's eye like a shutter closing on a camera. All over, she thought now, all done. Nothing left but the tidy-up. 'I never thought we'd ever be able to joke about those days; do you know that?'

He nodded. 'I know. Neither did I. And maybe we'll be able to joke about these ones too, someday soon. Mind you, I have to say that I already find Lisa's little outburst hugely entertaining.' He glanced over at her, not even trying to conceal a smile.

'Yes, well, just remember what I asked you.'

'Don't worry. I'll be all grave and fraternal. By the way, I called Dad.' Damien poured more tea into his cup, stirred it thoughtfully. 'I spoke to him yesterday evening.'

'How did it go?'

He shrugged. 'Quite cold, I thought. But I gave him the benefit of the doubt. I thought he might still be smarting after Lisa.'

He stopped. Rose didn't press him.

'I've agreed to meet him tomorrow afternoon, for coffee. He suggested the bar in the Westbury. I thought "The Joy of Coffee" would be safer.'

Rose rested her hand on his. 'I'm glad. Two wise decisions for the price of one.'

'I'm not looking for anything from him, you know? I'll meet him because you want me to. I've every intention of saying my piece – maybe not like Lisa, but I'm saying it anyway.' He sipped at his tea. 'I'm not pretending that he's to blame for everything I did.' He looked at her, quickly. 'I've learned enough to know that I'm responsible for myself. But by the same token, *he* was responsible for *him*self. And what he did to us was shitty; cowardly, selfish and shitty. I've every intention of telling him that.'

'I'm not arguing with you. Even your dad said that the other day, when Lisa let him have both barrels. "She's entitled," he said, and he let her have her rant.'

'Well, mine might be a bit different. I've no intention of even raising my voice. And if I feel that I'm not getting any-where, I'm walking out. One chance, that's all he gets. Just the one.'

'That's all I'm asking, Damien. And as I keep telling you, I'm asking it for your sake, not for his.'

He nodded. 'Yeah, well, I still don't believe that you're right about that. I have no sense of lacking a father in my life. But I'll do it because you want me to.' He drained his cup. 'And *you* have to accept that I might not tell you what happens.'

Rose nodded. 'I'm fine with that. It's your business. You don't owe me anything.'

He looked at her curiously. 'What a strange thing to say.'

She smiled. 'I mean it. Go figure it out.'

He stood up from the table. 'Another day's work, as you'd say yourself. Right, I'm off. I'm going upstairs to collect my stuff and then I'm gone. I'll talk to you over the next few days, anyway, okay?'

'Fine. Good luck. Now, I'm going for a shower before anyone else sees me like this.'

He grinned. 'Don't worry. I won't tell on you.'


Lisa knocked on the bathroom door. 'Mum? Phone call for you.'

Rose pulled open the door, exasperated, wrapping a towel around her wet hair. 'What? What did you say?'

'Call on your mobile. You left it in the kitchen.'

'Okay – thanks. Who is it?'

Lisa shrugged. 'Dunno.'

Rose took the phone from her, making a mental note to tell her later that not all calls were equally urgent. Teenagers were wedded to their mobiles; parents had other priorities.

'Hello? Rose here.'

'Rose? I hope I'm not disturbing you. It's Sam.'

'Sam! Good morning. No, no, you're fine. You're not disturbing me at all. How are you?'

'Good. Look, I'm really sorry about Thursday – didn't get in until almost nine o'clock. The best-laid plans, as they say.'

'That's okay – nothing you could do about it,' said Rose, easily. She knew what was coming, had already decided what her answer would be.

'I have the preliminary figures ready, and next week looks to be a bit crowded. Would it be possible to meet this afternoon, do you think?'

'Yes,' said Rose, at once. 'It would indeed.'

'Great! I was hoping you'd say that.'

She could hear relief, enthusiasm, just a little caution in his tone.

'Where would suit you?'

'I think our Thursday arrangement was just fine,' said Rose. 'But perhaps even a little earlier? Everywhere gets so crowded on a Saturday night.'

'Okay, yes, that's fine – say four o'clock, upstairs in Neary's?'

'Four o'clock it is. See you then, Sam. Thanks for calling.'

'See you, Rose. Bye for now.'

She slipped the mobile into the pocket of her dressing gown and went back downstairs. Lisa was eating breakfast, flicking through *Heat* magazine. 'Morning, Lisa.' She stooped to kiss the top of her daughter's head. 'Did you have a good night?'

Lisa nodded, her mouth full of cornflakes. She gestured for her mother to wait. Rose grinned. Another battle won: don't speak with your mouth full.

'Yeah, Alison and Carly came over, we watched two DVDs. I made popcorn.'

'Anybody call?'

'Just Damien.'

'What time did Brian get home?'

'He was here when I got in from school.'

'Did he go out again?' asked Rose casually.

'No, he was here all night, in his room. He asked us to keep the noise down, said he was studying.'

Rose nodded, satisfied. 'I've to go out this afternoon. I don't know what time I'll be back. I'm meeting a friend for a drink. Have you plans?'

'Yeah, we're babysitting Carly's little nephew, Jonathan. Her sister-in-law will drive the two of us home, but it could be about one o'clock. They're going to somebody's birthday party.'

'That's fine. You can text me later – doesn't matter what time. I want to know when you're on your way home.'

Lisa nodded. 'I *know*, Mum. It's the usual routine. You don't have to tell me every time. Anyway, Brian'll be here, too.

John is coming over to study with him tonight. He's going to stay over in Damien's old room.'

'Okay. I'll talk to him later, then.'

Lisa continued to turn the pages of her magazine. Rose caught a glimpse of the usual celebrities, the Pitts, the Anistons, the Spears of that other, vacuous world that seemed to hold her daughter in thrall. Lisa spoke, without lifting her eyes from the page. 'I've decided to give Dad a ring tomorrow. I've already sent him a text.'

Rose looked at her in surprise. 'Good. I'm glad you did that. Did he answer?'

'Yep. More or less straight away. Said he'd be delighted to see me again. That was all. I talked to Brian. He thought it was the right thing to do.' She turned another page nonchalantly.

It didn't fool Rose for a moment.

She smiled over at her. 'Well. Good for you, for both of you. I'm sure it'll all go well this time. Do you know when?'

Lisa shook her head. 'No. He said to text him when I was ready. That he'd come and collect me here.'

Rose thought quickly. 'I think neutral territory would be best, Lisa. Why don't you choose somewhere in town and meet him there? That means you're free to come and go as you please.'

'Yeah, all right. Are you finished in the bathroom?' She stood up, closing the magazine.

'Yes. Off you go. I left clean towels on the radiator.'

'Thanks. See you later, Mum.'

Rose climbed the stairs to her bedroom. She closed the door and sat on the edge of her bed. The sense she had had earlier, of her old black-and-white life passing swiftly out of the frame, returned to her again now.

Things could never stay the same: she knew that. Not as they used to be before Ben left, not even as they used to be *after*

Ben left. The future was now set to become something very different. She had the strongest sense of the next part of her life belonging somewhere else.

After all, now she was no longer a mother to three small children: Damien had flown the coop, his wings growing stronger all the time. Brian was only half likely to settle into home again after his summer of freedom in Paris, and Lisa was able to handle more and more independence all the time. Soon even her youngest wouldn't need her mothering any more, not in the traditional, needy sense.

Daughter, sister, wife, mother, carer, caterer, survivor.

All done, all past, all over.

It was time for Rose, now.

She pulled her black jeans out of the wardrobe, and her new silk blouse. She took two handfuls of bottles and jars off her bedside locker and rummaged in the drawer of her dressing table for a new tube of foundation. Then she sat regarding herself in the old-fashioned, three-way mirror. It was only midday. Plenty of time for a face pack, a bit of a manicure, some careful make-up.

There were some arts a woman just never forgot.


It was very pleasant, Rose decided, to be sitting in a quiet bar on a Saturday afternoon, with a pleasant breeze billowing the net curtains beside you. Were there really people who led lives like this all the time? she wondered – sipping chilled white wine, reading the newspaper, no sense of push or hurry tugging at their sleeves?

She watched two young people at the bar: university students coming up to final exams, to judge by their conversation. Must be nice, she thought. That would be a good life, an *interesting* sort of life.

'Rose, I'm sorry I'm late. Taxi never turned up.' Sam pushed his way along the upholstered seat beside her. She thought he looked almost nervous, on the verge of shyness.

'You're hardly late, Sam – I've only just arrived myself.'

He grinned, suddenly looking more relaxed. 'Good. I hate hanging around waiting for people. Don't expect anyone to do it for me.' He placed a leather folder on the seat beside him. 'Well, what would you like to drink?'

'I think I'll have a glass of white wine. I can't remember the last time I sat in a bar at this time of the afternoon – but I'm getting to like it. I've decided it's the start of the new me.' She smiled at him, looking him right in the eye.

He didn't answer. Instead, he went up to the bar and returned a few minutes later with their drinks. When he sat, he placed his large hands carefully on the table in front of him. Rose had watched him as he'd walked to the bar. She liked the solid way he moved, the way he held his body. She liked the air of substance he brought with him. Now he turned towards her, poured wine into her glass, and spoke quietly.

'So. Did you retrieve the offending documents from the kitchen bin that night, as we discussed?'

She grinned. 'I did indeed. I have them in my bag. And you were right. Ben *has* done a lot of the legwork. Judging by the contents of that brown envelope, my home – sorry, our *house* – is worth at least a million euro and change.'

Sam nodded. 'I'm impressed. Your portion of that should put a very decent new roof over your head.' He raised his glass. 'Here's to you.'

There was a small, charged silence.

Rose took a deep breath. Okay, Katie, Claire, Sarah: better late than never. I'm going for it. Something daft, remember?

'Sam, I wanted to ask you if—'

He raised one hand in the air. 'Stop, Rose. Stop right there, please. I can't do this any more.' He put down his glass, ran both hands through his unruly hair. It was a gesture she had become very familiar with over the past year.

She stopped and looked at him in astonishment. How had he known what she was going to ask? His eyes are really very brown, she thought suddenly, so much warmer than blue.

'Do what, Sam?'

'Be your friend,' he said bluntly. 'I'm not going to put this off any longer,' he said, shaking his head and trying his best to smile at her. 'When you said that you'd meet me today, I was determined not to let the opportunity go. I have to talk to you – I've been putting it off for far too long.'

She looked at him, half afraid, half hopeful. 'Go on,' she said quietly.

He sighed. 'I've been wanting to ask you out for months – ever since I first met you. I've spent – I've *wasted* – almost a year waiting for the right moment.' He shrugged, helpless. 'There never seemed to be a right time. When I met you first, you were up to your ears in financial problems. I didn't want you to think I was taking advantage of your difficulties, didn't want to cloud our professional relationship.'

He stopped. Rose willed him to go on.

'I tried to tell you again that time we were in the Espresso Bar, but just at the crucial moment, your daughter rang you on your mobile.' He grinned. 'I'm beginning to hate phones – when I think of the number of opportunities they've scuppered on me.'

Tell me what? thought Rose. What is it he wants to tell me?

He reached over and took her hand. 'I can see you're speechless – just stay that way for a minute. I don't know what it is about timing and me. As if the rest of it wasn't bad enough, now your ex-husband's back, and this is probably the worst possible moment to even think about being with another man.

'But I've had it with waiting, Rose. I'm nearly fifty – far too old to postpone the important any longer. If you say no, that you don't . . . that you couldn't . . . feel anything for me, Dónal will do all the financial advising you need. I can't be with you as the solid, suited money-man, dispensing advice and objectivity. I just can't do it any longer.' He took a large sip of his wine.

'That's what you wanted to say the last time I was in your office, isn't it?' she asked softly. 'When you snapped at the receptionist, and I thought I was taking up too much of your time?'

He nodded. 'And the time before that, and the time before that again.' He threw both hands up into the air. 'Even last Christmas, for Christ's sake, when you agreed to come for a drink with Dónal and myself – I thought "Great, perfect timing."' He turned to her again. 'And what happened on that occasion?'

She smiled at his unsteady grin, remembering, wanting to make it easier. 'My delivery man let me down. There were thirty Christmas cakes and thirty dozen mince pies sitting back at the Bonne Bouche. I'd to rush off and do it myself.'

'See what I mean?' he asked, halfway between exasperation and affection.

She smiled. 'I thought I'd offended you. I was upset over that, but there was nothing I could do.'

He took her hands in his again. 'I *know* that – I'm not blaming you. I'm just . . . trying to explain how I feel about you.' He shook his head. 'I can't just have a professional relationship, Rose. Can't do it. What I feel for you is far deeper than that, far more important.'

Rose watched him, saw him breathe a long sigh of relief as he took another sip of wine. She wondered if he could have any idea of how she felt, listening to him speak. Any idea at all.

He seemed to examine his own hands now as he spoke, very carefully not looking at her. 'I'm sorry if this makes things even more difficult for you. I know that this is a particularly sensitive time. Dónal knows you might be calling on him again. He'll steer you safely through everything, I promise. I trust his judgement even more than I trust my own.'

Now he looked up and met her gaze. 'I know it's all out of the blue, and I don't expect you to have an answer. All I ask is that you think about it, and call me if there's even a chance that you—'

Rose interrupted him. 'I don't need to think about it, Sam. I don't need to think about it at all.'

His face lit up at her tone. His eyes began to search hers.

'In fact, just a few minutes ago, I was going to ask if you'd have dinner with me, sometime soon. Like tonight. But you interrupted me.' She smiled at him, teasing. 'You might have saved yourself that long confession.'

He began to sit up straighter.

'Somehow, even with all that's been happening to me over the last couple of weeks, I've realized that I've been thinking about you for months without knowing it.'

Okay, Sarah, Claire, Katie: you win, you all win. I'm off the fence.

She paused, conscious of the dramatic effect her words were having, enjoying every second of it. 'The answer is yes.'

He looked at her, startled, his hands holding hers ever more tightly. It seemed to Rose that he couldn't believe what he was hearing, seeing. 'Do you mean that?'

'Yes,' she said, with a conviction that felt good. 'I do. I may not have been the brightest at picking up the signals along the way, but I have the wavelength now.' She lowered her voice, conscious that the two young students were looking over, curiously, at their corner of the almost empty pub.

They probably think we're having an illicit affair, she thought suddenly. The idea cheered her immensely.

Slowly, she retrieved one of her hands, although Sam let it go reluctantly. She stroked his face then, leaned towards him and whispered, 'And I'm very happy at what I'm hearing.'

What are we like? she asked herself, smiling. Two middle-aged people about to kiss in public – well, half-a-dozen or so people didn't count as much of an audience, but still – in the middle of a late spring afternoon.

She leaned towards Sam and took his face in both her hands. Then she kissed him, lingeringly, for as long as she dared, and then a little longer.

When they pulled apart, the two students at the bar whooped and the barman growled: 'Enough of that, or I'll have to bar the two of you young ones.'

Everyone laughed, and Rose felt giddy with happiness, a delightful fizzing of hope and expectation. This time, she thought, it really could be different.

'Walk with me?' Sam asked.

She nodded.

Sam picked up his leather folder and handed her her jacket. They headed out of the pub hand in hand, crossed the street at the lights, grinning at each other like demented teenagers, and made their way to Stephen's Green.

Afterwards, Rose couldn't remember what they'd talked about, what they'd seen, what they'd planned. All she could recall was bright sunlight, shimmering water, and Sam's mouth on hers. His large, warm hand on her back felt like the most erotic embrace she'd ever had. There was a sense of vast, rolling freedom all around her. She didn't care that it all might feel much more sober, much more restrained in the morning.

'I love you,' he said simply. 'I don't care whether you think this is all too quick, or how bizarre the whole situation is, I don't want to – won't – wait any longer. I think I've been in love with you since the first day you walked into Dónal's office.' He hugged her. 'Do you think all of my clients get this sort of treatment?'

'I should hope not,' she teased him. 'Or we'd have things to discuss.'

She felt almost limp with expectation and desire, felt that his arm around her was the only thing keeping her on the ground. 'I feel like a dizzy teenager – do you know that? And I'm a mature, middle-aged woman. What have you done to me?'

'Nothing to what I'm intending to do.' He pulled her closer to him. 'Come home with me? Time's too precious. I don't want to waste any more of it.'

'Yes,' she said. 'Yes, I'll come home with you.'

She kept being reminded again of the first day they'd met: the way his arm had scooped her along after him, drawing her across the blue carpet into the ordered interior of his office. It had made her think of a farmer, flocks of woolly white sheep following in his wake.

Well, she thought, he had her now, lamb to the slaughter.


'You okay?' Sam kissed her gently.

She smiled over at him. 'Never better.'

'You took me by surprise, you know. I thought I'd have a much harder fight on my hands.'

She adjusted the pillow under her, brought her face closer

to his. 'You said something earlier, about not postponing the important any longer. Remember?'

He nodded. 'Yeah. And I meant it.'

'I know. It just reminded me of everything I've been feeling since Ben came back. I think I've spent most of my life dealing with the urgent.' She stroked Sam's greying hair, smiling at its unruliness. 'It makes you lose sight of the important. Being with you reminds me of what that is. Today, earlier, when you rang, I was already thinking about you, about the end of my old life, about how things never stand still.'

He groaned. 'You mean I could have saved myself at least two sleepless nights, worrying over what I was going to say to you?'

She smiled and shook her head. 'No. I'd never want to be without those words.' She pulled him towards her, sank again into his warmth.

He spoke softly into her hair. 'I was terrified of what you were going to say. I was afraid of pushing it, particularly now that Ben's back. But I just couldn't wait any longer.'

She kissed him. 'I'm glad you didn't. Your timing was perfect.'

He held onto her even more tightly. 'I suppose it's absolutely out of the question for you to stay tonight?'

She smiled at him. 'Not all night. I'll have to do a Cinderella. I've to leave at midnight, or else I'll turn into a pumpkin.'

He threw back the sheets. 'Right. It's only eight o'clock. I happen to have a bottle of very good champagne on ice. Don't move: you're not getting out of that bed, not yet.'

He stopped. 'I've just realized we haven't eaten.' He grinned at her. 'Can you live on love, or would you like some strawberries with your champagne?'

She stretched luxuriously. 'Can't I have both?'

'You can have anything you want. Just don't go away.'

She looked over at him wickedly. 'I've no intention of it. It's not every day I get offered champagne and strawberries.'


Rose's taxi pulled up just as Lisa arrived home.

'Where were you?' said Lisa, looking curiously from the taxi to her mother and back again.

Rose thought there was a hint of disapproval in her daughter's expression. 'What do you mean? *I'm* the one who's supposed to ask that.'

Lisa grinned. 'Sorry – I didn't mean it like that. I didn't know you were going to be late.'

'I'm not. I'm home at exactly the same time as you are. You're always telling me that one in the morning isn't late for a Saturday.'

'Well, it's not. But it's late for you.'

Rose laughed. 'Well then, I guess I'm just full of surprises.'

Lisa looked at her strangely. 'Were you with Dad?'

'No, I was not. I was visiting a friend. Now, are you going to open the front door or am I going to have to stand out here all night? I'll start rummaging for my keys if you don't hurry up.'

'Relax, relax. I have it.'

Rose hung up her jacket under the stairs. 'Right, I'm off to bed. Don't stay up late.' She kissed Lisa on the forehead.

'Don't you want tea?'

Rose shook her head. 'No, thanks. Not tonight.' Her mouth was still tingling from champagne and strawberries. And kissing. 'I had some earlier.' She couldn't help smiling. But Lisa had already disappeared into the kitchen. Rose looked around the living room door. Brian and John were sprawled on the sofa, watching television.

'Night, you two,' she said.

They both looked up. 'Night.'

'How did the studying go?'

They looked at one another. 'All right,' they said in unison.

'Bit of a waste of a Saturday night, in my opinion,' said John, grinning at her.

'I see you haven't changed,' said Rose, 'despite your mature years.'

He shrugged. 'What can I say?'

She laughed. 'See you both in the morning. Don't have the telly too loud, Brian, okay?'

He nodded, looking at the screen. 'No problem.'

'Night.'

Rose climbed the stairs to her room. Images of the day she had just spent swirled everywhere, a heady, potent mix of champagne and happiness. She sent Sam a text: 'Home safely. Talk tomorrow.'

The reply was instant: 'Dream well. Call me early.'

She smiled. She didn't recognize the woman who looked back at her from the old-fashioned dressing-table mirrors. Was it really only hours since she had sat here, full of anticipation and hesitant, unformed desire? Slowly she removed her make-up, applied eye cream, night cream, hand cream. She grinned at herself. How predictable, she thought. How silly, how ordinary. How daft.

Rose knew that no matter what happened next, nothing would ever matter as much as today. The world had turned full circle. Her new life was everywhere, the old one turned into a pumpkin at midnight.

She felt the joy of ambush: she'd been felled, scooped along, gathered up willingly by a strength of feeling that might turn out not to be – but for now, felt something very much like love.

PART THREE

# Chapter Eleven

'MA?'

Rose looked up from her newspaper, startled. 'Damien! I didn't expect to see you today. I thought that was Brian coming in.'

'Are you on your own?' Damien made his way over to the sofa where Rose was curled, but he didn't sit down.

Not any more, thought Rose, with a rush of delight. I'm not on my own any more. 'No,' she said innocently. 'Lisa and Alison and little Katie are upstairs, doing girly things. Why?'

'I just want to talk to you for a minute.' Damien opened the door into the kitchen. 'I'll put the kettle on.'

Rose followed, feeling quite calm. Whatever it was he had to say, she'd be fine; she felt ready for anything. Memories of the previous night were still warm and vivid, and just now, she'd relived them again on the phone with Sam. Nothing could disturb this new and solid sense of equilibrium. She sat down at the kitchen table, quite content to wait.

'I've just come from Dad.'

She nodded. 'Right.'

'I called for him at the hotel, as we'd agreed. I was a bit early, so I just hung around the foyer upstairs, reading a Sunday paper.'

'Go on.'

'I actually heard him before I saw him. That surprised me: I recognized his voice straight away, even before his face. I dunno . . . I just didn't expect that. He was comin' up the stairs, talkin' to someone. I'm not sure why, but it was like I got cold feet, or somethin'. I kinda hid behind the newspaper.' Damien took the teapot off the shelf. 'The thing is . . .' The kettle clicked off, and he turned around, filled the teapot with boiling water.

Is he doing this deliberately? Rose wondered. Or can he genuinely not fill a teapot and talk at the same time?

He threw the water down the sink, and reached into the caddy for two teabags. 'The thing is, he was with another woman. I watched them. They went up to the desk together and asked for their key.'

For a second, Rose didn't understand what he was trying to tell her.

He walked towards her and put the teapot carefully on the kitchen table. 'Ma?'

She looked up at him quickly, and was struck by the anguish in his face. God almighty, she thought, with a shock of understanding, he's actually afraid I might *care*.

Rose answered him at once. 'Was she good looking?' she asked, archly, smiling at her son.

'What?'

'Don't look so surprised. I asked you if she was good looking.'

'Well, yeah,' he said, slowly. 'She was.'

'Pour my tea, will you, please?' Rose said, mildly. 'It'll get cold if you just keep on standing there with your mouth open.'

He stared at her, his face finally beginning to clear. 'You don't care, do you? You really don't care?' He sat down and concentrated on pouring tea.

Rose nodded at him, smiling. 'That's right. I really don't care. Tell me what she looked like, go on – do.'

Now Damien began to grin. 'That's the really funny thing,

and I wasn't going to tell you this bit – but she looked a lot like you.'

'A lot like me now, or a lot like I used to look?'

'Well,' he shifted a little on his chair, 'a lot like you used to look, I suppose – except that her hair was dark.'

Rose laughed at him. 'So was mine, fifteen years ago! Do you think I grew these blonde highlights for nothing?' She pointed at her hair.

He shook his head in disbelief. 'You can forget fifteen – I'd say there's more like twenty-five years between them.'

'How original,' said Rose. 'How very surprising.'

'You knew already, didn't you?' His tone challenged her, but relief was written all over his face.

'No, but it makes perfect sense.'

Damien held up one hand. 'Look, hang on. I don't know what sort of . . . arrangements you two are comin' to right now, and it's none of my business. The only reason I'm tellin' you about this woman is so that you have the full picture, in case it makes a difference to whatever happens between Dad and yourself. And that's how I feel about it: whatever happens is between you and him. I don't need to know.'

'Thank you for telling me. It's another piece of the jigsaw – and I'm really grateful for your concern. But it doesn't make any difference to me. I'm fine, Damien, truly. I'm fine.'

He looked at her curiously. 'You look different today.'

'Do I?'

'Yeah,' he said. 'You do. You look great, actually.'

'Thank you.' She leaned across the table, squeezed his hand. 'I feel great, and I've a strong sense that this will soon be over, and then I can enjoy the next part of my life.'

'Okay,' he said. 'So I don't need to worry about you?'

'Absolutely not,' she said firmly. 'Not for a moment.'

'Good. Then I'm glad I told you. And before you ask: Dad

and I have just had what is called, I believe, a full and frank exchange of views. He got quite snippy with me, said I wasn't old enough to judge him.' He shrugged. 'I said I wasn't judging *him* – just the impact that his irresponsibility had on all of us, the ones who were left behind. There's more, but you don't need to hear it.' He finished his tea, stood up, yawned and stretched. 'I'm pretty wrecked after it, I must admit. Kev an' Andy have convinced me to go to the gym with them later on, and we've a couple of new computer games to try out tonight. So I'm goin' straight home. That's the end of my exciting weekend.'

'Will you meet him again?'

'Dad? I haven't decided. He wants us to get over the "impasse", according to himself. Don't know if that's possible, myself, but I'll see. I suppose the first time is the hardest. I told him I'd leave it for a week or so, mull over what we talked about.'

Rose forced herself to be silent, not to ask any more.

'Brian all ready for the big trip?'

She nodded. 'Yes, but he has to get his exams over with first. He's really excited, though, really looking forward to it. He and John can hardly contain themselves.'

'I suppose he'll be all right for money?' His tone was too casual, too dismissive.

Rose looked at him in surprise. 'Yes. He'll be fine. Your dad gave him some, I've given him some and he's saved a pile from his part-time job. You know Brian.'

Damien grinned. 'Yeah – tight bastard. Still has his First Communion money. Not like his big brother, eh?'

Rose smiled. 'Comparisons are odious. Besides – things change.'

'Just as well. I'll give him a few quid, too. Can't afford too much, but every little helps.'

'I'm sure he won't say no. Come for dinner before he goes.' Rose stood up, gave him a hug and clapped him heartily on the back.

'Will do. I'll be talkin' to you before that, anyway.' He opened the door into the hallway. 'Take care of yourself, right?'

'I will,' she smiled. And so will someone else. 'Enjoy the gym, and good luck with the job next week.'

'Thanks. See ya.'

He stepped outside and Rose watched him walk down the driveway, bathed in the sunshine of a late April afternoon. She watched him go, glad, grateful.

No matter how hard she looked, she couldn't see them. He looked tall, straight, his arms swinging. His shoulders were broad, unencumbered.

No more monkeys clinging to his back.


When Rose arrived at work the following Friday, Katie was standing at the outer door, pungent cheroot in one hand. She looked pale, almost sickly.

'Don't tell me these are bad for me, okay? Otherwise, I'm likely to stab you and end my days in prison.' She tried to smile at Rose, but her eyes gave her away.

'Actually, I think you look most elegant.' Rose put her briefcase on the ground and stood beside her. 'Not too many women can carry off a cheroot with panache, but you're one of them. Besides, I love the smell. So, no prison cell on my account.' She gestured towards the car park. 'Not much of a view is it? Gritty urban chic was never my thing.' She waited, could feel the other woman getting ready to speak.

'We really have to do this, don't we?' Katie put her head back and expelled a plume of bluish smoke into the air. 'Because it's really shitty.'

Rose paused for a moment before she spoke. She could hear the tremble in Katie's voice. 'Yes,' she said quietly. 'We do have to, and it is truly shitty. But you don't have to be here, Katie. We've already discussed it, and the rest of us are fine with that: come back when it's all over.'

Katie shook her head. She took a last pull of her cheroot, then ground the butt under her heel. 'No, that wouldn't be fair. Nobody likes doing . . . this. It's just . . . Deirdre, my eldest, did a bit of shoplifting a couple of years ago. We were lucky: she didn't get caught. I keep thinking this could be her, you know?' Katie looked down, using the toe of her sandal to hide the remains of her cheroot among the gravel.

'I know that feeling all too well,' said Rose grimly. 'We've all been there, one way or another. But there's a hell of a difference between a bit of adolescent bravado and systematic, planned, well-executed *stealing* that has lasted well over a year, at the very least. Isn't there?'

Katie nodded, twisting her long hair back into its customary knot at the nape of her neck. 'I suppose so. But is it a difference of degree or kind, I wonder? That's what I'm not sure of.' She waved one hand in the air. 'Oh, don't listen to me. Of course we have to do this. I suppose it's like the guilt of the survivor, you know? We could have killed Deirdre when we found out what she'd been up to. I feel badly for Angela's parents, whoever they are.'

'Katie,' said Rose mildly. 'Deirdre was sixteen. Angela is nearly thirty. At what age do you suggest they become responsible for themselves?'

Katie's face brightened. 'You're right. Of course you're right. And Angela had to have known what she was doing. Come on, let's have a cup of tea first.' She opened the door and ushered Rose in before her. 'When all else fails, make a pot of tea.'

\*

Sarah was already on her mobile. Claire was leaning on one of the counters, absorbed in making a list. Betty was at one of the sinks, scrubbing at something vigorously with a Brillo pad. Katie went to fill a kettle.

'Morning, all,' said Rose casually.

Sarah waved, Betty raised one reddened, soapy hand in greeting. Claire looked up at Rose and smiled.

'Hi, there. You look great.' She looked at Rose quizzically. 'You keeping secrets from us, these days?'

'Of course not.' Rose returned her impish gaze, innocently. For one fervent moment, she hoped that Claire hadn't made her blush. 'What's on for today, then?'

Sarah finished her call and threw her eyes up to heaven. 'I'm going to strangle that bloody woman, I really am. That's the *fourth* time she's changed her mind. I've told her I'll have to charge her for the stuff we've already prepared: I'm not having this. I'm just not having it.'

The door opened and Angela came in. The kitchens went suddenly silent.

'What's her excuse this time?' asked Claire quickly, filling the gap.

'Oh, something about too few choices for non-fish eaters. It was vegetarians before that, then picky children, then people's wheat intolerances. We'd already worked all this out, *weeks* back. This is turning into a nightmare.' Sarah turned abruptly towards Angela. 'Morning, Angela,' she said.

'Morning, everyone,' said Angela.

Rose nodded her greeting, wondering at Angela's air of calm confidence. Claire waved and Betty hardly looked up from her sink. Rose thought what a wonderful relief it was to have Sarah's genuine irritation fill the air around them. She hoped that all Angela would see was another normal morning.

'Right, then,' said Sarah. 'Let's not get bogged down. Claire, even if that list's not finished yet, let's get going on the urgent stuff. Give each of us a job to get started on, and we can review things, say, in an hour and a half or so. Okay? Go for it. Katie, just fill the mugs and let everyone take one to wherever they're working.'

The kitchens became busy immediately. Angela was dispatched to do an inventory of the cold room while Betty continued scouring the oven trays. Sarah gestured to Rose to follow her into the office. She closed the door behind them.

'The Guards have confirmed for half ten this morning. I've already told Claire and Katie. We've just got to keep it all together until then.' She smiled at Rose. 'It's funny – I think Katie was the angriest of all of us when we found out about Angela. I was surprised: she's normally such a softie. Now, she's literally sick to her stomach.'

Rose nodded, feeling her own insides shift uncomfortably at the thought of what lay ahead. 'I know. I met her outside earlier, doing serious damage to a cheroot. I think we'll all be glad when this is over.'

'You sure you're okay to supervise those two today, in the circumstances?'

'Absolutely,' said Rose. 'It would be very odd to do otherwise. Angela might smell a rat, even at this late stage. She's no fool. She knows there's something going on. The four of us don't make very good liars.'

'Okay. Well, good luck. It's nearly nine – not too much longer to wait. I hope to Christ the Guards arrive on time. My nerves are about to snap.'


In the event, they arrived precisely on time.

At half past ten there was a knock at the outer door, which

Sarah went to answer. 'I'll get that,' she said. She walked through the kitchens quickly, without looking back.

Rose stood beside Angela, watching her. Part of her still hoped that this was all a mistake, some dreadful misunderstanding that the arrival of the police would somehow clarify, and then they could all get back to normal. Sarah made her way back through the kitchens, her eyes averted. Even though Rose had been expecting them, it took her a moment to register that the two tall figures in her wake were Guards. She wondered, briefly, what Angela must be feeling.

Suddenly, a large blue uniform stood in front of the counter.

'Angela Walshe?' its voice said.

Rose watched as the room seemed to fill with Angela's expression. Her eyes widened, she dropped the stainless steel bowl she'd been holding in her hands. It clanged onto the tiles, spinning a little before it finally settled into silence.

'Are you Angela Walshe?' the figure insisted.

Angela said something inaudible, her hands clutched wildly at the air. Rose saw Katie look away. Claire's dark eyes were troubled and startled in her pale face. Rose had the strange feeling that she was looking at an unfinished still life, or a bad photograph: something contrived and artificial which needed life, vigour, something to animate it.

Then Angela looked wildly from Rose to Sarah and back again.

'No, no, no,' she kept saying.

Something had released her words into the tense, shocked air of the kitchens and Rose let go of the breath she'd been unaware she was holding. The scene before her settled at once into a recognizable reality.

'Please,' Angela begged, her eyes round and huge in a

suddenly white face. 'I'll pay it all back, every penny. It wasn't my idea – it was David's.'

Her eyes pleaded for salvation as the taller of the two Guards intoned the reasons for her arrest. His female companion stood impassively behind him. Rose felt her mouth go dry, her stomach begin to weaken. Uncomfortable memories of her own kitchen surfaced: Sergeant Finlay's face swam before her eyes, Katie's words roared between her ears.

*This could be Damien.*

She caught Sarah's eye and then they both watched in horror as, without a sound, Angela's knees gave way from under her.

'Jesus, Angela!' Rose's arms shot out to catch her and she sank to the floor, too, holding onto the suddenly leaden body. It seemed to Rose that everything was happening in slow motion, that hours, rather than minutes had passed since Sarah had opened the outer door.

'Please, please,' Angela kept moaning, her voice suddenly hoarse, her hands searching the air uselessly. 'I'll pay it back. I promise, I'll pay back every penny. Don't do this to me. Please don't do this to me. It was David, not me. It was all David.'

Claire knelt down and pressed a glass of water to Angela's lips. 'Here, sip this.'

Angela obeyed, her eyes looking pleadingly into Claire's. Gradually, the colour came back to her cheeks. And then, somehow, the policewoman took over: Angela was back on her feet, someone handed her her handbag, someone else got her jacket and then she was gone.

The kitchen door swung quietly shut behind the three figures. Rose found a chair and lowered herself into it, her heart thumping. Katie dragged her hands through her hair and reached for the kettle. Sarah and Claire disappeared together into the office. The whole kitchen seemed to sag.

And then, as though out of nowhere, a stark, piercing wailing began. Rose looked up in alarm. What on earth was that? There, standing at the sink, looking hopelessly lost and vulnerable, was Betty, the Brillo pad still in her hands.

Rose went to her, put her arms around her, and allowed the girl to sob herself into silence. 'It's okay, it's okay,' she said, over and over, rocking the lumpy body as though Betty were a child. 'You did the right thing. None of this is your fault.'

God, thought Rose. What a day. What a dreadful, dreadful day. I want to be out of here.

I want to be with Sam.

He was waiting for her as she got out of the lift. 'You okay?'

She nodded. 'A bit shattered. But I'm glad it's over.'

He put one arm around her shoulders and drew her inside the apartment. 'Go and sit on the balcony. There's a bit of sunshine still in one corner.'

Rose put her bag and jacket on the bed and stepped out onto the decking. She smiled. The small, circular table had a vase on it, holding a single red rose. She sat in the sunshine, looking down on the garden below. The cream-coloured buildings all around her gleamed; the silence was fragrant, restful.

Sam stepped out of the bedroom, a bottle of wine and two glasses in his hands. Rose nodded towards the vase. 'You're an old romantic: did anyone ever tell you that?'

He looked at her sternly. 'Romantic, certainly; less of the "old", please.'

She smiled at him, accepting the glass of chilled white wine he handed her. 'Mmm. Thanks. I've been looking forward to this all day. You have no idea how much.' She sipped, leaned her head back and closed her eyes. When she opened them again he was watching her carefully. She gestured towards the garden below, full of early summer blooms. 'You know, when I was young, a "flat" in Dublin meant something very different from all this.'

He grinned. 'I know, I remember. But don't forget, these are *apartments*: the new, shiny Dublin doesn't have flats any more – or would like to think it doesn't.'

She shaded her eyes for a moment, looking around her.

'Well, are you going to tell me?'

She sighed. 'Of course. It was most unpleasant.' Rose told him, briefly, the events of her day. When she'd finished, she looked over at Sam, unable to hide her anguish. 'I know it had to be done. I know that Angela was dishonest and sly and that she took advantage of us. But all I could think of when they arrested her was something Katie said: she's someone's daughter, you know? Behind this, there are devastated parents somewhere. And I know what that feels like. It could have been me, one of my children.' She sipped at her wine. 'The panic on her face when she saw the Guards arrive was awful, just awful.'

'It's over,' said Sam quietly. 'And you had no choice. Even if you hadn't prosecuted, Maguire's would have.'

Rose nodded. 'I know. And the strange thing was, even Betty was distraught. She started sobbing when they took Angela away. I think if she could have taken everything back that she'd ever said about her, she would have. I didn't want her to be there in the first place. I'd have given her the morning off, but the Guards insisted we kept everything as normal.'

'Did you talk to Betty afterwards?'

'Yes. Sarah and I brought her into the office. We told her the case against Angela would have gone ahead anyway, even without her. Sarah calmed her down, reassured her. I'm afraid by that stage I was no use. I was in bits. Then we gave her the rest of the day off. Clean slate for all of us when we go back next Monday.' Rose raised her glass. 'Cheers. Or something.'

Sam stood up. 'You stay here. I'll just go and finish off the food, before something gets cremated. No dessert, though. My waistline has had it with strawberry shortcake.' He bent down and kissed her. 'Back in a minute. I hate seeing you upset like this.'

'I'll be fine.' She reached up and smoothed his mop of hair. 'Just give me an hour or so to get this out of my system. It's been a long day.' She grinned at him. 'Then we can discuss my real troubles.'

Sam laughed. 'I'd better put more wine in the fridge in that case. By the way, what's the story? Can you stay the night, Cinderella?'

She smiled. 'Lisa happens to be going to a birthday sleepover tonight . . . and, therefore, so is her mother.'

'I always knew there was a God.'

Rose put her glass on the table and clasped her hands around Sam's neck, drawing him closer. 'I don't have to be home until lunchtime tomorrow, at the earliest.'

He sighed. 'You're killin' me. Are you *sure* about this? I mean, what if Lisa changes her mind at the last minute? I know my sister's kids do all the time. Drives her nuts.'

Rose laughed, let him go. 'I doubt it; it's in my friend Jane's house, with Alison and Carly and all the usual suspects. Lisa's known them all forever. Besides, even if she did decide not to go, Brian will be there. He's home on Friday and Saturday nights from now until the exams are over.' She looked at him smugly. 'I'm a free woman, with all bases covered.'

'I'm just going to turn off my mobile.' He gestured to the bottle of wine in the cooler. 'Help yourself. I won't be long. We'll eat in here, though – gets chilly when the sun goes down.' He went back inside.

Rose topped up her glass. The last rays of the early May sun were strong. She closed her eyes against the glare and leaned her head back against the screen behind her. What a crowded few weeks, she thought. Ben had been back just over a month, a month that had been stretched and made fuller, denser with every passing day. Lisa had seen him again, and remained non-committal. Rose had decided not to press her. Brian was happy, Damien still tight-lipped.

And so it went, she thought, and so it would probably go, long into the indefinite future. Well, she thought: so be it. She'd done her bit.

Time for Rose, remember?

Sam set the table and put dishes and bowls on the counter behind him in the small, orderly kitchen.

'We've half an hour at least before that's done.' He walked over to the sofa and sat down beside Rose. 'I think we should talk, get some stuff out of the way,' he said quietly. 'I don't want your husband – ex-husband, even – hanging around between us any longer than I can help it.'

'What do you mean?'

'I've done out some new figures for you.' He pulled out several blue folders from a drawer in the coffee table. He turned and grinned at her. 'We didn't pay too much attention to the ones I brought to Neary's last Saturday, if you remember. We'd better do it now. Aren't you meeting Pauline again sometime next week?'

'Yes. Apparently Ben is getting impatient.' She gestured towards Sam's hands. 'Ah, the blue folder – I remember it well.'

'What are you smiling at?' he demanded.

'Oh, I don't know,' she said, teasing. 'I'm just wondering if figures are the accountant's only response to a crisis.'

He looked at her sternly. 'Don't mock me. My blue folders pulled you out of the shit before – or at least, helped you to see it when it was up to your ankles. Besides, with this out of the way, we can concentrate on much more important things.'

'Such as?' She leaned towards him, teasing.

They were both grinning now, Sam looking at her over the tops of his glasses, Rose's hand searching out his, each insanely delighted with the other.

'Oh, love, then more love, and other mysteries of life.' He pulled her close to him. 'You happy?'

'Daftly, ridiculously happy. If these are my fifties, I'm planning on staying here for a while. And to think I thought that I was middle-aged!'

Sam lunged at her, scattering blue folders everywhere. Rose saw the pages settle on the floor under the coffee table, under the television, and wondered how something so white, so innocent, so inanimate, could dispel so much menace.


Later, in dressing gowns, at the table, he said: 'So, here's what I propose.'

Rose sighed, putting down her cup. 'It's a Friday night, Sam – you know, one of those brief events called a weekend? Can't it wait just a little longer? I'd like to live in the cocoon for at least twenty-four hours.'

'Did your cur of a husband respect *your* weekends when he came back?' Sam's tone was mild, reasonable.

'Well, no, but—'

'Exactly. We have to be ready for him. We have no idea what he's planning. You need to be ready for next week.'

'You don't have to do this, Sam,' said Rose, quietly. 'If it muddies the waters between us, I'd much prefer to have someone else fight this particular battle with me. I know what my priorities are.'

'That isn't an issue. There's no question of it coming

269

between us. Call this cosmic revenge – a whole global feast of dishes best served cold.'

'Okay, then,' she said softly. 'Let's do it now. Let's do it to him before he does it to us.'

At two in the morning Sam indicated his laptop screen, handed Rose the latest printout and said, 'I agree with you – I think this should be your first offer. Bearing in mind that he wants money *now*, otherwise he'll have to wait for four years, or even longer. Tell him Lisa wants to be a doctor. That should soften his cough: four years left at school, and another seven at college? I think he'll want to look at this.'

'Oh, it can be the first shot across the bows, all right. But don't forget, I know this man. Nothing's ever *enough* for him.'

'Well, this way, with you buying him out, he walks away with between a quarter of a million and three hundred thousand euro, cash, with all his family debts paid, and no hanging around waiting for the house to be sold. With all the equity you have, you could easily borrow that amount.'

Rose shook her head. 'I don't want to. I don't want that sort of a loan in my fifties. Obviously, I'm glad the house is worth a lot, but one bit of me just can't help wondering . . . do you know that? One point one million euro for a house that once cost seventy-five thousand pounds? The whole country's gone mad.'

'Why do you think it's going to be about more than money for Ben? I'm curious.'

Rose nodded, slowly. 'Yes, it might sound strange to you, to someone who's never known him, but Ben will never agree to my buying him out. It was always *his* house, *his* achievement, *his* pride and joy. He wouldn't be able to bear the thought of me sitting there, no matter how much it had cost me to buy his share.'

'But legally he can't force you to sell . . .'

Rose shook her head impatiently. 'It's got nothing to do with legality. Look, *he* knows I want rid of him; *I* know he wants his money. What's stuck in the middle? That bloody house. I'd say he knows I'd sell my soul to see the back of him. Don't forget, if I know his buttons, he knows mine. We shared a home for twenty years, after all. No, the house will be the sticking point of any negotiation. If he can't have it, then he'll make damned sure I can't have it either.' Rose stopped. She wanted Sam to understand how this was about her own peace of mind, her sanity, as much as it was about financial security.

'He'll wear me down, Sam,' she said quietly. 'And I'm afraid that he might do it through the kids as well as every other way he can think of. Life's too short – you said so yourself. I don't want anything to do with him other than what I have to. I want this closed. I want it settled, my kids settled. Then I can move on, out of his orbit forever. And have him out of mine.'

'Okay,' said Sam calmly. 'Let's run the numbers again, and see what would happen if you did decide to sell the house, as long as you're absolutely sure that's what you want.' He smiled at her. 'Final answer, as Mr Tarrant would say?'

She laughed. 'Final answer, Chris. I *am* sure. I always have been, ever since this started.'

Sam looked at her. 'Okay. There's certainly an argument to say it would be cleaner, but you'd still have to haggle with him over his portion. Let's see what happens if we change the percentages a bit. Then you can take all of this to Pauline.'

'Do you know,' said Rose wistfully, 'for the last while I've been dreaming about somewhere small, somewhere quiet, somewhere where I can close the front door, and say "keep out".

Somewhere I can call my own. Do you know what I mean? It's just for me and Lisa, really. The boys are up and running. I doubt very much if Brian will want to live at home again, particularly after Paris, and sharing with other lads.'

Sam looked at her, his expression hang-dog, comical. 'Would there even be a small corner just for me?'

Rose leaned forward and kissed him. She knelt up on the sofa and wound both arms around him. 'Actually,' she said softly, 'I'd hoped you might share my corner instead. There's a bed in it.' And she kissed him again.

Sam took her face in his hands. His skin was warm, dry. He rubbed his thumbs gently along her jawline. She leaned into them, and rested her cheeks against his palms. He pulled her closer. 'Try getting rid of me,' he whispered into her hair.

She slept that night curled into Sam's large frame. One of his arms was draped protectively around her waist. She had never managed to sleep this close to Ben: he had been all awkward angles and restlessness throughout the night.

She felt that nothing *too* terrible could be aimed at her from Ben's corner next week. She should probably be cowering among the domestic sandbags somewhere, fearing imminent attack. But she wasn't: she felt energized, exhilarated.

As long as she had Sam, her ex-husband's artillery could do its worst, and she'd still be ready.


Pauline raised her hand. 'Hang on Rose, I know this is all bull – but I want you to listen to what he's saying, so that you're ready when you need to respond.'

'Sorry, Pauline. I really thought I'd got over most of the anger, but this . . . this really infuriates me.'

'"Furthermore,"' Pauline continued, looking at the pages in front of her, '"Mr Holden is most anxious to keep up the visits with his younger son, who will soon be in Paris, and of course, he cannot do so without resources."' She flipped through the pages. 'He now gets really stuck into the Bonne Bouche. He points to the success of your business, emphasizes that you've made far more money than he has over the last years and that he needs more time to make full reparation to his family.'

Rose shook her head in disbelief. 'Full reparation – who does he think he's talking to? Given the fact that he's already lied about maintaining the kids?'

'He thinks he's talking to a judge.' Pauline spoke quietly. 'To the system, which is still adversarial. We've talked about this before. If there was any way we could get him to mediation—' Pauline stopped, seeing the look on Rose's face.

'Out of the question. He's already refused, twice. It doesn't matter what I say; he refuses point blank to go that route. He wants his day in court. And I can see why. If you're prepared to lie that much, the world can be your oyster. And I cannot believe that *I* might have to support *him* just because I made a success of the Bonne Bouche.' Rose stopped and thought of Sam's words. Nothing personal, he kept saying. Just think of it as business. That way you don't need to get angry. Hold onto your energy, channel it, focus on the fight.

'Well, he may get more than he bargains for,' Pauline said grimly. 'If Ben wants money now, we can use that as our strongest bargaining tool. I suspect some of his eagerness to go to court is a smokescreen. He's sabre-rattling. And he's trying to hurry you up. He calls this an "unconscionable delay".'

'Does he, now? Well, I have a few sabres of my own. I'm considering digging my heels in and insisting that I couldn't even contemplate selling the house until Lisa's either finished school or finished college. Sam suggests that Lisa might like to study medicine. Let's see how much that pisses her father off.'

'Attagirl. You still working on those scenarios with Sam McCarthy?'

'Yes,' said Rose and couldn't help smiling. Nothing could stop her smiling these days when she thought of Sam. She slid one of his blue folders across the desk to Pauline and opened it up. 'These are the first two offers we've come up with. This one here is the smokescreen: the one that doesn't involve selling the house. And this is the one where I do sell the house, but all Ben's debts get deducted before he gets the cash he's waiting for. I don't expect him to accept either of these. They're just the opening salvo.'

'Am I missing something, here?' Pauline was looking at her intently. 'How come you're looking so happy all of a sudden?'

Rose could feel her cheeks begin to grow warm.

'Rose Kelly! I do believe you're blushing!'

'What am I like, Pauline? At my age!'

'Sam McCarthy?'

Rose nodded, feeling even more foolish.

'Good for you. I don't even need to ask if it's good – I can tell that by just looking at you. How long?'

'Oh, we're only on the nursery slopes. It seems we've been skirting around the issue for some time. Officially, only a few weeks.'

'And who's counting,' said Pauline, grinning.

'It makes a change from counting the years after Ben left, and counting the days after he came back. I know it's very early yet, but it's good. I'm really happy.'

'All the more reason to wash Mr Holden out of your hair.'

'I've more reasons than I could possibly need. I don't want to make Sam one of them. I'm a bit long in the tooth for that, arranging my life around a man.'

Pauline smiled at her knowingly. She didn't comment. 'I'll look through these proposals for Ben, and get back to you.

Remember, no more conversations in the meantime. I know, I know,' she said, seeing Rose was about to speak. 'I know we agreed you should ask him again about mediation. But that's done now, and he's refused for the second time. We need to move on.'

Rose stood up, sorting out her bag and her folder of papers with a briskness she didn't feel. Time for this to be over. She'd had enough.

'This business with Sam McCarthy: is it love?' Pauline was teasing her.

Rose smiled. 'Well, if it isn't, it's not far off it.'

'You deserve it, you know. The last couple of years would have killed a horse. I admire you.'

Rose looked at her in surprise. She'd never thought of herself as that – as someone to be admired. Survival came naturally, surely, all grim determination and the constant imperative of children. What was to admire? She'd just done what parents most often did: got on with doing their best.

Nevertheless, Pauline's words made her feel good about herself. Sam's love made her feel good about herself. Now all she had to do was get rid of Ben Holden once and for all, and she could then feel impossibly good about herself.

Lisa stood in the hallway, leaning against the banisters. Rose thought she was on the verge of tears.

'Are you sure you don't want to come, Lisa? There's plenty of room.'

She shook her head. 'I'm playing tennis with Alison in half an hour. Besides, I don't want to go.'

Brian grinned at her. 'Missin' someone to fight with already, are you?'

Her eyes filled suddenly. Brian looked taken aback.

'Ah, Lisa: I'm only teasin'. C'mere. Gimme a hug.'

She walked over to him and buried her head in his shoulder. He gave her a mighty bear hug, lifting her bodily off the floor. 'Put me down!' she protested.

'Only if you say you'll miss me,' Brian said, grinning, lifting her higher.

She squealed, thumping her fists against his shoulders. 'Okay, okay, I'll miss you! I'll miss you! Now put me down!'

He put her down gently and ruffled her hair. 'I'll bring you back somethin' fashionable from Paris, okay? Don't forget to write, and have a great time in the Gaeltacht. Keep away from all those spotty boys, ya hear me?'

She giggled.

'Are you right, Brian? It's time for us to go.' Rose had just found the keys to the van.

'Yeah. I'm right.' He picked up his rucksack off the floor in the hall. 'Be good, Lisa. See ya at the end of September.'

'See ya. Don't forget to email me – and send me all your photos!'

Rose followed her son out to the van. He turned and waved. 'You'd better email me back!'

Rose started the engine. Brian looked at his watch.

'Don't worry,' she said, smiling. 'We're in plenty of time.'

He nodded. 'I know that. It's just that Dad said he'd try and ring before I left.'

She reversed carefully out of the driveway. 'Have you got your mobile with you?'

'Yeah. It's in my pocket.'

'Have you enough credit to call him, just in case, before you take off?'

'Yeah. I got some this morning.'

There was a silence. Then they both spoke suddenly, at the same time.

'Mum—'

'Brian—'

They laughed.

'Damien gave me some money last night.'

'Did he?' said Rose, managing to sound surprised.

'Yeah – he gave me two hundred euro. I couldn't believe it. An' it was really nice of him to come over and say goodbye. I wasn't expecting it.'

'Changed man, your brother,' said Rose, lightly.

Brian nodded. 'Yeah. In all the ways that count. He says that he really likes his new job, too. I said I'd email him from Paris, so he gave me his address.'

'I'm glad. The two of you probably have more in common than you think.' She glanced over at him.

He made no comment. 'When we get to the airport, don't come in with me, okay?' he said abruptly. 'I hate goodbyes.'

Rose smiled. 'I won't. We can say goodbye in the car park.' She swallowed, taking her time before she spoke again. 'I'll miss you.'

He nodded. 'Me, too.'

They drove for sometime without speaking. Rose was reminded of that night along the quays, centuries ago, when they'd driven home together in the shocked silence of Ben's return.

'Call home and reverse charges if anything happens, if there's anything that you need; do you hear me?'

'Yeah.' He grinned. 'I bet John an' his mum are having this exact conversation, right this minute.'

Rose laughed. 'I bet. Well, here's the other thing we'll both say: be careful out there. Mind yourselves. It's a big city, Paris.'

Brian shrugged. 'Can't be any more dangerous than Dublin.'

'Maybe not,' she agreed. 'But in Dublin you grow up

knowing the places to avoid. You don't have that familiarity with Paris.'

'We'll be careful.'

Rose waited another few moments. 'Brian, is there something else on your mind? Whatever it is, say it. I'm not going to be upset.'

He shifted uncomfortably in the passenger seat. 'I wasn't goin' to tell you until I got back, but I don't see the point in keepin' it from you.'

'Go on,' she said.

'Well, it's just that me and John are hopin' to share a house together in October. You know Alan, John's older brother?'

Rose nodded. 'Yes, I've met him once or twice.'

'Well, he kind of caretakes a house for this guy who works in Brussels. Your man is fanatical about his plants and his garden, and Alan does all that stuff, loves it. He's had two others sharing with him up till now, but they're both graduating this year. He asked John if the two of us would be interested, 'cos he wants people he knows. It's really close to the university, and my job will cover the rent. Besides, I'll be earnin' really good money, Mum, over the next few months, an' I intend to save hard.'

Rose smiled at his earnestness. It was a long speech, for Brian. He'd barely drawn breath. She wondered how long he'd been cherishing that bit of information. She pulled into a space in the airport car park.

'I'm not a bit surprised. You two are as thick as thieves. And it'll be good for you, time for all of us to move on. Just remember, there'll always be a room for you, all three of you, no matter where I am. Will you remember that?'

'Sure? I mean, are you sure you don't mind me movin' out?' His relief was palpable.

Rose grinned at him. 'And miss all those smelly socks and bits of pizza under your bed? I don't think so. Fire ahead with your plans – enjoy them. We'll talk about it again when you come back from Paris. Okay?'

He nodded eagerly. 'Yeah, sure, of course. It's a really nice place Alan's got: you'll like it.'

'I'm sure I will.' She got out of the van and opened the boot for him. He hauled his suitcase out.

'Sure you don't mind not comin' in?'

She shook her head. 'I hate goodbyes, too. Besides, I'd hate to ruin your street cred.'

He allowed himself to be hugged. 'Thanks, Mum. For everything.'

That was what Damien had said, too, Rose remembered suddenly. Had she actually managed things, after all?

'You're welcome. Call me when you've arrived safely.'

Brian hoisted his rucksack onto his back. 'I will. Text me if you want me. I don't think the phone in this hostel is up to much, according to reports. In fact, I don't think the hostel is up to much.'

'Well, as long as it's clean.'

Brian grinned at her. 'You guys are so predictable. John's mum said the same thing. We'd never afford anythin' else in Paris anyway, so it'll be grand. Cheap and cheerful, as you'd say yourself.' He took a step towards her. At that moment his mobile rang. 'That'll be Dad.' He let it ring. 'C'mere. I never gave you a proper hug.'

'Don't lift me up,' she warned him.

'I can't – look at what I already have on my back!'

They hugged. She kissed his shadowed cheek. 'Off you go. Have a blast.'

'I will.' He began to walk away from her, fishing his mobile out of his pocket. At the door to the lifts, he turned around and waved, the mobile already at his ear.

She waved back, waiting, smiling until he had disappeared.

After all, she could always have a little weep on the way home.

# Chapter Twelve

'SURE YOU'RE READY FOR THIS?'

Rose replied at once. 'Absolutely. I want to move this up a notch. What have I got to lose? He's been bombarding us with requests for a meeting. Let's give him what he's looking for.'

Pauline nodded. 'Just don't *agree* to anything – put your offer on the table and wait and see what happens. Leave the negotiations up to me.'

'Don't you worry,' said Rose grimly. 'I will.'


'Sure you're ready for this?' Sam handed her her new jacket, easing it carefully off the hanger.

'You know I am. We've practised it a million times. I know it so well that if I don't do it now, over-familiarity will make me forget it. Do you know what I mean?'

'I do, indeed,' said Sam, smiling at her. 'All I can say is, I'll be thinking of you. And I'll be waiting here with champagne on ice, no matter what the outcome.' He turned around, picked a small, gift-wrapped parcel up off the table. 'This is for you.'

Rose was startled. She hadn't noticed it before. She looked at Sam. 'Can I open it now?'

He laughed. 'You can't wear it if you don't open it.'

Rose tore off the wrapping paper and lifted the lid carefully. 'Oh, Sam. It's beautiful.'

He took the slim, gold bangle from her and placed it carefully on her wrist. 'For luck,' he said, and kissed her.

She threw her arms around him, clung to him. 'I love you,' she said quietly.

He smiled. 'I'd hug you back, but I'm afraid to crease that outfit. Now, just remember what we said . . .'

'I know, I know,' she said, smiling. 'This meeting is business. Nothing personal.'

'Exactly. Keep thinking like that, and you'll be fine. I'll be waiting for you when you finish. Don't hang around – get a taxi back straight away. I'll be here. And my mobile will be on all day, in case you need me.'

She took a long breath. 'I can do this, can't I?'

'Yes,' he said, firmly. 'You can. Now, stop thinking about it: just go ahead and do it. Remember what we said: "Let's do it to him before he does it to us."'


Rose walked smartly down O'Connell Street, keeping an eye on the time. She'd be a couple of minutes late, but that was how she wanted it. She'd already been into the Gresham Hotel earlier that week and booked the table for lunch. She'd chosen carefully, so that a passing glance would be enough to tell her whether Ben had arrived before her.

If he hadn't, she would simply sweep past, make a leisurely detour to the Ladies downstairs and return once he was installed. She'd already decided, too, to allow him fifteen minutes' grace, no more. If he was later than that, she was gone, out of there.

Keep the upper hand at all times, Pauline had warned her. Seize the advantage – don't wait for him to initiate anything. Sam had concurred.

'Remember,' he'd kept saying, 'this man is not your husband any longer – think of him as a business adversary, a canny operator, well able to pull a fast one. If you keep thinking of him like that, you have a fighting chance.'

All weekend Rose had summoned images of wakeful nights, domestic battlefields, the desperation she had felt on all those five o'clock mornings after Ben had walked out. It wasn't difficult. She could access those times so easily in her memory, it made her shiver.

And so, armed with Sam's blue folder, his gold bangle and all the courage she could muster, Rose made her way into the deeply piled silence of the Gresham's dining room. Ben was there before her. In *another* fancy suit, she noticed, wearing one of those ultra-fashionable steel-grey, almost metallic-looking ties, and a white shirt whose collar told Rose it had cost a small fortune.

Charvet, she thought suddenly, the name coming at her from somewhere she couldn't remember.

She stood up straighter, conscious of her own smart suit – long jacket, skirt with seams so sharp they were dangerous – and a pair of wildly extravagant taupe leather kitten heels. Damien would have enjoyed that, the way she'd spent his Brown Thomas voucher. The only problem was, she'd never be able to tell him what proportion of her outfit it had actually bought.

But the shoes. The shoes were her *pièce de résistance*.

Ben stood up on her approach. 'Rose,' he said, pleasantly, with just the ghost of a chilly smile. 'So good to see you.'

'Hello, Ben.' She watched as the waiter approached and held out her chair for her.

'Can I get you a drink?' she asked her husband, signalling to the waiter to stay. Just as she had hoped, Ben was completely thrown. With that one question, that one gesture, she had made it perfectly clear who had just gained the advantage.

'Er – gin and tonic, please,' he said stiffly. He smoothed his expensive tie back into place, and by the time he sat, he had recovered his composure.

'Sparkling water for me, please,' Rose said sweetly, and the waiter vanished, all smiles and deference.

She allowed a silence to grow, contentedly looking around the dining room. She had steeled herself in advance not to be the one to fill in any gaps in the small talk. Looking at the other hotel guests, Rose couldn't help wondering how many other lunchtime meetings had murder as their first course.

Ben cleared his throat. 'It's good to see you again, Rose. How have you been?'

'Fine, thanks. Very well indeed. And you? How are all those business . . . *opportunities* . . . coming along?' She sipped at her water, looking at him innocently.

He flushed.

Gotcha, she thought.

'We're making progress . . .'

The waiter arrived to take their order. Wonderful, thought Rose. What a perfectly timed interruption. You'd think I'd paid him. She took her time, listened to the lunchtime specials with great concentration, asked knowledgeable questions about the salmon. At the same time, she saw, enjoyed – no, revelled in – her husband's obvious discomfiture. She could read every nuance of that facial expression: this was *his* role, *he* was accustomed to being the host, *his* was by rights the tone of sophistication, of geniality, of ownership. By the time Rose had ordered, and turned smilingly to see what her guest would like, Ben's face was shadowed with the sullenness she already knew so well.

Take it easy. Keep just this side of nuclear explosion, or everything I've planned will go pear-shaped.

Once the waiter had gone, Rose reached into her briefcase. 'Let's get on with what we came here to discuss, shall we?' she said, handing Ben a blue folder across the table. 'You told me nearly three months ago you'd come back to "regularize" everything between us – the house, the kids, the lot.'

He nodded curtly, not meeting her gaze.

'Well then, let's do it. As far as our grown-up children are concerned, you've now met with all three of them, with considerable help from me, I might add. Whatever happens in the future is up to you and them. I've done my part. And whether you believe it or not, I've never said anything to turn any of them against you.' She took a sip of water.

Ben didn't answer. She hadn't expected him to.

'I've thought about the house a lot, Ben, and I really don't want to sell it before Lisa finishes school. Brian will be coming home to go back to college in October, as well; it would all be too much of an upheaval.'

She stopped, taking the cap off her pen. 'I know you have your opportunities here, and that you need to finance them. I'm prepared to do that, to take out a loan for your portion of the property and finish everything between us. Take a look at these pages.'

She could see that he was agitated, that he resented the initiative having been wrested from him. He wanted to reply, but curiosity got the better of him, as she'd known it would. She watched the fury build across his forehead as he read. Good, she thought. Just the reaction I wanted. She was surprised at her own sudden ability to play this game. She felt curiously dispassionate, detached from any emotion. *Nothing personal, just business.*

'You're offering me twenty-five per cent of the value of my *own house*? You've got to be kidding.' His voice was tight, strained, holding onto his temper with some difficulty. Rose was immediately grateful that all of this was taking place in a neutral space, far away from her home. She had deliberately chosen a very public venue, one where no memories or hidden agendas lurked in ambush. Early that morning, she had visualized parcelling up all her feelings – love, anger, bitterness, tenderness – and wrapping them in gold paper. She'd placed them in her kitchen, on the table, and very carefully locked the door behind her.

I am nothing but a tough negotiation on legs, wearing a new suit and expensive shoes. That's all.

'It's not your house; it's the family home. You walked out eight years and four months ago and you've *still* never paid a penny towards it, *or* your family. You'll see that all I have deducted is what you owe.'

She watched the reply forming, watched as Ben shifted in his chair so that he could lean across the table at her. Now it would start. But she was ready for him: she knew this tactic too. Twenty years of marriage had prepared her.

In Your Face. She sat back. She raised her hand, just a fraction: but it was enough. Astonishment seemed to silence him.

'I'm not finished, Ben. There's not a court in the land that would force me to sell my children's home, not a judge anywhere that would absolve you of what you owe. This is a generous offer, and it's based on the highest of three estate agents' valuations – you've got the originals there in front of you.'

Rose pressed her hands into her napkin. She could feel their trembling getting out of control.

The waiter arrived, setting their food before them. Rose looked at her plate, filled with a watery nausea. Hurry up, she urged her husband silently. Hurry up and say "no" so that I can walk out of here while I'm still able.

'I don't accept these valuations. I don't accept them at all.' Ben pushed the pages away from him, his gesture signalling contempt.

Rose shrugged. 'Perhaps you'd like to send in your own experts? Perhaps the man with the measuring tape, the one who showed such interest in the width of the garden, the length of the driveway?'

But it was lost on him. He leaned even further across the table. 'You're not listening to me,' he hissed. 'I don't accept *any* of these valuations because they can't predict what a house like . . . like *ours* will fetch at an auction. These are all bullshit.' He stuffed the papers back into the blue folder and glared at her.

'Well, that's my offer, Ben. Take it, or wait eleven years until Lisa's finished college. Doesn't matter to me.' She picked up her fork and made a pretence at eating.

'You can't seriously expect me to accept two hundred thousand euro out of a house that I know is worth well over a million? Christ almighty, things can't have cost you *that* much over the last eight years.'

What a wonderful note on which to make my exit, Ben Holden.

'Tell that to the judge.' Rose picked up her handbag, her briefcase and stood up – a little shakily, but nothing that anyone else would notice. 'I'm not going to sit here and listen to any more of your fatherly concern. Stay as long as you like – I've already paid the bill.'

And she turned her back, counting the steps to the dining room door. She was left with a vivid image of her husband, red-faced, open-mouthed, just as he had been when she'd closed her door against him all those years ago.

Round one, she thought, as she hailed a taxi.

I think that went rather well.


'So what's next?'

Pauline poured another cup of coffee and pointed to the

papers in front of her. 'Well, he certainly won't accept your first offer, but we knew he wouldn't. He's looking for a minimum of *four* hundred thousand, according to this. He wants his own independent valuation.'

'Fine by me. Any time he likes. Although he told me last week that he didn't accept *any* valuations, because they wouldn't take "auction fever" into account. I don't care how many independent experts he gets. I just want him to continue believing I don't want to sell. I want this to be tough for him, and I want him to acknowledge what he owes his children. That's all.'

'And are you still quite sure that you want to concede? Are you really happy to live somewhere else? You don't have to, you know. Please remember that.'

Rose smiled at her. 'I'm already living somewhere else, in all the ways that matter. That house ceased to be my home a long time ago – I just didn't know it. It's got nothing to do with conceding anything: I just don't want to live there any more.'

'Do the kids know you're going to sell?'

'No, nobody else knows, except the two of us, and Sam, of course. I'll tell them all when I have to. I've already started house-hunting, very quietly. I've lots of options – even if we end up with a sixty–forty split. I want to string this negotiation out for as long as possible, and then agree to sell.

'Let Ben think he's won, that I've agreed reluctantly because I can't take the pressure of the negotiation. Then we can go to auction in September or October, which is supposed to be the best time, and then it's over, done with. I'll pay him off and I'll never have to see him again.'

'Okay. It certainly makes financial sense, as long as it makes emotional sense for you and the kids.'

'Don't worry, I'll handle them. Brian is planning on moving out in October, anyway, so it's really just Lisa I have to worry about. And she's grown up a lot through all of this. The important thing is that Ben accepts that some things are just not negotiable.' Rose paused for emphasis. 'He pays what is due to his children, that's all. I don't want anything for myself, but I'm not budging on that figure: that's their future.'

Pauline nodded. 'Okay again – we'll proceed on that basis. All the haggling is now over the percentages; the day in court seems to be receding somewhat after the last volley we fired across their bow. There was a deafening silence to my request for medical reports on Ben's depression, and for copies of his bank statements. We're making progress.'

'Good,' said Rose. 'Tell him to go ahead with his valuation and then we'll talk again.'

Rose stood up to leave.

'You okay? Mr McCarthy okay?'

Rose smiled. 'More than okay. It's – like a whole other life.'

Rose left Pauline's office and made her way out onto the street. It wasn't time to tell her of Sam's plan, not yet. Too many 'i's to be dotted and 't's to be crossed. It might even have to wait until the day.

September. Or maybe even October.

She'd tell her when she was sure the time was right.


Rose put Lisa's case by the front door and left her rucksack lying beside it. She had a quick glance around the living room, but the earlier thunderstorm of clothes and shoes and make-up seemed to have abated. The air had settled again. Calm after the storm.

'Lisa? Are you sure you have everything?' Rose called.

She appeared at the top of the stairs. 'Yeah. I went through the list again before I locked the case.'

'What about your rain jacket?'

'It's down in the hall, under the stairs.'

'Right. You've another ten minutes, no more.'

Rose opened the cupboard under the stairs and pulled out Lisa's rain jacket. Her new handbag came with it, its velcro clasp somehow having wedded itself to the fastenings on the jacket. As Rose tugged, the handbag fell away suddenly onto the hall floor, its contents scattering widely.

'Bloody hell,' she muttered, and bent to pick them up. A purse, lip gloss, a notebook and a hairbrush had all made their way under the hall table, along with several envelopes. Puzzled, Rose reached out for them. As she did so, fifty-euro notes slithered everywhere, disappearing further underneath the table. She got down on her hands and knees, retrieved them and counted, with mounting astonishment. Nine brand-new notes: four hundred and fifty euro, in cash. For a brand-new fifteen-year-old? For three weeks in the countryside?

Rose stood up to find Lisa looking at her from the bottom stair. She didn't even wait for her daughter to speak.

'Lisa, where on earth did you get all this money? You spent Damien's hundred on new clothes, and I gave you a hundred last night. Where did you get the other three hundred and fifty?' But she already knew the answer, or most of it.

Lisa looked at her defiantly. 'I saved fifty myself, from babysitting. Dad gave me the other three hundred.'

'Come into the living room.' Rose opened the door and gestured to Lisa to go in ahead of her.

The girl didn't move. 'We'll miss the bus,' she said.

'No, we won't. And even if we do, there is no way you're leaving this house with four hundred and fifty euro in cash in your handbag. Now, go inside.'

Lisa tossed her hair angrily and marched into the living room, where she threw herself onto the sofa.

'I asked you had your dad given you money, and you said no. Why did you lie?'

Lisa examined her nails. 'Cos I knew you wouldn't let me bring it. All the other girls are bringing way more than a hundred. Why do I always have to be different?'

Rose took her mobile out of her pocket. She highlighted a number from her contacts, pressed the call key, and waited. 'Jane? It's Rose. Yes, we're just ready to leave: we'll be with you in a couple of minutes. Just a quick question: can I ask how much cash Alison is taking with her?' She looked directly at Lisa. 'A hundred, and Carly the same. That's fine, Jane. Thanks. See you in a minute.'

She walked over to the sofa. Lisa wouldn't look at her.

'Lisa, you are going to a village in the middle of Donegal for three weeks. You'll be most of the day in a classroom learning Irish. We've discussed all this. You know that Jane and Margaret and I are coming up to see all of you on the second weekend. We agreed that if you needed more money, you could have it then. What is going on?'

Lisa shrugged. 'Then we must be the only three in the whole country going with that amount of money.'

Rose looked at her levelly. 'I really don't care about anybody else, or what *everybody* else does. That's all you're getting, Lisa. This is not negotiable. For one, you won't need any more than a hundred for the first two weeks: everything is already paid for. And secondly, you are *not* having that amount of cash hanging around either in your bag or in your room. That's asking for trouble.'

Still she said nothing.

'Okay, Lisa. We'd better postpone this trip until we sort this out. I'll tell Jane to go ahead without us.' Rose opened up her mobile.

'All right, all *right*,' said Lisa, her voice full of resentment. 'I'll just bring the hundred. Don't keep going *on* about it.'

Rose handed her the handbag, and put two fifty-euro notes into an envelope. Lisa took it without a word.

'Let's go,' said Rose quietly.


By the time they reached the coach, Alison and Carly had giggled Lisa all the way out of her bad temper. Once out of the car, the three of them were swallowed up instantly by a gaggle of shrieking, multicoloured teenagers.

'Trouble on the cash front?' asked Jane, smiling.

Rose nodded. 'You bet.'

'Don't worry – your call came five minutes after Margaret had the same row with Carly. I think that particular fight has been duplicated in every house in the neighbourhood this morning. Well, almost every house. There are the usual suspects with more money than sense.'

'It's not like her. I'll have to get to the bottom of it.'

'Don't worry about it. Come on. Let's bring the bags, or they'll go without them. They haven't an ounce of wit between them.'

A mêlée of bags and coats and girls and teachers followed. Rose could remember her own Gaeltacht days and her mostly fruitless attempts to speak Irish, despite sharp-eyed teachers and the encouragement of patient housemothers. She could still recall the chilly certainty of Donegal rain in summer, damp sheets, endless cups of weak tea. And the rowdy céilis, where the dances had strange, warlike names: The Walls of Limerick, The Siege of Ennis. Rose remembered the energy and military precision demanded by such dances. All thoughts of romance vanished as you held on, tight, nervous, to the sticky palms of your partner. The more daring boys would swing their girls faster and faster and the room revolved in a dizzying spin of lights and music and the stamping of feet. Terrifying, exhilarating, tribal.

And it was fun, she thought suddenly, real fun. Even at the time, she and her classmates had known it was fun. They'd enjoyed everything about it: the weeks of anticipation, the secret, delighted terror of meeting all those boys, the heady freedom of being away from home for almost a whole month. Despite – no, really *because of* – the apparent sophistication of Lisa and her friends, Rose was glad that the Gaeltacht rite of passage was still available to them: possibly the last marker of an older, more innocent age.

In all the confusion, Rose had had time only for one brief, silent hug with Lisa before all the girls were herded onto the coach. Now she searched along the windows for her daughter's face and found her almost at the rear of the coach. Rose waved at her, trying to ignore the lump in her throat. But Lisa wouldn't look in her direction.

Her youngest child's first time away from home. Leaving her like this wasn't right. Rose made her way quickly towards one of Lisa's teachers. She had to speak to her daughter again. This wasn't good enough.

At that moment, Rose's mobile bleeped. She looked at the screen. *Sorry, Mum. Dad said 2 treat myself. Just wanted not 2 have 2 B so careful. D€100 is fine. xx*

Rose looked up and saw her daughter smiling in her direction. She waved up at the window, blew her a kiss, then pointed to her mobile and gave the thumbs up. Call you later, she motioned. Lisa smiled again, and waved back.

'Would you just look at the three of them? Imagine having ten of those under your roof for three weeks.' Jane stood beside her. 'Jesus, those Gaeltacht women must be saints.'

Rose laughed. 'I know. It doesn't bear thinking about. We still going up to see them, the weekend after next?'

'Sure. Margaret couldn't be here today, but she said to tell you she's more than happy to share the driving. We'll sort the insurance out later.'

They both waved madly at the three faces pressed up against the window of the coach. The girls' noses were flattened against the pane; they stuffed their fingers in their ears, stuck their tongues out. They stayed like that until the coach pulled out of the car park.

Jane laughed. 'So much for worldly sophistication.' She turned to Rose. 'So, madam, what have you and the gorgeous Mr McCarthy got planned for all this free time ahead?'

Rose linked her arm through Jane's. 'I hope you've time for a very long lunch. You just come with me and I'll tell you. And I promise I'll spare you no detail.'


Sam took both suitcases out of the lift.

'What have you got here?' he complained. 'Your moon rock collection?'

Rose made a face at him. 'Just a few clothes, my make-up, a couple of books. Enough to see me through until the end of the week.'

'*The week?* Am I going to regret this?'

'Well, you asked me to move in while Lisa was away – you'll just have to put up with the consequences.'

He closed the door behind them and pulled her gently towards him.

'Welcome home.'

They stood in the hallway, neither of them moving for sometime. Rose finally pulled back and looked up at Sam. 'I can't believe it, do you know that? It's as though the last few years were some sort of nightmare and I've just woken up.'

He kissed her. 'The best is yet to come,' he said lightly. 'Come on – lunch on the balcony.'

Rose lifted her face to the sun. She could hear Sam in the kitchen, opening the fridge, the cupboards, the cutlery drawer. She knew the sounds of his home almost as well as she knew her own. She almost felt like holding her breath, afraid that what was before her would suddenly disappear, go up in smoke.

Now she had a whole, long, glorious month ahead of her, doing nothing. Sam had persuaded her that she could afford it, and Sarah had been more than willing to keep Betty ticking over. A slow month, August. She really should have taken it off before now, but those had been the years when every penny counted. Things were going to be different, now.

Sam arrived on the balcony carrying a bowl of salad, a bottle of white wine and two glasses. She made to get up to help him.

'Sit down,' he said firmly. 'This is the month when you do nothing, remember? Or at least the three weeks while Lisa's away. After that, well, I'm afraid you're on your own. Until then, you and I are going to play house, take a weekend away and lie low, hiding from your husband. Isn't it wonderful to have such an excuse to stay in bed all day?'

He handed her a glass of wine.

Rose smiled at him. 'It was a close-run thing, you know, this morning. We might have had my daughter come between us.'

'Why? What happened?'

Rose told him.

'What did you do?'

'Took it from her, of course. She has enough. And her teacher's holding some as well, just in case: although Lisa doesn't know that. But I felt a bit bad – I think she feels she's entitled. "Eight birthday and eight Christmas presents," was what she said Ben owed her, almost as soon as she knew he was back. I'll always remember that.'

'Did you part on good terms?'

'Yes. We did, eventually. I'll call her later.'

'Good. You'll miss her.'

Rose nodded. 'Yes, I will. She's infuriating and wonderful at the same time. But two weeks isn't too long. She can cool her heels and then she'll be glad to see me again.'

Sam handed her a plate. 'Help yourself to salad.'

'Thanks. This looks good.'

He grinned, glancing over at her. 'I'm afraid I don't have high-voltage serving techniques: you'll have to teach me.'

Rose slipped off her shoes and stretched her legs. 'Not this month, I won't.'

Sam raised his glass. 'To August.'

Rose smiled. 'A wicked month, I do believe.'


They'd sat in the sunshine for some time, hardly speaking. Rose had begun to doze when she heard Sam's voice at her elbow.

'Sorry to bring business up so soon, but when did you say you were meeting the estate agent?'

She kept her eyes closed. 'Next Monday. The sale of the house will be advertised at the end of this month, and the auction is scheduled for the third week in September.'

'So you're nearly there, then.'

She turned and looked at him. 'I've cleaned the house from top to bottom, thrown out an enormous amount of junk, and I'm ready for viewings. I don't care how many people tramp around it now – it's only a means to an end.'

Sam grinned his approval. 'And Ben was like a dog with two tails when you *caved in* to his pressure.'

Rose nodded. 'Cock-a-hoop. Couldn't contain himself. I

hammed it up a bit – said it was all too much of a strain. He's agreed to thirty-three and a third per cent – after all the fees and the mortgage are paid, of course – and what he owes for the kids. He knows he's getting a good deal. I'd have agreed to forty – must tell him that, on the day.'

Sam raised his glass. 'Well, Mr Holden, look out. Enjoy your crowing for now. *All good things come to he who waits.* Or is it *him*? I've forgotten.'

'Neither,' said Rose. 'All good things are coming to *her*,' she pointed to herself, 'and to us. I've waited long enough.'

They toasted each other.

'To the twentieth of September,' said Rose.

'To the twentieth – and to all the days thereafter.'


'Like it?' Sam asked, as he pulled out the chair for her.

'It's lovely. I had no idea so many places like this existed.' Rose looked around at the restaurant's soothing décor – all warm wood and light, creamy colours.

'You've been too long in the suburbs,' Sam grinned at her. 'Time you got out more, got to know your city again.'

'That's the funny thing – it's like it's no longer my city: certainly not the grim one I grew up in. You're spoiling me. You've spent the last three weeks spoiling me. I can't remember the last time I went to the cinema before this, and as for the theatre . . .' She smiled at him. 'You know all the attractions of this place better than I do – and you've only been home two years.'

Sam took her hand across the table. 'That's because I had to find my way around all over again, once I came back. I haven't done this in a good while, either. And as for spoiling – you were long overdue a bit of pampering. You've a busy few weeks ahead of you.'

'It's been great, Sam. This time together has just been wonderful. I can't believe I'm going home tomorrow.'

'All part of the service,' Sam said, handing the waiter back the wine list. 'Begs the question, though – when are you going to make an honest man of me?' Before she could answer, Sam grasped her hand again. 'That's a joke, okay? One thing at a time. I'm going to miss you when you go. But in less than a month, this will all be over.'

Sam tasted the wine and nodded at the waiter. 'That's fine, thanks. So,' he said, 'the advertising has begun and everyone's singing from the same hymn sheet.'

Rose raised her glass to him. 'Yep. I've told all three of my children, and there's no problem. Damien just said: "Good move." He's no attachment left to that house, anyway. That went a long time ago. I thought Brian was a bit taken aback. Not upset that the house was being sold, actually, but I gathered that Ben hadn't told him. And they're in touch quite a lot. I think he was upset about that. But that's between the two of them.' Rose smiled at him. 'As usual, kids are full of surprises. Lisa was the only one I was worried about, but she's quite excited. There seems to be a certain cachet to moving house, as far as I can gather.'

'Whatever works for you. Have you told any of them about our alternative?'

Rose shook her head. 'No, that's absolutely between the two of us. I haven't even told Pauline. Nobody needs to know. Besides, we mightn't even be able to make it work.'

'Well, it won't be for lack of trying, I can assure you. I think we'll do it. It might be touch and go, but I've done my homework on auction results over the past while. And it's possible, it's all more than possible. I want to make sure that you have what you want out of all of this, that you get what you're entitled to.'

Rose smiled at him. 'Seems like you're planning to stick around for a while.'

'Oh, only a few decades or so. But I do promise you this.'

'What?'

He held both of her hands across the table. 'I'll never try to be a father substitute to your kids – never. I'll never muddy those waters. And if it takes even a couple of years of this softly, softly until you and I can finally be under the same roof, so be it. You're worth it. I can wait.' He refilled their glasses. 'As long as you stay over a couple of nights each week, obviously. I may be a saint, but I'm no martyr.' And he grinned at her wickedly.

'Done deal,' she said softly, wondering what on earth she had done in all her previous lives to make her so very lucky in this one.

# Chapter Thirteen

IT WAS ALMOST three o'clock, and still the auction room was empty, apart from the chairs occupied by Rose and Pauline O'Brien.

'Come on,' said Pauline. 'Let's go and get a quick coffee. You don't want to be here like a sitting duck. We'll wait until Ben arrives and then come back in.'

'He's definitely coming, is he? I mean, he won't just send his solicitor?'

'He'll be here,' said Pauline grimly. 'Trust me, he'll be here.'

Rose knew she was right. Ben would be here to collect his money. And it was *his* house, after all. She followed Pauline into the coffee shop next door. She wanted today to be over: to look forward with complete freedom to finding her own new home, somewhere where she could choose the colours and the lampshades and the furniture. Somewhere with absolutely no memories stitched into its intimate fabric. Somewhere, eventually, for her and Sam.

'Take-away, or do you want to have coffee here?'

Rose started. 'Sorry, Pauline – I was miles away. Take-away, I think – I'm too nervous to sit here. I want to see what's going on.'

'Okay. Let me just check and see if he's arrived.'

Pauline was back instantly. 'He's there all right, with Mc-Gowan by his side. I see what you mean about his suits.' And she grinned at Rose. 'But you're looking pretty sharp yourself – love the shoes!'

'Window-dressing. I couldn't let myself down.'

'Come on; are you ready for this?'

'Ready as I'll ever be.'

She followed Pauline back into the auction room. She deliberately avoided looking in Ben's direction. Some of the other seats had filled up in the meantime. She could just see Sam, too, sitting in the third row, doing the crossword. He hadn't looked up as she entered. Rose glanced at Pauline, who was sipping her coffee, a file now open on her knees. Rose was sure she hadn't noticed, couldn't see Sam from where she was sitting.

There were seven other people in the room, Rose counted, all studiously not looking at the auctioneer. She nudged Pauline.

'There's very few people here. Do I need to get nervous?'

Pauline shook her head. 'Four people applied for the Conditions of Sale, that means you have at least four serious bidders. Others *can* bid without having seen the Conditions of Sale in advance,' she whispered. 'They like to be dark horses. They'll often just glance at the Conditions once they've bought. For some people, nothing will stand in the way of their getting the house they want. They're the ones for whom money is no object. Trust me.'

Rose nodded. She listened to the auctioneer droning on about the merits of what had once been her home: its four spacious bedrooms, light-filled drawing room, only minor decoration and modernization needed. Large front and rear gardens, plenty of room for extension, subject to planning permission. Oh, just get on with it, she thought impatiently.

'What am I bid for this very fine property . . .'

It's begun, she thought. Finally, it has begun. This, too, will end. And then the last eight and a half years of my life will be over.

She found it impossible to judge where the bids were coming from. She looked curiously around her, almost unable to hear the auctioneer's voice above the racing tide in her ears. She had squeezed her cardboard coffee cup so hard that foamy black coffee was oozing upwards through the lid. She sipped at it distractedly.

Nine hundred and fifty thousand. The auctioneer smoothed his tie. 'The reserve has been reached, ladies and gentlemen. I can declare that this property is now on the market.'

She risked a glance at Ben, who was avidly watching the room. He was nervous, eager – she could see it in the way he held himself. There could be no doubt but that he was the owner; even his gaze carried a proprietorial air.

Nine hundred and eighty thousand, she heard. Thirty over the reserve. Pauline smiled at her, gave her hand a comforting squeeze.

'Nine hundred and ninety.'

'One million.'

Still Rose couldn't make out who was bidding. One man had a pipe in his mouth; another appeared to be reading a book. Yet another seemed to be fiddling nervously with a pen. She was afraid to look towards the third row, where Sam still continued with his crossword. Yet the auctioneer went onto nod, almost imperceptibly, towards different corners of the room as the bidding continued unabated.

And then, suddenly, it was over.

'One million, one hundred and fifty thousand once; one million, one hundred and fifty thousand twice; one million, one hundred and fifty thousand – for the third time. Sold.'

Pauline turned to her, smiling. 'Congratulations, Rose – that's a great price. You're well out of the financial woods.' But Rose wasn't listening. Her eyes sought Sam's. He turned around gravely, put his newspaper on the seat, and glanced in Rose's direction. He nodded briefly, just the once.

'Pauline, come with me. There's something I have to tell you.'

She took her by the hand, making her way quickly towards Ben's corner of the room. Ben's solicitor was delightedly shaking hands with him. Rose saw the look of satisfaction on her husband's face, his *told-you-so* expression as he watched her approach. She stopped at the auctioneer's table and turned to Pauline.

'Just listen. I couldn't tell you earlier – I was afraid you might find the information . . . uncomfortable.'

'What information? Listen to what? Rose, have you lost your marbles?'

'No – I've just found a few more. Listen.' She squeezed Pauline's hand urgently.

Sam made his unhurried way towards the top of the room. He shook hands with the auctioneer and spoke to him quietly. Rose couldn't hear what he said. She saw the auctioneer gesture towards Ben, who moved forward eagerly. A young woman, dark-haired, suited, stood up from the third row and made her way towards the top of the room. Rose knew who she was, from Damien's description. She didn't need to be told. It was almost like watching herself.

Rose pulled Pauline closer. She knew that she had just spotted Sam. Pauline was looking suddenly bewildered. Rose squeezed her hand: wait, wait. Don't worry. All will soon be revealed. They could hear the voices clearly now.

'Allow me to introduce you to the vendor,' the auctioneer was saying. 'This is Mr Ben Holden. Mr Holden, meet Mr Sam McCarthy, the new owner.'

Pauline's chin literally dropped. She wheeled around to look at Rose. 'What on earth is going on?'

Rose grinned. 'Shhh – listen.'

They watched as, almost in slow motion, Sam reached his hand out to grasp Ben's. He shook it heartily.

'A fine house, Mr Holden. A very fine house. I'm proud to be the new owner – we both are. Please, meet my partner, Rose.'

The remaining five steps are the longest walk she has ever taken. Sam turns, puts one arm around Rose's shoulder, and says 'I know we're going to be very happy there.'

Ben simply looks from one to the other, comprehension taking a long time to percolate. His solicitor is looking puzzled, all bonhomie fading fast. The dark-haired woman's smile suddenly collapses, her expression uncertain, troubled.

Then, Rose watches as horrified understanding seems to begin at Ben's hairline. His face flushes and then pales suddenly, all colour leaching away. His lips become a thin, tight line. *My house*, she can see him thinking. *She's going back to live in my house.* For one long, dread-filled moment, Rose thinks that Ben is going to lunge at her, at Sam. His face becomes suddenly featureless; even his eyes seem to lose their definition. The moment passes.

He says nothing, just pushes his way past them and makes for the door. McGowan follows, hurrying after his client. The dark-haired woman walks after them, unhurried. She casts a glance in Rose's direction, hesitates, then follows the two men out of the room.

The auctioneer is looking bewildered.

Sam takes out his cheque book. The spell is broken. 'I believe you have a contract for me to sign?' he says.

The auctioneer was suddenly all business, pulling papers from a pile in front of him, sliding them towards Sam.

'Yes, yes, of course, Mr McCarthy. Please, if you'd be good enough to sign here.'

Pauline turned to Rose. 'Well, aren't you the dark horse!'

'I'm sorry, but I couldn't tell you. We didn't even know if the bidding would go beyond us. As it happens, it's just what we budgeted.'

'But – forgive me: I'm really confused now. I thought you didn't want the house? I thought you wanted to make a fresh start somewhere else?'

Rose smiled at her. 'I do – and I don't want the house. That's the best part. Sam has been very quietly negotiating with a couple who refuse to buy at auction. They've already offered me one point two million. But they're not in a position to close the contract for at least six months. So I'm going to keep on living there until they're ready. They're prepared to sign all the papers now, pay a deposit, and wait until it suits all of us to move. I'm more than happy with that. We'll move next summer sometime, during everyone's holidays.'

Pauline nodded slowly. 'A dish best served cold, isn't that what you once said to me?'

Rose smiled. 'Yes – and Ben still walks away with in excess of three hundred grand. So don't feel sorry for him. This way, my kids' futures are secure. I told you that they were my main priority. I was willing to fight like a lioness for them.'

'So you did. Remind me never to cross you, okay?'

Rose laughed. 'Only where my children are concerned. *Even the worm turns.* My mother used to say that, too.'

Sam shook Pauline's hand. 'Thanks for everything, Pauline. Rose has told me how well you've looked after her.'

Pauline grinned at him. 'Seems like I wasn't the only one, Sam McCarthy. You take my breath away, both of you. Congratulations. I'm still not over the shock. There is something truly wonderful about finally seeing the good guys win. I see that so little, these days.'

\*

It took hours for Rose to feel normal again. She was constantly surprised that 'normal' these days was increasingly coming to mean 'happy'. It's really over, she thought. Ben is out of my life, my kids are looked after, and now the best part of my life is just beginning.

Sam squeezed her hand. 'You okay?' he asked quietly. 'You're very pale.'

'I'll be fine. I love you, Sam McCarthy.'

'I love you, too. Now let's go home. You've a daughter to collect before we all do some serious celebrating. And just so's you know, Jane and Jim and Alison are all joining us. I'm not telling you where we're going for dinner. I want to see all of your faces when we arrive.'

Rose hugged him. 'Some good serving ideas for me to copy?'

He grinned. 'The best. And not a strawberry shortcake in sight.'

# *Epilogue*

ROSE LOOKS AROUND HER in satisfaction. She likes the way the evening sun fills the bay window, the way the wood gleams gold. Damien shoves the living room door open with his shoulder and staggers slightly under the weight of a large cardboard box.

'Jesus, that's heavy.' He dumps it on the floor. 'That's the last of the painters' rubbish from upstairs. We can put the beds back now, if you like.'

'Let's do that. Then we can sit on the patio and light the barbecue. Lisa will be back around seven; so will Brian. Will you stay and eat with us?'

'Sam coming?'

'Yes.'

'Yeah, I'd like that.'

'Dump that box in the boot of my car – I'll get rid of it tomorrow.'

'Anything else that needs to go in?'

'No, that's it. All done and dusted.'

Rose waits as Damien struggles out to the car. She watches him from the window, this tall, dark-haired young man. Hard to believe he has ever been a child; harder still to believe he was once a troubled youth. Almost twenty-six, warm, thoughtful, something so very *solid* about him now.

He comes back into the house. 'Right,' he says, rubbing his

hands together, 'let's light the barbie and get this show on the road.'


The patio is in just the right place to catch the evening sun. Rose reclines on her lounger – a gift from Jane and Jim, with a matching one for Sam – and closes her eyes; she thinks what a lovely month September always is. Nicer than summer.

The doorbell rings.

'I'll get it,' Damien calls, checking the barbecue, which is still glowing redly.

Lisa bounces in. 'Hi, Mum! Is my bedroom back together again?'

'Yes it is. Just be careful, the paint might still be a bit tacky.'

'Okay. Sam coming tonight?'

'Yes.'

'Cool.'

Cool. Is it still the ultimate accolade, Rose wonders, or has its place been taken by something else? Brian used to say it all the time as a young teenager. Brian, all sophisticated now, all serious, after his two summers in Paris. His return home is only temporary, he keeps telling her, he'll definitely be gone by Christmas. She listens. Again. She doesn't mind.

He and Damien still rub against each other from time to time, spatting occasionally in a way that no longer worries her. She's seen them together when it mattered, brothers above everything else.

Ben calls each of the three of them, from time to time. And from time to time, they call him. She doesn't know what they talk about, doesn't want to pry. She's seen him only once since the auction, bumped into him in Grafton Street the day after their divorce had come through. They were civil, polite, wished each other the best. It was enough.

The doorbell goes again. Rose loves the sound. There are no longer any shattered pieces of the past that come calling to her door.

'I'll get it!' Lisa shouts.

Sam and Brian come in together.

'Found this ruffian at the bus stop – thought I'd better bring him in and give him a decent meal.'

She doesn't need to look: she can hear the friendly punch that Brian gives his tormentor. He's too *sedate* for a young fellow, Sam keeps telling her. He needs to treat me with less respect, if you know what I mean.

'Hi, Mum.'

'Hi, Brian. Good day?'

She still doesn't open her eyes. She doesn't need to. She prefers hearing what they all look like, gathered around her.

'Yeah, starving, though.'

'How you surprise me. There's some quiche left over from lunch. Why don't you have that before dinner? It'll be a good hour yet.'

'Okay.' He disappears into the kitchen.

'Well, Lady Muck.' Sam sits beside her, taking her hand in his.

She smiles, opening her eyes now. 'That makes you Lord Muck.'

'But I've been out slaving over hot figures all day. I've not been sitting here in the sun, indulging in the good life.'

'More fool you.'

'Any word from Sarah?'

'Yes.'

'Well, go on, then – don't keep me in suspense.'

Rose has to shade her eyes from the slanting sun. 'She jumped at it. She's buying me out. She's very happy with my client list, even happier to keep Betty on. And as from January next, I'll be working a maximum of twenty hours a week – that's a *third* of my average over the last nine years or so.'

'How do you feel, then, milady?'

She grins at him. 'Absolutely wonderful. A five-year contract, consultation fees, part-time work – how else would I feel?'

He kisses her. 'Lustful?' he asks, hopefully.

She smiles at him, pulls him closer. 'Always. Stay tonight?'

He nods. 'Try sending me away after that.'

'And I made another decision today.'

'Go on.'

'I'm going to do something different next autumn. Haven't decided what it is, yet – but I want it to be something that's not remotely *practical* or *useful*. Something for me.'

'Such as?'

'Maybe history of art, or literature, stained-glass making – I don't mind. I want to stop my brain from atrophying.'

'I think there's two chances of your brain atrophying – but anyway. Go for it, young woman, go for it.'

Rose grins at him wickedly. 'I wasn't asking your permission, you know.'

Sam strokes her cheek. 'Nor was I giving it. I was just making some general, approving noises. Speaking of noises, I'd better take a look at this barbecue. Seems to be spitting at your elder son quite a bit.'

She watches as he crosses the small area of decking that separates the patio from the house. She loves the very bones of her new home, her new life. Loves its compactness, its welcoming light, its friendliness.

Damien and Sam discuss the technicalities of barbecuing. Music pours down from Brian's bedroom – more melodic, softer music since his return from Paris.

She can hear Lisa talking. Just turned sixteen: all grown up. Her summer life has been a constant round of parties, friends, long conversations on the phone, just like this one. Probably to a mobile, too, Rose thinks now, and suddenly doesn't care.

Life is . . . serene. She leans her head back, closes her eyes again. She can feel herself begin to drift.

She hears laughter, Sam's voice above it, and is consumed with love. How lucky I am, she thinks. How very, very lucky.

She hears Lisa again, closer now, discussing with Sam the merits of tongue-piercing, nose-piercing. He teases her about the perils of turning into a pin-cushion.

She hears Damien tell him about his recent promotion. And then Brian's heavy footsteps on the stairs, come to scavenge more food.

This is how it should be, she thinks. *This* is all I ever wanted. Unsummoned, the thought makes itself clear inside her mind: *I love my life.*

What else was there? It was here, all of it.

Tranquillity. Peace of mind.

This.

Love.

Or something like it.

Visit **www.panmacmillan.com** to read more about all our books and to buy them. You will also find features, author interviews and news of any author events, and you can sign up for e-newsletters so that you're always first to hear about our new releases.